Blood Ties

by

Gina Whitney

Dedication
To my two wonderful boys,
PJ and Drew, who believed in me even when I didn't. (Even though they thought I was turning into an emo chick.)

Acknowledgments

A very special thank you to Joel at Arbor Books for his wicked editing skills and insightful thoughts, and patience with my endless questions and deluded thoughts.

I want to send an enormous thank you to Terry for her magic fingers and creativity. Love you master Yoda!

To Jessica, for an awesome cover. You're kick-ass!

My thanks also to Aunt Sue and Alice (bff), who were thrusted into my preternatural world of fiction daily. You gave me an ear, a smile, a good talking to, and sometimes a "huh?"

My deepest gratitude to my little sister Laura, who pain- lessly listened to my vampire/witchy jargon. Although you had your hands full with Payton, you found the time to listen; for that I'm grateful, sis, and love you dearly.

A heartfelt thank you to my doll Eileen, for putting up with me, pushing me, and encouraging me with megawatt enthu- siasm. You're awesome!

To Rafael (who insisted on being listed), thank you for your enthusiasm, support, love, and sheer awesomeness that knows no bounds. I needed a push, and you kicked my butt. Man you're all sorts of fantastical!

Finally to my around-the-way team, Kenny and Geri, for your libations and countless invites to get me out of the house. I love you guys! When I started to rant about my book, you always encouraged me with smiles, hugs, and friendship. For that I'm eternally grateful. (Even though you shot each other looks like, "What a nutbag!")

Last but not least, to all my terrific friends who always have my back: love you all!

Table of Contents

Chapter One	8
Chapter Two	15
Chapter Three	23
Chapter Four	28
Chapter Five	35
Chapter Six	39
Chapter Seven	43
Chapter Eight	46
Chapter Nine	49
Chapter Ten	51
Chapter Eleven	57
Chapter Twelve	64
Chapter Thirteen	74
Chapter Fourteen	78
Chapter Fifteen	87
Chapter Sixteen	96
Chapter Seventeen	104
Chapter Eighteen	109
Chapter Nineteen	125
Chapter Twenty	141
Chapter Twenty-One	145
Chapter Twenty-Two	160
Chapter Twenty-Three	177
Chapter Twenty-Four	200
Chapter Twenty-Five	225
Chapter Twenty-Six	253

Chapter One

> Deep into the darkness peering, long I
> stood there, wondering, fearing,
> doubting, dreaming dreams no mortal
> ever dared to dream before.
>
> —Edgar Allan Poe

The four witches watched the birth, anxious to see if the baby was a monster.

It was more like a brutal assault than a delivery. Ilan Valois lost her delicate elegance as she squatted, splayed legs pulled back as far as she could take them. She bore down with a pain so great, it choked out the primal scream lodged at the back of her throat. It was as if the baby knew what awaited her and was fighting to stay within the safe confines of the womb.

Despite it being mid-winter, Ilan's searing body heat fogged off her skin. Every spasm caused her to lurch forward, leaving vapor footprints on the linoleum. Her pelvis cracked, unhinging from her hipbones. Her moist, pink flesh ripped to accommodate the gross mass of the descending child, bloody chunks preceding it.

Ilan saw that Addison Bolingbroke was keeping her distance, craning her neck to see what would pop out. Even though Addison had killed many times, seeing new life brought forth—especially this obscene life—was difficult for her to stomach. Despite her own agony, Ilan felt sorry that Addison had been drawn into this dreadful situation. She took no offense when Addison said to her, "You never should have conceived this child. It's an abomination."

"It's a baby," Evelyn Valois said to Addison while acting as midwife. Evelyn's attire looked like a kaleidoscope that had exploded. It consisted of items she had picked up during her world travels, like the scarf made out of aso oke fabric that held together the oversized bun on top of her head. She unfurled the scarf and wiped Ilan's soaking brow with it.

Evelyn then pushed her blue-sided Nulady glasses—worn for no particular visual impairment—off the tip of her nose. This action partially obscured Ilan's view of her eyes, making it difficult for her to discern Evelyn's emotions. However, the high pitch of Evelyn's apprehensive voice exposed her true feelings. Ilan understood Evelyn's concern; it was still a mystery as to whether Ilan had conceived their savior, a beast, or an ordinary child.

Ilan gave a final, concentrated push. Her perineum ripped open, and the hefty baby fell into Evelyn's hands, completely engulfed in the amniotic sac. Ilan stayed balanced on her heels just long enough for Evelyn to take the bloody mass to the bed, and then she collapsed to the floor. Suddenly, Addison snapped out of her dumbfounded state and rushed to Ilan. She picked her up and carried her to the bed, next to the moving sac.

Evelyn took a large hunting knife and poked through the tough, transparent sac. Its tawny fluid gushed out as Evelyn reached in with her eyes closed, not sure of what she'd pull out. Her hands retracted and she held a baby—a big baby, but not a fiend.

"She's beautiful," Evelyn said, putting the girl to Ilan's engorged, aching nipple.

The marble statue of a woman cradled her child in her cold arms. The infant's screams prompted Ilan's letdown reflex, and her breasts secreted sweet-tasting blood instead of milk. The voracious baby latched on with vigor, its bare gums almost chewing the nipple as it fed.

Ilan winced as Evelyn repaired her injuries with a taper-point needle and synthetic sutures bought from a pet-supply store.

Ilan had tasked James Bolingbroke with finding the witches a suitable hideout. After months on the run and the impending delivery of the baby, they'd had to make due. The bulk of their magical abilities had gone into cloaking Ilan. Her pregnant body had been a lighthouse emitting rays of energy to predatory witches. Her unrivaled power had been siphoned off to her baby, and she could hardly muster enough to protect herself.

The cabin James had chosen was isolated, claustrophobic, and musty. However, Ilan didn't mind its constant silence; it made her feel at peace. Despite this, she was not pleased with its vulnerability to attack.

She watched James as he kept vigilant guard at the window, scanning the black woods for any sign of Catherine. The incandescence of his cerulean eyes against the moonlight almost made him look demonic. This juxtaposed his fresh-faced, wholesome looks despite the fact that he was hundreds of years old.

In the window's reflection, Ilan could see James looking at his brother, Adrian. She regretted that her decision to have the baby had created an even bigger rift between the already feuding brothers. She tried to ignore their back-and-forth banter, but their voices carried all too well through the hollow room.

Ilan's sweat saturated the springy mattress, and she requested a towel. James, refusing to leave his post, ordered Adrian to get one for her. Ilan was disturbed by Adrian's casual reaction to the situation as he dropped a washcloth on her. He then put his hand to his chin with cool detachment as he watched Ilan, her body still convulsing from the birth.

Ilan rested with the baby tucked into the pit of her arm. The others slept also, except James, who had been alerted by a rustling in the woods. He opened the door just a crack, sensing the air. His skin blushed as his blood vessels dilated with a fight-or-flight response. He closed the door with an inhuman, accelerated motion and awakened the others.

"They're almost here," he said.

All were alert as if they had been awake the entire time; however, Ilan was still groggy and incapacitated from childbirth. James reached for the baby, but Ilan stopped him from taking her.

"Ilan, let me have her. I promise I will guard her with my life," James said with his arms outstretched.

Shoving his hands away, Ilan stated, "I'm not letting go of my child."

James raised his hand to the window, psychogenically assessing fluctuations in the atmosphere. "There're too many of them. We won't survive trapped in this house."

Adrian perked up. "So we go outside to slaughter? You know we don't have the power to fight them."

"We'll have a better chance in the open woods," James explained as he gathered a few essential items. "Addison, Evelyn, help Ilan. Adrian and I will take front."

"Why can't Addison be frontline?" Adrian asked. Addison looked at him, incredulous. "I mean, she's more powerful than I am," Adrian corrected.

James backed him up against a wall. He spoke no words, but Adrian got the message and fell in line.

The small coven escaped out the back door of the cabin, gliding over the ice-packed snow at hypersonic speed. Addison and Evelyn supported Ilan, adeptly positioning themselves on both sides so Ilan could maintain a grip on the baby.

As the group crossed over a hilly pass, a vertical shadow blocked their path. Catherine's physical form flowed into the shadow. They could barely see her thin, blue-veined face with her long, blonde hair cascaded over it. However, they all recognized her menacing, yellow eyes scorching through the strands like a blazing fire.

"It took forever to find you," Catherine said. She was accompanied by a group of lesser witches—coven radicals who supported her demented cause. Eager, they rocked back and forth, awaiting her orders.

"I have to say, it wasn't easy, but I have some special gifts of my own. My coven is best known for its tracking abilities. So for me it was only a matter of time," Catherine stated.

James, with lightning-bolt speed, placed himself in front of her. His face constricted into a feral snarl as he squared off with her. He was very careful, since her powers were so great—almost as great as Ilan's when she was healthy. James was so focused on Catherine he didn't notice Adrian quietly scooting behind a tree, being careful not to draw any attention.

"Cousin, I would think long and hard about what you are about to do! This is not right. We don't kill our own kind," James told Catherine.

"Really, James, I don't follow that impotent doctrine anymore. Besides, that creature is not one of our kind." Catherine wildly eyed the baby. "Yet, I must admit, the Valois blood that runs through her is extremely potent. If she is what her mother made her to be, I only need her flesh and blood to inherit all of their powers. James, you're too much of a coward to do something as brave as that."

Catherine spoke to Addison, who was protecting Ilan with Evelyn. "You can't really support this futile cause. You are still a Bolingbroke. I know you only followed James to protect him. If you join me, I will make you my second in command."

"Screw you," Addison snapped, never taking her eyes off of the enemy witches.

"Well, I can see *all* of you must die. So be it then." Catherine moved in on James, but he mirrored every step she made—a macabre dance.

Catherine smiled at him, confident she would win the fight like she had ever since they were children. She'd cheated most of the time; however, the closer she had gotten to womanhood, the more her true powers had come in. Eventually she no longer had to cheat. Her innate powers overwhelmed not only James, but all of her competition. That was except Ilan.

Regardless, James had to stop Catherine tonight. Too much was at stake. He addressed her minions, "You fools, we were once all in one fold. Klement, my brother, you remember."

Klement, a diminutive man, took a slight step forward. His raised hands were positioned, ready to throw magic at James. "Brother? Ilan's clan has conspired to keep us docile servants to them. Catherine has offered us freedom. Our own voices. Our own powers."

"She has offered you death," Evelyn interrupted. She raised her rosewood staff and shot off a wave of orange light, hitting Klement in the chest. All of the witches entered the fray, shooting lethal, fluorescent projectiles of light at each other.

Catherine sliced her hand through the air, throwing a hazy crystalline line of energy at James, making him stumble backward.

"Catherine, this is treason!" James said, now crouched in a fighting stance.

"You would side with a strange child over your own family? She is not of your bloodline. Why are you so protective of her?" Catherine asked. "We may both benefit from her blood. You must see she could possess gifts more powerful than any of ours."

"I don't need her gifts! Neither do you!"

"If you won't help me, then get out of my way, or I will do away with you myself. I have no problem with that, cousin."

James released a magical bolt of lightning at Catherine, who responded with a bigger one. Addison and Evelyn used their staffs to ward off the overwhelming swarm of witches. Even though they killed some, they were on the losing end because their magic wasn't honed in on specific targets.

Catherine held up her hands, her wrinkled palms facing James. She emanated a huge ball of pure, white energy that landed on him, suspending him helplessly in the air as if he were in the grip of a gargantuan, invisible hand. She then turned her attention to Ilan and the baby.

"Please, don't harm my child," Ilan pleaded.

"Ilan, you left us too soon," Catherine said a hair's breadth away from Ilan's face. Catherine picked up the baby and motioned to her few remaining supporters to follow. However, Evelyn and Addison joined hands and harnessed the energy of the waxing gibbous moon into their staffs. They pounded the ground at a rapid pace. With every thump, dynamic ripples charged out toward Catherine's witches, vaporizing them into puffs of smoke. In the midst of the chaos, Adrian came out from behind the tree, making it look as though he had been in the fight the whole time.

Just as Catherine was about to phase out with the baby, Ilan called upon the last strength she had. Her illuminated irises turned crimson, and all of her energy converged into them and shot out, striking

Catherine, who tumbled to the ground with the baby. Though stunned, she turned toward Ilan. Her eyes widened, the evil within her totally possessing them.

On one hand Catherine curled her bony fingers under, focusing her power to the tips, and flicked them forward. A spindly, plasmatic line of energy shot from her into Ilan's forehead, leaving an ashen imprint.

Catherine's hateful energy expenditure left her spent, causing her invisible grip to release James. He seized the moment by conjuring a molten fireball. As it moved toward Catherine, it turned dry leaves into embers. She tried to escape, but her exhausted body wouldn't allow her to get off the ground. The fireball consumed her like an infernal prison.

Through the searing pain of the flames, Catherine screamed at James, "I'll be back for her!" Then she was gone, fireball and all. All that was left was the stench of burnt flesh in the air.

Evelyn retrieved the baby, who was screaming uncontrollably as if she knew her mother was dying. With her other hand, Evelyn lifted Ilan's head. Ilan's voice was barely audible as she said, "James will accompany you as you take the baby to her father. I've already summoned her protector. With me gone, they won't be able to track her—until it's time."

With that, Ilan gasped a bit, and peacefully died.

Chapter Two

The most terrible poverty is loneliness
and the feeling of being unloved.

—Mother Teresa

I kept my head down as I made my way to the student counseling
services building, which stood at the far edge of Long Island
College.

Every so often I'd sneak a side glance at the more carefree students
hanging around. I thought that when I entered college, I would learn
how to be like them. I was now a senior and couldn't understand why I
was still so different from the rest.

My counselor, Dr. Graves, kept his wing-backed chair right in
front of the dormer window. This allowed for only the tiniest wedge of
light to come in, adding to the somber ambiance of the gray room. I
thought he did it on purpose, to elicit crying fits and eye scratching
from his patients. *Ah, yes, Ms. Valois, you've ripped your eyes out.
Now we're making progress.*

The doctor was a squat, ruddy-complexioned man whose nose
looked like a pig's snout. Whenever he spoke, I halfway expected him
to snort. This hog had been my counselor for the past six months. I
didn't like him, and found it irritating that he never made eye contact
with me, especially when I confessed the most intimate things about
myself. However, like a codependent junkie, I dutifully kept seeing
him. I mean, I didn't want to upset him by changing counselors.

I decided to enter therapy when I started experiencing chest pains,
hyperventilation, and a rapid heartbeat, as if my body were preparing
itself for some jeopardy. At first I attributed it to my natural
inclinations—a nervous personality flavored with a sliver of social
anxiety. That was until the hallucinations began.

The first one had occurred at Stop & Shop as I was scoping out the
candy aisle for a nutritionally sound college breakfast. As I'd reached
for the cherry-flavored Twizzlers, I'd felt a weird twinge in the palm

of my hand. The package had started vibrating, and then practically jumped off the shelf at me.

Let me tell you, I was more than a little freaked out. It might as well have been a king cobra the way I snatched my hand back. The candy was on the floor, and I was just ogling it, waiting for it to do something else. Some random customers stopped and stared at the Twizzlers, too. When they didn't see anything, they gave me a look and moved on.

Finally, the store manager came over like he was approaching an escaped mental patient. "Miss, can I help you?" he asked, maintaining a distance.

And I was still just standing there, waiting on the Twizzlers. "I'm okay," I said, but I was thinking, *Okay, now I'm just freaking losing my mind.* All I could do was rub my eyes and go grab some Red Bull. Obviously there wasn't enough caffeine in my system to keep me coherent. I needed some wings.

Six months later I was in Dr. Graves's office, watching him draw straight lines on his writing pad.

"You know, Ms. Valois, this is all very simple," he said. "Not only your hallucinations, but all of your emotional problems as well, primarily stem from your unconscious rebellion against adult responsibilities. Graduation *is* coming up soon. And your father's parenting style—smothering, overprotective—has plainly crippled your ability to cope with stress. You're twenty-one years old. Time to grow a spine."

Wow! I didn't realize I was so fucked up. Thanks, Dr. Graves, for pointing that out.

The doctor leaned forward like he was about to tell me a great secret. "And you really must get over Rafe." He leaned back with that smug, know-it-all look. Unfortunately, I couldn't argue with what he had said, especially the part about Rafe.

Rafe was my first *everything.* We'd met in high school and bonded over being two weird, little squids in an ocean filled with great white sharks. We spent weekends playing games on the computer, watching horror movies, or walking in the woods just talking about nothing. We'd decided to attend Long Island College together.

It sounded real sweet, but time was Rafe's friend. Once an ugly duckling, he'd experienced a sudden growth spurt at age twenty that had resulted in a buff body and the disappearance of his cystic acne. He had constantly perused the drugstore aisles in search of the perfect product for his highlighted hair. To me he'd started looking like a damp puppy as he chased the ultimate wet look.

Tiffany, a perky Delta Rho Rho, had seen the changes in Rafe, too. Shortly thereafter I'd found it hard to get him on the phone, let alone see him. Hell, the last time I'd seen him, Tiffany had been tonguing him down at the student union. *Fuck.*

And why wouldn't he want Tiff? He had a choice: a hot chick, or some loner who had apparently gone fucking crazy. I was resigned to the idea of never finding love again and becoming the ultimate cat lady.

"You have been hiding from the world, Ms. Valois. Why do you think you chose accounting as a major? Stop trying to hide behind numbers in a ledger book."

Mr. Graves had gotten me again. I hated motherfucking accounting, but numbers never teased me. Numbers never cheated on me. And numbers never made me feel like I had to apologize for taking up space on this earth.

"Find out who the real Grace Valois is," Dr. Graves finished.

I stood up, and had to screw my ass back on since it had been handed to me. As I walked to the door, Dr. Graves looked up at me as if I were a memory he had forgotten already. I whipped around, scraping my arm against a wooden shard protruding from the doorframe. I didn't even notice the tiny drop of blood my abrasion left behind.

And then, Dr. Graves said something else to me.

The next morning I was determined not to let anyone or anything—especially my apparent mental illness—put a damper on my day.

I shared my cubicle of an apartment with Julie, my best friend since preschool. She was already in the kitchen with a bowl overflowing with Fruity Pebbles, chewing like a horse eating confetti. "Hey, Jules. Helping yourself to my cereal again? You know that stuff's like five dollars a box, right?" I said, a little miffed.

She plopped her size-eleven, flip-flopped feet on the table. "Just sit your ass in the chair. What are you wearing to the beach today?"

I had forgotten all about that—more like kicked it into my subconscious, hoping like hell it wouldn't come to pass. "Julie, what ever are you talking about?" I innocently fluttered my eyelashes at her.

"Don't be funny, Grace. I packed all of your stuff in your duffel bag … including your 1920s-style bathing suit. You will not have me stop back to get it. That's called stalling."

Shit, she figured out my maniacal plan, I thought.

Julie was not one for detours. If she was on a mission, it was full steam ahead. She swung her feet off the table, and slammed her fist down with enough force to create a current that rustled the curtains.

"For fuck's sake, Grace, you're going to have a good time," Julie demanded. "Do you understand me?" Suddenly, she jumped up out of her chair and grabbed me. I struggled to break free of her death grip.

"Oh, sorry," she said. "I'm just so stoked. Besides, you need some meat on those bones."

Julie had no problem displaying her strength, and constantly encouraged people to challenge it. Some boys thought she was a little butch, and yeah, she probably was a girl trapped in a boy's body—not that she liked girls or anything—but she constantly craved competition. She loved fast cars and arm wrestling, and was very athletic. She had a rock-hard body, with well-defined legs and nice tits.

If it weren't for her beauty, one might have assumed she had gender issues.

My father, Ed, had never been a fan of Julie's daredevil antics. It wasn't that he didn't like Julie; he was just protective. When we were kids, whenever Julie had stopped by, Dad had looked over his glasses, his eyes telling her to handle me with care. And boy, when Julie got her driver's license, I thought Dad was going to have a stroke every time I got in the car with her. So did I, the way she sped up and down Sunrise Highway like mayhem on wheels. Regardless, she was my best friend and alter ego; I always ended up having a good time anyway.

Julie gently shoved me out the door and into her car. I gave her a look of warning, but before I could even get my seatbelt on she floored the gas, leaving a set of tire marks in the parking lot. She let out a hearty laugh. "Sorry, I forgot you lack the need for speed."

"No problem. I love starting my day with my eyes sucked back into my head."

I scanned the radio stations before settling on classical. Vivaldi was Julie's clue that something was up.

"Spill it, Grace. What's on your mind?" she asked, pretending she didn't know.

"Do we really have to go to this party? I'm so done with these flakes, it's not even funny. I can honestly do without seeing these fake-ass people for the rest of my life."

"Seriously! What's your problem with everyone? Graduation's a month and a half away. After that it's all downhill. I mean *really* downhill. Would it kill you to let loose a bit? This is our last day being with all of our friends."

"*Your* friends."

"Damn it, Grace. If you'd get your head out of a book every once in a while, maybe you'd have friends other than me. Geez, let's just eat, get a tan, and have some fun. Okay?" Julie threw a towel at my face. We both laughed, but I had something else to tell her.

"I saw Dr. Graves yesterday. I'm having those dreams again."

Julie knew those dreams well. She had lost many a night's sleep running to my room to stop my screaming. I was thankful she took care of the numerous noise complaints angry neighbors had delivered to the landlord. Still, I never felt comfortable enough to tell her the dreams' contents. They were so disturbing, so perverse. I didn't want her to think I was a psychopath.

"He told me, 'Have a good life while you still can'," I said.

Julie looked at me like she was expecting something else to come out of my mouth. When new words weren't forthcoming, her eyes narrowed, and she let out a ghoulish laugh. "Ooh, have a good life ... How sinister."

"It wasn't what he said, jackass. It was how he said it. Like he knew something."

"What do you expect from someone who talks to crazies all day?" Julie caught her faux pas. "Aw, sorry, Grace."

"Christ on a cross, Grace. Don't tell me you're going to analyze that all day. Paranoia will destroy you." Typical Julie; she wouldn't allow me to wallow in my well-deserved pity party. She pushed button number two on her radio and cranked up 30 Seconds to Mars. However, she gave the lead foot a break, opting to drive at a more acceptable speed to make me feel better.

Pulling up to the beach, Julie parked her Volkswagen in the outermost spot, forever mindful of any potential damage to her car. She bounded out with two beach chairs in one hand. Her stride was quick and long.

Julie ran down the beach to get right in the middle of the action. I hung back, surveying the surroundings for a quiet spot.

"Grace, are you going to sit with me or by yourself?" she yelled from all the way down the beach. I thought she was pretty much being a nag at that point. She should've been thankful I was there at all; this was for her benefit, not mine.

"Fine! Be a loner!" she grumbled, and immediately immersed herself in a volleyball game.

I adjusted my chair to face the sun. Getting a tan was at the top of my list. I would live on the edge that day and use a sunscreen with an SPF of only ten. My SPF-fifty-preaching father would have killed me if he knew, but you can't get a decent tan slathered in paste.

I blissfully reclined in my chair, taking in the salty ocean air. It was heaven. The heat of the sun combined with the cool breeze coming off of the water was an awesome blend. Burying my toes in the warm sand, the sound of the waves started lulling me to sleep. The cries of the seagulls cradled my thoughts, allowing me to fall even deeper.

Then a sudden cloud cover sent a chill down my spine. I opened one eye, assessing when the sun's warmth would return. I chuckled at Julie's big mouth as she challenged a group of boys to a flag football game. Unfortunately, that wasn't all I heard.

Tiffany's catty, suburban–girl, shrill voice was coming up behind me. "Rafe said I was the best fuck he ever had," she squealed, making sure I heard every word. "He can't even remember why he was with such losers before. Oh … sorry, Grace. I didn't see you there."

The demoness dropped her crap mere inches from my chair, surrounded by her it-girl goon squad. "Grace, would you mind sitting somewhere else so my girlfriends can hang with me? You'd be the best," Tiffany said, glowering down at me.

As I looked up, all I could see were the bottoms of Tiffany's braless, newly fitted tits peeking from underneath her cut-off shirt. And those were two of the reasons I'd always been intimidated by her. Seriously, she was such a perfect physical specimen; there was no way she could've been born to Homo sapiens parents. This diabla enticed her prey with her deceptively angelic face, like a prototype Precious Moments figurine. And her pheromones smelled like cotton candy— usually. That day she smelled a lot like rancid bologna and sulfur. I instinctively put my hand to my nose to prevent the thick odor from coating my nostril hairs.

Tiffany saw this and became highly offended. "What the hell are you doing? I know some lowlife trash like you isn't implying I stink."

That was my cue to leave, like the other times Tiffany had gotten in my face to establish dominance. I didn't care about those things. I just wanted to be left alone.

I was about to get up when she slapped the top of my head. "You hear me talking to you, chick?"

Goose bumps raised the hair on my arms. All of the sounds around me became jumbled up. The world constricted right before my eyes; all I could see was Tiffany. I stood up on slightly shaky legs. My equilibrium went haywire for a few seconds. When it steadied, my vision was intensified. Tiffany's outline was crisp, sharp—like I was looking at her through the eyes of animal. Oddly, I was no longer afraid of her or intimidated. Rather, I felt challenged and exhilarated.

Tiffany gave me a peculiar look. "Well?" she snapped, unsure whether she wanted to continue the fight.

My palm began to burn, like someone was holding a blowtorch to it. I refused to acknowledge the pain, and remained on target. My fingers locked, moments away from being wrapped around Tiffany's neck. A shockwave exploded in my mouth, and I could feel fangs trying to bust through my gums. I immediately covered my mouth.

Julie saw Tiffany and practically torpedoed out of the water, coming to my rescue. Little did she know that this time, it was Tiffany who needed help. Good ol' Jules ran up, waving her hands with a 'DON'T JUMP OUT OF THE WINDOW' look on her face. She had no clue what was really happening, and assumed I was getting messed with again.

Tiffany walked backward, never taking her eyes off mine. She knew if she stayed one more minute, something really fucked up was going to happen to her. She scooped up her belongings as quickly as she could, all but running off the beach and leaving her friends behind.

"Grace, it's okay. I'm here now," Julie said, panting.

My dissociated mind came back to me, and brought with it a brain-slicing migraine. "I don't know what just happened," I muttered, rubbing my temples. Julie put me in the car and drove us home. I stared in the side-view mirror, tracing my gums with my tongue.

"What are you doing?" Julie asked, *not* keeping her eyes on the road.

"Nothing." I kept looking at myself, thinking, *Just another fucking figment of my screwed imagination.*

Chapter Three

Hell is empty and all the devils are here.

—William Shakespeare

*S*omething was searching in the dark, and caught a whiff of what it was looking for. A scent led the phantom figure to a door that was top-paneled with glass and had Dr. Graves's name on it. It smelled around the old, wooden frame, its painful appetite growing stronger. It tried to open the door, but it was locked, so it used a fraction of its fantastic strength to rip the door lock out of the jamb. It pushed the door open hard, with no regard to the glass slamming against the office's interior wall.

Grace's blood had dried into a purplish-crimson stain on the shard of wood, which still jutted out like a porcupine spine. The figure sniffed and tapped the quill with the tip of its leathery tongue. Ravenous hunger contractions squeezed its stomach tight.

The figure heard the Vietnamese janitor, Bao, rounding the corner. Bao had recently immigrated to the United States, so his attention was divided between the ESOL app on his iPhone and trying to maneuver the bulky industrial buffer. His earbuds and the whir of the clumsy machine prevented him from hearing the wispy movements of the phantom figure. Bao had turned on a single light—forever mindful that electricity was a precious commodity where he came from—and was working at the dark end of one of two abutted hallways. He didn't notice that the shadow figure had caught sight of him and was spooking around in the darkness like a wraith.

Bao came upon Dr. Graves's door, perplexed that it was broken. He looked around, but saw no one.

Spider-crawling up the wall, the figure took a keen interest in Bao's confusion. It crept up to the dropped ceiling and hung upside-down, with its hands and feet adhered to the tile … all the while staring down at Bao.

It watched as Bao hesitated, then committed to taking a small step into the office. He didn't dare turn on the lights for fear of what could have lurked inside. Instead, Bao pulled out his earbuds and listened to the darkness. The janitor heard nothing except the eerie hum of the air conditioner; he reasoned it was not his job to look for trouble, and quickly exited Dr. Graves's office.

All the while the mysterious figure wondered what Bao tasted like. It scaled back down, positioning itself like a living wall sconce only inches away from Bao, its milky, thickly veined fist about to punch a hole through Bao's chest. Suddenly, the figure remembered its orders not to bring any attention to itself. All the stalking stranger could do was inhale the tang of the sweat that beaded off Bao's skin.

The phantom figure watched Bao swat at his raised neck hairs before grabbing the buffer and hotfooting it to the elevator. The janitor's frantic finger kept hitting the "close" button as he looked deep into the immeasurable darkness of the hall. Finally the car came, and Bao jumped in. As the door closed behind him, the figure heard the muffled voice of the translator through Bao's dangling earbuds: "*Tôi đói,*" it said. "I'm hungry."

Later that night Samantha Beckon got off work. She hated smelling like a bag of Fritos. Like Grace, Samantha's family had no money to speak of, and she had to work at the Galaxy 10 movie theater to pay her way through college. Tonight she had been pulled to concessions—her least favorite job—where the intermingled smells of buttered popcorn and jalapeno nachos had not only conquered her uniform, but had actually seeped into her pores.

Normally Samantha worked the ticket booth, where she spent most of her time staring aimlessly out the window. She had seen Grace a few times and recognized her from Chemistry 301. In class Samantha sat in front of Grace, but was unaware that her cheap perfume choked Grace out. Moreover, her lion's mane of curly, red hair blocked Grace's view of the chalkboard.

It was well past two in the morning, and all Samantha wanted to do was get back to the dorm. The bus pulled up, and she was surprised that her old friend Jack, the regular driver, didn't greet her. She presented her pass to the gruff replacement, and—despite being overwhelmingly tired—offered a genuine smile.

"Where's Jack?" she asked.

"Just go sit down, will ya?" said the brusque driver, who resented the fact that he had to drive all the way out to LIC—on the outskirts of town—to drop off one person.

Samantha took a seat at the very rear of the bus. She avoided looking at the driver's reflection in the rearview mirror, with the corners of his mouth pointing downward. She scooted down and prepared mentally for the long, tense drive, wishing Jack were there.

Samantha did not expect to be dropped off at the actual bus stop two blocks away from LIC's campus. She heard the whoosh of the compressed air cylinder as it opened the doors—her audible cue to hurry up and get off the bus. She took a step down the stairs and looked into the pitch-black night. Something didn't feel right to her, and she turned back to the driver.

"Could you please drive me up to the gate? Jack always does. He never drops me off here."

The driver stared straight ahead. "I'm not Jack."

Samantha had barely touched the sidewalk when the driver closed the doors and drove off. "Fucking asshole," she said under her breath as she waved her way out of a cloud of black exhaust, coughing diesel fumes. However, she felt that was the least of her problems.

LIC was definitely not a party campus. This was the weekend, and the bulk of the students had either gone home or to New York City. The streetlamps barely lit the cobblestone street, which was totally devoid of life. However, there was one small storefront window with a blazing neon fleur-de-lis. Its scarlet haze lit Samantha's way to the back gate of LIC's campus. She was unnerved, thinking she might actually have fared better on some desolate, backwoods road populated by raving, inbred hillbillies. Her stomach fluttered, and she glanced to her side as she quickened her steps.

In her peripheral vision, Samantha thought she saw something in the distance, coming up fast. She broke into a jog, the plasticky tapping of her cheap work shoes filling the air as they hit the cobblestones. She looked back and saw a tall shadow of a murky figure gliding toward her on the buildings' brick walls. The shadow seemed to be alive, not naturally conforming to the bends and corners of the buildings.

Samantha took off into a full sprint toward the gate, calling out to whoever would hear her. Unfortunately, no one heard her pleas, and the gate was still far, far away. It seemed like the figure was right upon her, and Samantha knew she had to take a life-or-death stand. She turned and swung wildly with her junky purse, but no one was there. She found no relief in that, and immediately started running again, digging through her purse simultaneously. She found her phone and tried to dial 911 as she ran, but her bouncing steps and trembling hand kept making her misdial.

Samantha hurled herself to the gate, making a judgment call to hide in the guard shack. It hadn't been used in decades and was more ornamental than functional. Time and weather had worn down its lock, making it easy for Samantha to enter. She dropped down—afraid even to breathe for the noise it might make—and huddled deep in a corner, keeping the door closed with her foot.

The doorknob rattled. Samantha covered her mouth to keep from screaming. Suddenly, a loud thud shook the door. It was followed by a series of scratches and pounding overlaid by Samantha's manic screams. Then, all at once, everything was silent outside the guard-shack door.

Samantha quieted down. Her eyes, mascara dripping and running from them, stayed on the door. Not seeing anything, she slowly leaned forward. The glass window behind her crashed in, and the figure's hand grabbed the back of her shirt, then the nape of her neck. It yanked her back, slamming her against a small, metal shelf populated with safety manuals from the 1970s. They fell on Samantha like blocks of colored snow.

She threw them off and escaped the shack, running as fast as she could toward her dorm, which was on the other side of campus. Breathless, she came upon the student counseling services building.

She could vaguely see Bao through the window. He was on the first floor, and his back was turned to her.

Samantha was about to scream bloody murder when the figure's massive arm clotheslined her neck, collapsing her trachea. She was laid out on her back, but could still see Bao as he turned in her direction. He looked like he was already scared of something. Samantha kicked at the air, but kept missing the figure that loomed over her.

At the window, Bao just missed the figure dragging Samantha into the darkness. By then she was suffocating from her collapsed trachea, but death was too slow in coming.

Even though the figure had been instructed not to feed, it was just too hungry. It took near-erotic pleasure in snapping Samantha's bones in its mammoth hands—first pulverizing her legs, then her arms, and finishing with her back. Before the merciful unconsciousness of death arrived, Samantha's bleary eyes saw the killer's canines growing longer as its face came down upon her.

And that face belonged to Grace.

Chapter Four

You can spend minutes, hours, days, weeks, or even months over-analyzing a situation; trying to put the pieces together, justifying what could've, would've happened ... or you can just leave the pieces on the floor and move the fuck on.

—Tupac Shakur

Shocked out of sleep, my screams echoed through the apartment. Julie rushed in—forever my rescuer.

"Another dream?" she asked as she rocked me in her arms.

All I could do was weep. "It seemed so real this time. So real."

Later that morning, I stood in front of the mirror. "All right, Grace, get your shit together," I repeated over and over again. However, I couldn't get that dream out of my head. I took a deep breath, formulating yet another apology. *Sorry, Jules, about waking up like a maniac. You know how I am before that first cup of coffee. Tee-hee.*

I made some ramen noodles and joined Julie, who was already in the living room watching TV. I could tell she was irritated with me because of her squinty-eyed smirk. She was tired of losing sleep and having to eat crow with the landlord. "You're up early. You must be pretty rested, huh?" she said sarcastically.

"Whatcha watching?" I asked, trying to change the subject.

Julie huffed a bit through her nose as she flipped through the channels. "Nothing."

I made a peace offering with the noodles. She brushed them off, but gave me an *I forgive you* smile.

Julie landed on a news conference already in progress. I sat on the floor, fixing my eyes on the police tape draping the area around LIC's student counseling services building. The camera panned to the highly stylized reporter from New York City, who was unaware she was being broadcast live at that moment ... while she was adjusting her Spanx.

"That's a first," I said. "A news conference in this Podunk town? What happened? The cows robbed a bank?"

The reporter straightened up when she finally saw the cameraman motioning to her. She was flustered, but carried on with her report, her shirt haphazardly tucked into her exposed undergarment. "Local police made a shocking discovery last night. A young woman was found dead on the bucolic campus of Long Island College. She was last seen alive in the early morning hours, after getting off work. The murder may be connected to a string of gruesome attacks across the country—possibly the work of a serial killer who has been operating for more than twenty years. The body of the girl has not been recovered yet, but her head was. It was displayed on the stairs of the counseling building—a possible taunt to police. A janitor has been taken into custody as a person of interest, but is not considered a suspect at this time. The manner of death is still under investigation."

I could only think, *Really? The manner of death is not obvious to you?*

The reporter cut to Police Chief Carl Murphy, who stepped up to the podium. He was a tall, gaunt man—whose normal demeanor was controlled and calculating—but today he was shaking.

"Hello, I'm Chief Murphy. First I'd like to say my thoughts and prayers go out to the victim's family. I'm so sorry they have to endure this tragedy. To my right is Mayor Bataglia."

The mayor just nodded and didn't say anything; he was still over the legal limits of alcohol consumption from his overnight binge.

The chief continued, "And to my left is Special Agent Adams of the FBI. Please hold any questions until the end of the conference. Thank you."

Chief Murphy kept it short and sweet. What else could a man, who only ever dealt with burglaries and the occasional rowdy student, do?

Agent Adams was not merely cute. He was not merely handsome. This man was the kind of good looking that could make you say, "Oh my effin' God" loudly and inappropriately in the middle church—at your mother's funeral. He swagger-walked to the podium, making everyone forget about Chief Murphy. Agent Adams's deep, resonating voice caused all of the female reporters to swoon ... and a few of the men, too.

"The FBI has been tracking and collecting information about this potential serial killer, and putting it all together in a crisis management database," said Agent Adams.

I looked back at Julie, who actually seemed worried; that was a first for someone who never let anything get to her. Then I turned back to the TV and that stud of a man.

"Any current or new leads will be cross-referenced against all of the other data to try to connect the dots," he continued. "We are asking the public to call in with tips. Even if you think something is inconsequential, please call. Most solid leads come from tips that do not appear to be relevant initially. Also, let me reinforce the importance of communication. We are recommending a temporary curfew for children and young adults. This initiative is designed to deter copycats and prevent other related crimes. At this time, I'll take questions."

As Agent Adams pointed to reporters, I noticed he was wearing a silver ring with an inordinately large lion's head on it—something that would be found on a family crest.

He finished up. "Now with that, let me give the podium to Mayor Bataglia for some final thoughts."

The mayor was taken aback that the microphone had been passed off to him. He blinked his eyes fast, as if that would sober him up quickly, as he and Agent Adams switched places. "Uh, I would like to let the people know I will do whatever possible to bring justice to those responsible," the mayor said, hoping his inept assistant would put some words up on the teleprompter. Chief Murphy passed him a photo, and the mayor continued, "And we will remember Samantha Beckon in our prayers." He raised the photograph of Samantha, showing it to the crowd.

That looks like the girl from my dream! I dropped my ramen noodles and didn't even hear Julie fussing about the mess on the worn-out, green-shag carpet. I stopped breathing for what seemed like hours. My heart tried to pound its way out of my chest. I tried to collect my thoughts, believing this was another hallucination. I kept thinking, *Okay, I'm just imagining this.* Yeah, yeah … This chick just happened to look exactly like a girl in my chemistry class; the one who sometimes had that funny smell. She sat in front of me, but I'd never gotten a good look at her face. No, that couldn't be the girl from my dream. It just couldn't be. Ugh, maybe I was just stone-cold, fucking crazy.

I stared at the TV screen, which showed a close-up of the red-headed girl's face, and rubbed my eyes, trying to make her look like somebody else.

Fuck. Dream Girl still looked the same.

For the rest of the day, Samantha haunted my every thought. If I was going to have any peace, I knew I had to confront this.

I *had* to go down to the school and see. Just to look at the crime scene. If nothing was familiar, I'd tell Julie about my dream. Then we'd go to a real psychiatrist and get me on some drugs fast, quick, and in a hurry. However, if it *was* familiar … well, I'd cross that bridge when I got to it.

I snuck out of the apartment while Julie was in the shower. I knew she'd be in there for at least an hour because she'd said she was going to shave. For a female, Julie had a massive amount of body hair, and it always took her that long to scrape the moss off.

We didn't live too far from campus, so it only took me a few minutes to get there. The closer I got, the more it felt like I was reliving the dream—a morbid déjà vu. There was just enough dusky sunlight to see the campus yard. Police tape hung like laundry on a line. The cleanup crew had done a shitty job of power-washing the blood off of the sidewalk and steps, leaving a dried river of pinkish streaks behind. If I saw the fleur-de-lis, it would confirm that it hadn't been a dream—that in some way I had actually been there during the murder. I scanned the area and could not find anything resembling a fleur-de-lis. *Phew* … It had been only a nightmare.

I laughed despite my neurosis, satisfied that I could hold off on the crazy pills a wee bit longer. Turning around to walk home, I heard dried grass crunch under someone's feet. Suddenly, I was hit with a concussion-inducing blow that pushed me forward about five feet. I saw what appeared to be a man. His hideous face could have passed in a crowd of regular people, but upon closer inspection you'd see something was off. He stood there looking at me for a moment, as if he already knew who I was, with a strange combination of awe and hatred on his face. His mouth pulled back over his teeth; I could see some caked-on blood on their pointy tips.

In the next instant, he knocked me down and straddled my legs. I was trapped by the overwhelming weight of his large body. In turn, my body reacted, and my fangs emerged from my gums.

Just then something flew out of the twilight and crashed into my attacker, smacking him off me. A humanoid, wolf-like creature appeared. Its graceful, almost feminine beauty momentarily struck me. It stood about seven feet tall and had chocolate-brown fur that lay smoothly on its skin. Its yellow eyes had midnight-black irises that strobed brightly in the dark. They were scary as hell … and yet oddly familiar.

The wolf wrestled with the killer. They effortlessly picked each other up and threw one another around the yard. The wolf slashed at the killer with its mammoth claws, leaving fleshy gashes behind. The killer, in return, bit into the wolf and tore out bits of hairy skin.

I wasn't sticking around to see which monster would win the fight. Despite my head injury, my body took full advantage of the excess adrenaline, and I ran all the way home. Usain Bolt had nothing on me.

Julie wasn't going to believe this!

I slid into the apartment like it was home plate. Securing the chain, I dropped to my knees to turn the lock on the knob. I was far from being a religious person, but since I was already kneeling—and had Freddy Krueger and a big-ass dog possibly chasing me—I clasped my hands and spouted out a random prayer: "Hail Mary. The kingdom and the power. Santa Claus. Easter Bunny." I tried to make the sign of the cross, but was so scared I couldn't remember how.

I waited a moment, trying to get my mind in order. Then I steeled myself and looked out the peephole. Luckily, the fisheye view showed nothing except the fire-escape door across the hall.

My head felt like it was about to explode, and I had to get to the couch. I touched the back of my head where that Section 8 had slugged me; it was saturated with blood. Wiping it on my clothes, I sank into the couch like I was the Titanic.

"Julie," I called out. "Julieeeee!"

The sliding glass door opened, and in walked the she-wolf—the one from campus—morphing into Julie. "You called?" she said.

And I faded to black.

I woke up feeling the high-speed velocity of a car underneath me. "Oh, my fucking head. Julie ... Advil." I was disoriented, and thinking I was still at the apartment. I glanced over to see Julie—no, Wolfy— was driving. I jerked back, trying to wedge my body between the door and the seat.

"Okay, I know you're fully about to wig out on me. But can you just chill for a moment before you do?" Julie pleaded as she flew around curves. I opened the door and tried to jump out of the car, but Julie's oversized hand dragged me back in.

"Are you trying to fucking kill yourself, you big dummy?" she snapped, warding off my prissy hand slaps.

"Deputy? Seeing eye? Snoop Dog? Exactly what kind of fucking canine are you?" I said with my back pushed hard against the door.

Julie raised one eyebrow. "All right, keep it up and see if I don't pop you one."

"*Oh*, I don't have permission to say anything, right? Yet you can go all Teen Wolf on me." Yeah, I was glib, but my mediocre world had just been turned upside down. What else was I going to do? Fight? Talk about my feelings? Being a smart ass was all I could think to do.

Julie pulled off to the side of the road. "I'm not upset with you. I sympathize, really." She took a deep breath. "This is going to be really hard for you." She kept hemming and hawing, and I was in no mood to guess what she was talking about.

"Just tell me what's going on," I demanded.

Julie got out of the car and leaned back into the driver's side window. "Wait till we get to your dad's." She went to the trunk and brought something back around for me—some of her sweaty-smelling athletic gear.

"I don't want to wear your funky duds," I said.

"Yours have blood on them. You don't want your dad to get any more upset than he will already be."

Chapter Five

Truth is stranger than fiction, but it is because fiction is obliged to stick to possibilities. Truth isn't.

—Mark Twain

The wolf and I arrived in Massapequa around sunrise. Dad was pacing on the porch. He had given up smoking years ago; however, it was obvious he had been chain-smoking all night from by the scrunched up cigarettes scattered about. He was joined by our ever-faithful beagle, Hercules, who thought he was ten times bigger than he really was. I could see now why Hercules and Julie got along so well. Cousins maybe?

"Hey, Mr. Thomas," Julie said as respectfully as she could. I saw in Dad's face that he was blaming her for whatever was going on, but I suspected that was because Julie was the only one at that moment he *could* blame.

"You all right, baby?" Dad asked.

Apparently this whole situation was not new to him. Like Julie, he had been keeping secrets from me.

"Dad?" I asked. "What's going on?"

He tried to lead me to the house, thinking if he didn't say anything I wouldn't ask any more. So sorry, but he was wrong. "Dad! What's going on? Stop blowing me off."

"I gotta make a phone call. Let's go inside." He looked around, making sure we weren't being followed, and led Julie and me into the house. I made sure to stay on the opposite side of the room from Julie, and stared at her with suspicion. I just *knew* Dad was calling the police. Julie was going to be arrested for kidnapping and thrown into a cage. Hell, she was probably already used to that.

Instead, I heard Dad talking to my aunt, Evelyn, on the phone. He was rambling on about it being "time," and something about me waking up. Under different circumstances, Aunt Evelyn would have seemed like an odd choice to call ...but not that morning.

Dad put the phone on speaker, and I heard Aunt Evelyn instructing Julie to bring me over to her house. Aunt Evelyn owned this awesome occult store just outside Massapequa, and lived in a house right behind it. She catered to New Age freaks, and teenagers who dabbled in Internet spells.

Of course! Evelyn was going to give us a free supply of wolf's bane and mandrake. *Like that's helpful.*

Dad looked out the window. "I think it's best if we lay low here. Everything seems clear."

"Ed, Grace's awakening is being sensed right now by only the most powerful witches. It's too dangerous for her to stay in her childhood home. Her energy is too strong, too pure there. She's got to get out now, because when the rest of the witches sense her awakening, it's really going get hectic."

"I guess we'll be right over," Dad said, and started to make his way to his bedroom to pack.

"You can't come, Ed. You have to stay away from Grace for a while. It's easier for us to protect her that way. We can't watch over Grace and you at the same time. All of our energy has to go to her."

Dad smashed the receiver against the wall and spoke to the heavens. "Damn it, Ilan, why did you do this to our little girl?" He got back on the phone. "I've spent her whole life protecting her, and now you tell me I can do nothing? What kind of father can't protect his baby? I'll let her go, but you'd better take damn good care of her."

I went over to Dad, who was trying to hold back tears. "I've dreaded this day ever since they brought you to me. If things were different, I'd never let you go. Unfortunately, we're up against people ... evil people ... Just go."

Julie pushed me out the door. "C'mon, Grace. We've got to leave." She forced me into the car, and we peeled out of the dirt driveway. I still remember my dad as he waved good-bye until the car was out of sight.

"Grace, it will all make sense when we get to Evelyn's," Julie said.

I listened to her dribble off at the mouth as the trees blurred past us. I chuckled to myself at the irony of the situation. All this time I'd thought I only had to worry about hater girls, a retarded ex, and schizophrenia. Meanwhile, I'd been living with a girl who should've been eating out of a dog dish.

Julie tried to keep a poker face, but I wasn't buying it.

"How did you know where I was?" I asked. "You were in the shower when I left."

"I'm not a mind reader. However, I am assigned to you, and gifted to know when your life is in peril. Basically, you pinged."

"Great, now I'm pinging, too."

We both sat in silence. I was wondering what my aunt could possibly tell me that would alleviate this crisis. I tried to make sense of the last few hours by replaying them over and over again: *Murderer. Wolf. Waking up. Murderer. Wolf. Waking up.*

Finally, we pulled onto a steeply inclined, graveled road; it led up to Evelyn's store and house. At the end of the road was an old, wooden mailbox embossed with the name Evelyn Valois. On top was an iron sculpture of a witch on a broomstick.

I had spent many summers hanging out with Aunt Evelyn. Her store and home were old, totally refurbished farmhouses. She filled them with odd family heirlooms, antiques, and strange items she picked up along the way. Around town she was known for specializing in fulgurites—also known as lightning glass. It was the closest thing you'd get to holding real lightning.

To make the glass, Evelyn would head down to the beach in her truck filled with long, metal tubes. Obviously no normal person would be caught in a storm with a metal rod on a beach. However, Aunt Evelyn was not your average person. She placed them carefully into the sand, and when lightning struck them, it produced a long rod of sand crystals in elaborate shapes and colors. Aunt Evelyn pulled them out, polished them, and sold them as wind chimes. She couldn't keep them on the shelves.

As we approached the store, I could hear the familiar sound of the wind chimes. The pleasant melody usually calmed my soul, but today nothing would to give me peace. Julie parked the car in front and hopped out. She looked back at me, knowing I'd need a moment, before she went inside. I tried to prolong my time in the car as long as possible, just staring at those wind chimes. I knew that as soon as I got out, my life would change forever—and not in a good way.

Chapter Six

Call it a clan, call it a network, call it a
tribe, call it a family. Whatever you call
it, whoever you are, you need one.

—Jane Howard

A unt Evelyn greeted me at the door in a calico sarong and cork
sandals. "Aw, baby girl, I heard you had a rough day." She
ushered me in, enveloping me in a tight bear hug. Her store
was filled with Books of Shadows, herbs, candles, and crystals. The
dark mahogany trim and veil of incense gave the space the feel of a
temple.

Before I could speak, Aunt Evelyn and Julie started talking. Evelyn
said she had glamoured her property with a protection spell.

Damn. I'd always thought Aunt Evelyn was a bit eccentric, but
never a real witch.

Julie told her about my attacker. "It wasn't Catherine. I didn't
recognize the scent."

"Sounds like one of her protégés. It looks like Catherine has
figured out the general area of Grace's whereabouts, but couldn't
pinpoint it. She probably didn't want to expend any energy going after
Grace herself, since she isn't sure if Grace's powers have kicked in
yet."

I did the referee time-out signal. "Excuse me. I didn't hear that
right. Did you say 'powers'?"

However, they kept up their own conversation as if I hadn't
spoken. "A girl was murdered on campus," Julie explained. "They just
found her head. It was the same guy who attacked Grace."

"Oh, he needed a snack," said Aunt Evelyn.

I stood between the two. "You mean *eating people?*" I exclaimed.

"Yes, I mean exactly that," Aunt Evelyn said as nonchalantly as
she could, to prevent me from going into total meltdown mode. She

pulled me to the white-chenille sofa on which she performed tarot card readings and started pushing my clothes around, looking for something.

"Have you seen any strange marks on your body?" she asked, her examination getting a little too personal.

I pushed her hands away. "No. Same ole, same ole."

"We told you your mother died when you were born, but we didn't tell you how. That was for your protection," Aunt Evelyn said. "We come from a long line of witches dating back to the Middle Ages. There was a division, and your mother was ultimately killed because of it. Before she died, she had an indiscretion with a mortal, Ed, and you were born. Not only born, but created with a purpose. You were born to lead. It is your destiny."

"So let me get this straight. I'm some sort of half mortal and half witch savior?"

Aunt Evelyn sighed and gently cradled my face in her hand. "Grace, since you're the first of your kind, we really don't know what you are. We weren't sure you'd Awaken like the rest of the witches, but it appears you are doing just that. Past this point we really don't know what's going to happen. Regardless, we hope you are ready for what's coming."

She paused for a moment, bracing me. "Your blood may be so potent that a single drop could open the doorway to the many gifts and abilities of our clan. Because of that, supernatural forces are plotting your demise. They will stop at nothing to see you dead, but not before they take your powers. We are the only immortals who can protect you, honey."

I jumped up. "I'm a guinea pig! Is that what last night was all about? Is this what I am now? A girl who rides on brooms with fucking fangs? And seriously, what kind of witches have fangs? Never ran across that in Grimm's Fairy Tales." I started to walk away, but felt the need to express myself a little more, a little louder. "Oh yeah, let's not forget the killer who tried to eat me. Now witches eat people, too?"

Aunt Evelyn stood up, keeping her emotions close to the vest. "Grace, you need to calm down, or I will help you calm down."

"What does that mean? Is it a threat? Are you going to silence me with your magic?"

I was about was to say more when Aunt Evelyn lifted a finger and murmured, *"Mouth so big. Quiet now. Listen up. I'll show you how."* She pointed at my mouth, and I couldn't open my lips; it was like they were superglued together.

Julie laughed. "I thought she'd never shut up."

Aunt Evelyn approached me with a motherly smile on her face. She didn't know that my right hand had started burning like it had at the beach, or that the sting in my throat had returned. A sudden rush of electricity shot through my veins, just enough to blush the surface of my skin with a warm, tingly feeling. I pointed at my mouth and mumbled. Aunt Evelyn saw I was upset and reversed her spell. I clenched my teeth as my fangs poked all the way out of my mouth.

Julie got excited and started having a reaction of her own; her hands trembled violently, followed her arms, and finally by her head. The vibrations became blurred, as did Julie. Even though she broke through her clothes, she wasn't naked. Her skin was replaced by fur—dark brown from head to toe. I was horrified, yet totally entranced. Julie's face turned upward, and she belted out a howl.

Aunt Evelyn elbowed me. "Close your mouth, dear," she said, chucking it up. "Isn't she beautiful? Grace, you have no idea what a gift you have been given. Julie has been placed here to keep you safe and sound. I guess you can call her your own personal sergeant-at-arms."

Julie shook like a dog after a bath and was back to normal, clothes and all.

What a sad moment for me. The friend I'd known was no more. The ugly fact was that Julie and I were both monstrosities.

"I didn't ask for any of this. I'm leaving," I snapped, and ran out of the house.

The chirping of crickets filled the forest as if warning the woodland creatures of some strange beast in their midst. As I hurdled over brush, I noticed I could run faster than normal, almost gliding through the air. I caught the scent of some freshly killed animal's blood ... and it smelled good. The iron-y scent wafted into my nose and shrouded my entire being. My palate responded by moistening, and I thought about following the scent and getting a taste.

What?

As I snapped back, I heard Julie's voice pleading in the distance. "Grace, please don't do this. Come on back to the house."

"Stay away from me, Julie. This is not your life."

Somehow she appeared right in front of me. "Do you really think you're faster than me at this point?" She bucked me with her chest, pushing me in the opposite direction. Now that was the Julie I was used to; not that kumbaya chick at Aunt Evelyn's house.

However, that didn't matter to me. I wasn't going to let her talk me out of my breakout. "You heard I have some special powers. You sure you want to mess with me?"

Julie cracked up. "You're brand new. What the fuck are going to do?"

While I contemplated that, I heard something huge and powerful running toward us. Suddenly three coyotes rushed out of the woods. I was hit with the blunt force of Julie's arm pushing me out of the way, knocking me into a tree. A little dazed, I watched her toss each coyote in the air like rag dolls, and they immediately scampered away with their tails between their legs.

Julie turned her attention back to me. Fortunately for her, my body was numb from being thrown into a tree. I was unable to move right away, and I had to listen to her.

"Those were just a few coyotes, but there are more powerful predators out there, and they're coming for you, no doubt. So get a grip and deal with the situation, because there's no place for you to hide, and the only thing you can do to change it is fight."

I guessed she was right, but I wasn't letting her off that easy. "Um, maybe if you hadn't launched me into that tree I would be able to walk home on my own." Winking at her, I held out my hand, and in return Julie gave me a sly grin and helped me up.

Chapter Seven

A verse from the Veda says, "What you
see, you become." In other words, just
the experience of perceiving the world
makes you what you are. This is a quite
literal statement.

—Deepak Chopra

Stapleton. Thompson. Williams. Boudreaux. Winstead. These
were the aliases the Bolingbrokes had assumed over the past
twenty years. Well aware of their family's vendetta against
them, not to mention the threat of Catherine, they never let their guards
down. Their most recent neighborhood—Southern Shores in the Outer
Banks—was quiet, and thankfully filled with transient residents who
didn't stick around long enough to ask too many questions. The house
was a cozy craftsman-style cottage complete with an ID-card printing
machine. James was in charge of it, and was the one who came up with
their new names.

Even though James found the wild horses, bird-watching, and
fishing to be ideal, Addison found the OBX intolerable. In her former
life, she had been an icon in the immortal world, where her beauty and
other talents had always gotten her exactly what she'd wanted. She'd
used her short, black bob, endless legs, and dazzling aquamarine eyes
to turn many heads. She'd enjoyed being the center of the universe and
had taken every opportunity to bask in the admiration of her fanatic
following. Plenty of immortal girls had begged to be her apprentices.
However, Addison had always refused; she didn't like the thought of
potential competition. In her old life, she had lived by these famous
words: "If you're not living on the edge, you're taking up too much
room."

Addison had also been an unapologetic feeder—that was until
James had become involved with Ilan. During Ilan's pregnancy more
than twenty years ago, Ilan had forbidden the four other witches to eat
human flesh in her presence. No matter how hungry Ilan got, she had
refused to let go of this principal. That decision had left the others
somewhat in a state of malnutrition. The spirits that inhabited their
bodies had been famished and held their enormous powers hostage,

refusing to share with the witches until they fed them—which was how Catherine had almost defeated them.

Now Addison resented the fact that James continued this abstinence during their years in hiding; she had grown tired of steak tartare and the occasional bleeding cattle late at night. However, she had to refuel somehow. Lately her discontent had grown to the point that she was considering leaving James and his cause behind. She missed her old life and was exhausted from trying to keep their secret from the world. This was even more difficult because of Adrian's outlandish antics, which constantly threatened to expose them.

Addison joined James at the end of a long pier that had battled way too many nor'easters. She could tell his mind was elsewhere, but was not deterred from what she had to say.

"You're thinking about Grace again, aren't you?" She tried to ease into the conversation.

"Yeah. I think I feel her." I also felt my cock twinge, but I wouldn't share that with my sister.

She gave him a doubtful look and leaned on the railing, focusing her eyes on the horizon. "It's been more than twenty years. Witches Awaken at puberty. If she were going to do it, she'd have done it by now."

"She's unique. We don't know what she's going to do."

"So what are we to do in the meantime? Sit around, waiting for something that may or may not happen? For eternity? Come on, James, let's be realistic for a change."

Addison refused to look him in the eye as he turned her toward him.

"What the fuck's wrong with you lately? You know we have an assignment … a mission," James snapped.

"No, James, I don't have any mission. I only agreed to come because I wanted to make sure *you* were safe. It had nothing to do with Ilan or that baby. I'm here only because of you. I really think this is wasting time at best, and death sentences for us all at worst. You know I live my life quite literally on the edge, but this is just plain retarded."

Addison started walking away from James, but felt bad for being so hard on him. "Next time we move, could you pick a better name for me than Sally?" she called over her shoulder.

Chapter Eight

Neither love nor evil conquers all, but
evil cheats more.

—Laurell K. Hamilton

The envelope had a New York City return address—33 W. 55th Street—and contained instructions to be there at seven o'clock sharp, followed by an obnoxious comment: "I do not suffer fools, tardiness, or mistakes."

Chetan, a low-level witch, felt it was an honor to serve Catherine as one of her protégés. Catherine had been missing for years; many believed her to be dead. Following the invitation, she sent a driver for him, and he was overly impressed by the luxury treatment he was receiving. And why not? If anyone were asked to describe him, most wouldn't have been able to. He was unremarkable in every way. Beige. Vanilla. White-bread. His only distinguishing feature was that no one could seem to remember his name.

The limo arrived at the Shoreham Hotel, where Chetan was ushered into Catherine's lush penthouse suite. It had a magnificent view of the heart of New York City. The floors were marble, the walls adorned with suede. It was spacious, and decorated in a modern Art Deco style. Vases with fresh, sweet-smelling flowers were positioned in corners. However, the heady scents of jasmine and gardenias hardly masked the stench of decomposition somewhere in the penthouse.

A tall "man"—Samantha's killer—came from one of the back rooms. Chetan was unsettled by his presence, but offered up a casual high five. The man just looked at him and walked down a long, narrow hallway. He knew to ask no questions of the mystery man, and just to follow.

Chetan entered a sprawling, purple room—purple walls, purple carpet, purple sofas, even purple curtains—And Catherine sat in the middle, on a throne-like peacock chair. Samantha's killer, Catherine's most ruthless protégé, stood behind her and awaited further orders.

"Welcome, Chetan," Catherine said in her purring, Italian accent. "Not a minute late. I like that. Oh, let me introduce you to my friend."

Chetan waited for Catherine to tell him the killer's name, but it seemed Catherine thought "friend" was enough.

"As you know, I have a small problem named Grace Valois. It seems she is on the verge of awakening, and I need something from her. Now, she is most likely guarded by a group of witches ... some from my old coven. Can you believe that?"

Even though Chetan was honored to be one of Catherine's protégés, her reputation preceded her. He knew whatever answers he gave, he would have to tread lightly. "No, I don't understand how someone could betray you like that."

"Exactly! I must admit I have lived a good life, but I've had to avoid detection until the awakening. Now I have the opportunity to consume all of that girl's power."

Chetan kept his eyes on the protégé, who seemed to be looking right through him. "Uh, how are you going to do that, Catherine?"

"*Consummatio in quinque puncta.* I will entrap her in a prison-like pentagram and simply drain her of her power. Then I will consume her flesh."

"No disrespect, but what is the purpose of all this? You're already so powerful." Chetan could see he had gotten Catherine's hackles up, but she answered him anyway, her voice cold.

"Power, you silly, insignificant thing. To take over the council. As a side benefit, we'll all be able to hunt humans for sport and feast as much as we want. No more restrictions."

Catherine pushed the key on a nearby intercom. "Could you bring in lunch?" she asked of the dead air on the other end before looking back at Chetan. "You are going to help me take Grace Valois down. However, there's one thing: remember I don't suffer mistakes. Regardless, it seems my friend has made one." The stoic figure squirmed a little at that comment.

A mind-controlled helper, Jacklyn, entered the room with a room service cart holding several silver cloches. Jacklyn uncovered the dishes, revealing some of Samantha's body parts.

Catherine pointed for the figure to stand in front of her. "See, Chetan, my friend could not control his hunger and brought unwarranted attention to us. That's a *big* mistake." She waved her ghostly white hand, and an invisible sword sliced off the protégé's head.

Chetan gulped as Catherine stared at him. "You won't have that problem with me," he stated.

Chapter Nine

People are like stained glass windows: they sparkle and shine when the sun is out, but when the darkness sets in their true beauty is revealed only if there is a light within.

—Elizabeth Kubler-Ross

When Julie and I returned to the house, Aunt Evelyn was sitting on the porch. She seemed unconcerned, like she'd had foreknowledge about how this whole deal would work out. She was carefully hollowing out a wooden staff.

"I see you decided to come back," she joked. "Julie, thanks for getting her."

"No problem. That's my girl," Julie replied. I was just glad she and I were cool again.

Aunt Evelyn inserted a fulgurite inside the staff and sealed it off. She tapped it on the ground, and a tiny spark flickered. I stood there, amazed and terrified by the world in which I now found myself. Aunt Evelyn, on the other hand, was as giddy as a mother whose daughter had just gotten her period. Too bad this wasn't as fun as a tampon commercial.

Julie fixed me a cup of oolong tea with lemon, heavy on the sugar.

Evelyn rummaged through a few items—saint statues, worry stones, witchy bumper stickers, athames—and found a small, black box. She blew off the dust and opened it with a tiny key she always wore on a necklace. A small piece of stiff parchment paper was inside, with an incantation on it.

"Your mother wrote this," Aunt Evelyn said, handing it to me. The Latin words were handwritten in calligraphy. It didn't matter what they said; the paper itself was so beautiful. A work of art.

"What's it for?" I asked.

Aunt Evelyn took the paper back. "It's a summoning spell. We're calling the others." Walking over to an ornate cabinet, she pulled out a chalice, a pin, and rubbing alcohol. She came back to me and took my hand.

"This will only hurt for a second." She pricked my finger and squeezed droplets of blood into the chalice. Raising her hands, she recited the words of the spell.

I looked around, expecting some army to crash through the walls, but nothing happened. "Well, that's it?" I felt totally disappointed.

"Yes. It is done. Now we wait." Evelyn burned the incantation in the chalice. She dumped the ashes into her palm and then blew them into a cauldron in the fireplace.

And to think, I used to make s'mores in that.

Chapter Ten

You can't stop the future. You can't
rewind the past. The only way to learn
the secret … is to press play.

—Jay Asher

"**G**race, do you like it? I made that recipe up myself," Aunt
Evelyn said, fishing for a compliment about the dinner
spread she had put out.

"Oh, yeah … great," I replied, pushing my dry meatloaf around the
flower-trimmed Correlle plate. I didn't want to hurt her feelings. My
fork scraped through the sugary, ketchup-ed snail trails of some
strange concoction Aunt Evelyn called a glaze. Whatever it was, two
more bites of it would have induced a diabetic coma. That didn't
bother Julie, though. She gobbled down her chunks of beef like her life
depended on it.

Inside I was feeling like the female counterpart to Atlas, and was
wondering how I would navigate this new life as some kind of crazy
hybrid. Pondering the surrealism of it all. On one hand I was being
initiated into some hidden magical world, populated with crazy-ass,
cannibalistic assassins and Morpheus-and-Trinity-type protectors. On
the other I was asking Aunt Evelyn to pass the mashed potatoes and
lumpy gravy.

Because I was still in such a state of shock, my mind had not seen
fit to list the thousand commonsense questions it should have …
except one. "Why did I dream about Samantha's murder? You know,
as it was happening?" I asked, watching Aunt Evelyn cut her meatloaf
into perfect squares.

She put her fork down and wiped a bit of ketchup from the corner
of her mouth. "Grace, that is because we all descend from the original
coven. We are all *somewhat* connected to each other. Some witches,
apparently, have more of a psychic tie to the group than others … like
you for instance."

"Oh," I said, now prepared with a more substantial question. "Aunt Evelyn, who exactly *are* we? You gave me a little background, but it's obvious I need to catch up a wee bit more."

Aunt Evelyn pushed back her chair and began to speak like she was a shaman telling little children a story. "In the late 1600s, we were one large coven of peaceful witches, descendants of others who came from many continents. One big family, so to speak. We had maintained the magical traditions of our ancestors even though we were regular mortals. We lived quiet and contented lives, only using our magic for worship, and if the need arose, for continuance of the group.

"That was until one of our men returned from a long journey speaking about rumors of religious killings in Salem. At first we couldn't fathom such atrocities being committed by so-called civilized people. Taking no chances, we decided to sequester ourselves from the general population, not knowing how the Salem executions would affect us. However, that didn't help. Some of those pious fanatics made their way to the area near our settlement. At first the interlopers came with smiling faces and good cheer ..."

Aunt Evelyn started stroking her hands, as if the recollection of events frosted her skin and she was trying to warm back up. "They began encroaching on the lands of the natives, stealing it through deception and brutality. Justifying their actions by saying it was some kind of divine right ... that their lord had blessed them. And maybe what happened to us was some retribution for not taking a stand when others in our midst were in trouble."

I watched Aunt Evelyn squirm in her chair, trying to find a position that would somehow make the story easier to tell. None of them worked; she got up and made her way to a large bookshelf on the other side of the room. Her fingers ran across different subjects such as astrology, history, politics, and mythology.

"Aunt Evelyn, are you okay?" I asked, genuinely concerned about the washed-out look on her face. She was so focused on telling me what had happened that she didn't answer.

She continued, "The outsiders engaged us, trying to figure out exactly what our beliefs were. Not sure exactly what master we bowed down to, they set about their mission to convert, and became hostile when their aggressive attempts to 'save' us didn't work."

She pulled out a book. The cover featured the painting *Saturn Devouring His Son*. Aunt Evelyn's eyes did not move from that book, as if it had some special connection to what had happened back then.

"Now, it came to pass that some of their children started exhibiting strange illnesses and behaviors. Because we tried so hard to keep to ourselves—never getting involved in *their* rituals—they needed a scapegoat, and we were it. In the middle of the night, they ambushed us, murdering some of our members in the name of their god. We were totally caught off guard by this act of barbarism. We had no time to cast protection spells or anything. They primarily sought out the children, to ensure our lineage of so-called demons would end. They lined them up and impaled them one by one with knives, sticks, whatever they could find … Ritualistic sacrifices they were. After the children slowly bled out, the so-called godly ones buried the bodies underneath one of their churches."

I sat there utterly transfixed by Aunt Evelyn's story, horrified and sickened by what had happen to my people. Was that the type of life that was in store for me? Having to worry about superstitious morons, on top of witches?

Aunt Evelyn went on, "The rest of us, so ravaged by our fury and sorrow, sought revenge for our brethren. However, *all* energy is real … in its own way magical, and we were still mortals. The fundamentalist fanatics overwhelmed us in number. They were fueled by an all-powerful, consuming rage, essentially against all life that did not conform to *their* way. Whatever goodness we had wasn't enough to overcome them. So we debated whether or not to invoke the Ancients—a malevolent group of disembodied spirits. It's tricky to invoke them, because the Ancients usually require some kind of grotesque trade-off in exchange for their assistance."

"The worst kind," Julie interrupted, shivering a bit.

A faraway look drifted over Aunt Evelyn's face. I could tell these memories were just as vivid to her now as when they had happened. She drew her arms in close to her torso. "A schism developed between two factions: one supporting the idea of using the awesome power of the Ancients, and those who believed that not only was it morally wrong to do so, but dangerous to the coven itself. The majority decided to invoke the Ancients, and the dissenters left the coven."

Based on what I had heard so far, I wasn't impressed by the goody-two-shoes faction of the coven. I blurted out, "I agree with the ones who invoked the Ancients. Really, what is the point of having all of this magic if you're not going to mess up the people who hurt you? I mean no disrespect, but I think they totally punked out."

I swore I heard Julie think, *Oh, shit.* Aunt Evelyn's nostrils flared, and every muscle around her eyes tightened. She walked over to me slowly, deliberately, like she was about to kick my ass. Before I could take a step back, she suddenly ghosted to me, totally invading my personal space, and kept poking me in the chest. I had never seen her like that before.

"Oh really, missy? You think they were weak? You think they were dumb? That the others were the heroes? Let me tell you what happened. The ones who stayed invoked the Ancients, and there was a horrible trade-off. To receive the Ancients' great magical power, the witches had to allow the spirits to inhabit their bodies for eternity. To maintain these bodies, the witches would have to kill humans and cannibalize their flesh. *Forever.* Do you understand what I just said? You think demon possession is cool? Is that the life you think is good? If so, we've got a lot of work to do."

Well, damn. All I was doing was expressing my opinion. I didn't realize the First Amendment ended at this farmhouse. "I'm sorry," I said. Aunt Evelyn took her finger away from my dented-up chest and commenced with the rest of her story.

"The possessed witches annihilated the fanatics with phenomenal ease, and used their flesh to feed the disembodied spirits within. To this day people talk about a group of missionaries who suddenly, mysteriously disappeared from their camp—hundreds of them. Really, they just became supper … After the massacre, most of the possessed witches went back to their homelands, while a small portion stayed in the Americas."

Julie, who had said very little, adjusted her chair and turned my way. "Meanwhile, the members of the original coven who refused to participate in the invocation intermarried with Native American tribes, creating what is known as the mythical Thirteen Tribes of Long Island. Like the others, they called on spirits to inhabit their bodies, but these were benevolent Native American ones who gave them the ability to shape-shift into humanoid wolf-creatures."

I looked at Julie in amazement, with a deeper understanding of who she was. She shook her head with pride and said, "Yeah, we did it the right way. We wolves managed to blend into the tribes, keeping our true identities a secret. We recognize each other by symbols and items we hang outside our homes. And that, Grace, is some history for you to digest along with Aunt Evelyn's world-famous meatloaf."

I was grateful that Aunt Evelyn and Julie had given me some background, even though Evelyn had tried to take a chunk out of my ass. But I couldn't help it—I still felt like a spiraled pile of dung sitting at the bottom of a rest-stop toilet. I mean, knowing the history didn't change the fact that I was mentally connected to a bunch of stranger-witches in parts unknown, some of whom were death-dealing degenerates. Just knowing that made my body cold shudder and my spine tingle like right before I have to vomit.

However, this time that spine-tingling sensation traced its way to the nerve endings right beneath the surface of my skin. It felt like the color electric green would feel if it were solid. Suddenly the invisible sensation shot out of my pores and knocked over my half-filled mason jar of Sangiovese.

I looked at Julie, expecting her to make some smart alecky comment about my being drunk. Instead, both she and Aunt Evelyn sat there like babies looking at bottles—with their mouths wide open.

"How long have you been able to do that?" Aunt Evelyn asked.

"For a couple of months, I guess," I replied, brushing off my forearm; it felt like it had some sort of charge on it.

"Why didn't you tell me, you jackass?" Julie asked, mad and a little surprised.

"Well, obviously all this started happening before I knew what *you* were. I seriously thought I was delusional. C'mon, you have to admit it's weird to have things jump out at you. I thought I was a little … you know … loony."

"Loony? No, no, my dear. Far from it. Can you do it again?" Aunt Evelyn asked.

Putting my fingers to my temples—like I had seen in hundreds of B rated movies—I focused on my fork. I squinted my eyes and tried every variation of fluttering lids I could think of. Nothing.

"That's okay, baby girl," Aunt Evelyn said as she stood up. "What you've already shown us is fantastic. In fact, this event calls for a celebration." With that she disappeared into the kitchen.

Julie looked at me with a toothy grin, but I didn't share her happiness. I was in a void, a kind of unrelenting netherworld between being a young lassie and a ma'am ... and I was absolutely terrified. Despite my reluctance to come off like a blubbering fool, I had to confess.

"I'm scared, Jules." After my simple statement, all I could do was lower my eyes and be embarrassed by my emotional weakness.

She came over and crouched at my knee. "Yeah, I know." She looked over her shoulder for Aunt Evelyn. "I'm scared, too. But I'm here, and I'll do whatever it takes to help you. Not only because it's my duty, but because you're my best friend."

Aunt Evelyn breezed back in with my favorite dessert: strawberry trifle, heavy on the whipped cream. You'd think after the glaze, I'd want nothing more to do with sugar, but trifle ... I couldn't let that pass.

"Grace, after dinner I have something to show you," Aunt Evelyn said, scooping out my humongous portion with a giant soup ladle. I couldn't fault her attempt to use the syrupy confection as a device to make me forget the shit that was now called my life.

And things *were* okay, because for a few moments—as I savored every bite of that spongy sugar high—I did forget.

Chapter Eleven

Am I my brother's keeper?

—Cain

James had suffered through it all day. A desperate nagging stuck in his diaphragm. One of those aches that always seemed to herald the arrival of something.

The feeling was momentarily interrupted by a phone call. Henry Dodson, a barely functioning heroin fiend, was on the other end. James had learned years ago that if you wanted to live incognito, you had to enlist the services of many unsavory characters along the way. This was because even though a magical ability was a gift, it came with limitations.

James was aware that, like humans, witches were confined to the material world—which was ruled by the laws of space, time, and matter—and it took a tremendous amount of supernatural energy to transcend these laws. Some magical workings required so much force that performing them could result in the witch's death. Physical and ethereal recovery were real issues no matter how great or small the conjure was. So James always employed mundane efforts, whenever possible, to achieve his goals—even if those actions were felonious.

The Bolingbroke siblings had racked up an impressive list of underworld mortal connections: dirty vice cops, venereal-disease-ravaged prostitutes, hired killers, closeted politicians, and hardcore drug addicts. These were the types of people who got them what they needed without all the scrutiny and paper trails that came with legal methods. James preferred the addicts because he found them to be the least likely to become turncoats ... as long as the drugs kept coming in.

Henry was James's current snitch. Henry basically lived at a hopping nightspot called Club Entice, way over in Chesapeake. He always gave James the heads-up whenever Adrian somehow managed to escape the confines of the Southern Shores house. James didn't care if Adrian thought the clubs around the OBX were dull compared to the big city ones; he had given Adrian explicit orders to remain low-key.

Regardless, Adrian somehow always managed to travel the 120 miles to party and act like a raunchy hot-alpha at Club Entice.

"James, man, your brother is down here acting all rowdy and loud. I think he's had way too much to drink, and he's drawing a pretty big crowd," Henry said. James could hear his excessive yawning, an early symptom of heroin withdrawal.

"Damn it!" James snapped, not wanting to deal with Adrian's shenanigans once again. He stormed toward Adrian's room, rubbing his twinging stomach. "How long has he been there?"

"Not long," Henry answered, sounding jittery. "Hey, uh, if you're coming by, some cash would be appreciated. Even if it's just a little."

James was barely paying attention to Henry. "Sure, whatever." He was more interested in getting to Adrian's room at the end of the hall, and just hung up on Henry.

James hated going into Adrian's room. The vibration in there was frigid and hollow, just like Adrian. The four walls enclosed a lifeless space void of décor. The only furniture was a king-sized bed covered with a lonely, black fitted sheet that was always raised at the corners. James swiped his hand. Instantly, the room hazed over where he and Addison had placed a binding spell to keep their wayward brother trapped in there. James thought it was ridiculous that Adrian, who was hundreds of years old, still acted like a seventeen-year-old kid. No matter. James was still his big brother and felt obligated to watch over him. James called out to Addison.

Addison practically ghosted into the hallway. "What's up?" she asked with an extremely rare burger in her hand. James didn't feel it necessary to tell Addison about the strange feeling in his stomach, in case it was nothing.

"Adrian is being a prick and acting out again. We've got to go get him," James said.

"Aw … I guess I have to get dressed."

James knew Addison was faking displeasure and controlling her urge to turn cartwheels all the way to her room. Even though she was tired of reining Adrian in, she often suffered from cabin fever, which manifested in a mild form of OCD—usually pathologically arranging canned goods in the cabinets for hours on end. James figured tonight would be a well-deserved outing for her, considering all she'd been through, even if it was just to Club Entice to drag Adrian back home. Something was better than nothing.

James snickered as he watched Addison go to her room. She was forcing herself to walk stoically; she didn't want to let James know how excited she was. However, her internal exhilaration was brimming so much, she looked like a kindergartener holding her pee, trying to make it to the bathroom.

The slight smile that had appeared on James's lips melted away. It was replaced by that feeling—that gnawing feeling. He knew that the off-putting knot was not caused by Adrian's mischief, but he couldn't quite locate the source no matter how hard he tried. And he didn't have time to contemplate it either. He needed to focus his attention on uncovering how Adrian had gotten out.

James continued swooshing his hand around the room, looking for any weak spots in the vapor. Then he saw that the closet door was cracked open a bit. He pushed it and saw a hole in the binding cloud, right at the attic door. James climbed up, pushing the small door open. He peered in and discovered that the tiny, round attic window had been Adrian's mode of escape.

"That bastard."

James squirmed on the velvet fainting couch, waiting on Addison to get dressed, and clicked his tongue to alleviate the tension that had spread throughout his body. It had taken him two minutes to get ready, but he was well aware of Addison's prolonged routine. She would fastidiously shave off every single hair that was not on her head, and douse her slender body with Chanel No. 5 just in case she stumbled upon some handsome male witch from her old clan—which never happened. She'd even gotten a clitoral piercing for such an unlikely event. James found it utterly deplorable his sister would tell him such personal details about her *potential* sex life, but he also knew she was shameless.

Addison popped into the living room decked out in a black mini skirt, fishnet stockings covered by thigh-high boots, and an impossibly tight top. James thought she looked like one of Anna Gristina's girls.

"What took you so long?" he asked, as if he didn't know. "We're just retrieving the prodigal brother. And by the way, you're going to call too much attention to yourself with that getup. Go put on jeans and a T-shirt."

"What? Did you think I was going out looking like a troll? Besides, we're going to Club Entice. A T-shirt and jeans would pull more attention than this. Duh."

"I can see the horny wheels spinning in your head. Remember, we're just picking up Adrian. So whatever wild fantasies you have swirling around in that brain of yours, put them to rest."

"Brother, I haven't left your ass yet, but that option still exists. So I'd shut up if I were you." Addison stepped back and got a full view of herself in the hallway mirror. "Oh my God, Addison!" she said to herself. "Look at you! You're so damned hot."

James interrupted her display of self-love and pushed her out of the house. He watched as she almost quantum leapt to the car. James was about to take a step off the porch, but something in the air caused him to hang back. He looked around, scanning the darkness for whatever was causing his ill feeling. He thought he heard a voice—a small whisper. Simultaneously the dull pain in his stomach became razor sharp.

"What's wrong with you?" Addison asked, impatiently waiting for him to open the car door.

James listened closer to the night air, half expecting something to jump out at him, but he only heard a peculiar rustle bristling through the trees.

Club Entice was the hottest spot in Chesapeake. It was housed in a stand-alone building that was noticeably taller than the others on the street. The creepy exterior was made up of large, gray stones that were weatherworn and dirty. The muted sounds of death-industrial music thumped from inside, causing the ground to quake to its rhythm. Club Entice's patrons clustered on the wrong side of the velvet rope in front of a Gothic, arched black door while two depraved gargoyles looked down at them in judgment, as if they were God himself.

James and Addison strolled past the pulsating crowd and showed the burly bouncer a gold VIP card. The bouncer unlatched the rope and let them pass, no questions asked. As the Bolingbrokes made their way into the club, the restless crowd hissed and threw an assortment of items they found on the street.

The ringleader of the rebellious crowd was a wanna-be-cool redneck taking out his blue-collar frustrations on the Bolingbrokes. "You fucking assholes," the redneck said through his yellowing teeth. "You think you're special or something? That you don't have to stand in line? Fuck y'all!" The redneck threw, with all his might, an unopened forty-ounce bottle of beer, straight at James's head.

From James's perspective it appeared as if it were happening in slow motion. He calmly closed his eyes and used the slightest bit of magic to block the impending torpedo. The glass bottle fell to the sidewalk like it had hit an invisible wall. The crowd heckled the redneck; they were all too drunk and stupid to know they had just witnessed a nifty bit of witchery. The bouncer snapped his fingers, summoning his buddies. Picking up the redneck by all four of his limbs, they tossed him into a trash container in the alley.

Addison took the whole thing in stride. "What an asshole," she said, adjusting one of her stray hairs.

The door opened, releasing a pent-up barrier of sound. James and Addison followed the long hall of flying buttresses, lined with stained glass images of red devils and statues of demons. The hall led to a cavernous space in the center of the club, complete with seizure-inducing lights and eardrum-piercing music.

James could see Addison resisting the urge to dance. "I'm going to go look for Adrian," she shouted and was quickly swallowed up by the crowd. James scoured the room as he made his way through the packed horde of wildly dancing clubbers. The mortals could sense something was different about James, and they parted like the Red

Sea. He noticed out of the corner of his eye a tall, blonde tart slinking over to him.

The inebriated young woman spoke with a whimsical voice. "Hi there. I'm Zoë. You wanna get me a drink?"

At that moment, a stifling shriek pierced James's ear, as if someone had placed a plastic megaphone to it and screamed. His face contorted, and he looked—involuntarily—at Zoë as if she were the most atrocious thing he had ever seen.

"Fucker, if you didn't want to hang out with me, you could've just said so," she said, miffed and walking away in search of her next target.

Through blurry vision, James could see Henry rushing over to him. Henry was flushed and needed a fix.

"Adrian is going onstage," Henry said, holding his hand out, making a *give me* motion. James placed a few brand-new bills into his palm. Henry didn't even stick around long enough to say thanks; he had an urgent date with his dealer.

Glancing over, James saw Adrian as he stepped casually out onto the stage. He knew right away that Adrian was using his charisma—his magical, magnetic appeal—to arouse bewitched admiration in others. It was similar to what mortals call *je ne sais quoi*.

Adrian was clad in plain, black leather pants with a marquisette shirt. He wore no shoes to showcase his unusually attractive feet. He fingered his longish, wavy, brown hair, playing coy as he took the microphone.

James, unimpressed by Adrian's spellbinding hypnosis, watched the crowd. These people could hardly contain their worship of this false idol, and at any moment could have turned from an energized throng into a full-on riot mob. James decided he'd had enough of the farce and headed toward the stage just as Adrian started to drone a hauntingly poetic song. Suddenly, a discarnate voice yelled inside James's head, dropping him to the sticky floor.

"James!" shouted the voice again, getting louder and louder, like it was drilling itself out of his skull. He finally recognized who it was:

Evelyn. He hadn't heard that voice in more than twenty years. Her summoning spell was working.

Adrian saw James when he fell to the floor, and didn't appreciate how some of the crowd had gathered around him. Adrian believed James was muscling in on his charisma spell, and it would be a couple of days before he would have the energy to conjure it up again. So, as he went on with his song, he channeled the force of James's pain to fuel his spell. Adrian knelt down on one knee with the microphone stand between his legs and stroked the stand in a masturbatory manner, sending the audience into a frenzy. James could feel Adrian draining his energy. At the same time, fleeting images of Evelyn and Massapequa crashed through his mind.

Addison scrambled over to him. As soon as she touched him, a spike of pain pounded her head.

"I saw her, too," she said as she placed James on a chair.

"We've been summoned. We've got to go immediately." He could see the disappointment in Addison's eyes.

"I know," she muttered in a low voice. She hesitated a bit. "We don't have to do this, you know. This is our last chance to turn back."

James did not answer her. He was tired of the same old conversation, and his mind was made up. Right then Addison gave up fighting against his plan.

"So we're leaving right this minute, huh? Guess that means I can't even go back to the house and get any clothes. All right, I'll get Adrian."

Addison rushed the stage and yanked the microphone away from him. "Show's over," she yelled to the crowd over the mic's screeching feedback before dragging Adrian off the stage. "Come on, lover boy."

"I swear! Don't you have anything better to do than to chase me around, Grandma?" he yelled, standing his ground.

"First off, you aren't even supposed to be here. We've all agreed on that point a *million* times before. Second, Grace's awakening is happening. We've got to go. We'll pick up the other one along the way."

"Damn," he said, following Addison over to James, and waving a final good-bye to his enamored groupies.

Chapter Twelve

I think somehow we learn who we really
are and then we live with that decision.

—Eleanor Roosevelt

Aunt Evelyn led me to the rear of the house, where we ended up standing next to a door that had always been locked as far back as I could remember.

"So I get to see what's behind the magic curtain," I said, pointing to the door.

"Not yet, Grace." Aunt Evelyn pushed a wide wall panel. It popped open, revealing a hidden, narrow staircase. She put her hand on my shoulder like she was bracing me for something, and urged me forward.

"Follow me," Aunt Evelyn instructed.

My lungs took in the dense, stuffy air as we ascended the creaky, wooden steps.

"Who even knew you had an attic?" I let my hands guide me up the poorly lit corridor.

We reached the top, and it was like stepping backward in time. I ducked to avoid the low, vaulted wooden beams that were mere inches from my head. The attic was filled with items left behind by previous owners long since passed. An antique sewing mannequin stood to my side like she was the attic's guardian. Dust-smothered quilts and a decrepit rocking chair sat in limbo, waiting to become useful again. Miscellaneous drape-covered items stood around the room.

"Let's start with some family heirlooms. I have a few of your mother's baubles as well," Aunt Evelyn murmured as she treaded to the other side of the attic. "There's so much to tell you."

She threw a very old, white sheet off some large object. "Aha! Grace, help me pull this trunk to the middle of the floor." She beamed. I helped her slide the heavy, leather trunk and noted it had a fleur-de-lis across the front in pink and burgundy.

"This is the same symbol I saw in my dream, right before Samantha …" I said, unable to finish the thought. My fingers traced the pattern of the delicate flower.

"Grace, that particular flower represents our family, our ancestry … the most honorable Valois coven. When we awaken, the symbol usually manifests on some part of our body. To those not initiated, it may very well look like a beautiful tattoo, a birth mark, or even a scar."

"That's why you checked me when I got here. You were looking for the fleur-de-lis."

"Yes. I must admit, it is highly unusual for a witch not to have her mark by the end of puberty. But you aren't a by-the-book witch, now are you?"

Aunt Evelyn opened the large steamer truck, and the relic released a vacuum of stale air. It was filled with yellowed parchment paper so decayed it disintegrated with the slightest touch. Containers of dried Dragon's Blood ink, stamps and waxes, rattles, and a druid robe had been carefully placed inside.

I picked up the robe and held it up. "This was my mother's?" Aunt Evelyn nodded.

As I stood to try on the robe, I noticed a box at the bottom of the trunk. Even though it looked as old as the world itself, it had managed to retain its faultless refinement and grandeur. Opening it, I discovered it was actually three nested boxes, like matryoshka dolls. The smallest container held an antique jewelry box that looked like it belonged to royalty. Gently, I placed the jewelry box on a nearby Boulle-styled desk that was raised on bronze cabriole legs. I caressed the box with my fingers, savoring the moment.

I carefully opened it, not daring to rush and possibly break this treasure. Tucked inside the velvet lining, a five-carat ruby was set atop an artfully crafted platinum ring. Another piece was a cameo pin with a rose-colored backdrop, with a fleur-de-lis adorning its bottom. Next there was a ruby pendant, again featuring the fleur-de-lis and enshrined by pave diamonds. I held it up, inexplicably drawn to it more than the other items.

"Grace, all of these jewels belonged to your mother. The pendant was her favorite. If you're feeling a particularly strong connection to it, that's completely normal. In fact, it's better than normal. Being able to connect to your deceased mother on a physical level gives me hope that your powers are indeed great. I'm going to leave you alone with your gifts. Call if you need me," Aunt Evelyn said with a knowing look on her face. "Go ahead and try on the pendant. It suits you," she added as she slipped out the door.

After placing the pendant around my neck, I found a full-length floor mirror clouded with the whitish film of age. Even through the mirror's fog, I thought it looked awesomely good on me. As I admired my reflection, my head began spinning faster and faster. My legs were knocked right from under me. And then … I was out.

I woke up in a castle somewhere in the past. This place must've been built at a time when kings and queens ruled the lands. How had I gotten there? I didn't know. All I knew was I was scared and alone. My almost paralyzing fear kept me from screaming for help

If ever I'd needed Julie, it was right then.

"Okay. Okay. Just breathe," I told myself, struggling against hyperventilation. I looked down at the cold, marble floor, each tile different from the next. My eyes moved up to the oversized oil paintings of severe-looking people hanging on every wall. There was a double staircase, one on the left and one on the right. Their railings were delicately engraved with fleur-de-lis, flowers, and multitudes of intertwining vines.

Six large, evenly spaced stone pillars kept the castle standing. Each was carved to perfectly accentuate the structure's noble feel. A majestic wooden door led to a grand library, while another one went to an emerald room that housed an immeasurable amount of fragrant roses in all shades.

Despite the castle's beauty, the brutal markings of some sort of violence were etched into the cold, stone walls.

Someone's fast footsteps echoed off the marble, shattering the ubiquitous silence. Not knowing to whom those steps belonged, or even where I was, it was imperative I find a hiding place.

In the nick of time, I hid around a corner; whoever it was just barely missed me. I peeked around and saw a passing feminine shape wrapped in a cloak. She looked familiar to me, and I was bizarrely drawn to her. Overcoming my common sense, I followed her.

My heart raced as I trailed her. The rounded hallway seemed to go on forever before darkness swallowed it. I stayed back as the young woman entered a pair of large, amber-colored French doors.

I heard two voices arguing, one male and the other belonging to the young woman. I figured since I had been dumb enough to follow this girl instead of trying to find a way out of the castle, I might as well go all the way. As I inched toward the door, every step seemed to reverberate throughout the macabre palace. Taking a deep breath, I opened one of the French doors and peered in.

Our family crest was elaborately displayed over a gigantic, stone fireplace. I turned my head and saw the young woman appealing to an older man. Suddenly, I was hit with a bolt of recognition! That young woman was my mother, Ilan. Aunt Evelyn and Dad had shown me a few cherished photos of her, but in no way had they done her justice. She was the most striking creature I'd ever seen. Her long, blonde locks cascaded over her cloak and were tied off with a ribbon at her waist. She was lithe and fine boned, yet it was obvious she possessed a massive fount of strength.

My mother passionately engaged the man, an authority figure to her. He looked at Mother with eyes of the deepest red. He had a middle-aged face, though he was not as young as he looked. I made myself quiet and listened to their conversation.

"Your Honor, Maximus. I speak to you not as a subject, but as your daughter. Father, please, you must listen to me. You cannot ignore this forever," Mother said, the palms of her hands facing up, engaging my grandfather. "Yes, I do understand the ramifications of committing the most egregious sin of our clan—falling in love with a human."

"I have no more patience for you, Ilan," Grandfather said. "Once more you have disgraced this family, me in particular. To me you do this? You have put me in an impossible situation, and now I cannot protect you any further."

Grandfather paused, then went on, "I loved you more than my entire existence, Ilan. You have broken my heart into a million pieces, my only daughter. It was your destiny to be at my right side on the council. You were to be my successor, the future of this coven. No other witch possesses the gifts and abilities you have, yet you have chosen to discard them."

I wanted to run over and wipe away the huge tears streaming down my mother's face. However, my body couldn't move; some power kept me in my place as an impotent observer.

"I cannot say how sorry I am, Your Honor. I know I have offended you. It was not my intention to do so. It grieves me to cause you so much pain, and for that, remorse engulfs my heart. I know what my punishment is by our law. I do not ask you lightly for this favor, but I must. I beseech you to grant me one final request."

I could tell it was not in my mother's nature to grovel, but for some reason she felt it was warranted.

"You ask too much of me, Ilan. I have nothing more to give," Grandfather said as he turned his back to her.

"Please, Father, I am not asking for myself, but for the life of your unborn granddaughter," Mother said, her cloak becoming soaked with tears.

My grandfather's body went totally still, like he was petrified. My mother's last words had stunned and devastated him. He walked away from her, treating her like she was nothing more than a common subject. "Laws have been broken. The council will decide your fate. I can no longer protect you, Ilan."

Mother grabbed his arm like a death-row prisoner seeking pardon from a governor. "You can, Father! I have been careful to keep my thoughts to myself. Therefore, I am sure the council knows nothing. I am no longer asking. I am *begging* you," she said as she fell to her knees.

Grandfather sighed, his heart heavy. "What will you name this fetus?"

Mother's eyes shined with the tiniest sliver of hope. "I will name her Grace."

"You will name her *Grace?*" Grandfather said, his rage bellowing forth.

"Yes, Father, it is a family name. Our family!"

"You dare give a half breed our family name? This plague, this bane you call a child?"

"How can you speak of her that way? She is one of your own, is she not? She may even possess more outstanding qualities than we do."

"The Seers warned me of a possible future where Catherine Bolingbroke took over the council, with massive bloodshed of both witches and mortals as the result. However, their abilities to see the future clearly were clouded. Of course I didn't believe them … I found their prediction ridiculous. And most certainly I did not believe my own daughter would have anything to do with it if it were true. Now look at you. You've developed doubts about feeding on mortals like we've done for centuries, knowing that is how we survive, how the Ancients give us our powers. Then you go and have an affair with a mortal and allow yourself to be impregnated. Woe, this is how Catherine takes power."

Grandfather sat down, as if he could take no more. He spoke with his hand over his eyes. "How have you been eating?"

"My lover allows me to feed on his blood to offset this problem, but it's not enough. So occasionally he offers up bits of his flesh to quell my hunger," Mother said.

Grandfather moaned. "It gets worse and worse. You need to explain something to me. How can it be possible that a half witch, half mortal child can be more powerful than a full-blooded immortal?"

I watched as my mother wrung her hands, getting ready to confess something. "Well, I have more to tell you. I could see the rapidly increasing influence and power the Bolingbrokes were having over the other witches. That psychotic banshee, Catherine, posed the biggest threat of all. Her magical abilities are nearly as great as mine, and she is the main instigator of conflict and dissention in all the coven families. I decided to end the Bolingbrokes' quest for power. In my way, not yours. I secretly rummaged through forbidden grimoires and found an obscure spell to create a magical child with a mortal. Normally that wouldn't be possible, as witches and mortals are unable to reproduce with each other. The spell warned that the child could be a gift to us, a curse, or have no special abilities at all. There is no way to know until the child's awakening ... if indeed it has one. I took a chance on even the slightest possibility of my baby having greater magical powers than I do—powers for the good."

"Such stupid, needless risks. We were dealing with the Bolingbrokes," Grandfather said.

"No disrespect, Father, but *we* weren't doing anything, and they were rapidly rising up," Mother shot back, her fighting spirit making an appearance.

"It is too late. The spawn is here, and she will be a curse upon the earth. Witches on all sides will attempt to kill her because none of them will know what she is. It is the law to put her to death. I want you to know *you* gave her this sentence when you decided to consort with that mortal."

I slumped on the door, totally dejected. However, my snarky inner self couldn't help but think, *Damn ... this shit gets better and better. Who forgot the party streamers?*

"Don't worry. She will not sully the rarified air of Valois castle. She will go to her father in the Americas and *will* be raised with our name," my mother stated.

Oh, apparently I'd gotten that snarky gene from my mother, because I heard it all through those comments.

"A human with no abilities or gifts to protect her." Grandfather laughed, while Mother could only heave a frustrated sigh.

I saw my grandfather lift my mother's chin—finally there was some compassion in his face. "You're always thinking, my child. I can only blame myself for your ambitious and defiant nature. I groomed that warrior spirit into you, and now I am so sorry for that."

"Do not fret," Mother said. "I have a plan. I will leave at dusk. No one in the coven will see me go. I will take the baby away from here on the night of a full moon. I will not involve you with all of the details, so as not to put you in any more danger. I know you have risked so much already, Father. If anyone should ask, a simple 'she's away' should suffice. All I ask is for some time to make sure Grace is safe and never tied to this coven or you—until it's time."

"And what becomes of the child's father?" Grandfather asked. "A mortal man raising an immortal child? He is not a mother, and the child will need one. Surely even you can see that."

"I have planned for Evelyn to assist him. If and when Grace embraces her gifts, Evelyn will be there to guide her," Mother explained.

"Ilan, maybe someone along with Evelyn should act as a buffer between Grace and the mortal world."

"I've found her, too. One of our old clan mates. Julie Glentworth."

"What? One of the heretics who left us? I can see I won't be able to reason with you any further—you are as stubborn as always. No matter how I feel about you, I am still leader of this coven, and I play no favorites. After you birth the child, you will return and face the council. I will have no choice but to vote with them. Go, Ilan. It pains me to look at your dear, sweet face."

I saw Mother kiss Grandfather's thick, platinum ring adorned with an intricate fleur-de-lis pattern and the letter V in calligraphy. He looked at her as if he wanted to sweep her into his arms and whisk her to a safer realm, but all he could do was walk away.

Then Ilan—Mother—looked directly at me and started walking my way. I quickly yanked my head back and hid behind the door. I heard her voice right on the other side.

"My dearest daughter," Mother said as she pulled the door. My eyes flew open like window shades. There she stood right in front of me.

I had been denied my mother's touch, and I had always longed for it. When she stroked me, my body became weak and rubbery. All the grief I had stored for twenty-one years poured out into a painful cry.

Mother knew exactly what to do, caressing my hair and lightly kissing my face. If she had lived, she would've been the perfect mom.

Even though she was an apparition, I saw she was just as affected by our lost time as I was. Right then she wasn't a witch or the leader of some coven. She was just a woman reunited with the child she'd had to give up so many years ago.

The ethereal cord to the past was wearing thin. Mother knew her time was limited, and had to get down to business.

"Grace, I allowed you to listen to the past so you can start to connect with your future. You're wearing my pendant. It is a temporary portal allowing us to communicate briefly. Wear it well. When you're ready, it will yield all of my power to you," Mother said.

She leaned over and crushed her lips onto my forehead. They were ice cold and hard, like they were mummified. I didn't matter to me; they were still part of my mother's touch.

I saw her fading away. Panic set in, and I pleaded with her, "No, please don't go. I've missed you my whole life. You can't leave me again. And I can't do what you want me to do. Can I stay here with you?"

"Oh, precious, as much as I would like that, it is not an option. Aunt Evelyn is waiting for you. Remember, always and forever, I love you." She wiped a single, red tear from her eye. With a smile and a wink, she vanished.

Then my body felt like it was freefalling through a wormhole, with flashes of colored lights streaking past me. I was as light as a feather, and the spatial trip seemed to go on for days.

I opened my eyes and was laid out on the attic floor, next to the trunk. I could hardly catch my breath. However, I felt like I had been reborn, and was filled with some unexplained delight.

Aunt Evelyn sat calmly in the rocking chair. "Quite a jaunt, huh?" she said with a mischievous grin on her face.

"How long was I gone?" I checked my body to make sure I had all of my parts.

"I left the attic one minute ago and came right back in to check on you."

"One minute? You've got to be kidding," I murmured, standing up and flexing my muscles. They felt like they had been built up a bit.

"Yeah, I'm some kind of comedian," Aunt Evelyn said as she did a silly dance toward the trunk. We put it back in its place, exactly where Aunt Evelyn had found it. She spoke to me, but now with all kinds of seriousness on her face.

"Whatever happened between you and your mother, I hope it was beautiful. But I'm sure you learned some unpleasant things, too. Tonight, rest up, because the real work is about to begin." Then she matter-of-factly walked down the stairs, leaving me with that thought.

Ugh, really? Aunt Evelyn absolutely had to go and kill the mood by reminding me of ... *everything*. Couldn't a blossoming messiah catch a break?

Chapter Thirteen

Sophisticated persons masturbate without compunction. They do it for reasons of health, privacy, thrift and because of the remarkable perfection of invisible partners.

—P.J. O'Rourke

A late-night storm hovered over the farmhouse. Flashes of lightning gave way to fleeting glimpses of huge raindrops splashing in and out of mud puddles, which were situated like potholes all around the property.

I stood at the large picture window, the sheer curtains pulled open wide. Despite Aunt Evelyn's instructions to rest up, I'd found it impossible to drift off to sleep. I had a mad case of insomnia and was killing time, hoping the night would fast-forward itself.

My wakefulness didn't make any sense. I was hella drowsy, and my whole body ached; with not only physical exhaustion, but mental fatigue as well. The bedroom was straight out of Bed Bath & Beyond; there was an ultra-plush down comforter with the thick smell of long-term storage, and a king-sized, cherry wood sleigh bed. Battery-powered tea lights dotted the blackish corners of the room, giving it a relaxing ambience. A large bowl of lavender potpourri sat on the nightstand, its heady fragrance permeating the air.

All of that, combined with the glow of moonlight breaking through the deluge, would have been enough to lull most normal humans to sleep. Unfortunately, the insomniac in me could only concentrate on the constant stream of raindrops thumping into a rusted-out tin bucket under the window. *TINK. TINK. TINK.* I got into bed and folded the pillow over my ears, but could still hear the settling house creaking like an old woman's hip. I looked up at the vague outline of the ceiling fan going around and around in an endless carousel. With an exasperated sigh, I pulled the down comforter up to my shoulders ... and was too hot. I kicked it off and was too cold. I twisted onto my back, then my stomach, then my back again.

I tried every mind trick I could think of to induce sleep. I replayed episodes of favorite television shows in my mind: *Dexter. CSI. Snapped.* When that didn't work, I started making plans for my future. Five years ahead ... Ten years ahead. I quickly became frustrated when I realized I couldn't even plan for the next hour of my new life, let alone years down the road. Then I played the game of counting sheep. I got up to 566 before I started repeating numbers and forgetting where I was in the sequence.

I decided to play a final game—my own version of solitaire. Masturbation always put me to sleep, but I rarely used it as a somatic tool. I always felt like such a skeevy perv afterward. *Tonight,* I reasoned, *it was necessary.* After all I had a lot of work ahead of me. So I popped open a few top buttons of my nightgown; an XX-large, striped men's dress shirt I had found at a garage sale. The shirt's armpits still had a lingering musky scent—that testosterone odor found in all men's shirts after they'd been worn a few times. Its smell you can't even fully remove in the wash. I had just enough room to stick my hand in and stroke my hardening nipples.

I relaxed my body, from my toes with the flecked nail polish to the top of my scalp, which was still a little damp from my shower. Sinking into the mattress, I allowed it to mold around me like a firm marshmallow. I felt safe, embryonic even. And I closed my eyes.

Usually I fantasized about guys around campus I crushed on and, regrettably, even Rafe. He was the only man I'd ever been with, and I thought for sure I'd never experience the love or touch of another human being after him. So I learned how to love and touch myself instead.

Before I could go through my mental Rolodex of guys, an image I'd never seen before entered my mind. His appearance was crystal clear ... Technicolor vivid. It was almost like he was really there. His face was overly serious, but sexy nonetheless. He had otherworldly eyes that were the strangest shade of blue I'd ever seen. His body was rocking—slim, athletic—yet it had many scars on it.

I started to rub my lower belly in a small, circular motion.

The dream lover stood at the foot of my bed and stared at me for a moment ... *in that way*, giving me notice that things were about to get really erotic. My pussy began to ripple with slight contractions in anticipation.

This fantasy was so real, I thought I could actually hear the bed squeak as the phantom lover climbed over the footboard and parted my bent knees. He slithered his body between my legs and kissed me. At first his full lips were slightly opened, teasing me. The wetness moistened my eager lips. He opened his mouth wider, and then closed his warm lips around mine. I couldn't hold back and kissed him, drawing his hot breath into me. He pulled back, taking control, and returned us both to a more measured pace.

As I hallucinated that he was nibbling on my lower lip, my hand continued acting as a substitute for him. My index finger went down … all the way down. It made its way through my pussy lips. Their softness felt good to me, and my wetness grew. Suddenly, I felt the need to bear down. Even though my eyes looked straight at the ceiling, in my fantasy they were squarely on the face of my lover. I imagined him entering me with his big cock, gyrating with perfect rhythm and pace. I rubbed my clit toward ecstasy. My fingertips became slick as the strokes became longer, deeper, harder. *Damn, I needed him in me.* I wanted a real cock, not just some fantasy. I wanted the full feeling of real maleness. I thought the friction was warming up my palm, so I didn't pay too much attention as it grew warmer, then hotter. When the heat became uncomfortable, I jerked my hand out of my panties and saw it was glowing red.

Running to the bathroom, I turned on the light and stood in front of the old, scratched-up porcelain sink with the rusty drain hole. The fuzzy lightbulb above me dimmed and gave a jaundiced haze to the small space.

My hand felt like I had dipped it in a vat of acid. A ghostly, white-hot knife blade sliced through the skin, etching something on my palm. I closed my hand, afraid to look at it directly. Instead, I held it up to the medicine cabinet mirror and opened it up. The shining fleur-de-lis reflected back, illuminating the bathroom with an eerie, red hue.

Unbeknownst to me, at that same moment, witches from all over felt that the world had shifted somehow. To some this revelation was subtle, like the soft buzz of a mosquito around the ear. However, others had a more visceral, disturbing effect.

Chapter Fourteen

Leadership: The art of getting someone
else to do something you want done
because he wants to do it.

—Dwight D. Eisenhower

C atherine paid no mind to the distant clamor of New York City's
rush-hour traffic. Instead, she sat motionless in her sunken,
concrete tub inlaid with intricate, blue and black mosaic tiles.
The water had been perfectly transparent, but as Catherine's dead cells
sloughed off, it turned a sickening yellow.

She looked at her bony body. It resembled a Sphinx cat's—
wrinkled, leathery, thin-skinned—and she was like an alien within it.
The body was a foreign entity to her, an inconvenient vessel she
inhabited for the time being. Otherwise she was just numb, devoid of
any real feeling, trying to remember emotions like the ones she'd had
before the Ancient spirit had become a co-resident in her body.

That stoic attitude abruptly changed when a feeling of odd portent
caused Catherine to sit straight up. A dreadful, prickly sensation
bristled under her skin. Bulging, blue welts rose to the skin's surface.
Her blood temperature rapidly dropped way past normal to an
unnatural low. The blood became so cold, it started to form the tiniest
shards of ice right in her veins, causing minute cuts as the blood pulsed
through her body. Catherine's body involuntarily seized up on her, and
she slipped under the water.

As she struggled to regain her bodily control, she saw a vision of
Grace. The girl held up her hand, blazing with the fleur-de-lis symbol.
The vision cut to a future event: Grace and Catherine engaged in a
battle to the death, throwing magic rays at each other. They both let go
of their final rays, knowing one of them would die. However, the
vision ended before the winner was revealed.

Catherine bounded to the water's surface, gasping for air. She got
out of the tub, her body heavy like she had just stepped back on land
after being in the ocean all day. Lumbering over to a black hutch, she
rummaged through its multitudinous drawers, and found a small, red

sachet. It contained the herb agrimony, used to reverse hexes and curses. She untied the bag and dumped its contents straight into her mouth. She gagged on the dry, twiggy concoction as it scratched its way down her throat.

"Chetan!" she yelled, coughing up bits of agrimony. Chetan rushed in as fast as he could, knowing there would be hell to pay if he made Catherine Bolingbroke wait.

"Yes, Catherine?" he asked, caught off guard by her panicked expression.

"Get the car. Grace has awakened, and I need more backup."

"Where are we going?" Chetan desperately tried not to look at Catherine's crinkled, naked body.

"Jersey, you fuck."

Chetan drove the black Mercedes GL550 through Elizabeth, New Jersey. Catherine sat quietly in the backseat, glaring with superior repugnance at the city's denizens. To her, this place was nothing more than a filthy wasteland of 7-Elevens and Dunkin' Donuts. However, Catherine also believed the best hunting grounds for protégés were in places like this.

Environments like law practices, venture-capital firms, and Wall Street would seem to contain an unlimited pool of protégé candidates. The problem was those people embraced their demons and used them to get what they wanted with no remorse. Consequently, Catherine had nothing to tap into. That was why she found the so-called innocuous environments to be the best places for finding protégés. In these safe havens, wickedness abounded. It was simply obscured, masked by the veneer of civility. It festered beneath the surface, where it took on a delightful malignancy. Wickedness grew exponentially with the effort it took to keep it down. Therefore, in most of these "good" people there were powerful alter egos that somehow always managed to express themselves in road rage, gossip, passive aggressiveness … the list went on and on.

As the Mercedes arrived at the pickup loop of a popular outlet mall, Catherine carefully examined herself in a compact mirror. She had performed a beauty spell for the occasion, which had cloaked her body in an illusion of adorableness. Her craggy skin was now dewy and youthful, all peaches and cream. Her scraggly hair appeared voluminous, with a slight wave. The scent of her flesh was a bit soapy, with hints of citrus and vanilla.

Chetan turned toward her. She could see he wanted to ask her something, but was afraid to annoy her. He bravely asked anyway.

"Pardon me for my ignorance, but why don't you just recruit other witches? Why use humans for such a dangerous endeavor?" Chetan crouched as if he were expecting a frying pan to come flying over the seat.

"It is impossible to turn another witch into a protégé—especially one who's already inhabited by an Ancient. Only humans can be used for that purpose. However, not just any human. The protégé must have something in them … a certain ruthlessness, immorality, selfishness that goes beyond the norm. Most humans don't qualify for the job, as being a typical asshole is not enough. The ones I seek are truly extraordinary beings. Much more extraordinary than you even."

Catherine smirked, knowing Chetan was irked by her insult and could do nothing about it. He got out of the Mercedes and tried to keep a straight face, making sure his expression didn't betray him. He did not want to give Catherine any reason to cut him from what he considered a prestigious position as her helper. And, most importantly, he didn't want to rile her up, thereby causing his own demise.

"Would you like me to accompany you?" he asked after he opened Catherine's door and offered her his hand.

"No. This task I must do alone."

Catherine refused to touch the escalator railing, which was sticky from candy, snot, and other unidentifiable fluids. As the escalator ascended, mall patrons on all levels focused in on her—the obvious fish out of water. The pot-bellied shoppers wore the standard suburban uniform of cargo shorts, unflattering graphic tees, and tired sneakers or sandals. Catherine sported a tailored pencil skirt, a taupe silk shirt, and six-inch stilettos.

She arrived on the second floor—next to one of those clothing stores that Pied Piper-ed teenagers in with their pedophilic advertising—and decided to stroll in the middle of the walkway, against the flow of pedestrian traffic. This allowed her to casually bump into people, skimming their skin to pick up on their auras. Within five minutes, Catherine reckoned, she had touched about ten people. She picked up on someone who had just cheated on the SAT, another who had shoplifted a scarf, and still another who let a cashier undercharge him at the GAP. Unfortunately, no one with the special gifts.

Catherine wound up in the food court, which was littered with chain restaurants offering up a gross hodgepodge of MSG-laden, lard-infested chemical cocktails they called food. As she passed a server handing out samples of syrupy Chinese food on toothpicks, she suddenly sucked in a breath—a signal that her protégé was somewhere in the vicinity. It was now just a matter of finding them. Catherine quickly made her way around the perimeter of the food court, rapidly bumping into people and getting a sense of who they were.

First she bumped into a teenage girl who just wasn't having it. The girl wore a belly shirt, which showed off her spray tan, and Daisy Dukes that showed off everything else.

"What, stupid bitch? You don't see me standing here?" she barked before taking a bite of her greasy pizza.

"How can I *not* see you? You're bright orange," Catherine came back, all the while scanning the food court for the protégé. Tan Girl put her pizza down and whipped her dishwater-blonde hair into a ponytail. Suddenly, she pumped her fists at Catherine.

"Aw, Uptown wants to fight. Let's go," the girl said.

And Catherine did want to go. On a different day, she would have used her powers to grab the girl, toss her in the air, and send her careening over the crowd. However, Catherine needed to conserve her energy to capture her protégé, and settled on a more moderate retaliation. She winked one eye, causing Tan Girl to trip and land face first in the custodian's bucket of dirty water.

As that section of the food court burst into riotous laughter, a hand brushed across Catherine's. Her senses went into overdrive, as if she were a plug being stuck into a socket. She didn't even have to look at the human to know this was her protégé.

"She got what she deserved, talking to such a gorgeous woman like that," said a nebbish voice.

Catherine had to stretch her neck to look up at the man staring down at her. "Oh, I'm okay. I just let petty things like that roll off me," she said, doing her best impersonation of coy.

The stranger's towering height was his only attractive attribute. His voice was whiny and high-pitched. Catherine unconsciously put her finger to her ear, doing a suctioning motion. She figured he had just gotten off from some lame office job, considering he was dressed in a cheap sports jacket and khaki pants. She fought to not focus on the smudge of mayonnaise he had neglected to wipe off his chin.

"Italian?" asked the man, squinting in a failed attempt to give his eyes a bedroom look.

"Yes, I've been in this country for … well, let's say a very, very long time. Do you speak Italian?"

"Uh, yeah," the man muttered, fiddling to take off his wedding ring behind his back.

"*Ho intenzione di uccidere e mangiare le interiora con salsa picante,*" said Catherine, testing him.

"Hey, yeah, sounds good to me."

She knew beyond a shadow of a doubt that he was the right one. How many people would agree to let someone kill them and then eat their entrails with hot sauce—as she had just asked him to do?

"I'm Catherine," she said, holding out her hand for a shake.

"Nick," the man responded, lying about his name. He kissed Catherine's hand instead of shaking it, and left behind some of the mayonnaise from his chin. Catherine quickly drew it back as she painfully smiled with clenched teeth.

Catherine invited the potential protégé back to her penthouse. She was pleased with her selection, and with how easy he had been to acquire.

However, Catherine understood that one of the conditions for making a protégé was that the intended had to be in complete compliance with his transformation. In other words, he had to decide with his own free will to be subjected to the whims of his future master. From past experience, Catherine knew most humans would not agree to such a hideous fate, so a witch had to use a certain amount of subterfuge. This usually entailed romantic gestures if the potential protégé was a woman, and the promise of sex if it was a man.

On the ride to the penthouse, Catherine cock-teased Nick to the point where he was willing to do just about anything to get her on her back. Yes, it was entrapment, but it worked every time.

Upon their arrival, Chetan made himself scarce, and Catherine took Nick to the purple room.

"Would you like a drink?" she purred.

Nick looked around, wondering where in the penthouse Catherine kept the bed. "Sure, anything you got."

Catherine was more than satisfied with that answer. It gave her permission to serve him up a magical mixture of Jack Daniels and Grey Goose spiked with a dash of a potion she had spent years developing. The potion contained a unique blend of micronized herbs and Haitian zombie powder derived from puffer-fish toxin. With the sleep-inducing drink in hand, she swayed over to Nick, who was loosening up his tie and kicking off his shoes.

Taking the drink, he guzzled it down. He immediately started feeling the effects, and his few inhibitions disappeared. "Damn, you are smokin' hot. I'm going to fuck the shit out of you tonight." He patted the couch. "My fucking wife never wants it. Oops ... I wasn't supposed to mention her. My bad."

Catherine sat down next to Nick. "Oh, you big romantic, you," she said, allowing him to slobber on her neck—his poor excuse for kissing. She could see why his wife rejected him, with his pitiful, amateur technique. Catherine barely wrapped her arms around him, knowing the more excited he got, the quicker the toxin worked. She looked past him at her watch. The drink typically took no more than five minutes to kick in. It was already minute two.

Nick went for his zipper, and put Catherine's hand into his pants. "Oh, yeah, you like that, don't you, baby?" he panted as he pawed at her breast. Catherine could only think how pathetic it was that his hard-on was about three inches long. She looked at her watch again and began counting down in her mind. *Five. Four. Three. Two. One.* At zero, Nick conked out.

Nick woke up naked, with his arms and legs staked to a pentagram on the floor. He instantly began to struggle to release his wrists from the tight shackles that cut off his circulation. When that didn't work, he tried to scream, but he was gagged with a terrycloth rag. He saw an open door at the back of the room. Catherine entered, dressed only in a priestess robe and the same six-inch stilettos she'd had on earlier. She crossed the room, holding a large Book of Shadows to her chest.

The walls resonated with the desperate, muted sounds of the backs of Nick's feet banging the floor. His throaty, muffled screams were barely audible through the gag. Then his eyes widened as Catherine pulled out a sharp, heavy-bladed knife from the pages of the book.

"Do you know why you're here, *Nick*? And no, it's not to fuck," she said as she removed the gag from his mouth.

Nick coughed hard. His larynx was inflamed from his frenzied screaming; he could only release a faint, hoarse wail. He started to weep. "I don't know. Is this some sort of weird sex game? What do you want?" He watched Catherine put the book on the floor and pull a feather out of it.

"I'm not an authority on what is good or what is bad. I only know what is useful to me. You have very special attributes that can serve me well. Yes, you are a liar and a cheat, but what you have kept hidden from everyone is that you have killed … A young woman in college who didn't find you so sexually desirable. You took not only her virginity, but her life. Poor girl. Her undiscovered remains are still in those woods."

"How did you know about that?" Nick asked. He was shaking, thinking that all of these theatrics were part of some elaborate plot to set him up for blackmail. "What do you want? Cash? Stocks? Just tell me."

"Nick, you barely have two nickels to rub together. Besides, look around you. Does it look like I need money? I just want you to agree to do my bidding." Catherine held the knife in one hand and the feather in the other.

"Whatever, whatever! Omigod!" Nick said through his sobs.

"Great. I have your full cooperation. Now I have to measure your heart against this feather." Catherine straddled Nick's thighs and laid the feather on his navel. Raising the knife over her head, she said, "This is going to hurt … a lot."

Nick saw the knife come down and go straight through his ribcage; Catherine cut him from clavicle to sternum. He then felt her powerful hands separating his ribcage and ripping his still-beating heart out of his chest cavity.

Catherine only had four minutes to perform a speedy Weighing of the Heart ritual before Nick would be clinically brain dead, and she needed him to be alive for the ceremony. She took his heart in one hand and the feather in the other. Her hands moved up and down like a justice balance, determining that his heart was heavier than the feather. He was a bad boy indeed.

"You and I are going to do great things together," she said, wiping Nick's blood off of her hands on his stomach.

Nick felt his life exit his body. His last moments consisted of perfect fear and the knowledge that Catherine had done this to him. This knowledge would bind him to her forever.

Catherine opened her Book of Shadows and recited a necromancy spell over Nick, capturing his soul before it left him. His body twitched as it came back to life with horrific agony. The muscles contracted and relaxed in a rapid fashion, and he nearly bit off his tongue. His body was undergoing some sort of metamorphosis. The facial bones rearranged themselves into a hideous caricature of the former Nick. His gnarly fingers grew longer and clawed at the empty space.

Nick's eyes had turned a dead gray color and were full of abject terror. He looked at Catherine, his gaze pleading with her to help him, but she just stood there taking utter delight in watching a new protégé being born.

Nick was now powerful enough to yank up the stakes that bound him to the floor. However, he could see that Catherine was not intimidated by him in the least. He accepted his fate, then his rational mind shut down its own will and forced him to become a servant to her.

Chapter Fifteen

A woman knows the face of the man she
loves as a sailor knows the open sea
—Honore de Balzac

"They're here!"

Aunt Evelyn's giddy declaration was way too much for me to handle at that time of morning. My head was completely cocooned in the comforter; the rest of the blanket hung off the side of the bed and made a nice heap on the hardwood floor. I managed to crack open one eye, and it didn't even matter that rogue threads poked the white of it. When I didn't hear Aunt Evelyn say anything else, I started drifting back to la-la land.

Then it hit me: who *they* were. The ones Aunt Evelyn had summoned in that spell.

Oh, snap. I bumbled out of bed, of course getting my foot caught in the comforter. After I recovered from my spill to the floor, I ran over to the window and saw an unfamiliar silver car in the driveway. From my second-floor vantage point, I could make out a woman's legs in the passenger seat. The driver's hands, resting on the steering wheel, were obviously male.

Probably some old, haggy witch and a crotchety warlock.

I guess I really should've been ready for their arrival at any moment, but I kind of hadn't expected that kooky spell of Aunt Evelyn's to work. Although, after all I'd seen so far, I shouldn't have doubted it.

I could hear Aunt Evelyn's Børn clogs clacking like little mouse feet to the front door. Meanwhile, I ran over to my suitcase and sat on the floor with my legs tucked under me. My arms started wind-milling, throwing clothes out of the suitcase I had never bothered to unpack.

"Grace, come on down. Hurry!" Aunt Evelyn shouted from downstairs with nervous excitement all through her voice.

"Coming," I responded, not finding anything good to wear. When Julie and I had to get the hell out of Dodge, I hadn't exactly had time to pack an extensive wardrobe. I'd left Dad's house with a few shirts, shorts that didn't match any of them, socks without mates, and an armful of cotton granny panties. None of it was appropriate to make even a mediocre first impression.

I decided to bank on Aunt Evelyn's closet; surely she would have something I could borrow for this nerve-wracking moment. When I surveyed the abyss where unfashionable clothes went to die, the only appropriate response was bewilderment. Aunt Evelyn's wardrobe choices consisted of checkerboard shirts, a punk-rock leather jacket, a T-shirt with an iron-on decal reading "hot tamale," and nine pairs of culottes circa 1978. I knew she was a bit of a wack-a-doo, but goddamn. This was the kind of shit I had read about in microfiche copies of *Life* magazine. I was obviously going to fare better with my own ratchet clothes.

The doorbell buzzed, and I knew I had to get it in gear. I threw on the first thing that smelled clean—with absolutely no consideration of looking in a mirror—and hopped to the door on one foot, trying to get my shoe on while wondering what they'd be like. Surely they'd have Third Reich temperaments. They'd need personalities like that to take on the dangerous task they'd been given: protecting me.

I walked slowly down the long hallway, hoping the creaking, wooden floorboards wouldn't give me away to the crowd gathering below. I could hear Aunt Evelyn talking to a young woman with a Received Pronunciation British accent. Wow, what happened to the German accent I was expecting? I hid in a nook, steeling myself. My ego made an appearance and was wondering why I was tripping out over making a good impression on these people. They were there for me, not vice versa. However, my cowardly *Id* quickly reminded me I didn't want to be a disappointment to them.

From the nook I could kind of see Aunt Evelyn and Julie standing at the door. The British woman, for some reason, had not yet entered the house, and I could hear some hesitation in her voice. I could tell she was being polite but really didn't want to be there.

"Addison, get on in this house," Aunt Evelyn chirped, sounding actually happy to see the young woman.

I left the safe confines of my little corner and covertly looked over the railing, to see down below. In walked this really cute girl. She looked like she had just come home from a club or something. She did look little whorey. However, despite her ensemble, she had a regal air about her. She tilted her head back ever so slightly, so she could look down her nose at Aunt Evelyn and Julie. Her lips were pursed like she really couldn't have been—rather shouldn't have been—bothered.

That didn't stop Aunt Evelyn from grabbing and hugging her. "Oh, Addison, it is so good to see you. It has been too long." Holding Addison in a bear hug, she shook her about.

Addison tensed up and gave her a rigid pat on the back. "Mm-hm. It is nice to see you again, too."

Julie and Addison greeted each other like two gun slingers about to draw. I didn't know what the deal was, but no love was lost there.

"Addison, it's so awesome you managed to show up. What, no mani-pedi?" Julie snapped, glaring at her.

"Oh, Julie, didn't you hear? I moved it to next week. When I heard you were actually still in the game, I had to come and see for myself. Now that I've seen your lovely face, I can go have hundreds of manicures. I think I'll start with some OPI 'Don't Pretzel My Buttons' and think about you the whole time."

Before Julie could say anything, Addison switched gears. Oh, she was a clever woman. Not giving Julie a chance to respond was a hand-to-the-face maneuver that instantly made Addison the victor. Then she pulled an even cheaper trick. She gave Julie a surly, superior smile and proceeded to be … nice. Yeah, she was faking it, but it worked.

"Julie, let's not fight. I have a surprise for you," she said.

Julie didn't know what to do. She was ready with an aggressive defensive move, but she didn't know how to counteract nice. All she could do was blurt out, "What?"

"Come on in. Julie's ready for you," Addison called, looking toward the front door with a winner's grin on her face.

Hari, Julie's younger brother, leapt from the side of the front porch. I could barely make out his features, but clearly saw his attire.

He looked like he had just come from a Hawaiian vacation, complete with flowered shirt and loose khaki shorts. He didn't understand the concept of socks, preferring high-tops with their tongues pressed down instead. And Hari kept his sunglasses on top of his head, which was thickly covered by a mop of curly hair.

Julie was silent for a moment, stunned that Hari was standing in front of her. When she came back to her senses, she hollered, "You've got to be fucking kidding me!"

Hari dropped his bag on the porch and stood in a V stance, leaning back with his arms wide open. "Get over here, bitch!" he yelled back with the biggest smile. Julie ran onto the porch and jumped into his arms, wrapping her muscular legs around his waist. Hari had to hurry and grab the doorframe to keep from falling.

After a bunch of chicken-peck kisses all over his face, Julie slid off him. "Why didn't you tell me you're a helper, too?"

"You know all this had to be kept on the down low. I couldn't say a word." Hari attempted to move his face away from Julie's. She punched him on the arm and let him go.

Now that she was no longer blocking my view, I got a better look at Hari. He was rather short and thick. Not fat, just powerfully compact. His dark hair and olive skin made him racially ambiguous like Julie. I could remember many times when Julie had been mistaken for Sicilian, Mexican, Louisiana Creole, or Middle Eastern.

Hari actually hadn't changed that much since I had last seen him years ago. Julie had taken me to her house only a handful of times since our childhood. When she had, no one else had been home, and the visits had been as quick as a premature ejaculator. Though I'd thought it strange, I'd never dwelled on it. I'd assumed Julie just liked hanging out at my house instead.

But now I knew why. There were secrets that needed to be kept, and if I'd hung out at her house too often, they could have slipped out. That would have been really bad for me. No child should accidently discover she's a witch with a deadly destiny while she's playing Chutes and Ladders at her buddy's house.

Aunt Evelyn caught sight of me trying my damndest to hide, and ordered me to come down to the foyer. I grabbed the banister and gripped it so tight I cut off the circulation to my fingers. I didn't give a shit; I was making sure I didn't take a tumbling roll down the narrow staircase.

It might as well have been prom night the way everyone was watching me. All that was missing was a taffeta gown and a dried-up corsage. I descended slowly, taking my time, making sure to hit every step. I couldn't take my eyes off Addison, who looked at me with contempt. Her stank facial expression gave away her thoughts: *The fuck. This is what's expected to save the world? Really? I came all this way for this bullshit? This is going to be such an epic fail.*

After I managed not to fall down the stairs, Aunt Evelyn placed right me in front of Addison. I was so intimidated I couldn't even look at her directly. "Uh ... hi. I'm Grace," I said, sounding like I was twelve. *Get it the fuck together, Grace.*

Addison pointed at my shirt and smirked. "You put it on wrong."

I glanced down; I had not only put it on inside out, but backward as well. *Oh my God.* I stretched the collar out in front of me and fiddled with it as if that were going to help anything.

My mind instantly went into panic mode, and I started to pull the shirt over my head so I could turn it around. *What?* Not only was I embarrassed, but I was going to try and remedy the situation by stripping in front of everyone. Just one of those moves you make when you're retarded. Auto Response kicks in.

I'd already lifted my shirt over my face when I felt someone pulling my arms down. I thought it was Addison doing something compassionate. However, when my shirt was back down over my torso, I saw a male face instead.

The way Adrian just showed up out of nowhere was right out of a clichéd horror movie. The one where the girl goes to her locker alone. She opens it up, casually putting her books away, totally oblivious to the danger around her. As soon as she shuts the locker door ... *BOOM.* Some random dude materialized from the ether all creepy-like, and now he's just standing there. Yeah, that was how this guy was standing before me.

Adrian cheesed all in my face. *He'd better be glad he's so cute*, I thought, because if he'd been fugly he would've been irritating as hell.

Yes, that was shallow on my part—I admit I wasn't above it—but hey, hotness can make up for dense any day … at least until the sex gets boring.

"I like fashion trendsetters," Adrian said, quite convincing in his smoldering way. "I'm Adrian."

"I'm—" I said, but he interrupted.

"Babe, I know who you are." He raised a meticulously groomed eyebrow. Addison then stepped between him and me.

"Enough, Adrian," she snapped, shooing him away.

"What's the problem? I was just talking to her." Adrian put up his hands like he was surrendering to the police.

"Yeah, I know about your talking," Addison responded. Adrian backed off, but never stopped giving me that mischievous leer.

Even though the others didn't necessarily get along, I felt like the odd man out. They had already-established terms and conditions, unspoken rules through which they engaged each other. I had to play social double-dutch, trying to jump between two ropes that were swinging fast and furious.

Addison looked around and started to say something. "And where is—"

"James," said a particularly low-pitched voice. From the way it sounded, I thought James Earl Jones had walked in, but it turned out to be a young man. My heart fell into my stomach as I saw him for the first time: this was the guy from my intense fantasy the night before.

His very presence caused me to have some sort of bizarre vertigo attack. Even though he was only about five feet from me, the foyer seemed to elongate itself, placing him at the other end of it. And I actually heard the THX Deep Note. I figured he must have had some sort of instant recognition of me too from the way he gave me a disturbing double take.

Aunt Evelyn introduced us, "Grace, James. James, Grace."

I couldn't speak. I literally couldn't say a word. I could only make a sound resembling a cat coughing up a fur ball. Aunt Evelyn took my hand and brought me closer to James. He didn't speak either, just gazed at me curiously. *Fuck! My fucking shirt. He can't take his eyes off it.*

Eventually our eyes met, and I became lightheaded and dizzy. I felt like I was being smothered. I could tell James was uncomfortable too from the way he squirmed around. He kept adjusting his clothes, needing a place to disperse that nervous energy. I swear we must've looked like two crackheads, as twitchy as we were. However, nobody else seemed to notice this bizarre undercurrent flowing between James and me.

"Grace, these are your wonderful teachers. Aren't you excited?" Aunt Evelyn stated, clasping her hands in delight.

I wanted to tell her "hell-to-the-no" as my heart palpitations grew stronger.

"I'm sorry, guys. Please excuse me," I murmured, making a mad dash out of the foyer. I ended up in the den, leaning against the wall. As I thought about James and tried to catch my breath, my mouth filled with saliva and my stomach tightened. Before I knew it, I retched into Aunt Evelyn's lovely wicker trash can, but not before spraying some upchuck on the wall as well. From the foyer it probably sounded like an exorcism.

"Are you okay, honey?" Aunt Evelyn called out, not daring to come in and experience the horror of my vomiting.

I wiped off a long line of vomit-spit mix from my mouth. "Yeah, everything's cool," I said ... right before I hurled again.

Addison crossed her arms and grimaced. "Now that's just nasty."

James was in the basement unpacking his things with Addison's help. He saw Adrian waltz in and put his duffel bag on one of the two twin beds.

"That's for you," James said, pointing to a pitiful blowup bed in the middle of the room. James figured that was all Adrian deserved after his antics in Chesapeake.

"Whatever," Adrian replied as he reluctantly took his bag off the bed. He then proceeded to plop down on the halfway-inflated blowup. He almost sank to the floor, but was too lazy to do anything about it.

As James put his clothes away, he couldn't keep his mind off Grace. The last time he'd seen her, she was a newborn. So, despite the twenty-plus years that had passed, James had somehow expected to see a girl, not a full-grown woman. His reaction had been a surprise to him, and he didn't like surprises. Although he was normally reserved, he now felt the need to talk about Grace like any man who just met a woman he was interested in. However, he was trying to convince himself he wasn't. He decided to get some input from Addison, albeit in a roundabout way.

"She really grew up, didn't she?" he asked, trying to be as subtle as possible.

"Who? That bitchy cunt Julie?" Addison sharply responded.

"No … Grace. For some reason I kind of expected her to still be a little kid."

James glanced over at Addison and could see he was starting to overstep. She kept hanging up the clothes while looking suspiciously at James out of the corner of her eye. Despite that, he just couldn't help talking about Grace.

"She seems okay, barring the vomiting," he said, smiling some.

Addison huffed, "I wouldn't know, James. I didn't take the time to notice how all sunshine and lollipops she was … unlike you." She paused for a long second before speaking again, somewhat more calmly. "Our lives are about to be consumed with Grace. Can we have these last few moments of peace without talking about her?"

"I was just trying to talk to you," James said, now wanting to end the conversation.

Adrian piped in, "Yeah, I think she's real hot. I might have to give that filly a ride."

James marched over to Adrian and picked him up by his collar. "Don't you ever talk about her that way," he growled.

Adrian was still tired from his charisma spell and knew he was no real physical threat to James at that time. He backed off, appearing to be meek and mild, but James saw in his eyes that this encounter wasn't the last of it. James looked over at Addison, who was shaking her head back and forth like a mother trying to rattle the incessant noise of boisterous children out of her ears.

"Enough already," she said, pointing a hanger at James and Adrian like it was a loaded gun. "We are here for one reason and one reason only: to train Grace for her mission. You boys better not even think about getting twisted up with this chick in any other way. We do our job, and we try to get back home. *To our people.* To not having to save anymore Valoises."

"I know what we're here to do. I asked you to come. It was my idea, remember?" James stated.

"No, *you* just remember that," Addison snapped back as she tossed the hanger on the bed and went upstairs.

Chapter Sixteen

> You can always tell a real friend:
> when you've made a fool of yourself, he
> doesn't feel you've done a permanent
> job.
>
> —Laurence J. Peter

I sat at the kitchen table with Hari, Julie, and Aunt Evelyn. I found myself feeling more comfortable about everything, especially about being a witch.

We cracked jokes about Aunt Evelyn's lack of cooking skills, my weirdness, and Julie's big-ass feet. In the middle of the laughter, we saw Addison trying to rush past us in the hall. She had just come from the basement and looked flustered.

Aunt Evelyn waved her in. "Join us. We're having some hot cocoa. I can make you coffee if you'd rather have that."

"Naw, she looks like she's in a hurry to be somewhere else," Julie said before swigging a thermos-sized cup of Swiss Miss.

"You know, I'm quite tired," Addison replied, trying to slip away.

I tried not to be obvious, but I kept looking past her for James. I figured he would be right behind her, so I sucked in my stomach and tried to position myself in my best sexy pose.

"No, thank you. I'll just go to my room," Addison stated. Her head was the only part visible to us at the edge of the doorway as her body tried to get away.

"Our room," Julie corrected.

Addison looked incredulous. "I'm sharing a room with you?"

"Yup," Julie answered with a shit-eating grin on her face. Hari laughed under his breath.

"I really wish you'd let me get you something. You came all this way. I just feel like I haven't done enough for you," Aunt Evelyn told Addison.

Addison didn't even look at Aunt Evelyn as she responded. She glared at me instead. "No, I'm fine. You've done more than enough already." And she walked away.

God damn. Addison sure knew how to throw shade.

"Brrr, chill factor," Hari said, rubbing it in.

I turned my attention to Julie. She was mocking Addison with a sourpuss face. "You've done more than enough already," Julie joked, imitating Addison in a ridiculous British accent. I laughed, but still felt slighted by Addison.

"Grace, I know Addison has her ways, but she came through for you. After all, she did help save your life when you were a baby," Aunt Evelyn reminded me.

Julie hurried up and said, "I would've too if I had been there. If I had been told early enough."

"I know, Julie. I know. Grace, you need to get to know Addison … and James as well." With that, Aunt Evelyn got up to clear the table.

"What about Adrian?" Hari asked slyly.

I saw Aunt Evelyn taking her time to formulate a safe response. "Well …" That was the best she could come up with.

"All right," I said. I accepted the inevitability of having to communicate with Addison, and I wanted to get it out of the way. I went to her bedroom, trying to think of topics to talk about. Hair? Weather? Celebrity gossip? Yeah, Kelsey Grammer!

What in the hell am I thinking? Kelsey Grammer? Wow, that's so dumb.

As I approached the bathroom door, I could hear a high-frequency noise emanating from the room. The door was ajar, and I peeked in. Addison stood at the sink.

"Knock, knock," I said while simultaneously doing so.

I heard Addison let out a hard breath. Geez, she was acting like I was a stalker or something.

"What do you want?" she asked with her hand on her hip.

I immediately felt the need to apologize, but that urge went away rather quickly. Why should I apologize? I hadn't done anything to her, even though she may have thought my very birth was a bane to her existence.

"I just want to tell you thanks for being here," I said with a little salt of my own. That was surprising to me—it definitely was not my way.

"Don't thank me. Thank James," Addison snipped.

Oh, that name ... James. The very sound of it still made me feel a little ill, but made me want to drop my panties at the same time. However, Addison was still glowering at me.

"Look, Addison. I kinda know you don't want to be here. And yeah, I get it. But seriously, you don't have to be such a bitch about it," I said.

From the confounded look on her face, I could tell not many people had dared to speak to her that way. I got a little scared when I remembered that she was a seasoned witch who had the power to zap my ass right then and there.

Addison went back to brushing her teeth—her vain attempt to get her composure back. She didn't respect many things, but she did respect a big pair of cojones. And I had just earned some points thanks to my female version of swinging balls.

Addison held an oscillating electric toothbrush up to her mouth—the source of the buzzing I'd heard. It was a brilliant red, and had a base with multiple slots for strange-looking attachments. The brush's head barely touched her teeth, but left them spectacularly white.

"What kind of toothbrush is that?" I asked, trying not to sound totally brand new.

"It is a Sonicare Elite e9500 series. You know, for the whitest fangs."

"I didn't know Sonicare made anything like that."

"They *officially* don't. During our time on the run, we managed to meet a few witches here and there. Let's just say one of our kind is on their board and had this specially made for us." Addison handed it to me. "Want to try?"

I put it in my mouth cautiously and pushed the button. Addison stopped me with a light touch of her hand. "Grace, the toothbrush is already programmed. You barely even need to hold it. It does the work for you. Hell, I've applied makeup and brushed my teeth at the same time without any effort."

The toothbrush glided over my teeth and gums. It felt like a massage in my mouth. "Wow, this is fucking sick! They could make a freaking fortune selling something like this to the general public."

"General public?" Addison said like I had just asked her to eat trash out of a dumpster. "Silly girl, this isn't for humans. It's strictly for witches like you and me. You did get your fangs, right?"

"Yeah, I did … This must cost beaucoup greenbacks. I'm sure you had to pay *something* for it. Since you've never worked, where'd you get the money?"

Addison gave me a "whatever happens in Vegas stays in Vegas" look.

"Never mind," I said.

The toothbrush and I were getting along just fine until I accidently pressed a gray button. Suddenly, water shot out all over my face like a lawn sprinkler. Addison laughed, letting her defenses down.

"Let me help you." After she got towel and wiped my face, she told me to look in the mirror. My teeth were so white, it was like someone was shining a flashlight behind them.

Addison rinsed off the toothbrush. "Don't think this makes us friends."

It didn't matter to me what her words said. When she looked at me in the mirror and gave me a look of reassurance, I knew I was in there.

The next morning I woke up with a migraine caused by lack of sleep. I had tossed and turned all night knowing James was just two floors below me. Before I went to bed, I had nonchalantly made myself available to him on my many trips to the kitchen for glasses of milk, soda, and water. I would stand at the front door, staring aimlessly into the distance, hoping he would pop up. I practically stomped as I walked on the ground floor, trying to compel him to come up and see what the hell was going on. However, James stayed sequestered in his room all night long.

The smell of breakfast had two fingers in my nostrils, pulling me to the kitchen. As I rounded the corner, I saw James walking in from the opposite direction. He had just come up from the basement. He was putting his shirt on, and I caught a glimpse of his block-stacked abs with fine baby hair along his happy trail. His thick, gaping thighs sported in basketball shorts made my mouth water. I wondered if he went *commando*. I hid so he wouldn't be freaked out by my watching him, waiting for him to go into the kitchen. Just as I was about to do so myself, I heard a "boo." Julie had snuck up behind me.

"You little voyeuristic hussy," she said.

"I'm not. I just didn't want to bother him."

"Yeah, right. Let's go get some breakfast, horny toad."

Julie and I went into the kitchen and were greeted by what could only be described as a paleo lover's wet dream: eggs, bacon, sausage, ham, even protein drinks. I wasn't bothered one bit by the lack of carbs. I had been craving a lot of meat lately; I figured I was anemic.

Julie took the seat next to Hari, leaving me with the only open chair left; the one next to James. He and I both mumbled something resembling a morning greeting to each other.

Adrian sat directly across from me. He was in full-on player mode and winked at me every two seconds.

The clanging and scraping of the forks on the plates sounded extraordinarily loud to me that morning. In fact, all sounds seemed to be amplified. I brushed it off, attributing it to my throbbing migraine.

"Grace, James is going to show you some ropes today," Aunt Evelyn said as she bit into a juicy sausage link.

I gulped, swallowing a chunk of ham I hadn't even chewed yet. "Okay, sure," I replied, trying my best not to look at James. It was at that moment, I realized unfortunately I liked him a little too much.

And lusted to the point of perversion. Honestly, it went beyond mere *like*, and I had to be careful with that.

Aside from this being a business arrangement, I knew what it was like to fall in love with everything you've got and have that love betray you. After Rafe, I'd resigned myself to being alone. On the off chance that another guy happened to show up in my life, I'd sworn I'd keep my emotions in check. If that meant not loving to the fullest, not giving unconditionally, so be it. I might have sacrificed true love, but at least I'd still have my soul … no matter what went down.

That was why I was attracted to and repulsed by James at the same time. He *felt* like he'd be good for me, but that was the way Rafe had felt once upon a time. Anyhow, I didn't need to get involved with anyone at that time. However, a girl occasionally wants to get carnal, and Adrian was a safe bet. I was certain there would be no intellectual or emotional connection there. Just sex. That line of reasoning may have made me a slut, but I'd be a smart slut.

I started eating like a hog that had just finished a joint, pulling handfuls of meat off the serving plate and eating without utensils. I was making nom-nom sounds as I filled up my mouth. The eating was proof of the rapid changes within me; my cells were begging for fuel. I didn't notice everyone else at the table intently watching me. They all knew what was going on—something more than what I knew. The insatiable hunger was a sign of something they were keeping to themselves. They knew I wasn't ready for that revelation yet.

I was on my way out the door to meet James for our training session when Adrian stopped me.

"I'm sorry I wasn't your first," he said, stepping to me. He had no clue how to disguise his innuendos. "Your first teacher that is."

I could see James leaning back on his car and knew he was wondering what was going on. The longer I stood with Adrian, the more James pursed his lips. I didn't want to give him the wrong impression.

"I gotta go," I said to Adrian as I circumvented him and headed to James. He smiled at me nervously as I walked toward him. I, on the other hand, thought I would lift off at any moment with all the butterflies battering around my stomach.

"Let's go over to the barn," James stated, putting his hands in his pockets. As we walked to the barn, we didn't say anything, and stayed far apart from one another. No matter how awkward it may have been, I felt a sense of safety I hadn't in years—even though he still made me feel a bit nauseated.

We arrived at the old barn, and I thought we were going to shoot the breeze a little, but James got right into training.

"All witches vary in the amount of magical power they have. Some have very little. Their powers resemble those of sensitive humans— enhanced intuition, ESP, charisma. Others are supremely powerful, with the ability to affect the physical universe through sheer will. Also, we each have one particular talent we excel in. Have you noticed any special abilities?"

"Things move by themselves when I'm around."

"Telekinesis. Can you control it?"

"No, it comes and goes."

"Show me."

"I tried to show Aunt Evelyn and Julie. Nothing happened."

James came up behind me and took my hands. "Now, I want you to concentrate on that old can on the ground. Move it," he said softly in my ear.

Oh damn, he felt so good. I could see I was going to have to work extra hard to not let this guy get to me. I redirected my attention to the can. I didn't try any fancy tricks or gimmicks. I just said "move" in my mind.

The can shimmied a bit. James urged me to keep going. *Move*, I thought. The can did a 180-degree spin.

James let go of my hands. "Do it again."

This time the can popped up into the air.

"Now make it fly," he said.

I really wanted to please him, and tried with all of my might to make it soar. However, the can fell flat. I tried to get it to move again, but it was dead.

"That's okay. We'll work on it," he said.

James passed me a haunting lascivious smile. His eyes were so clear and sparkly. I knew I was in trouble. I could handle Adrian—my feelings for him were a shallow stream—but the ones I had for James were turning into the Mariana Trench.

Julie stood on the porch waiting for me and saw too much bounce in my step for her comfort.

"So, how'd your little session go?" she asked.

"Fine. We got a lot done," I responded, trying my best not to say it in a sing-song way. "James is still at the barn."

Julie was edgy. "You know this isn't about getting you laid. You have a job to do. And besides, they are Bolingbrokes, and you know the history. Remember where your loyalties lie." With that she went into the house.

That brought me back to reality. Julie was right; this was about a mission, and James did come from a rival family. It got me to thinking. Why was James—a Bolingbroke—even there? What was his deal? And why did my mother bring in one of the enemy to help us?

Chapter Seventeen

> Trust is hard to come by. That's why my
> circle is small and tight. I'm kind of
> funny about making new friends.
>
> —Eminem

Catherine sat in the back of the Mercedes drinking a vintage bottle of Krug Brut champagne with Chetan, who was thrilled that he was indulging in the fabulous life and being driven around by Nick. Catherine knew Chetan's initial attitude toward Nick was jealousy, though.

When Catherine had informed Chetan she would be creating a protégé, Chetan had wondered what was wrong with him. Why did Catherine need a protégé? But now he watched Nick with a sideways glance and was relieved not to be him. To Chetan, Nick was the walking dead. Chetan made mental notes, comparing the two-timing man Catherine had picked up at the mall to this empty shell driving the car.

With all the bottle popping, Catherine understood that Chetan couldn't grasp the fact she was playing him for a fool. She had employed a divide-and-conquer tactic that powerful people had used since the dawn of time. She knew she'd be able to manipulate Chetan even more by giving him two things. One, a carrot. She dangled the potential prestige in front of his face, giving him just a taste of it. Once he had a bite of that, he'd chase it forever. Two, she gave him the illusion of superiority. She would never let him feel above her. However, if Chetan felt he was better than someone else, it would keep him satisfied and working on her program. With those two things, she'd have a flunky for life.

The trio arrived at Long Island College with the intent of locating Grace. Catherine had tried all manner of magic spells, trances, and astral travel to find her. Unfortunately, no matter what she did, she could not get a clear picture of Grace's location. Old-fashioned detective work was Catherine's final option.

As the car made its way over endless speed bumps, Catherine was surprised by how bucolic the campus was. It was so much better than Jersey. She closed her eyes and breathed the air deep into her lungs, trying to soak in any remnant of Grace's essence. The car passed the campus washateria. Catherine got a ringing in her ear that sounded like tinnitus.

"Stop! Stop the car right now," she commanded Nick. The car screeched to a halt.

"Is something wrong?" Chetan asked, trying to recover from the mild whiplash he'd just gotten.

Catherine pointed at a young Indian woman, Naisha Samala, who grabbed a container of laundry detergent from the backseat of her Toyota Corolla and zipped back inside the building.

"That girl," Catherine said, her voice displaying rare excitement. "She can tell me where Grace is."

Catherine got out of the car and noticed another vehicle next to Naisha's. It had a flat tire.

"Nick, you park the car over there, out of sight," she instructed, then she stepped into the washateria.

As soon as Catherine got through the double doors, a blast of hot air circulated by ceiling fans hit her in the face. It smelled like burning cleaning solvent. She strode onto the black-and-white checkered floor, careful not to slip on the liquid fabric softener someone had spilled.

Down a long row of double-stacked dryers, Catherine could see Naisha. She was the only one in the place; Catherine ascertained the driver of the car with the flat tire was out getting help. Catherine knew she had to act fast before that person came back.

Naisha sat in front of two dryers and was engrossed in something on her computer screen. She didn't hear Catherine's footsteps coming toward her because of the dryers' loud tumbling and rumbling.

Catherine was no social-media butterfly, but she could tell Naisha was. She found it funny that humans left themselves so open to attack through these means. She guessed that youthful obsession with these mediums diminished the gift of instinct; it was nearly impossible to develop or use over a computer screen, and that carried over to in-person interaction. And without instinct, everyone becomes your friend. Therefore, Catherine knew that this young woman wouldn't know a predator until it had her in its mouth. Unfortunately for Catherine, Grace had no profiles on any social media to speak of.

"Excuse me, miss," Catherine said.

She saw Naisha quickly closing out a window to a lesbian dating site and switching it over to a photo of a handsome, young Indian man her parents were trying to arrange a marriage with. Naisha had not yet fully embraced her homosexuality and considered her frequenting of lesbian websites a harmless pastime.

"What do you need?" Naisha asked with a childlike voice.

Catherine did a quick once-over of the girl's immediate space. Naisha was an editor of the college newspaper, and despite being a nice young woman, she was a rabid busybody. She had a legal notepad, articles she was proofreading, and the most recent copy of the paper. The headline article was about Samantha's murder.

"Oh my. That's awful," Catherine murmured, picking up the newspaper.

Naisha didn't seem bothered by Catherine's handling of her personal property. "I know. The killer left her head and took the rest of the body. Isn't that deranged?"

"Let me tell you, this world is filled with demons. Yet here you are, all alone. You must be very brave." Catherine pretended to be interested in the article.

"Not really ... just laundry. Uh, did you say you need something?"

"Yes, I'm looking for a friend of mine. Grace Valois. I haven't seen her in a very long time, and it's a surprise that I'm here."

"I know Grace. We have a mutual friend—Julie." In reality, Naisha thought Julie was a lesbian too, and had a serious crush on her. However, Naisha had backed off when she'd found out Julie and Grace were living together; she'd assumed they were lovers.

"You won't find either of them here on campus, or even in their apartment. They just got up and left all of a sudden. A moving van picked up their stuff the other day." Naisha knew this because of the many hours she spent driving past their apartment and looking through their windows. "You said you're a close friend of Grace?"

Catherine could see Naisha was starting to get suspicious. After all, Catherine had walked into some random washateria with no clothes to launder, asking a stranger for information about someone who was supposed to be a friend. She opted for the blitzkrieg approach. "Do you know where they are?"

If Naisha was anything, it was compliant. She immediately got on her computer and pulled up a campus directory. "Don't tell anyone I have this. I got it from an informant in student admissions. He comes in handy when trying to get the scoop on a story."

The computer screen came back with Julie's last known address—the apartment. "You don't want that. They don't live there anymore," Naisha explained as she searched for Grace's information. She pointed at the screen. "Here it is. Grace's home address. I'm sorry, it's in Massapequa. I guess you won't be able to surprise her."

"Massapequa? That's no problem. I love Massapequa," Catherine replied, trying to contain herself. "What's the address?"

Naisha tore a piece of paper out of the legal pad and wrote down the address. "Sorry I couldn't do more."

Catherine stared at the paper. "This is just fine. Thank you." She knew she would have to kill Naisha, just in case the girl decided to run her mouth about this encounter—that whole six degrees of separation thing. As Catherine's fangs started to pop out, however, the owner of the vehicle with the flat tire came in. He had a bottle of Fix-A-Flat in his hand and proceeded to make his way to his dryer.

While Catherine tried to escape out the door without the young man noticing her, Naisha shouted, "Tell Julie I say 'hi'!"

Damn it, Catherine thought as she looked at the young man. Luckily, he was so absorbed by his clothes, he didn't even look up.

Good. Then I only need to kill one.

Later Catherine sat in the Mercedes with Chetan. She saw Naisha putting her scorching-hot clothes into the trunk of her car. The car with the flat was gone.

"Go get her," Catherine said, sending Nick to retrieve the girl.

To Naisha, Nick's hand was like some big, hairy paw coming out of nowhere and covering her mouth. He picked up the frail-boned young woman and tried to drag her to the Mercedes, but Naisha had some fight in her. She managed to bite Nick's hand, causing him to drop her on the concrete. She noticed his blood didn't taste right. It didn't have the normal metallic undertone; it was more like soured milk.

"Nick, really, you can't capture one little girl?" Catherine yelled.

Naisha tripped and scraped her knees as she tried to run back into the washateria. With her on the ground, Nick took the opportunity to grab her again, this time breaking her arm in the process. He threw her into the back of the Mercedes. Naisha screamed bloody murder, but the soundproof windows prevented anyone from hearing it.

Chetan looked at her like she was steak and a baked potato. The protégé was too young to have developed his hunger yet, but Chetan was starving.

Catherine slapped Naisha across the face. "Dear, you really do need to shut up."

"What are we going to do with her?" Chetan asked. He expected Catherine to say they were going to eat her. Instead, Catherine stuck a pencil through Naisha's temple, killing her. Then she directed Nick to drive, and they wound up in a heavily wooded area, at a rickety bridge that had not been used in decades.

"Nick … Chetan … toss her," Catherine said from inside the Mercedes.

Chetan grabbed Naisha's legs while Nick held her arms. They lifted the body over the rail, but Chetan had to ask Catherine, "Why aren't we eating her? Isn't this just a waste of meat?"

Catherine put her sunglasses on and said matter-of-factly, "I'm not in the mood for Indian food."

Chapter Eighteen

To be trusted is a greater compliment
than to be loved.

—George MacDonald

I looked down my red nose at the thermometer that dangled out of my mouth.

My whole body was fatigued and heavy, like it was being crushed. I had a mad case of the chills, complete with blueberry-colored lips and icy fingertips. My mind was totally disconnected from my body, and I couldn't seem to remember how to properly move it. It just kind of laid there in a lump, making reflexive, erratic movements like a sleeping newborn does.

James knocked on my door and stuck his head in. I quickly stashed the thermometer under my pillow, not wanting to alarm him.

"Hey, sleepyhead. Ready to get the day going?" He actually had a tiny bit of cheer in his voice for a change. Then he entered the bedroom and gasped at the death mask called my face. "What's wrong?"

I was glad to see James and welcomed him in—until Julie's words popped into my head: *Don't trust him. He's a Bolingbroke.* My face instantly transformed into the embodiment of spite. James halted in his tracks, and he looked at me with the most bewildered expression on his face. For a second he went back into his mental file to see if he had done something to offend me.

I sucked my teeth and snapped, "I'll be down in a minute." I was being a bitch, but until I knew his true intentions, that attitude seemed to be the most appropriate way to deal with him.

"All right. I'll meet you in the kitchen," he stated cautiously as he backed out the door. He never took his eyes off me, just in case I decided to pounce.

I pulled the thermometer from underneath my pillow and read the mercury through bleary, crusted-over eyes. The shitty way I felt, I knew my temperature had to be way past 100 degrees.

"Ninety-one," I said, shaking the thermometer, sure it was a mistake. I thought about retaking my temperature, but felt too much like shit to do it. I wanted to go back to sleep, but for some reason my stomach had other plans. I was hungry … No, starving … No, ravenous. I *had* to eat something.

Slow as a snail, I moved my heavy legs to the side of the bed, finally ending up on my hip with my arm hanging off the side. With a forceful thrust, I somehow managed to sit straight up for a few moments. However, the room started spinning, and I found my face buried in my sweaty palm. As I looked at the backs of my eyelids, even though I did not want to I thought about James. I wondered, *Can I trust him? And if I can,* should *I trust him?*

I had somehow managed to make it to the kitchen without actually lifting my feet off the floor. Dragging—the new walking.

James was at the stove frying up some breakfast. The smoky smell of applewood bacon and the sizzle of fried eggs made my salivary glands go berserk. Nevertheless, I wasn't going to let breakfast and James's handsome face win me over.

"It's just us two for breakfast this morning. The others went into town," he said, flipping the hard-cooked egg like he was an expert chef. I didn't respond, determined that he wasn't going to get to me. James plated the food and brought it over to the table where I was.

"Voila, Madame. Breakfast is served." He waited for me to take a bite. I did, and it was delicious, but I couldn't let him know that. He joined me, and we ate in the most horrible silence ever known to mankind. I wished the others would hurry back so they could break the seal on that vacuum of quiet. Regardless, my funky attitude toward James did not diminish my appetite in the least. In fact, after the slab of bacon and a dozen eggs, I started to feel a little better … but my stomach was still queasy. I didn't feel that total sense of renewal I had the other morning when I'd scarfed down every part of the hog. What was wrong with me today?

I scooted my chair back across the chipped linoleum and started to go get some Pepto-Bismol. As I was about to disappear out the door, James hurried over and gently took my arm.

"Is there something wrong?" he asked, getting his face close to mine to stop me from avoiding his gaze.

I shook his hand off me. "There's nothing wrong with me. Is there something wrong with you?" I noticed that the angrier I felt toward James, the sicker I got. And I was getting quite used to feeling like shit. After all, I had become the undisputed queen of puke over the last few days.

For the day's training, James and I ended up at the large, manmade pond at the edge of Aunt Evelyn's property.

I stood at the end of the narrow pier, looking into the water. Light penetrated the sparse water hyacinths enough that I could almost see the bottom. The pond was stocked with fish that jutted in and out of an underwater forest of Anacharis. Along the edge, Aunt Evelyn had created a stone garden filled with statuettes of angels and frogs, and she had hung some her famous wind chimes made of lightning glass. I was mesmerized by the absolute beauty and peace of this place. For a minute, I forgot I was out there alone with a potential threat named James. I came back to reality when I heard him clanging around the battered rowboat.

"Come on," he said, waving me over. I walked slowly down the pier, wondering if a double agent was waiting for me. I was watching my back, all the while pretending to go along with the whole thing. I didn't want to tip him off. Man, where was Julie when I needed her?

"Be careful. It's slippery out here," James said, coming toward me. He seemed like he was going to help me walk down, but how could I be sure? I reluctantly let him put his warm hand on the small of my back and guide me to the other end of the pier. And damn, wouldn't you know, James's touch, soft and sensual, still felt good to me. I *so* had a split personality when it came to this guy.

He stepped into the boat, steadied it, and reached his hand out to me. The thought still ran through my head: *Can I trust him?* However, I took his hand, got into the boat, and sat on the slightly wet bench— all pouty lipped. James untied the rope from the pier. He sat opposite me and started to paddle, attempting to make light conversation. I just stared at him, scrutinizing his face for any sign of betrayal—seeing if he was a friend or a foe—but his eyes, those big, blue eyes, kept drawing me in. And the only response to that was to be an ass.

"Why are we out here anyway?" I snapped.

"To see if you can walk on water," James joked, trying unsuccessfully to lighten the mood. When he saw I wasn't laughing, he said, "*Ookaay.*"

He was totally perplexed, but he went on with the lesson. "Since you're having trouble with telekinesis, we're going to try to move water instead of a solid object. It's lighter and should be easier manipulate than something with compacted mass. Once you master that, we'll gradually increase the density of your practice objects."

We made it to the middle of the pond, and James said, "Grace, now move the water." I made a half-assed attempt at it. My mind was too preoccupied.

"Why are you here? I don't understand why a Bolingbroke would decide to help me—a Valois heir—to overtake the council. That would keep you and yours underneath us. And no one likes to be on the bottom if given the choice."

James finally understood. "Oh, *that's* what all the attitude is about. You don't trust me." He rested the paddle across his lap. "Grace, I wasn't going to say anything, but you've backed me into a corner." He paused, searching for the words to make his revelation less shocking. "I'm not a Bolingbroke by blood. I was adopted. All I know about my real mother was that she was an extremely close friend of your mother, Ilan. For some reason I had to be adopted out. It had to be kept very quiet, and much subterfuge was used to cover up my real identity."

I listened intently, using anything and everything I had to ferret out whatever lie he might have been telling. So far I hadn't been able to pick up on anything that would have caused a spike on a lie-detector test.

"I grew up in the Bolingbroke house not fitting in—a misfit. I always felt out of place with them, I just didn't know why. Even before the religious bigots killed members of our coven and the invocation of the Ancients, the Bolingbrokes were well on their way to becoming a greedy, power-hungry group. In that family those traits run on a sliding scale from mild to pathological, with Catherine at the far end. But that's who they are at the core of each of their beings. It's in their blood. They can't help it."

I still had questions. Some things still needed explanations. "And what about you? When they invoked the Ancients, you went along with it. Did you not?" I asked, sure he would trip himself up with the answer.

"Regrettably, when the decision was reached, I sided with my family. Now, my body is possessed by some spirit—I know not what. Luckily, my soul isn't. It's pure, and I still carry the blood of my genetic lineage, whoever they are. Grace, you've got to believe me when I say I did not agree with the Bolingbroke agenda. I sympathized with Ilan and her cause. That was why she chose me. And if you can't trust that, there's nothing more I can do. "

My instinct told me he was telling the truth. At that moment, I learned a valuable lesson: It wasn't James I had to learn to trust. It was me. I needed to trust my own gut reactions. I could no longer depend on someone else's observations or opinions to be my guides, even if they came from well-meaning friends like Julie.

"Do Adrian and Addison know about your past?" I asked, my body aching to get closer to James.

"No, they don't. I didn't even know about my adoption until Ilan told me, when we were on the run. No matter what, Adrian and Addison are still my family, and I love them. I always will. However, Ilan did tell me she would reveal my true heritage to me when you took your place on the council. She said it was too dangerous to divulge at the time. I trusted her and didn't press the issue. But when she died, she took that information with her. Ever since, I've kept my adoption a secret, and have had to deal with the knowledge that I have missing pieces. Sometimes I wish Ilan had never told me in the first place."

I sympathized with him. I knew what it was like not to have a parent. It was a bottomless hole that, no matter how much shit you tried to fill it with, only seemed to get bigger.

All of that confessing and my epiphany must have really gotten to me, because next thing I knew I was having a hot flash and rigor at the same time. Then it felt like my heart stopped beating.

"I can't breathe," I managed to squeak right before I passed out.

I woke up in a supine position, greeted by fluffy clouds that looked like cotton balls tacked onto a turquoise note board.

"Ugh … What happened?" I whispered, my head consumed by grogginess. I tried to get up, but my body hurt too much, as if it had been dropped from the Empire State Building.

"Grace, listen to me. Your heart stopped. You almost died. I brought you back with a little CPR, but you need blood," James said as he took a small knife and sliced deep into his index finger. "Please, trust me and drink it."

His blood, the prettiest shade of pinkish red, squirted out. "It may taste strange, but it will help you," he explained.

I looked at his finger and was repulsed by the thought of consuming his blood—*initially*. "No, I don't want it," I stated, quickly turning my head away.

"You don't have a choice." James grabbed my chin and turned my head back to him. Once my nose caught wind of his blood, I smacked my lips in anticipation. Despite my denial, I did want it—and lots of it.

James put his finger in my mouth. I sucked it cautiously at first, not knowing what to think of this situation. The blood tasted so good to me—a cross between iron and calla lilies. I sucked his fingertip longer and harder. My cheeks sucked in as I coaxed as much blood as I could into my mouth. As I lay there, still on my back, with James's finger in my mouth, I couldn't help but think, *Oh, the makings of a nice hardcore porn. Bom chicka wah wah.* But when something is that good, you just don't care.

"You're doing fine," James said warmly. "It seems as though your transition is having some unexpected side effects. Normally witches turn at puberty, and as we go through our teens, we naturally obtain and master our powers. We don't get sick like you just did. Because of your hybrid status, we don't know how this is all going to work out. I guess we'll just have to see. Take it day by day."

After about five minutes of my drawing blood, James had to steal his finger back. I got so into it I drooled—a lot. Luckily, it didn't seem to bother him, not in the least. He wiped my wet chin with the edge of his shirt, leaving flecks of blood on it.

"How did you like it? Do you feel better? If you need more, I'll let you keep drinking," he said.

I did feel better. In fact, I felt great. The near-constant nausea I'd had ever since I'd met James had transmuted into an indescribable connection to him. Though we were two bodies, it felt like we were one. Up until that moment, I hadn't believed in the concept of soul mates, but I finally knew the reason why I was sick all the time … my soul was trying to unify with his. And until that happened, I was going to feel like puking my brains out every other minute.

James and I didn't need to fall in love because we had *always* been in love. Even the term *falling in love* was inappropriate. It was more like rising up to it. However, I could see he regretted what he had done.

"What's wrong?" I asked, not understanding how I could be so deliriously happy while he seemed so sad.

"I didn't want to do that to you. I should have asked your permission first. But you were dying. I didn't have a choice," he said with his head down.

"James, I feel great, and you saved my life. What's the problem?"

"I knew the moment I saw you that we were destined to be together. Still … even when fate is involved … a man wants to be certain a woman made the choice to be with him of her own free will. This is why witches do not drink the blood of another. They become linked to each other in an unbreakable bond whether they want to or not. I want you to love me on your own. I never want to wonder if it was just the blood that made you want to be with me."

"When you walked through Aunt Evelyn's door for the first time, I knew it then. So you don't ever have to wonder if it was the blood or not. I do love you. I've always loved you."

James looked at me for a moment, and then suddenly reached for me. I grabbed him in return. Our lips met like they had been searching for each other for a thousand years. We pressed our bodies together as hard as we could, like we were trying to merge into one person. The boat wobbled with our movements, and James steadied it with a swipe of his hand. Ripples started to extend from underneath the boat, and the water heated up with the intense energy we generated. The water became agitated like a small-scale hurricane on the pond.

James slowly rubbed his cheek against mine. Then, with one hand, he cupped my face, which was flushed with desire. With the other he pulled my hair back until my neck was exposed, and slid his fingers to hold it firmly in place. Then he kissed and gently caressed it with his tongue. He stopped at my chin. I raised my head to see why, and he gazed deeply into my eyes. I could see myself reflected in his. James parted my lips with his tongue, and mine met his anxiously. I let him take the lead like the man he was, and I loved every minute of it.

I'd heard about people feeling like they were melting when they kissed someone. I'd thought that was an exaggeration. Not anymore. I literally felt like I had melted into James, the boat, the water ... I was one with everything.

We pulled back and looked into each other's eyes, unable to deny it any longer. There was no way we could fight the base urge to become one soul, one body. James rowed us to the bank of the pond, and we got out as fast as we could. He took me by the hand, and we ran into the forest like little children. I trailed him to a clearing in the middle of a group of massive oak trees. He swung me around in front of him, never letting go of my hand.

My skin flushed, and my body trembled with anticipation. I could tell he wanted me, too—the dampness of his hand and his dilated pupils gave it away. He stepped toward me and placed his ember-hot fingers on my hips. However, as James leaned in to kiss me, something stopped him. He held me at bay with a pained expression on his face.

"What's wrong?" I asked. I was practically lunging at him as I attempted to make lip contact.

James held my body stationary. His grip was firm and resolute. He pushed away a wisp of hair that had been covering my eye. "Grace, you are so beautiful. The last thing in the world I want to do it is hurt you, but ..."

Aw, no, I thought. *The dreaded 'but.' Nothing good comes after that.*

"I don't take the idea of making love to you lightly," he continued. "And trust me, you and I making love is nothing to trifle with. We just can't do it right now, if ever."

He couldn't fool me. I saw through that stoic look, straight to his hidden torture. A battle raged inside of him. One side wanted to take me right there, and powerfully so. The other struggled against it with all its might. James, for some reason, was trying to inhibit his desire and stay in control.

I was still on fire, though, and wanted to totally lose control. My lust was an F5 tornado rolling over an old trailer park. "I want you," I panted as sweat burst out of my pores. "I'm pretty sure you want me, too. What harm could it do?" As I started feather-kissing James on his neck, he grabbed me by the shoulders and gave me a slight shake. I could see the anguish on his face as his half-closed eyes gazed back at me.

"Tell me what you need and I'll give it to you. Tell me what you want and I'll go to the edge of the universe to get it. But for your benefit, making love is the one thing I can't give you right now. I am not going to allow this to go any further. Damn it, Grace, my entire being wants nothing except to be with you. Unfortunately, I can't do it. You've got to believe me when I say I've got your best interest at heart."

Then he looked away, toward a crumpling sound coming from the woods. "Did you hear that?"

"No, nothing," I said. The truth was that a freight train could have run through there and I wouldn't have heard it. That's how much I was into James at that moment. The very essence of my being was totally zoned in on that man. It was more than mere sexual arousal. Something in the blood I had ingested had *enhanced* me. I didn't just want him … I *needed* him. Needed his hands on me. In me. His tongue licking my wet slit in preparation to be *taken*.

James dropped my hand and walked over to the clearing's perimeter. Forever vigilant, he scanned the woods for *something*. And indeed there was an unwanted spectator in our midst. Adrian lurked behind a tree; he'd been watching us the whole time. His blood had grown so hot with jealousy, he singed the tree where his hand touched it. With thoughts of revenge, he ghosted out of the woods.

"Something's there," James stated. He had seen a streak of Adrian, but did not know what it was. Neither did I at that point.

I sucked my teeth, disappointed that James wasn't going to let it go. "Where?"

"In the woods. We've got to go."

"Why? We just got here," I argued. At first I was convinced this was some ruse to distract me, but now I could see that James was genuinely concerned. I had to learn to trust his instincts as well as my own.

"All right then. Let's go," I reluctantly said. If I had been male, I would have been standing there with a massive case of fucking blue balls.

James hurried us out of the woods; I could barely keep up. Though we didn't know it, we passed right by the tree Adrian had been creeping behind. The burnt-on imprint of his hand still smoldered a bit.

In my ignorance, I said to James, "Do you smell something burning?"

When James and I arrived at Aunt Evelyn's, everyone else was back from their excursion, and we were trying to pretend nothing had gone down between us.

Julie was in the kitchen with Aunt Evelyn, but when she saw James and me together, she just walked out. I blew it off, making an excuse for her behavior: *Obviously I didn't hear her say hello. Yeah, that's it.*

"Where have you two been?" Aunt Evelyn asked as she unpacked groceries. All of the cabinets were wide open as she filled them with cans of tuna, sardines, and Vienna sausages. Fucking gross.

James and I looked at each other slyly and answered in unison, "Training." Aunt Evelyn gave us a suspicious look.

"I think I'll go take a shower," James said. He gave me a light squeeze on the hand and was off.

Aunt Evelyn pointed at a chair. "Sit."

I sat down, trying to act as nonchalantly as possible. "You want some help with the groceries?"

She waved her hand, and all the cabinet doors shut. "I know."

I got a little scared. "Know what?"

"I know about you and James. I can feel it. I should've talked to you about this possibility before he got here, but I just didn't get around to it … considering everything else that's been going on. If it were going to happen, I didn't think it would happen this fast."

"What are you talking about?" I asked, feeling extremely uncomfortable.

"You two like each other … a lot. I won't tell you what do to in regard to the relationship, but I will say, don't let it become a distraction. Not only for you, but for the group as a whole."

"It won't." I felt relieved that I wouldn't have to hide it from her. Aunt Evelyn hugged me and started to tear up.

"What?" I said, trying not to cry as well, especially since I didn't know why I would be crying.

"You're really grown now. With so much work to do," she whispered with pity in her voice.

"I'm okay. Really. I'll be fine." I returned Aunt Evelyn's hug, hoping she wouldn't smell James all over me.

With the emotion in there getting way over the top, I just had to get out. I went to Julie's room and walked in without knocking. Addison wasn't there; she was relaxing on the porch. Julie lay across the bed reading *Popular Mechanics*.

"What's shaking, Dog Soldier?" I said, popping her on the behind. Normally this would have elicited an awesome comeback, but she ignored me and just kept turning the pages of her magazine—which she wasn't really reading.

"Julie, what's up with you? If you have something to say to me, just say it."

"Well, Grace, it's not hard to figure out that something disturbing went down between you and James. My question is what?" Julie finally decided to look at me. "What did he tell you? What could he have said to make you cavort with the enemy? That's your fucking problem, Grace. You are so damn trusting. And top that off with selfish. You didn't even care about my part in all of this. My sacrifice."

"First off, Julie, you really have no clue what you're talking about. Second, I am well aware of what you've sacrificed to be here. Don't you dare say I'm not."

Julie got off the bed and started toward me. I could see little hairs starting to sprout on her body. "What happened this morning between you and James?" she asked with all sorts of accusation in her tone.

"I got sick, and he fed me."

"Aw, shit. You can't be serious. You ingested his blood? You are so fucking stupid. Do you have any clue what you did? Now you're bonded to him. Forever!"

"I could have died, Julie."

"If he couldn't summon Evelyn or me, he should've let you."

I couldn't believe she said that. And I could tell from the mystified expression on her face she couldn't believe it either. I swore, this shit with James. First Aunt Evelyn had to warn me about its impact on the mission, and now Julie was losing her mind over it. James and I must have been the witch equivalent of Romeo and Juliet. All I could do was shake my head and refuse to acknowledge Julie anymore by not looking at her. Unfortunately, she wasn't having that. She raised my head and started to read my face.

"Aw, man, Grace. Did you fuck him, too?"

"No, I didn't, but I wanted to. Now what?"

"Grace, this is getting worse and worse. Please tell me you are not in love with him."

I didn't want to disappoint her, but there was no way I could deny what I felt for James. "Julie, I'm sorry, but I am."

She collapsed into a chair. "Why did you let this happen?"

"Is it so bad? James saved my life not once, but twice. There has always been a connection between us."

"You mean like soul mates?" Julie said, mocking me. "Let me tell you something. You aren't soul mates. How can you be? He's hundreds of years old. You're twenty-one. And you weren't there during the bad times, when those fucking Bolingbrokes decided to be total assholes and set out to destroy the Valoises." Her eyes glowed yellower the more she talked about James. She was about to turn; I just knew it. Her body shook uncontrollably.

"Please! Stop!" I yelled, but she phased right there in the middle of the bedroom. She didn't look like the beautiful wolf she had morphed into before. She was now just a hideous monster. *The fuck?* I was scared to death. If we were bound for life and I was going to have to deal with this werewolf bullshit, I needed to stand up to her and make a statement.

I knew she couldn't control me as my immortal self. Every last conversation I'd had with her flooded my head, and now my life was about choices. Who had I been? Who was I now? Who would I be? Acceptance was now the rule. I would own it all. And from then on I did. I closed my eyes and let anger take hold of me. It was the quickest way I knew to change. My fangs descended, and the vibration from my snarl nearly knocked me over.

"You don't scare me," I snapped at Julie. She growled at me, furious that I was challenging her.

"Now what? Do you want to fight?" I asked. "Whatever. I'm not backing down. But does it need to go that far? I'm fairly certain once my aunt finds out, she'll be pissed. Less at me, more at you. So I advise you to phase back, or fight your best friend. Either way, I'm staying with James."

Julie wasn't backing down; she had an excess of testosterone and pride. Then words slipped out of my mouth that I'd never thought I'd say: "You will stop this nonsense and phase back now! As your ruler, I command you."

Julie phased back to human form, but she was different, and something had changed between us. I knew the dictatorial posture I'd taken with her was probably not the best course of action. She was my best friend and my faithful shadow. Regardless, if I had a mission, I had to assume my rightful position—a leader, a ruler, or whatever the frig you call it—but to Julie I was simply power tripping and putting her in her place … as a footstool underneath me.

"So today you finally decide to embrace your destiny. And to think I couldn't help you do it, nor could Aunt Evelyn or anyone else. This is all for James. And you willingly put down our friendship over this man. So typical," Julie said, her words full of venom.

"Julie, this has something to do with him, but only a small part. I've been asked to embrace my destiny for a while now. So why question what day, month, or year I do it?"

"It's his blood, Grace. That's what you're embracing. Can't you see what it's doing already? It's turning you away from me." Julie held back her tears.

"Never ever, Julie. I will always be your best friend. You will also always protect me—when I need it of course. Do we have an understanding?"

"The *only* understanding we have is that I have a mission, too. That is to protect you when need be, and to train you. Otherwise, we don't have anything else to talk about."

James fell onto the bed, relieved the strange ruckus in the woods had interrupted an extremely volatile situation. He regretted how he had almost allowed himself to become vulnerable to Grace.

Addison bounded in. "How'd training go? Is she getting the hang of telekinesis yet?"

"Yes."

Addison was suspicious of James's curt response. She squinted her eyes and looked at him sideways. "Spill it. What really happened?"

James realized there was no need to hide it anymore. "I'm in love with Grace." He could tell she was disappointed, but not surprised.

"Like I couldn't see that coming." Addison let go of a chuckle—one of those laughs to keep from crying.

James's demeanor became more somber. "There's more."

"You sound like I need to sit down."

James pointed to a chair.

"Just give me a chance to brace myself," Addison said. She took her time walking to the chair, purposefully prolonging the wait before she heard the news. She sat down in a very businesslike manner. "Okay, let me have it."

"It's becoming obvious that Grace may have a dormant Ancient spirit in her. Now that she's awakening, it is, too. And it wants to be fed. She almost died because it's starving and trying to force her to feed. She is unaware of what's going on, and I don't know how she'll take it. So today I had to give her some of my blood."

Addison shot up like she was a Jack-in-the-box. "James, no! You know you've been forbidden to do that. That's the first step in establishing *blood ties* with someone and permanently marking them. First it's the blood exchange, then sexual consummation. You'll be sealed forever. I'm not saying I like Grace or anything, but I have grown to admire her somewhat, and I don't think it's fair to put such a burden on her."

"You think I don't know that?"

"James, did you fuck her?"

"No, I didn't. The last thing I want to do is bring harm to her."

He could feel the air leaving his lungs as Addison's body tensed up. The more upset she became, the more a vortex of energy formed around her. The air wasn't being sucked out of the room so much as being drawn into her vacuum.

"There's nothing we can do about the blood now. Go ahead and have your flirtation with Grace. Boys will be boys. But I suggest preparing for the inevitable. We are going back home after this ordeal, and you two can't be together there. That's just the way it is."

"Don't worry, Addison. I know my duty, my role. I won't jeopardize it."

Addison looked at James and knew he loved Grace too much to keep that promise. Between duty and love, she knew which one would ultimately win.

Chapter Nineteen

> When written in Chinese, the word
> "crisis" is composed of two characters.
> One represents danger and the other
> represents opportunity.
>
> —John F. Kennedy

A new civil war was brewing in America. Not between north and south. Not between conservatives and liberals. Not even between Mariah Carey and Nicki Minaj.

The unwitting opponents of this contention were Julie and me. Avoidance was our main line of defense, as if the other had just eaten a three-course meal of Ebola, herpes, and anthrax and washed it down with a leprosy cocktail.

Though surrounded by the smoke of our detonated emotional bombs, Julie and I somehow managed to keep our spat between us. Our strained cordial front left the others totally unaware of the angst simmering barely beneath the surface. To Julie's credit she kept her word and gave me help when I needed it, albeit grudgingly and in deathly silence. However, if I dared enter a room and she was alone in it, she would promptly gather her things and leave.

I wasn't about to tell James anything about the tiff. I didn't want him to feel guilty or, worse yet, have resentment toward Julie. As a result, he continued to carry on with copious but respectable amounts of PDA. Every hand hold or hug he and I shared in front of Julie was a Judas kiss to her.

As much as I loved James, I desperately missed my friend. Unfortunately, I could see no way to reconcile the damage I had done, except by breaking up with James. And I wasn't about to do that.

Hell, I couldn't wait for all the training to begin. It would be a welcomed relief from the tear-jerker drama.

My first training session was scheduled with Aunt Evelyn for the morning of the new Aries moon.

As soon as I stepped out of my room, I was greeted by the aroma of freshly baked blueberry scones. And they actually smelled like Aunt Evelyn had done a decent job of baking them. She was becoming a real Ina Garten.

The scones were a welcomed change from the new *refreshment* Aunt Evelyn had been forcing me to drink since that day I'd collapsed at the pond. It was a vile solution of unidentifiable red chunks floating in a cottage-cheesy, putrid liquid. I asked about the contents, but Aunt Evelyn went all secret agent on me—*if I tell you, I'll have to kill you* kind of shit.

I was practically running down the hall on my way to grab one of those scones, especially since my appetite for carbs had made a vengeful comeback. However, I came to a sudden halt, causing the floor runner to slide and bunch up under my feet.

The mysterious door next to the attic had caught my attention once again. By then I was really tired of Aunt Evelyn's evasiveness about what was behind that freaking door. I looked around to make sure it was all clear, and turned the doorknob. However, Aunt Evelyn was totally on point when it came to keeping that *one* door in the house locked. Pissed, I grabbed the knob tighter and tried shaking it as quietly as possible. I could hear jangling. Something was hanging off it on the other side. Then I heard a *TINK*. The hidden object hit the floor. Its hollow clang reminded me of tiny sleigh bells.

What was Aunt Evelyn hiding in there? Hansel and Gretel? An S&M chamber? KFC's eleven herbs and spices? Really, what?

I swore she must have had supersonic hearing because she appeared at the top of the stairs like two seconds later, all wide-eyed and breathless from her sprint. She proceeded to wipe a dust storm of flour off her old-lady-in-lingerie themed apron.

"I thought I heard something. Are you okay?" she asked while trying her best to put on a smile.

I gave her a sklent. "Yeah, fine. Why wouldn't I be?"

"All right then. Breakfast is ready. Come on down while it's still hot."

Though Aunt Evelyn was already on the stairs, she didn't go down. Instead, she skirted to the side and waited for me to go first, but I wasn't about to move. So we kind of just stood there looking at each other with weird smiles on our faces.

She ended up being the one who flinched. "If we're going to have a session, we need to get on it. No time to waste." She went back downstairs, but kept looking over her shoulder to make sure that damn door was still secure.

Aunt Evelyn and I had our session in her store. She shut it down temporarily so no wayward customer would catch sight of the magical happenings going down on the property. Though it never failed that some determined, self-proclaimed magus would ignore the big-ass "CLOSED" sign at the end of the driveway and show up anyway. I was seated at a small, round, abnormally tall table similar to one you'd see in a bar. As my feet freely dangled about a foot off the floor, I saw colorful mounds of what looked like sand on the tabletop.

"This is pixie dust," Aunt Evelyn said.

"No, really, what is it?"

She poured another mound of dust out—silver this time. "Really, it's pixie dust. Every color has a magical correspondence. Take blue for instance. It is used to bring about tranquility, truth, and good fortune." She presented the rest of the dust like a game show hostess. "Go ahead. Pick some up."

I went for the pink. It wasn't hard and gritty like I expected. The texture was fine, and it was warm to the touch; it smelled predominantly like vanilla and sweet apples.

"Pink is for love and romance. Why am I not surprised you chose that one? Toss it up," Aunt Evelyn said.

I hopped off the stool and threw the powder up and away from me. The particles suspended in the air and sparkled like rubies against a beam of sunlight streaming through the window. Slowly they came together like granular puzzle pieces. The result was a life-sized, pink effigy of James.

"The powder has the capability to concentrate the energy of whatever color, rather emotion, it represents. To do battle with Catherine, we obviously won't be using pink. Black and red will be our colors—the colors of courage, power, and destruction."

Aunt Evelyn started to cross the room. She stood next to "James" and shook her head, amused that I had conjured him. She lay her index finger on the figure, and it instantly disintegrated into a mound of dust on the floor. She then glided over to a rolltop desk and raised the tambour. Pulling a pair of startling-white cotton gloves out of a drawer, sheslipped her hands inside. Out of another drawer, she retrieved a rectangular box made of pure ivory.

"What's that for?" I asked.

"It's your wand," Aunt Evelyn said, sliding the box to me across the table. "From now on no other hands should touch it—witch, human, or otherwise."

I lifted the box's heavy lid and saw what would become my lifeline. It was an expertly crafted rod of three twisted woods: hornbeam, makore, and wenge. It was about seven inches long with a thick, cherrywood handle attached to a tapering shaft. I was afraid to pick it up at first. The power emanating from it seemed too intense for me to deal with.

Suddenly, the pendant my mother gave me lit up in some sort of symbiotic response to the wand. A sense of calm came over me, and I took the wand in hand. The powerful energy surging through it made my hand involuntarily do a *swoosh* or two.

"Though it is your companion, you must learn to control your wand," Aunt Evelyn instructed.

The wand released little bursts of lights as I pointed it at various items in the room. "I'll be able kill a whole bunch of protégés with this bad boy."

Aunt Evelyn teetered around me like a mother waiting to catch her baby as it took its first steps. "That's not *your* job."

"But they're coming after me."

"That's not *their* job. The protégés are for us, your helpers. They are interference. As they attack us and occupy our attention, Catherine will try to kill you. See, Catherine is banking on a confrontation before your powers fully kick in, leaving you absolutely vulnerable. And even if you get your powers, she is an awesomely formidable opponent."

The wand discharged a violent burst of fiery light that exploded a vase. Aunt Evelyn motioned for me to lower it. "We won't be talking about Catherine anymore today."

Hari was up next. I had no reason to believe that spending time with "Hang Loose" Hari would be anything but fun. The most work I anticipated was a little light jogging, swimming in the pond, and maybe getting some pointers on nutrition.

I figured there was no need to dress the part of an athlete in training. So I pulled my hair into a messy bun and put on a pair of ratty, cut-off jeans, like I was about to spend the day at Coney Island. I should've known something was about to go down when I saw Hari fully decked out in a military-style white T-shirt and BDU pants.

And I was right. Somewhere between the house and the boot camp he'd set up, gentle Hari turned into Gunnery Sergeant Hartman. We spent hours on repetitive hand-to-hand combat, calisthenics, and gymnastics. Then he continued to torture me with a ten-mile jog and thousands of push-ups and sit ups. He started calling me cute pet names like worm, loser, and maggot turd when I did nonsensical shit like trying to catch my breath. I swore if he yelled at me one more time, I would go all Private Pyle on him.

After what seemed like a millennium, my session with Hari mercifully ended. He then went all Sybil on me and switched back to his old self, as if his drill instructor alter ego hadn't made an appearance. And that was a good thing, because I had been planning a nice blanket party for his sadistic ass.

I taped some ice packs to my thighs and went on to my next teacher. Addison was a welcomed relief after enduring Hari's brutality. She was the magister of glamour, so I was all geeked up for a trip to the MAC makeup counter at the mall, or at least at Ulta. Wrong! Apparently witches have a different dictionary, and *glamour* doesn't mean the same thing as it does in the human world. I was once again stuck in Aunt Evelyn's den.

Addison started to teach straightaway. "Grace, glamour isn't about making you appear beautiful or sexy. It merely assists you in appearing *however* you need to in any given situation. The point is to use the illusory power of image to tap into a person's greatest motivation, whether that is sex, fear, greed, bigotry, or what have you."

"So if I want to scare someone, how do I do it?" I asked.

Addison motioned with her head for me to follow. We quietly went outside and stood a ways from a flock of wild birds that were busy pecking at the grass.

"Focus your gaze on them. Project into their group mind. Become one of their thoughts and you will become *it*," Addison said.

"*It*? Seriously, right now I don't have a clue what you're talking about."

"That's the wonderful thing about glamour. You don't have to know what the *it* is. Their thoughts control the image you become—the *it*."

I did exactly as Addison said, and the birds abruptly flew away. If that was all glamour could do, I wasn't impressed.

"Okay, so. The birds flew away. Big whoop-de-do," I said as I faked a yawn.

Addison broke into hysterical laughter. "Big whoop-de-do indeed." She reached into her pocket, pulled out a compact, and handed it to me. "See?"

I saw my reflection and let the compact crash to the ground. "What the fuck!?" I yelled in total horror. The glamour had transformed me into a principal cast member of *Cats*.

Addison gawked at me in utter amazement. "Now_*that's* how glamour works. You obviously tapped into their thoughts of what they feared the most."

I picked up the compact and stalled for a moment before slowly moving it back in front of my face.

"Whew." I had transitioned back into my plain-Jane self. I gladly handed the compact back to Addison.

"Glamour is a wonderful tool, but it must be used in moderation. It has a tendency to exhaust the user. Let's go in and I'll show you some more," she said while checking herself out in the mirror.

As we made our way back into the house, I felt a sudden urge to belt out a chorus of "Memory."

Adrian had scheduled a daytrip to New York for our session. Needless to say, this did not go over well with James. Me? I just tried to lay low for the impending fireworks.

"Is it necessary to drag her to the city to teach her what you know?" James asked. I could tell by Adrian's flared nostrils that he didn't take too kindly to James's condescension.

Aunt Evelyn, who had been sitting in the corner with her needlework, noticed Adrian's reaction, too. She looked over her glasses. "James, we are all Grace's teachers. And if Adrian believes it best to take her New York, so be it."

"I'm going with them," James insisted.

"No, you are not. You're going to stay here and help me take care of some loose ends. Capiche?" replied Aunt Evelyn.

No matter what James wanted, he understood that Aunt Evelyn was running the show. He clenched his teeth and said, "Capiche."

Adrian drew his lips across his teeth in a Mr. Grinch type of smile. He made no effort to disguise the fact that he thoroughly enjoyed making James uncomfortable. Then he turned to me. He caught me off guard with a happy, genuine grin. "Grace, you ready to go?"

I could see the wavy motion of feverish currents engulfing James's body like heat rising off cement. I tried to hug him, but his body was so stiff, so rigid, I knew to withdraw. He was a sauna, and I broke into a light sweat just being next to him. I backpedaled and tried to make a fast break to my bedroom. "I think I'll go to upstairs and get ready," I said while patting the wetness off my forehead and easing out.

James came to my room as I was putting the finishing touches on my hair.

"You look good," he said. "Too good."

My cheeks turned the loveliest shade of crimson. Over the course of my life, I had never really gotten any compliments. James gave them to me all the time, and I was still getting used to it.

"Thank you kindly, sir. Your sentiment almost brings tears to my doe eyes. Do you have a handkerchief?" I said like an antebellum debutante.

My comedic act made James belt out a hearty laugh. "That's one of the reasons why I love you. You always bring a smile to my face."

I looked at my watch and saw it was time for my appointment with Adrian. "I gotta go. Walk me to the car?"

His laughter instantly ceased. "Whatever you do, don't look into Adrian's eyes too much. He'll spellbind you."

"I think I can handle Adrian."

"Actually, you can't. Just be careful. He's not to be played with."

I luxuriated in the passenger seat of the Bolingbrokes' Lexus LS. The car screamed "big baller shot caller." Platinum body, pitch-black interior with espresso-wood trim. The super-black limo tint darkened the windows so much, it wouldn't have been a stretch to think a dignitary—or drug dealer—was riding inside. I couldn't help but moan as I sucked in the factory-issued new-car scent, while my ears filled with the classical music wafting from the premium surround sound system. And to think I'd thought Julie's jalopy was the shit.

James leaned into the car, breaking the spell like a record scratch. "Remember what I told you. Don't look too deeply into Adrian's eyes."

I gave him a reassuring kiss on his pillowy-soft lips. Peripherally, I could see Adrian strutting over to the car with his cocky attitude in tow.

"What? Still saying your good-byes? Don't you worry, James. I'll take good care of Grace."

James's face tightened. "Adrian, can I talk to you for a moment?"

"Grace and I have a lot to do. We've really got to get to it." Adrian winked at me in a successful attempt to provoke James.

I could see that James was trying with all of his might to maintain his composure for my sake. "Grace, if you'll excuse us," he said in a low tone. He yanked Adrian aside and dragged him behind a large oak tree. James knew I was watching, so he put on a sober face. Adrian smirked as usual. I couldn't hear what they were saying, but I could read their lips.

"I'm not going to let you push me in front of Grace. I will not give you the satisfaction. But, as kin, I offer you a fair warning. Don't try anything with her," James said.

"Afraid of a little competition, brother?" Adrian asked.

"Hardly. Remember, you are not to infringe on her will with charisma. It is forbidden."

Adrian chuckled arrogantly. "You're not scared that I'll use charisma on Grace. You're scared that I won't *have* to."

I could see Adrian ever so lightly bump into James as he headed back to the car. I almost chewed a hole through my lip as I waited for James to give him a supernatural smackdown. James closed his fists, his blue veins bulging. I knew if he opened those fingers, something bad would happen. I called out to him, "James!" It didn't work; he still glared at Adrian.

"James!" I yelled again. "Please. Please."

He heard me that time. Relaxing his hands, he headed to the car.

Adrian moved smoothly into the driver's seat while James stuck his head in the passenger-side window. "Remember what I told you," he said to me. Before he could give me an adequate kiss, Adrian pressed on the gas. The car accelerated, and we went from zero to eighty just like that.

Thank fuck James had reflexes like a mongoose, or else he would've been decapitated.

Times Square was nearly impenetrable with tourists. From what I could gather, most were middle-aged Ohioans crossing New York City off their bucket lists. They rabidly swarmed Broadway and Seventh, scooping up "I Love New York" T-shirts, videoing the giant 'M' of the McDonalds, and jockeying for the best position to see the Naked Cowboy.

Adrian and I got comfortable on the TKTS bleachers. I wondered how the crowd would react if they knew there were a couple of genuine witches amongst them—one of whom was going to save them from becoming part of a human buffet.

"The technique of charisma is actually quite easy," said Adrian. "You've heard photographers telling models to make love to the camera? Well, that's basically all you do with humans. You must visualize your target falling in love with you. Pretend with your mind's eye that you're making love to them. And be the best fuck they've ever had."

"So I just close my eyes and imagine someone crushing hard on me."

"Not exactly. You have to be adept enough to visualize it with your eyes wide open. No matter what or who is physically in front of you, disregard what you really see. Instead, see them making you their lover, savior, whatever. You will basically become the erotic projection of their god. Watch."

Adrian directed his glance at an old woman. There was no doubt she was a tourist. Her ill-fitting Velcro sneakers aggravated her bulging varicose veins, forcing her to take a break on the bottom bleacher. She took off her sun visor—yellowed from an overabundance of facial oil—and wiped her brow. Then she rifled through her fanny pack and pulled out a small map of the city. As she read the directions to her next stop, Adrian uttered a spell through his smile like a ventriloquist: "Know who I am. I'm passion's key. You can't help it. You want me."

"That's fucking corny as hell," I said.

"Maybe, but it works."

"Do spells always have to rhyme?"

"It helps, because nature likes rhythm."

The old lady looked back as if someone had called her name. She searched the crowd with her eyes and deadlocked on Adrian's. In the throes of a hypnotic trance, something drove her to climb the bleachers. She pushed the heads of random people out of her way as she let her internal homing device lead her. As if something clicked in her head, she plunked down right in front of Adrian and leaned back on his knees. Adrian's charisma was driving her subconscious impulse to touch him in any way she could. Finally, she turned around. I was freaking out at how she just stared at him.

Adrian puckered his lips and gently blew like he was blowing the seeds off a dandelion. The old woman simply got up and went back to the bottom bleacher. She snapped out of the enchantment and was left scratching her head with a befuddled look on her face.

"Wow! That was amazing. Can you do that with anyone?" I asked.

"Sure, but the results depend on the intellectual capability of the receiver. The less intelligent the victim, the more effective charisma is. Intellectual people are more difficult to influence. Independent minds fight manipulation. That's why the masses can never be *real* witches. Yes, they can dabble in magic. However, their nature is to believe what they see and what they are told. Television makes it way too easy for me to do what I do."

Even though I was enjoying my lesson, I thought I had covered these bases with Addison. "So glamour and charisma are the same thing."

"Charisma and glamour have much in common. Both are based on illusion. There are key differences, though. They work on different levels. Glamour brings about material illusions, the third dimension. That's why you were able to turn into a cat, so to speak. Charisma is abstract and takes advantage of one of the most powerful forces on earth: sex."

"So I can use glamour to stay beautiful and young forever?"

"If you continue using the same glamour effect, it will become permanently etched on you. Unfortunately, youth and beauty are glamour's exceptions. No one, not even witches, can stay young and beautiful forever. Witches still age, and our looks wither, even though at an extremely decelerated pace."

"What a cruel irony."

There was another paradox at hand. I was deeply in love with James. However, the more Adrian talked, the more fascinating he became to me. I found him to be well spoken, knowledgeable, and capable. The Bolingbrokes had underestimated his ability. He turned out to be a pretty good teacher. Still, I remained cautious and heeded James's advice to avoid his direct gaze.

I was eager to give charisma a go. I rubbed my hands together and asked, "Can I try?" I could tell Adrian was attempting to look deeper into my eyes.

"That's what we're here for," he replied.

We walked down the congested sidewalk. At the horizon of the sea of people, I scoped out a man in a Valentino Newman suit. He carried a Montblanc briefcase in one hand and a Carve club sandwich in the other. I recited Adrian's spell and made sure to smile. Smiling, Adrian said, was one of the best ways to entice people.

The man stopped in his tracks and dropped his lunch right on the sidewalk. He swung around as he looked through the crowd. His prominent, fishlike eyes landed on me. Tilting his head to the side, he grunted, "Hmph." A second later, he swiveled back around and continued on to his destination.

Adrian put his hand on the small of my back. "You got it. You're a natural," he stated in a breathy voice.

We went on for hours, spellbinding men, women, children, even a sewer rat. I finally understood why James said to use magic sparingly. The charisma drained me to the point where I could no longer garner any magical response.

"You're tired. Let's go back to the house and get you rested," Adrian said.

I think I was turning green from exhaustion, and the noxious fumes from the buses didn't help either. As we waited to cross Broadway, Adrian took my hand. I didn't know what to make of that. Was he just helping me because I was tired? Or was it something else?

I didn't have too much time to think about it. As I was about to step off the curb, a bat-out-of-hell taxi nearly took me out. It got so close to me that its wind shear billowed up my shirt when it passed. Adrian yanked me back and took me into his arms. At first I didn't notice that he had rescued me; I was too busy screaming epithets at the long-gone taxi driver.

"Are you all right?" Adrian asked. He stood back and examined me for injuries. After the last "stupid-ass shitface motherfucker" slipped from my mouth, the reality of what had happen set in. I didn't have to worry about Catherine. Fucking traffic was going to get me first. I shook my head in response to Adrian's question, and he pulled me in close to his body, swaying gently in an effort to relax me. I started to feel better, but then panicked when realized I was too comfortable in his arms. A tiny sexual rush shot through my body, and I shamefully let go of him.

"I know my shit with James is disturbing to you. I guess I act like a dick because I like you. I like you very, *very* much," Adrian said. He paused for a moment to gather his thoughts. "Tell me something. If James weren't in the picture, would I have a chance with you?"

Deer in the headlights! Deer in the headlights! I absentmindedly patted my head, searching for those antlers. I had to think fast. Adrian would know if I wasn't telling the truth. I had to be super careful with my response. "It wouldn't be appropriate for me to answer that question."

He gave me a knowing grin. "You already did."

Look, I had found Adrian sexually appealing from the start. I couldn't fool myself by pretending I didn't. James, however, was the man for me, and I had no desire ever to cheat on him—especially with Adrian.

Nonetheless, I was fully aware of Adrian's growing compulsion toward me. He might as well have been a pyromaniac with a pocket full of matches.

And I was the paper.

I felt so guilty about my fleeting lust for Adrian in Times Square. And I was hoping like hell that James would be nowhere in sight when we got back to the house.

Adrian drove well below the speed limit in an obvious ploy to increase our time together. He reached over and lightly touched my knee.

"Thanks," he said.

I put his hand back on the steering wheel. "For what?"

Adrian playfully smirked at my modest gesture. "For trusting me."

We made no more effort at conversation all the way back to Aunt Evelyn's house. The only sound in the car was KJOY 98.3 playing an eclectic mix of artists including Eric Clapton, Shakira, and Taylor Swift.

When we arrived at Aunt Evelyn's, I could see James waiting on the front porch. *Damn it.* Now I had to pretend nothing had happened, and I was horrible when it came to lying. James walked toward the car while Adrian took his time parking it. Adrian wasn't being at all subtle about his intentions to incense James. No matter how kind he had been that day, his base character still was operational.

James hurriedly opened my car door and helped me out. Instantly, he kissed me with such passion his body was shaking. It felt so good, I dug my fingernails into his arms.

"Are you all right? You're okay?" he asked.

I was still trying to recover from that flaming-hot kiss. "Yeah, I'm great now," I said, my body all wobbly.

Adrian slammed his car door. "Why wouldn't she be okay? Do you think I would hurt her?"

James tuned Adrian out and focused on me instead. "You're two hours late. I tried to call. Why didn't you answer?"

I looked at my phone and saw he had called three times. Did Adrian use charisma to make me miss the calls? After switching to another screen, I realized I had accidently sent all calls straight to voicemail.

"It was my fault, James. Everything's fine. And I did great today," I stated in a weary voice.

Adrian winked at me, but this time he wasn't so irritating. I had seen another side of him today. A vulnerable side. The one that had been living in his brother's shadow. No, I didn't want a relationship with Adrian—he was no James after all—but I did have a new understanding of him, whereas James still had the same one.

"Grace, Aunt Evelyn wanted to see you as soon as you got back," James said.

That may have been true, but it was *truer* that James wanted to have some privacy to fuck up his brother. I truly didn't want a fight to break out on my account.

"I can stay out here with you, babe. Aunt Evelyn won't mind." I was desperately trying to divert his attention to me.

James kissed me again while keeping his furious eyes on Adrian. "Grace, just go inside." Aunt Evelyn crossed in front of the window at that very moment, giving credence to what James had said. "Go get yourself something to eat. You look pale."

"Yes, Grace. Get some nourishment. We've got to make sure our girl is well taken care of," Adrian interjected.

I had a decision to make. The first option was to stay there and amp up a volatile situation with my very presence. The second was to go inside and let these two men beat their chests and get whatever agitation they felt out of their systems. I opted for choice number two.

"I'll be waiting for you inside. Don't make me wait too long," I told James, and hurried to the house, though I stopped on the porch so I could hear their conversation.

"Did you do it?" James demanded.

Adrian played dumb. "Did I do what?"

"Charisma. Did you use it on Grace?"

"It really burns you up that she actually could've had a good time and learned something today. Really? Do you find me so inept you believe I can't do anything?"

"Adrian, she is too—"

"Too what? Too nice to me? Too kind to me?"

James curled his lip. "Too good for you."

"Did it ever occur to you that she may like me, too? Or that I might sincerely care for her?"

I knew from James's face that was a real concern for him. He saw in Adrian's eyes something he'd never seen before: affection for another person. Adrian was still a manipulative cad, but he did have a soft spot for me.

"I will ask you one more time, Adrian. Did you use any charisma on Grace?" Adrian stepped into James as he savored the moment. "I didn't use charisma on Grace. It wasn't necessary."

A hellish rage surged through James's body. I could see he wanted to go all apeshit on Adrian. Adrian may have been asking for it, but I didn't want his blood shed over me.

Just then, Aunt Evelyn stepped onto the porch. "James, where's Grace?"

She couldn't have come at a better time. Her soothing yet commanding voice gave James the impetus to draw upon his own phenomenal self-control and bring himself down.

He lowered his voice so Aunt Evelyn couldn't hear. "I'm letting you be. Not for you, but for Grace, the woman I love. *My* woman," he said to Adrian.

"You might have Grace all caught up with you now, but I want her, too. Enjoy her while you can," Adrian responded.

James had never had to think of Adrian as any sort of competition before. However, Adrian had never had a good enough reason to challenge James until now. Love is a potent motivator that inspires idlers to become conquerors.

Chapter Twenty

There is no hunting like the hunting of man, and those who have hunted armed men long enough and liked it never care for anything else thereafter.

—Ernest Hemingway

"Take the Sunrise Highway exit," Catherine told Nick.

Chetan woke up from his catnap just as the off-ramp dumped them onto a busy street. He looked out the window and surveyed the surroundings. "So this is Massapequa."

It was very early in the morning, and rush hour was in full swing. However, Catherine's Mercedes traveled in the opposite direction of the traffic, headed east toward Grace's childhood home.

Catherine occupied herself with filing her dragon-claw nails. With every swipe of the pointy emery board, she enjoyed a thought about stabbing Grace in the throat with it.

After a relatively short drive, the Mercedes entered an unassuming residential neighborhood. Catherine could tell from the houses that the people who lived there weren't rich by any means, but their manicured yards and well-kept homes indicated they were hardworking folks who took pride in whatever they owned.

After a few turns, they located Grace's house on a dead-end street lined with a scant amount of trees.

"Pull into the driveway," Catherine said as she kept a close watch on the house.

"Don't you think that's dangerous? What if Grace is in there? I'm not ready to get into anything," Chetan whined.

"Grace hasn't seen me since she was an infant. I hardly think she'd remember my face. For all she knows, I'm just a harmless Avon lady."

Catherine's salivary glands squirted with the prospect of killing and eating Grace right then and there. Taking a breath to regulate her growing hunger, she got out of the car. "Stay here. Signal me if anyone comes up." She started to walk away, but Chetan stopped her.

"What should I say?" he asked with a profoundly confused look on his face.

Catherine was breaking one of her own rules—she was suffering a fool. This was a temporary hassle, however, as she had nefarious plans for him later.

"Just yell, '*The bitch is coming! The bitch is coming!*'" Catherine said with a sarcastic edge.

Chetan had no idea she was belittling him. "Okay," he replied in all seriousness.

Catherine stood there incredulous for a moment. Then she shook it off and took a few steps up the driveway. It was difficult for her to avoid getting her heel caught in the deep cracks of the paving stones, so she tiptoed to the threshold of the 1950s-style Cape Cod house.

Compared to Catherine's humongous penthouse, Grace's home was gerbil-cage small. The tacky aluminum siding did nothing for its plain face. It had no central air conditioning, as evidenced by two window units on the upper and lower floors. Catherine ascertained that no one had been in the house for a while by the knee-deep grass and wildly growing shrubs that needed pruning.

She also smugly noted the difference between her privileged upbringing and Grace's humble middle-class roots. An anger rose in her as she realized a peon had the potential to annihilate her.

Keeping her guard up, Catherine got closer to the house. As she did, her steps felt more and more like she was walking in quicksand. Moreover, she could smell the remnants of Grace's scent and see the indigo residual of her aura.

She slowly climbed the creaky steps to the porch. Pulling open the storm door, she knocked on the scratched-up, hollow aluminum inner door. This was a show for any nosy neighbor who might have been snooping out a curtained window. Placing her ear to the door, she heard nothing and decided the best course of action was to break in. So she nonchalantly made her way to the back of the house on a well-worn path through the dying grass, passing cheap plastic lawn chairs and a card table.

"Goodness! Am I fighting bunch of hillbillies?" she muttered to herself.

Catherine stepped onto the weathered deck. Tracing her finger around the back door, she closed her eyes to activate her second sight. When she opened them, she could see into the past, to when Grace and Julie had rushed out of the house. They looked like lines of electric currents forming vague human figures. Catherine stop-motioned the image, and the phantom forms hung frozen in the air. She walked around Grace's 3-D hologram, trying to get a clear view of her facial features, but they were just too hazy.

When she reached out and touched Grace, the image zapped and knocked her back some, which profoundly disturbed Catherine. If Grace's image was that powerful, the real person had to have phenomenal magical assets.

Wrath welled up in her, and she kicked in the door. She became even more tempestuous when, upon entering, she discovered the house had been totally vacated. There was no furniture, no dishes, not even pictures on the wall. The house was nothing more than empty rooms and stained rugs.

Regardless, Catherine knew forensic traces were always left behind. She scoured the floor for a random strand of hair, a clothing fiber, or a nail clipping. Her radar hit on something down the hall, and she followed the signal until she ended up in Grace's room. Catherine's fangs popped out in a reflexive action to being in Grace's personal space.

She walked around the room and stepped on a loose, squeaky floorboard. That little board piqued her interest, and she lifted it. Underneath, Grace had stashed a trove of erotic photographs taken by Rafe.

"Oh, you naughty, naughty girl," Catherine said as she shuffled through the pictures. However, she wasn't interested in Grace posed in strange positions and various stages of undress. What she examined was the background. The walls, where a ton of pictures of Aunt Evelyn and Julie hung.

As Catherine continued to go through the photos, one stood out. This particular picture was just a close-up of Grace's face. While Catherine studied it, her eyes turned a demonic red. She stuffed the picture in her pocket for safekeeping. As she did so, she heard a pop of static electricity and turned around. James and Evelyn's astral images floated across the room. They were ethereal, silvery, with the blackest of eyes. These powerful projections of James and Evelyn's souls appeared to Catherine *without* their owners' permission or knowledge.

"Leave her be," James's projection said with a ghostly voice. "You already failed once. Go on your way."

Catherine was cocksure and not intimidated in the least. "You *are* mad. Tell you what I'm going to do. I'm going to eviscerate, dismember, and consume every bit of your precious Grace as I promised. And when I have all of her power, I'll kill the rest of you just for fun. You'll all make tasty side dishes."

"This will be the end battle. Once and for all," said Evelyn's projection before disappearing into the ether. James's projection evaporated, too.

Even though Catherine was sure of her own prowess, she was daunted by how apparently strong James and Evelyn already were due to their dedication to Grace. All she had was Nick and Chetan.

"I'm going to need more protégés."

Chapter Twenty-One

How can a woman be expected to be happy with a man who insists on treating her as if she were a perfectly normal human being.

—Oscar Wilde

My father had a funny superstition he had picked up from his mother. He said that May heat waves were an omen that the devil was coming.

I could not verify or get the background on this tidbit because my father had estranged himself from our family before my birth. He'd said it was for my safety. I guess now the reason was obvious. And, lucky for me, it was May, and Massapequa was suffering from bizarrely hot temperatures.

Of course Aunt Evelyn's bootleg air conditioning was acting up. I had my bedroom window raised in a vain attempt to find relief from the sweltering heat. The steamy breeze that gushed through did little to cool down the room, but was sufficient to clear out the stale winter air.

The blazing weather did have some benefits, though. I had been nursing a particularly strong cough, and the warmth helped me to breathe a little better. The coughing had started about a week earlier, irritating but mild. Now I was hacking so hard and so much, my diaphragm felt like it had done a round with Mike Tyson—the in-shape version that is. I tried everything to get rid of the choppy cough. Humidifiers, zinc, orange juice—none of it helped a bit. All NyQuil did was induce an awesome coma.

I had the TV tuned to one of those twenty-four-hour news channels. An exposé about violence on college campuses was running. The fresh faces of young women brutalized or murdered at higher institutions of learning scrolled across the screen. I took note of how they were all from the same cookie cutter. They were the archetypes of upper-middle class: cute, toothy, surprisingly fit, equestrian/crew team/lacrosse playing chicks. I was sure Tiffany's face would pop up at any moment. It didn't. Darn.

Growing tired of the news, I decided to direct my attention to the warm, living body next to me—James. Even though he was *beyond* old in human years, he was respectful of Aunt Evelyn's surprisingly old-fashioned notions about coed sleeping arrangements. He complied for the most part, but every so often he'd sneak up to my room in the middle of the night to spend some alone time with me. We'd watch DVDs of horror movies and play daffy card games. Our sublime and ridiculous conversations lasted all night, and even though we'd rehash the same topics, they always seemed brand new.

James was on his back, shirtless. Unfortunately, he made sure to leave on his cock-blocker jeans. I, on the other hand, was trying my best to be as tempting as possible. I purposefully wore a gauzy cami top and butt-crease-exposing pajama shorts—a marked change from my usual oversized T-shirts and slouch socks.

I rested my head in the crook of James's armpit, inhaling the slightly pungent odor overlaid with bergamot and ginger accents from his deodorant. His ankles were crossed, and he rubbed his feet together with contentment. I ran my finger up and down his torso, thinking about how he had a way of making life feel easier and lighter. With him, during fleeting moments like this one, I could relax into a state of *normalness*.

However, an awful, goose-honk coughing spell ruined it.

James gave me a few pats on the back. "Whoa! You sound like you have a case of whooping cough. You okay, baby?"

"Fine," I said right before I coughed up a chunk of salty, metallic phlegm. It tasted like blood. I let it stay in my mouth as I tried to figure out what to do with it. Spit it into a Kleenex? No, not in front of James. Like a nasty bitch, I swallowed it so he wouldn't be grossed out. After the gulp, I said, "Whooping cough? That was just me being sexy." He was none the wiser.

But I really was trying to be sexy. During the past few months, I had pulled out all the *Penthouse Forum* tricks I could think of to entice James. And they'd almost worked. We had gotten incredibly close to doing the deed. The problem was that it was *not* close enough for me, but *too* close for him.

The closest we'd ever gotten was the other night. There'd been so much sex in the air, it was like my room had taken Viagra. The room was inky black; we couldn't see a thing. Our playful teasing gave way to extended foreplay that was particularly intense. Instinctively, we peeled away our clothing while kissing with hyper urgency. We got up on our knees with our palms pressed together. He pulled back from me, and I felt his face like I was a blind woman. I could feel his mouth open with desire, shallow breaths leaving it. I pressed my naked torso against his, and he clutched me hard. He started pushing me down on the bed. Suddenly, he stopped ... as fucking usual. He was motionless for a long time, and then quickly got out of bed.

"I've got to go," he'd said. He'd put on his clothes while walking briskly to the door. As it opened, I could only see his black silhouette against the light spilling in from the hallway. He'd rattled off some apology before retreating into the house.

I was thrilled he was back tonight. He was staring down at me like he had a million thoughts rushing through his mind. Although we had not been totally intimate, I dared to ask a strictly after-sex question: "What are you thinking about?"

"There was a time, for a very long time, when I had no faith in the world. I couldn't see any goodness in it or a reason to help it exist. Aside from my family, there was nothing to love. Then, months ago, you came back into my life. I couldn't run or hide from what you brought out of me. Finally, I felt alive. So I was just thinking about one word to describe you. Could it be *heart*? Let's try *soul*. Or could it be *amour*? Only one came to mind: *life*. You are life itself to me. You were a long time coming. I had to go through much heartache and trauma to be here with you right now, but I'd do it all again."

As he caressed my cheek, his faintly glowing eyes flickered. It was a relief to hear that I meant so much to him. Sometimes it was hard figuring him out. The vast majority of the time, everything seemed right between us. He was the ultimate when it came to being smiley and affectionate. Other times I'd catch him watching me with a look of sadness on his face; the kind people have when they're about to tell you good-bye forever.

I forgot all of that when James rolled over and kissed me. Joy and desire overwhelmed my body. Even though Catherine was still lurking around out there, for now James and I could be just like two *regular* lovers. I wished these moments could be bottled. That way, in the midst of chaos, I could have them at the ready, like aspirin for a heart attack victim.

As I tried to pull James on top of me, I caught a sound bite from a television reporter. He mentioned something about Long Island College. I abruptly stopped kissing James and sat up to look at the screen. "Turn it up," I said.

James found the remote in the crumpled sheets and increased the volume. The screen filled with Long Island College's most recent graduating class. The camera panned over all of their beaming faces and the proud mamas and papas wiping away tears. The screen fast-forwarded to tight shots of graduates crossing the stage in black gowns and mortarboards studded with craft-store rhinestones reading "Thanks Mom," "LIU," or "Hire me."

Off-screen, the reporter stated, "It has been three months since the gruesome death of Samantha Beckon."

Samantha Beckon—the only girl featured on the exposé who was like me. It was a travesty that she was only profiled because of the extreme heinousness of her death.

The reporter went on, "But it seems life has gone on for these students." A montage of seconds-long interviews followed. Graduates lamented Samantha's death and various campus safety issues. One even mentioned another female—a missing Indian student. To me they seemed more interested in the celebratory activities going on around them than discussing the death of some previously little-known student and some foreign girl.

The reporter's faux-concerned voice played over snippets of gleeful students moving out of dormitories and sad, empty rooms. "An initial suspect has since been deported, though not charged with the crime. Will the perpetrator ever be brought to justice? Will new students have to live under the constant threat that the killer will return?"

I started feeling regret. That was my graduating class. If things had gone as planned, I would have been getting ready for grad school or working some lame accounting job where I got to wear dowdy clothes and sensible shoes. I knew most humans craved extraordinary lives.

Some sought activities that gave them constant adrenaline rushes. Others needed to make a difference by some great feat or altruistic deed. When all else fails, infamy will do.

Well, in my defense, I wasn't quite human. And my "extraordinary" demigod status had been thrust upon me. Even though I had come to terms with my abnormal circumstances, I still mourned being ... well, normal. Not that I had ever been normal in the classical sense, but there was a degree of security in my *regular* oddball world. Now every day was like jumping out of an airplane with a Russian roulette-style parachute.

While James concentrated on the TV, my eyes started to water, and I hid them from him. I knew I had to stay centered on not what I had lost, but what I had gained: James. When I turned to him, he smiled, and a sense of relief came over me. Maybe this new normal wasn't so bad after all.

Just when everything was about to be all right, I felt a scratching sensation in my eyes as if they'd been blasted with shrapnel. I rubbed furiously, but the debris wouldn't dislodge. I got out of bed and headed straight to the bathroom.

"Where are you going?" James asked, propping himself up on his elbows. Shit, he looked really fucking sexy right then. However, he started to warp as my vision blurred.

"The bathroom. Be right back," I said while bumping into the door I couldn't see. I stretched my arms out as I made my way cautiously to the bathroom mirror. I tugged at the chain pull of the hanging lightbulb and it swung like a pendulum, taking my reflection from lightness to darkness.

My vision cleared up just enough to see red eyes with vertical slits staring back at me.

Okay, all the coughing made me burst a blood vessel in my brain, and I'm hallucinating—for real this time. I blinked, but the coin-slot slits didn't go away. "Agh!"

James rushed into the bathroom—Mr. Rescuer himself. He took one look at me and shook his head with remorse. "My blood has interfered with your awakening."

My arms flailed, emphasizing my point, and I paced rapidly across the floor. "What the fuck? I can't go out like this," I yelled between coughs. James tried to calm me down by wrapping his arms around me.

And I bit him.

Shocked, he released me. Hell, I was shocked, too. James remained calm and maintained control as blood trickled down his arm. "It's okay. It must all be part of the plan."

What plan? I didn't care about destiny, fate, karma, or any bullshit words James used to spin this situation. I was on the verge of growing a forked tongue and slithering. *Oh, hell fucking no!* I closed my eyes and willed them to go back to their ordinary state. They did. Fuck kismet. I won.

As soon as I was about to bust into an old school break dance, my eyes glowed and turned a milky white. *What? Now I'm a demon-girl!*

I gripped the sink and closed my eyes again, trying to repeat the magic trick of changing them back. The sink started to quake as I focused with all of my might. I kept telling myself, "I'm in control. I will determine the outcome of this." The vibrations loosened the sink from the wall. I opened my eyes when one of its screws hit the floor.

James looked over my shoulder. Both of our reflections stared back at me. "Stop it," he said, turning me around. "Right now your eyes are not your problem. Your situation is not your problem. Catherine is not your problem. You are."

"That's easy for you to say. This is not your fight. The burden is not on you."

"All of this training ... all of this magic you're learning will be for nothing if you don't get your mind straight. If you can master yourself, you can master everything. Submit to it all. No more resistance. Now, to change back, control your emotions. That's the only way."

Who the hell did James think he was? That Zen crap only worked in self-help seminars. And seriously the people who attended those didn't deal with shit like this. The worse things those people had to deal were bitch bosses, trying to get laid, or, excuse the irony, finding their stupid path. James was supposed to be indulging my dismay, and instead he was telling me to buck up. I wanted to slap the piss out of him.

He squinted and stared into my eyes. "Look."

"Screw you."

James whirled me around and forced me to confront the mirror. "Look!"

My pupils were round again, even though they were an animalistic, creamy amber color. I lowered my head, knowing I had been totally out of place with my outburst. "Forgive me?"

"You don't have to apologize to me. I understand." There was nothing more he could say. We both stared at me in the mirror.

James had played two specific roles in my life up until that point: bodyguard and leader. But now he wasn't standing behind me as a bodyguard. He wasn't standing in front of me as a leader. He was standing at my side as a partner.

I didn't want to tell Aunt Evelyn about my eyes. Mind you, there were flaws in my plan to wear sunglasses all day long—indoors—hoping no one would notice. I knew as soon as she found out, there'd be some other training or ritual I'd have to endure. I just wanted a break.

James didn't see it that way, and told Aunt Evelyn immediately. And just like I'd thought, I was about to be subjected to some more witchy rigmarole.

Aunt Evelyn pulled out an old doctor's bag she had procured from an antique store over in Amityville. The black leather was dry and cracked, with a well-developed patina. Its smell, reminiscent of an old library book, was strong, having endured at least a century of previous use. Aunt Evelyn handled the artifact with a light hand, opening the scaly, crocodile-skinned split handle with kid gloves.

"I'm not even going to ask why you have a doctor's bag," I said.

"You never know," Aunt Evelyn replied, searching through it. She nicked her wrist on a small scalpel and bled a little. "Sit," she told me. The whole time I was stifling a cough; I didn't want one more thing to worry her.

The bag was filled to the brim with holistic treatments: copper bracelets, marble cold stones, herbal concoctions, spices, and oils. Aunt Evelyn pulled out a doctor's pen light. "I'm coming in," she stated as she held my eyelid open.

My eyes changed, and I looked like a human-lizard crossbreed. I couldn't help but notice the thin trickle of blood running down Aunt Evelyn's arm, originating from the cut on her wrist. My heart beat faster the closer her wrist got to my face.

She studied my eyeball. "I've never seen anything like this," she muttered. "We have changes in our eyes at puberty, but not like this. Your pupils aren't even responding to light. You're undergoing tremendously rapid changes. Your eyes … Do you have *any* control over them?"

"Not really. Can you make it better so I can at least go out in public?" I could smell her blood—not only what was coming out, but what was in her veins as well. It made me hungry, and I wanted to eat her. My fleur-de-lis lit up, and my fangs popped out. I lunged forward, grabbing Aunt Evelyn's wrist, and bit her. She yelped, not so much in pain, but more frightened. My teeth clamped down on the bone and cracked it some. James pried my mouth open while Aunt Evelyn yanked back her wrist.

"I'm so sorry. I'm so sorry," I said, weeping through a hacking cough. Blood spurted out of my mouth. "What's happening to me?"

Aunt Evelyn was at a loss. "I don't know, sweetie. I need some counsel on this one."

James, Aunt Evelyn, and I sat around a crystal ball. The large, glass orb was on a three-legged pedestal atop a fringed satin cloth. A black tapered candle, the only light source in the room, allowed me to barely make out the embroidered pattern on the fabric. We held hands and our knees touched, forming a hexagon around the tiny table.

"Close your eyes," Aunt Evelyn said. She and James did. I kept mine open. She tilted her head back and opened her mouth like one of those carnival gypsies channeling spirits. I waited for the table to tip.

"So we're about to wake the dead," I wisecracked.

Aunt Evelyn opened one eye and looked at me. "Stop kidding and close 'em up." She closed her eyes again. This time I took the directive so I could see what was going to happen next.

"Pool your energy," Aunt Evelyn stated; she sounded strange, wraithlike.

The table began to move a little, then shake harder, and rose up without the crystal ball falling off. It then slammed back to the floor.

"Now open your eyes," Aunt Evelyn whispered. We all had fuzzy spheres in front of our foreheads. The balls floated away and met up above the crystal ball. They circled, then joined into a larger ball that dropped into the crystal ball. Grayish clouds started to swirl inside, then gave way to light-pink coils winding their way through some kind of *nothingness* in the crystal ball. I thought it would foretell a lovely future for James and me. However, the pink turned crimson red and then black. A frosty image came into view, distorted like a funhouse mirror.

"Catherine … She's not alone," Aunt Evelyn said with a grave look. "She's been making protégés. Lots of them." The crystal ball clearly revealed Catherine. She was surrounded by dead bodies covered in blood. "She has been feeding … Gathering the soul energy of those she has murdered. She has become powerful. Almost unstoppable. The spells to hide you are no longer effective."

My childhood home appeared in the crystal ball. "Catherine has been in town. She's been to your house. She's hunting, and she'll be here soon," Aunt Evelyn finished.

Catherine stared right at me. Suddenly, the apparition in the crystal ball rushed the glass. It was trying to break out so it could tear me apart. The glass cracked, and a puff of sulfuric smoke escaped in Catherine's place.

I pushed the funky refreshment out of my face. Aunt Evelyn brought it back.

James intervened. "You're coughing up blood because you're changing into some *thing*. We're not even sure what. Catherine is on her way. We need you strong. So drink it."

"Tell me what's in it," I demanded.

He and Aunt Evelyn looked at each other like the jig was up. James broke the news. "Well, I guess it's time. When you ingested my blood, your Ancient's appetite was whetted. It wants more. On top of that, your body needs blood to complete its awakening … Its transformation. What you've been drinking is fresh sheep's blood."

I couldn't believe what I was hearing. "What the fuck? Sheep's blood. Really?"

"Catherine has been feeding on live humans, which makes her infinitely stronger than you are. In fact, she's stronger than all of us put together. The sheep's blood has worked to sustain you for the past few months. Now its potency is dwindling. It's now only effective for a couple of hours. In the next stages of your evolution, you must feed on something else."

He stepped away from me and walked around the room, holding his chin as he thought of the gentlest way to tell me the rest. "The first time we all saw you at the table a few months ago, eating all the bacon and sausage … you were ravenous."

"Stop beating around the bush, James," I said, though I didn't really want to hear the rest.

"Our first objective was just to keep you alive during your awakening."

"And the second?"

"To satisfy your indwelling Ancient spirit so you'll be able to battle Catherine. We have to feed you."

"James, what will I be eating?"

"Tonight. You'll see tonight."

Addison was my designated babysitter for the evening. Her only task was to keep me out of the house for a couple of hours. I hardly spoke to her, still peeved that she'd known what was in that drink and had been keeping it secret from me.

We were on our way back from a very, very long walk on the desolate road leading to Aunt Evelyn's house. The nearest neighbor was miles away. Thanks to Hari's drills, the hike was no problem at all. Even though we had lanterns, our path was mostly lit by the waning gibbous moon. I looked into the trees and saw the glowing eyes of woodland creatures dotting the darkness like Christmas lights. I wasn't too concerned about the animals, but I sure was glad to see the driveway of Aunt Evelyn's house.

"Why did you drag me around all day? It seems pointless," I said as I swatted mosquitoes.

"They had to get ready." Addison pursed her lips; she was nervous as hell. "You'll see soon enough."

Aunt Evelyn's house was swallowed up by absolute darkness. Thank goodness for the electric candles blazing in the windows. Unfortunately, it still looked like a haunted house; the only thing missing were the carved-out pumpkins.

Hari, who had been sitting in the parlor, hurried to meet us in the foyer.

"It's time," Addison told him.

He nodded, and with no words went back to the parlor and put on his headphones. He cranked AC/DC up as loud as he could, as if making an attempt to drown something out.

Aunt Evelyn emerged from the basement with Adrian, both looking like executioners from the Inquisition. They were so serious with their sullen faces. Maybe the black druid robes they wore made them feel gloomy.

James was nowhere in sight. I hadn't seen him since earlier that day.

Adrian handed me a robe. "Put it on," he said. Addison put hers on so fast I didn't see how she'd done it. I struggled with mine. Step into it? Pull it over my head? Adrian came over and gave me a reassuring wink. He opened it up and slid it right on me.

Aunt Evelyn had two tall candles in her hand, and she gave me one. I was about to speak, but she held her finger to her lips and shushed me.

We all made our way up the stairs in what felt like a funeral procession. Aunt Evelyn was in front of me, and Addison and Adrian took up the rear. I'd had no idea the steps made so much noise, but I guess in deathly silence you pick up on such things.

We arrived on the second floor and passed Julie's room. She stood there like she was watching a sinister parade. I made eye contact with her, in a way asking for help in all that weirdness, but she simply closed her door.

The rest of us made our way to the mysterious door. Aunt Evelyn pulled out a skeleton key to open it. The smell of old incense wafted out. We stepped into a tight area at the bottom of a narrow staircase. As we proceeded to climb the steps, I stepped on something. I could hear the sound of collapsing metal under my foot, and bent down to retrieve the item. It was a tiny bell. That was the origin of the clanging I'd heard the other day. It had been a primitive alarm system to signal the presence of an incoming intruder.

It was extremely dark in the stairwell. I ran my hands against the wall for guidance, since my eyes hadn't adjusted. However, as we got closer to the top, a source of light lit our way.

I thought I heard the low moaning of an animal. It sounded like had been caught in a trap.

We reached the candlelit upper room—a marvel of ingenious architecture. Anyone standing outside would have been led to believe the secret, windowless room was an extension of the attic. On the far side, a black curtain hung from the ceiling. A red pentagram was carved into the floor, and next to it were butcher's knives and a machete.

I heard that moaning again. It sounded like it was coming from behind the curtain.

Aunt Evelyn spoke softly, as if we were in a church. "We are all possessed by the Ancients we summoned and invoked for revenge. Therefore, these spirits are all evil. We have been living on borrowed time by not feeding them what they demand. That was Ilan's wish—for us to abstain—but the time of reckoning has come. We do not eat for pleasure, but for sustenance ... survival ... power to fight. That is why we feed. We only do it under ritualistic conditions. Unlike Catherine."

The moaning grew louder. No one else seemed even to be paying attention to it.

Aunt Evelyn went on, "Catherine is possessed by a particularly sadistic Ancient that has made her psychotic. She has bonded with its evil so much, she does not even need ritual to invoke it anymore. It is operating within her at all times. She's not just a cannibal—she's the Jeffrey Dahmer of witches. She has a real taste for human flesh. With every kill she gains the life force of her meat for her malevolent Ancient to use. Even though we appear strong, we are at a tremendous disadvantage because we haven't been feeding properly. To fight her we have to appeal to and strengthen our own Ancients."

"Aunt Evelyn, you're starting to scare me. What are you really saying?" I asked.

James came from behind the curtain with a pathetic little man, the source of the moaning. The man was covered in bruises. His hands were tied behind his back, and he was blindfolded.

"Please, dear God, whoever you are. Please don't hurt me," the man said.

James removed his blindfold. His eyes were blood red from subconjunctival hemorrhaging. He looked at me directly. I had never seen an expression of terror like that in my life. "Please help me," the little man begged of me.

"Don't feel sorry for him. He's a bad man. I captured him as he was in the process of luring a five-year-old boy off a playground," James said as he threw the man to the ground.

"I wasn't going to harm him. I just wanted to be his friend," the man lied.

Aunt Evelyn looked at me. "Because of your heritage, you too have an Ancient spirit residing in you. It's now time you understand what that means."

All of a sudden, James and Adrian started kicking and battering the man. This had to be the only time those two had ever cooperated with each other. The man rolled up into a ball in a feeble attempt to protect himself. James and Adrian stretched him back out, lifted him up, and dropped him on the pentagram. Addison staked his feet and hands to the corners. The pedophile looked like the Vitruvian Man. The room took on an eerie glow as Aunt Evelyn chanted a spell from an ancient book in some language I'd never heard.

James kissed me. "This is going to be difficult to watch. When it's over, just remember I did it for the love of you."

Aunt Evelyn looked like a judge as she took her post at the little man's head. The others took the knives and started chanting with her. Then they stabbed the man repeatedly. The little man didn't make any noise at first; I figured he was in shock. Then the unrelenting pain crested in his body, and he wailed the most awful cry I'd ever heard. I covered my ears; I could not bear his ungodly screams.

The witches started to shake violently and convulse as their fantastically long fangs emerged. Their joints unhinged as if they were double-jointed. The witches' faces, though retaining their original features, took on gargoyle-like ghoulishness. Aunt Evelyn looked down at the man with her hellion eyes and chopped off his head with the machete. Chunks of flesh and puddles of blood surrounded the carcass. The only thing left of his body was a mushy pulp. The witches then devoured the flesh like crazed animals. They were frenzied, overcome with bloodlust. As they ate, I saw the little man's soul enter each of them.

Horrifically, I felt my own hunger rising, and I wanted to eat, too. I had to get out of there. I scooted backward to the stairs, watching the others ingest every piece of that man. My foot slipped off the top step, and I tumbled to the bottom of the stairs. Thankfully I had a hard head, because I landed square on it. A bit dazed, I crawled out into the hallway.

James ran down the steps with his whole face and body covered in blood. At first I thought he was coming to get me and make me dessert. But he reached out to me with a hand dripping blood.

I backed into the wall. "Don't fucking come near me," I yelled, making a cross with my fingers.

"I'm not a vampire," James said. He approached me ever so slowly, like he was about to capture a frightened kitten. "I didn't want you to find out like this, but there was no way to ease into it." He knelt beside me, his eyes still glowing from the arousal of his feeding free-for-all.

Of course I knew the history of the Ancients, but since the beginning of this journey, I'd been able to conveniently keep certain realities out of my mind. When the subject of feeding came up, I discounted it as something other witches did centuries ago. However, the past was now the present, and I had to admit what kind of monster James was. And what kind of monster I would be.

Girdled by all this carnage, I had an epiphany. In my frantic desire to be normal again, I finally understood that, since the day I was born, *this* had always been my normal. I just hadn't been aware of it until now.

Chapter Twenty-Two

> I prefer to characterize rape simply as a
> form of torture. Like the torturer, the
> rapist is motivated by the urge to
> dominate, humiliate, and destroy his
> victim. Like a torturer, he does so by
> using the most intimate acts available to
> humans—sexual ones.
>
> —Helen Benedict

Lingering dregs of the little man's soul still clung to the house, phasing in and out like multicolored motion blurs. They tried to hang on to their last bit of earthly existence by attempting to merge into the electrical system. This forced the house's light sources to seesaw between burning overly bright and dwindling to the barest illumination.

It was only a few minutes after the sacrifice, and my shell shock was just beginning to manifest. My legs trembled underneath me as I haplessly tried to process what had just occurred. James propped me up and escorted me to my room. As we slowly moved down the dark hallway, my mind began to splinter in an attempt to erase the traumatic carnage I had just witnessed. The world became one gigantic carnival mirror, distorting into harsh, jarring images. I reached out into the empty space before me to get my bearings as the hall stretched upward and suddenly snapped back into place.

James was talking to me, but there was some sort of time delay between his lips moving and the sounds of the words hitting my ears. From what I could make out, he was repeating my name and asking if I was okay. I loved that man, but that was a seriously dumb question. After about a thousand "are you okay," he led me into my room and parked me in the middle of the braided rug.

"Stay there," he demanded. "I'll be back as soon as we're done."

"Yeah, sure," I muttered, all spaced out of my mind.

James jetted out, and I was left alone, catatonic and staring at the door. Through the wee portion of lucidity I had left, I made out the fast and pounding thuds of his feet as he raced back up the attic stairs. A few moments later, I heard the mumbling of faraway voices counseling each other about waste management.

They made a decision, which resulted in a macabre symphony coming from the portion of the attic above my head. The opening sonata was the long drags of body parts to different areas of floor. That was followed by the cringe-inducing adagio of hacksaws cutting straight through bones, and their jagged teeth embedding into the wooden floorboards. Next up was the scherzo. This was composed of the *thwop*-ing of trash bags being shaken open and the accompanying blunt thuds of body parts being dropped in. The last movement, the allegro, couldn't come fast enough. The musical selection ended with the dull thumps of mops dunking into plastic buckets and the swooshing of water across the floor.

The deceptively calm splashing somehow awakened me from my transfixed state. I looked down at my arms and saw flecks of dried blood all over them. Its strong ferric odor excited my appetite once again. I staved it off the best I could, and became actively engaged in a tug-of-war between instincts and will. My arm made its way to my hungry lips; my tongue came out for a taste of the blood. However, I refused to indulge this animalistic desire.

Was this what it was going to be like? Constantly craving other people's blood? There had to be another way for me to avoid feeding. Hell, I'd drink that damn sheep's blood for the rest of my life if I had to.

Still, that blood smelled so good.

I had to get it off me right away. I promptly propped a chair under the doorknob. It wasn't that I didn't trust the other witches; I just couldn't take any more surprises. I went to the bathroom and flipped the light switch.

The overhead bulb exploded due to the still-pulsating, residual energy of Aunt Evelyn's spell and the little man's rapidly deteriorating noumenon traveling through the wires. Luckily for me, the dull light over the medicine cabinet still worked. I looked up, still hearing the other witches cleaning—that dreadful noise. I turned on the shower, hoping the water would drown it out.

I started to remove my clothing and realized I was covered in more blood than I'd thought. In fact, my clothes were stuck to me. I practically had to peel my shirt off my skin due to the massive amount of dried blood. I shucked off my pants and undergarments too, and stood there looking like a mottled piece of peppermint candy.

My stomach churned at the sight of death covering me. Even though the little man was scum, he was a human being—a person who had died because of me. I might as well have eaten him myself. I prayed a shower would wash away the squishy blob of guilt encapsulating me. When I stepped in, the glow of my flickering eyes reflected on the tiles. I turned my head; I so hated seeing myself that way.

The water heated up quickly, but it wasn't scorching enough for me. I desired self-punishment, some atonement for what had happened to the dead man. I turned the knob to its hottest setting—basically scalding. Like lava the water rolled off my hair and down my body. However, the dried, crusted blood would not let go of me that easily. It stayed plastered on like superglue. I grabbed a leftover sliver of soap and swabbed my skin with hard strokes. The scant amount of foamy bubbles failed to liquefy the blood.

Frustrated, I sank to the floor and wept bloody tears. The water finally loosened the tiny, solid pieces of the man's blood, allowing the flecks and my sanguine teardrops to intermix and swirl down the drain.

I don't know how long I huddled in that shower, but it must've been a long time. My soles and palms had wrinkled into plump, red raisins, while the rest of my skin was ruddy from the constant hammering of the super-heated water. I contemplated staying in the safe confines of the cave-like sauna for eternity … until I heard a ruckus coming from the bedroom. I scrambled up to turn off the water and listen more closely.

The bedroom door's knob rattled and shook, then the propped-up chair hit the floor. I popped out of the shower like a spring had boinged under me. There was no way I was going to get caught unaware—basically ass out.

I grabbed my bleach-splotched pink robe off a hook and steeled myself. Cringing, little by little I opened the door. I didn't see anyone in the room, but when the fuck did that ever mean anything? Like a fencer I lunged out, totally forgetting the en garde.

Without warning the attic fan kicked on, causing the bathroom door to slam shut behind me. I looked back and saw James standing there. He was freshly showered and hadn't dried off all the way; his thin shirt was slightly sticky on his skin. I didn't appreciate his sneaking around; quite frankly, it scared me a little. However, the night's events did not diminish the strangely charged bond between us. We were still hopelessly attached by a tight and tense invisible wire that was always pulling us closer together.

"What are you now? A fucking creeper?" I said. "You should've given a heads-up that you were going to get all cannibal on me."

James drew closer to me, but I kept my distance.

"Grace, I have a confession," he said. "We used you. Your fear actually amped up the spell. We regret doing that, but some actions are necessary."

I know I should've been angry as hell, but his sparkling-blue eyes penetrated me. Whatever misgivings I'd had melted away. Maybe it was my desperate need for comfort, but I felt myself succumbing to him.

"James, I saw you kill and eat a man. I'll never be able to erase that from my mind. Things are too heavy for me right now … moving too fast. Just when I accept the situation, something *more* bizarre happens and throws everything off kilter again. I want to be light and content. I want to be happy. Can you make me happy again, even if it's just for a little while? Even if the happiness isn't real? Please."

I needed to disappear into James, and fell into his arms in an attempt to become one with him. We both knew there was only one way for us to merge body and soul.

He rocked me while kissing the top of my head. "All right, baby, all right."

My body relaxed into safety again as he lifted my face and kissed me deeper, with his own sense of desperation. Normally this would have been the point where he'd back off—before things got too heated—but now he swooped me up like a bride on our wedding night and carried me to the bed. With unbroken eye contact, he not too gently laid me down. Untying my robe, he slipped it off and let out a satisfied gasp.

"You are so beautiful."

I sat up and began the process of undressing him. Both of our eyes glowed with pure love and anguished arousal. However, I who pulled back this time. I started thinking this was really the *worst* and *weirdest* time for our first lovemaking session.

Then I thought about the bottom line: James and I had been brought together to destroy evil. That responsibility did not include leisurely walks on the beach, Whitman's Samplers of assorted chocolates, or mushy rose petals on the bed. Our life together was ordained to be quite the opposite. No cotton-candy romance here.

"What's wrong?" James asked, wondering why I had slowed up. I was mulling over a question: when would there ever be a good time for us to make love? The answer: never. But a temporary opportunity for escapism existed now, and I was going to take it.

James guided my body back down toward the bed and gently stroked the side of my face. "I'm in love with you, Grace. I've loved you for a very long time. Before I even met you."

I don't know what it was about hearing those words. I had heard something similar to them in the past, and it had been a lie. However, since they were sincere this time, my insides hummed with two feelings: perfect love and sexual desire so great it physically hurt.

James took his time getting to know every inch of me. Starting at my head, he kissed his way down my stomach, following the thin line of downy hair going from my navel to my pussy.

"You have hair on your belly." He grinned.

I playfully ran my fingers through his hair. "I am human, you know."

"Well, half human."

I felt his cock growing thicker and longer against my leg. He rose up on his knees, making my mouth water at the sight of his velvet steel cock. I wanted to taste it, run my tongue all over it. And so I did. I sat up and engulfed him with my mouth. James was way too long and girthy to take in at one time; I didn't want to induce my gag reflex. So I licked the bulging vein on the side and made a special effort to tickle the sensitive spot under the head. My tongue made a trip down the shaft and feathered his ball-sac. I went all the way down until I reached the G-spot behind them, simultaneously stroking his shaft and twisting on the uptake. If his growl was any indication … he loved it.

James, being all man, pushed my head back. It was evident he liked to be in charge, and opted to take over. And I liked that. Fuck yeah. Full of vigor, he put me back down and sucked my nipples while alternating pinching them. His middle finger found my clitoris, and rubbed it until I nearly came. Two of his thick fingers were forced into my hole, vying for my G-spot. He pumped me with the intensity of a seasoned Olympian. The sounds of my pussy greedily suctioning his fingers filled the room. My lips made an O as I slowly pushed air out of my mouth in response.

"Don't stop," I begged as the pressure built inside of me.

James was like a drummer—brilliantly able to perform two actions at once. He stimulated my nipples, which had engorged so much I thought they'd crack, and below my waist his fingers worked physical magic, nearly taking me to the brink. I grabbed his hand.

"Stop. I want your cock inside of me," I said, panting.

James had an intense, dangerous look on his face, so extreme in its focus on me. Spreading my legs, he came down on top of me and slid into me … hard as steel. I took all of him in.

With every controlled thrust of his hips, we moaned and moved with each other in harmony—perfectly synchronized. The pace was purposefully measured, at some points rock-star fast. Then, when we were about to reach the verge, James pulled back, making me ride a wave of ecstasy. When I could no longer hold back, he brought me to climax and let himself release deep within me. Every spurt of his come brought about new goose bumps on my skin. It was fucking hot.

James stayed in me for a while, just staring at me and stroking my sweaty brow. Although this was post-orgasm, my heart wasn't beating fast. It was soft and easy. I was free, flying like a bird.

Finally, some peace.

"What in the hell?"

I was definitely not a morning person, and did not appreciate being awakened by an irritating, fast knocking at the door.

James wrapped a sheet around his waist and answered. It was Aunt Evelyn. Her mouth dropped with disappointment when she saw his morning-after glow. She looked over at me, surprised I'd had the audacity to sully her sheets. However, the prude in Aunt Evelyn knew she had no room to talk—not after I had seen her chomping down on a man the night before. She quickly regrouped, but was ruffled by something else.

"Amari is here."

All of the color drained from James's face. "When did he get here?"

"Just now. You and Grace need to get down there immediately. You know he hates to wait," Aunt Evelyn said, already halfway to the staircase.

James was flustered, and ghosted over to his clothes. "Get dressed."

I followed his anxious lead and bounded over to the laundry basket. "Who is Amari?"

James wasn't paying much attention to me; his mind was on Amari. He absentmindedly put his left shoe on his right foot. "Uh, he's the second-most respected witch on the council, right below Maximus. Think of them as the president and his vice."

I got excited. "You mean Maximus, my grandfather, actually sent help for me?"

James put his shoe on the correct foot. "I doubt it's that simple. He's not that altruistic."

I searched the basket, which was full of freshly washed clothes, for a pair of panties. I still didn't understand what the problem was. It sounded like good news to me that my estranged grandfather was concerned about me. "Dude, chill. Why are you buggin' out?"

"Because if Maximus sent Amari, something is really ... terribly ... wrong."

There's more! Super!

James was now fully dressed, and I still had just one leg in my underwear. But the way he was acting, he was the one with his panties in a bunch.

James did a quick double-check of himself in the hall mirror.

"Vanity, thy name is James," I said.

"This has nothing to do with vanity. When meeting with one of the royal court, you must present yourself in a respectable manner."

"What about me? How do I look?" Until then, I'd felt all right in my skinny jeans and clunky, black boots. James looked me up and down. As he made his critical assessment, my foot turned inward like an insecure schoolgirl.

"It doesn't matter what I think. Remember, you are royalty, albeit in training."

And ... I thought.

James took my hand and guided me down the stairs. Thankfully, he turned around and said, "And oh, by the way, you look terrific."

At the foot of the stairs, I glanced down the hall leading to the parlor. I could see everyone else was already in there, looking all strained ... Hell, even constipated. I was surprised to see Julie was there as well. She sat on the fringe of the room, closest to the door, and could see James and me headed her way. He didn't notice the smug look she gave me, but he was not its intended recipient anyway.

God, how long is she going to hold this grudge?

My heart tightened as we got closer to the parlor. James entered first and bowed. I was prepared to do the same. However, when I crossed the threshold, the first person I saw was a stranger with a familiar face. As the outlander made his way to me, James stepped to the side like he was handing me off in a dance. I recognized the stranger from the press conference regarding Samantha's death. He was the federal agent; his lion's head ring verified it.

The man took my hand and genuflected. He kept his head bowed as he spoke. "It is truly an honor to make your acquaintance. I am Samuel Adams."

"Seriously, like the beer?" I asked.

"It is a family name," Adams said, the humor escaping him.

James whispered in my ear, "He's a forerunner for Amari. He makes sure all's clear before Amari arrives."

I looked to the others to give me a clue on how to respond. This man was treating me like the queen of England. They just nodded as if saying "go with the flow."

"Adams, rise," I commanded, not knowing what else to say. He stood up, but was still careful not to look directly into my eyes. "I know you. From college. You commented on Samantha Beckon's murder."

"Yes, I was there on behalf of the FBI," Agent Adams confirmed.

"You went on television and told the world that a serial killer was among them. Guess that was a big lie."

"Witches in high places protect the world from the ultimate knowledge. Humans are not equipped to deal with the truth," Agent Adams responded.

I thought to myself how crappy that was to purposefully mislead the FBI and the general public about the truth, and manipulate them into chasing down shadows. Maybe it was best not to say anything at all.

"Allow me to introduce you to the master," Adams said.

That whole time I hadn't even noticed the silent figure sitting on the largest chair in the room, behind a desk. He was in the darkest corner, and had been observing me. I followed Agent Adams to the man.

"This is His Excellency, Amari," Adams stated. Everyone in the room bowed. I just copycatted.

Even though Amari was sitting, I could tell he was extremely tall from his elongated arms and rangy fingers. His well-defined muscles were evident even under his tailored, pinstriped suit. He was bald, and his black skin was dewy with oil. In human years, he appeared to be a well-maintained fifty, with jowls just beginning to sag.

I didn't need a genius intellect to know Amari did not want to be there. The commonness of the air was contaminating him. He was convinced that every breath he took coated his lungs in a thick coating of filth.

All eyes in the room widened as Amari placed his hands on the desk and pushed himself up. His hands didn't leave the desk as he leaned forward in an adversarial position. With a full, rich voice, he said to me, "Time to have a look at you."

He came toward me with a pompous stride, and stood behind me. I could feel him mentally categorizing all of my flaws.

"This? This is the one who is to destroy Catherine? What sort of creature are you? No wonder Maximus kept you a secret from me all of these years." In an excruciatingly slow manner, Amari came around to face me. "Maximus has made a grave mistake sending me here."

I could see James twitch at Amari's gall, but he held his tongue in reverence.

"Nonetheless, I will follow through on my assignment," he stated.

Amari *tsk*ed me and walked back over to the chair Agent Adams had pulled out for him. After instructing Adams to wipe away some microscopic dust particles, he flipped the tail of his jacket. Settling into the chair like he was sitting on a bag of rocks, he leaned back as far as the chair would allow, and steepled his hands across his abdomen.

"As you all know, the future is not set. Different outcomes are activated based on moment-to-moment decisions. This whole situation has caused quite a dilemma for our seers. They have never had difficulty determining the probable outcome of *anything* until now. We cannot predict what your *supposed* savior or Catherine will do. We have tried to solve the Catherine problem ourselves, but there appears to be a veil on her. We can't even find her. However, some things are clear. There is trouble at this house … Trouble that can impact the outcome of events, either in our favor or Catherine's. Julie, stand."

She didn't move at first, and couldn't understand why she was being called out. She took her time getting to her feet. "Yes, Your Honor?"

"Julie, you are troubled, and a cause for much concern. Speak on it."

"I have done my duty to the fullest, sir. I will continue to do so without hesitation. You don't have to worry about me."

"Those are mere words. True, you were reliable in the past, but something has happened. Something you and Grace are keeping secret."

Everyone in the room was surprised by this revelation—everyone except Julie and me.

"What is he talking about?" Aunt Evelyn asked.

Amari smirked. "Oh, Evelyn, you did not know. It is not my place to tell you. Perhaps the young women will confess it later. For now we will continue on. Catherine is devastatingly powerful at this moment, and the present timeline is growing more in her favor. This ultimately will result in the destruction not only of the Valois council, but the Bolingbrokes and all other council families. If that happens, Catherine will gather the most-sadistic witches as her support and rule the world as ultimate dictator. Witches will be her slaves, and humans will be her cattle. Maximus is desperate, and has entertained the ridiculous notion that Ilan was right and Grace is the one to set us free, so to speak."

I watched closely as Amari pulled something out of the black lining of his jacket. His pocket must've been deep, because whatever it was, it was long. "A gift from Maximus."

It was wrapped simply in a velvet cloth. Amari reluctantly handed it to me. "Well, just don't stand there. Look at it." He scowled.

It was a knife—more of a work of art than a killing tool. Seven precious metals elegantly forged and honed. The blade was so laser sharp, even the lightest tap on the blade resulted in a cut.

"That is the only thing in existence that can kill a witch possessed by an Ancient spirit. And, according to our seers, only two people have the power to use it. You—"

"And let me guess. Me," I said.

Amari didn't groove on me finishing his sentence. "Yes, you," he said with a superior attitude. "I am assuming you are well prepared for battle?"

Aunt Evelyn stood up and immediately answered, "Well, she's learning."

Amari let out a sardonic laugh. "What? Learning? So you have no idea if she can perform or not?"

Aunt Evelyn made sure not to overstep her boundaries, but she defended me the best she could. "Again, she's learning. She's come a long way."

"Maximus is putting his faith in a maybe," Amari snapped. He addressed Agent Adams. "He *is* getting very old. Perhaps it's time for him to step aside and let me run the council."

Adams was very careful not to let his opinion be known one way or the other.

Amari shook his head and looked at me. "You. Do you have any questions?" he asked, his eyes brimming with contempt.

Questions? How about a million of them? Mainly I wanted to know about my grandfather, but there was no way I was about to bother this asshole. "No, none."

Amari strutted to the middle of the room with Agent Adams in tow. "Our time here is over. Heaven help us," he lamented. He bent his forearm and rotated it in small circles. A tiny tourbillion formed around his arm and grew to encompass not only him, but Agent Adams as well. Small whatnots and pieces of paper scattered about the room got sucked into the swirling current. The tornado-like cloud began to obscure Amari and Adams. It funneled to the ceiling and disappeared, leaving the paper and whatnots to fall to the floor.

Everyone exhaled a collective sigh of relief, but the breather was short lived.

"What is this about? Are you plotting a betrayal?" James asked.

Julie stood, with a huge chip on her shoulder. "I am doing no such thing, and I do suggest you back up."

"I always knew you were trouble. This just proves it," Addison weighed in.Hari jumped into the fray to defend sister. "You Bolingbrokes! Always jumping to conclusions. Amari didn't even say what the problem is between Julie and Grace. You automatically take Grace's side."

The Tower of Babel was rebuilt in that parlor as they all shouted at each other. I took refuge on the couch and rested my chin in my hand. It was the best way I could disconnect from the hoo-ha. When Adrian came over and offered his hand, his smile was a welcomed relief.

"You look like you need a break." He pulled me up and led me to the hall. "Can I get you something?"

I was emotionally exhausted, and leaned back against the wall to recuperate. "Sure. Lemonade with extra sugar."

"Will do," Adrian said, and made his way to the kitchen.

I closed my eyes as if that would stop up my ears. Unfortunately, I could still hear everything going on in the parlor. Aunt Evelyn seemed like she was trying to be the voice of reason.

"Everybody, just calm down. We can't break down now. We've come too far. We're going to work this out. Julie, we'll start with you. Are you sure you're with the program?"

"I cannot believe what I'm hearing. Amari obviously is a prejudicial troublemaker. I've always been here since Ilan recruited me. I've only done my duty. How can you question my loyalty?"

Aunt Evelyn hugged her. "I'm not. This whole thing is just making us crazy."

James saw that neither Adrian nor I were in the parlor. He made a straight line to hall, arriving just in time to see Adrian handing me the lemonade.

James's protective jealousy rose up. "What's going on out here?"

"I'm shielding Grace from all of that noise," Adrian responded.

"Being her bartender is not your job."

"Maybe not, but while you were in there duking it out with Julie, you should've been attending to Grace's needs instead."

James knew Adrian was right. It was pointless to argue with Julie. All that did was create more bitterness in an already tenuous alliance.

Aunt Evelyn knew we needed more help, and decided to recruit Julie's people—the shape-shifters. However, bad blood still ran deep between our two factions, just as fresh as the day the decision to invoke the Ancients was made.

Initially Aunt Evelyn tried to meet Chief Chandranth Weylen in person to hash out their differences. However, he was understandably leery of allowing the Ancient-possessed on his tribe's sacred land. And he definitely wasn't too keen on the idea of my existence.

After days of making fruitless, impassioned pleas to the chief, Aunt Evelyn asked Julie for help. Julie was eager to prove her faithfulness to the mission, and was more than willing to act as a go-between. After much discussion and debate, she convinced the chief to relent, and we were all invited to a bonfire the next night.

Aunt Evelyn sat everyone down and handed out papers—a grocery list of peace offerings to be presented to Chief Weylen. Hari and Addison, though still not all the way cool with each other, were charged with getting wampum: hand-carved disc beads, prayer pipes, and a warrior headdress. Aunt Evelyn would go to the farmers market and pick up fresh fruits and vegetables to make a gift basket. Adrian would buy a top-of-the-line computer for the reservation school. James, however, was assigned to bring me much-needed sheep's blood, as I was growing weaker by the hour.

I had nothing to get. My only job was to stay home and rest up, since I'd be the guest of honor at the reservation. I was more than happy to stay behind and take advantage of a rare moment alone.

When it was time for the others to leave, I tried to be as low-key as possible. However, inside I was saying, *Hurry it up already!*

As soon as the last car left, I ran through every room in the house shouting, "Yippee!" Then I fell on the couch and talked to myself. "You hear that? No, you don't, because you can't hear silence, baby."

Yet after a couple of hours of bouncing around like a kid hopped up on caffeine-infused Kool-Aid, I grew tired of the quiet and loneliness. I hadn't realized how much I'd gotten used to having the others around, and I started to miss them. To occupy my time, I went out to the old barn. Stumbling across the bottles we'd used in my first training session with James, I picked one up and reminisced about how innocent I used to be.

I decided to test how much my telekinesis skills had improved. Standing the bottle up, I shook my body to loosen it, and thought about how happy James made me feel. A light wind began to flow around me and wafted over to the bottle. It rolled around on its bottom edge and then started to levitate higher and higher. I couldn't believe it; I was actually holding it steady in midair. However, the bottle crashed back down when the quiet air was broken by a voice.

"You've gotten much better with that. Just a little more practice and you should be a pro," Adrian said.

I was embarrassed. "How long have you been standing there?"

He came toward me. "Long enough."

"I thought you had a computer to buy."

Adrian slipped into my personal space. "It's in the car. I came as soon as I could. Thought we could spend some time together … like we did in New York."

The hairs on the back of my neck stood stiff. I could tell he was not himself. His eyes were scarily piercing, and to me he felt like he was pressurized. Instinct told me to make myself scarce.

"That's okay. I didn't mind being alone. It wasn't necessary for you to come back so soon." I started to walk away, but Adrian flashed in front of me, blocking my path.

"I've been thinking about us a lot lately. We have something special between us—a connection. We need to talk about it."

I started feeling queasy. "Adrian, I think you misunderstood the nature of our relationship. We're friends. Just friends."

"I know you have to say that because of James, but I know the truth. You want me just as much as I want you."

The fleur-de-lis started to blaze on my palm, inundating it with searing pain. "Adrian, I don't want you. I'm with James. You can never have me like that. What part of that don't you understand?"

I could tell my words still didn't register with him. He thought I was pretending to be hard to get. I tried walking away again, and this time Adrian grabbed my arm. "Ow, you're God damn hurting me," I snapped, struggling to break free.

"Oh, so we're playing games now. How about chase?" He let me go. "I'll give you a head start."

I stood there for a moment, not knowing what he really wanted me to do. When I looked past his eyes, into his mind, I could see what he had there. A voice in my head screamed for me to run, to get away as fast as I could.

With my new powers, I ran swiftly, my feet barely touching the ground. However, Adrian was a more seasoned witch than I was. And today he managed to harness his lust to summon a magical power out of his normal range of abilities: flying. The air suctioned under him as he shot up vertically. I could hear the whir of the breeze as he grew nearer. Adrian flew over my head, blowing my hair forward with his tailwind, and landed right in front of me.

"Don't you have any feelings for me?" he asked, sounding sincere. His head was tilted down, his eyes looking up. He was coming to the painful understanding that I really did want his brother instead.

"No, I don't have any feelings for you. Sorry." *Fuck me.*

With those words, I delivered a fatal wound to Adrian's heart. It killed him to be rejected by the only woman he'd ever cared for. His emotions took a sharp turn, going from raw pain to unbridled fury. He pushed me backward with such force that I flew about fifteen feet.

"I have done nothing except love you since the day I met you. And you—you bitch—strung me along like a puppet. You are not getting away with that."

Adrian pounced on me. He was heavier than his thin body suggested, and he weighed me down. He was turning into that monster I'd seen at the killing ritual. His nails started to claw up as he ripped my shirt apart, and left deep cuts. He kissed my chest savagely and covered my mouth so I couldn't scream. My fangs came down, and I fought to open my lips so I could bite him. I tried to use telekinesis to get him off me, but my terrified state blocked it.

"I'm taking what's due to me," he said with a little froth in the corner of his mouth. He ripped the zipper out of my pants as if it were made of papier-mâché. When he moved his sweaty hand away from my mouth, I bit wildly at the air, hoping to land my teeth in his flesh.

During the wrestling match, I was able to slam Adrian in the nuts. He rolled off me, clutching himself. I staggered to my feet and booked it to the house. Meanwhile, Adrian fought through his pain, ran me down, and tackled me. I landed on my stomach with him on my back, a puff of dirt rising around us. He straddled me, his knees digging into the backs of my spread thighs. I thought they were going to break. When Adrian got full control over me, he got between my legs and started pulling my pants down. Then I heard the sound of his belt unbuckling. *Oh fuck me.*

Suddenly there was a massive *thump*, and I felt Adrian's weight abruptly lifted off my legs. I looked to my side and saw Julie beating his ass. She was in full shape-shifter mode. She tossed him about, taking him from the dirt to the trees and back. Adrian had used the bulk of his magical energy to fly, and had no real strength left to fight her. All he could do was give in to the whipping and get knocked out.

With a mouthful of dirt and a couple bruised ribs, I pulled up my pants. I watched as Julie shifted back to normal. "Thank you," I said.

"Don't thank me. When Ilan came to me, it was understood that I would protect you if you were in grave danger—no matter what. That means if I ever have to choose between my life or someone else's and yours, I am soul-bound to save you. I can never override that. My protection will be automatic and unyielding. And like I told Amari, I will hold up my duty. I have no choice in it."

Julie threw Adrian over her shoulder and carried his battered body to the house. Right before she slipped inside, she turned back to me. "But don't get it twisted. This doesn't change anything between you and me."

I stood there—alone, vulnerable, and violated. More than ever I needed my friend to console me. How could she be so cold-hearted and merciless, especially at a time like this? But I remembered an old African proverb that fit Julie and me to a tee: the ax forgets; the tree remembers.

Chapter Twenty-Three

Probably the toughest time in anyone's
life is when you have to murder a loved
one because they're the devil.

—Emo Philips

N o one had to say a word. James knew what had happened as soon as he walked through the door. The chemical traces of Adrian's hormones gave it away; they were all over me.

I was in the parlor, wrapped mummy-style on the couch. The sedative Aunt Evelyn had administered had anesthetized me into a comatose sleep. James stood at the door at first. He stared at me, not wanting to believe I'd been attacked and he hadn't been there to protect me. He then slowly approached as if he were identifying a loved one at the city morgue. Pausing, he squatted down next to my head. He carefully pulled the wool blanket down to my neck. My puffy face and bruised body told him the full story. As he digested the awful truth, his fangs jutted out, and the entirety of his eyes became volcanic red. His wrath grew exponentially with every shivering breath I took. The house vibrated with him as his body quaked with hatred.

Despite being asleep, I could hear everything as if I were dreaming it.

James's adverse reaction sent reverberations through the house, causing pictures to fall off the walls and windows to crack. Aunt Evelyn knew she had to take immediate action before he ruined her home. She whisked over to him with a whir of current swirling under her feet. "James, bring yourself down. Now, young man."

Unfortunately, James didn't give a shit about anything Aunt Evelyn had to say. He looked straight past her, expecting to see Adrian entering the room at any moment. "Where is Adrian?" he grunted.

Aunt Evelyn grabbed him by the chin and turned his face to hers. "Don't worry about him. Maintain control."

James wasn't himself; a vengeful sentinel had taken his place. He snatched Aunt Evelyn's hand off his face. "What? Am I to be passive right now? Take a noble stance perhaps? You may be in control of this endeavor as a whole, but if you think I'm going to sit idly by after this defilement, you are out of your mind."

Aunt Evelyn sympathized with his raw emotion—the woman he loved had just been the victim of a brutal beating and near rape at the hands of his own brother—but Aunt Evelyn's first priority was me. And she was well aware of the devastating consequences James's volatile anger could have on our undertaking. If left unchecked, his focus would be siphoned to Adrian, and he wouldn't have the capability to shepherd me.

James stormed to the basement with Aunt Evelyn helplessly trying to pull him back.

"Look at me," she implored, stepping in front of him. "Adrian, he's not a problem anymore. Just relax."

I twitched and moaned, trying to wake up from this nightmare. However, I couldn't shake off the drug. All I could do was listen.

"Get out of my way," James growled. I had never heard him sound that way before. His voice had taken on a nefarious, otherworldly timbre and pitch. He pushed Aunt Evelyn aside forcefully, but not enough to hurt her.

Determined to get Adrian, James ripped the basement door off its hinges. His heavy footsteps left deep indentations in each stair as he descended. Large blood droplets from the beating Julie had administered led James to Adrian's limp blow-up mattress. However, Adrian was nowhere in sight.

The tang of Adrian's overabundant testosterone mixed with my fear-engorged epinephrine must've have been all over him, because it was so heavy in the room. When James caught a whiff of it, he was so deeply affected, his rational mind totally left him. All that was left was a time bomb with one second on the clock.

James wasn't speaking anymore; he was making primal, guttural sounds. He tore into the sheetrock as if Adrian were plastered behind it. When he saw there was nothing there except studded beams and wires, he raged out even more.

The other witches and wolves, who'd been instructed by Aunt Evelyn to leave me be, ran from all corners of the house when they heard James's resonating screams. He grabbed whatever wasn't nailed down and threw it about the room. Scraps of shattered lamps, torn furniture, and broken vases piled up on the floor. In the middle of his fit, James noticed the door that separated the main part of the basement from the laundry room. He barreled through it, finding only a washer, a dryer, and half-used boxes of detergent and fabric softener.

By that time the others had rushed down the stairs. Running at full speed, all of them went after James. They slammed him against a wall to subdue him.

"Goddamn you, Adrian!" James yelled, now growing hoarse. He managed to push the others off. However, he took out his frustration on the closest warm body. James picked Hari up by his collar and held him high in the air with one hand. "Where is he?" James said in a low and controlled voice.

"Enough," Aunt Evelyn demanded as she threw invisible projectiles—basically magic bullets—at James. His body jerked as they pelted him, but that didn't stop his cyclonic response. Julie crashed into him, causing him to drop Hari. Aunt Evelyn and Addison immediately started chanting. They conjured a magical vice grip that clutched James, forcing his arms to his sides.

He fought against the restraint. "Why are you protecting him?"

"We're not protecting him," Addison stated with tears in her eyes. "We're protecting you." She squeezed her hands, tightening her magical grip on him. "You know it's forbidden for a witch to kill another."

"Not true. We can kill Catherine," James said.

Addison was not going to let James get away with that incorrect explanation. "Don't even try it. Stop trying to convince yourself this display is okay. You know the council made an exception for Catherine. Adrian is your brother. The council will not condone your plans to do him harm. Father especially will never forgive you for the murder of his child. And you know there is no telling what he would do to you."

"I'll risk it," James bellowed.

"*We* can't risk it," Aunt Evelyn snapped back.

James knew he had to put on a show if he wanted to be released from the invisible straightjacket. "See? I've calmed down. Now can you let me go?"

Addison and Aunt Evelyn looked at each other. Aunt Evelyn shrugged—her way of conceding to Addison that it was safe to release James. The two witches nodded in agreement and set him free.

James's plotting against Adrian had made him quite crafty. He appeared to stretch out his arms innocently, all the while scanning their eyes. He was searching their minds for Adrian's whereabouts. Luckily, the group had veiled their thoughts long before he'd arrived home. James smirked at their forethought. *Touché.*

However, he was not deterred, and knew his next move had to be quick. Before the witches and wolves could intervene once again, James waved his hand, casting a spell on the room. It hazed over; he could see the last glimmers of Adrian, but he couldn't get a full picture for some reason.

James had been quick with his room swipe, but Addison's observation of him was quicker. "We veiled the room, James."

That didn't matter, because outside the window James spotted the murky residue of Adrian's essence. He pulled back his lips and exposed his long fangs. In a flash of light, he bolted up the stairs and out of the house. The other witches didn't even have time to process what had just happened.

I woke up from unconsciousness as James streaked out of the house. The front door slammed shut just as I sat up. Yanking the curtain back, I saw James outside. He was blood-hounding Adrian's fading vapor trail. The other witches and wolves flew out the door behind him.

James's nostrils flared as he sniffed the air, but Adrian's scent disappeared at the end of the driveway.

"He's gone, James. Let it go," Addison begged.

He saw me watching the happenings from inside the house. Though groggy, I pressed my hand against the window, urging him to come in.

"I'm going to check on Grace," he said. The others got out of his way as he walked right through the middle of them. He was halfway to the house when he made a declaration.

"The next time I see Adrian, I will kill him. You can be most assured of that."

Adrian couldn't believe the other witches had left him on Tobay Beach without any money, food, or clothing.

A few hours earlier, they'd literally tossed him out of the car with nary a word, and kicked up dust as they drove away. His last memory was of the car's taillights, and doe-eyed Addison looking out of the rear window at him. Once again, James had won. Not only did he have Grace, but he'd also caused Addison to disown Adrian, too.

He sat on the sand and watched the outgoing tide of the Atlantic. The sky was still glowing with a sliver of the setting sun behind him. The sun's clear, then yellow, then orange rings radiated out, but were not able to lift the gloom he felt.

Instead of being toasty, the remaining rays were cool on Adrian skin; his body was having a hard time recovering from Julie's assault. His injuries were extensive. He was missing a patch of scalp where his head had bounced off a tree trunk. His eyes were swollen, with black, viscous fluid ballooning under the skin. Multiple splits in his lips stung as salty sweat dribbled into them. And he had three of his teeth in his pocket.

Humiliated and vilified, Adrian ruminated on how Grace had manipulated him into loving her. The player wasn't used to getting played. He also couldn't deny that he really had fallen in love with her. He hated himself for pining for her. Moreover, he could hardly bear the thought of James touching, kissing, and making love to Grace. It was a gut punch when he imagined how much she liked it.

Adrian knew Grace would never truly love him, and this severed his heart in two. The more he thought about it, the more he wanted to eat her. Not so much for revenge, though. He figured if he consumed her, she'd always be a part of him, like a biological trophy.

Now, concerning the other witches and wolves, he did want revenge. And he was going to take it.

Adrian closed his eyes and repeated a name: *Catherine*. Like music on airwaves, his voice traveled from the beach, down the highway, to Massapequa proper. Its final destination was a large, foreclosed home with a lockbox on the door. The house was one of only two on a winding street. The other, directly across the road, was occupied by Michelle Ross, a night-shift night nurse and full-time student working on her practitioner license. Today she was exhausted. She had overslept, and was in a mad dash out the door.

She paused, though. There was a strange odor seeping into her house—had been for the past few days. It smelled like a festering sore. She blew it off, thinking it was the stench of decaying sea life coming in from the bay. The truth was she hadn't been paying much attention to anything going on in the neighborhood. Not even the supposedly empty, foreclosed house across the way.

Michelle stood on her porch and searched her junky purse for her elusive house keys. The bag was an ever-changing hodgepodge of receipts, lipsticks, broken cell phones, and that-time-of-the month essentials. Heaving heavy sighs, Michelle was unaware that Mrs. Delores Davenport had been watching her from the sidewalk. A power-walking retiree and recent widow, Mrs. Davenport seized whatever opportunities she could to hobnob with her outlying neighbors. She lived three streets over and always managed to catch Michelle in a frantic rush to work.

"Hello, Michelle. Nice weather we're having," said Mrs. Davenport as she marched in place.

Michelle sighed even heavier; she had no time for Mrs. Davenport right now. "Sure was. Going to work now," she stated dismissingly.

Mrs. Davenport put two fingers to her neck, making sure to maintain her target heart rate. "Did you hear about all of those missing people?"

"No." Michelle dropped her purse and spilled its endless contents. She partly blamed Mrs. Davenport for ruining her concentration.

"Yes, for the past few weeks, people from here to New York have been disappearing."

Michelle found her keys. "Hot damn!"

"Damn is right. We must be careful. Especially you out here on this street all alone."

Michelle locked her front door and hopped into her Hyundai. She backed up, flooring the accelerator, without looking in the rearview mirror—and nearly ran over Mrs. Davenport.

"Oh, I'm so sorry," Michelle said, but thought, *Not really.*

"That's okay. You did hear me, though?"

Michelle's car was already on the street, ready to go. "Uh … say it again."

"Be careful."

"Sure." Michelle peeled out.

"Such a sweet girl," Mrs. Davenport murmured to herself. Just as she turned to power walk back home, she thought she heard a noise coming from the empty house. She listened more closely. Now all she heard was an airplane passing overhead.

"You must be getting old, Mrs. Davenport." As she passed the empty house, she too noticed the smell of rotten meat, but ignored it like Michelle had.

If anyone had taken the time to investigate, the putrid odor would have led them straight to the empty house. The back sliding-glass door had been broken into a few weeks earlier. Low noises always seeped out at about three a.m., but because of Michelle's night shift and the desolation of the street, there was no one around to hear them.

The house's below-ground bonus room was the home of ten sleeping protégés. Newly formed, they were resting in somewhat of an embryonic state. The protégés had been well fed. All around them were the rotting carcasses of the missing people Mrs. Davenport had talked about.

Their mother, Catherine, was wide awake. She had been covertly peering out of the bonus-room window at Mrs. Davenport and Michelle, whose absentminded tiredness had been a blessing to Catherine. A more observant neighbor would have noticed the almost too obvious signs that someone had taken up residency in the abandoned house.

Catherine had seen Michelle and Mrs. Davenport numerous times since she had broken in. And each time she had thought about eating them, especially that irritating Mrs. Davenport. She opted not to; they were too close to home. Catherine couldn't afford to draw the scrutiny of law enforcement to the enclave.

After Michelle and Mrs. Davenport left, Catherine swiped her hand and created an orb of light that rose to the ceiling. It illuminated the maze of baby protégés. Like a nanny watching over her sleeping charges, Catherine strolled the rows between them. It had been a time-consuming task to change each one individually in ritual. She relished the time when she would be able to confiscate Grace's powers. Then she'd be able to create protégés at her whim.

As Catherine passed each one, she recollected how she had acquired them. One she had abducted after he'd robbed a convenience store. She'd kidnapped the sadistic school principal with a penchant for paddling after he'd brutally disciplined a young girl. Another one Catherine had taken after he'd smothered his cancer-stricken wife for a $500,000 life-insurance policy.

However, Catherine's favorite was Tamara. Catherine saw so much of herself in her. Tamara was the featured act at a sleazy strip club. Abused as a child, she had turned into a sociopathic killer after a lifetime of suppressing anything remotely resembling love. Her victims of choice were muscular and dark-haired males—just like her daddy. She was highly transient, and her hunting grounds were the clubs where she worked. One night a customer wanted some after-hours activity. However, instead of giving him a quick screw in the bed of his pickup truck, Tamara shot him in the eye. Catherine captured her right after.

As Catherine reveled in her children, she felt an itch inside of her ear. Not really paying attention, she reflexively rubbed it. However, she took notice when the itch grew more intense and spread over her body. Red patches appeared on her skin as if she had run through a poison-ivy field. She looked straight ahead through the darkness and saw a blob of static electricity coming toward her. As it got closer, it took the shape of Adrian's body. His spell finally had reached her.

Adrian's specter form pointed to a black wall where a montage of images began to play. The pictures were of Aunt Evelyn's house, Chief Weylen, and a bonfire. The final image was of Catherine standing in a vortex of energy, with Grace—near death—at her feet.

Meanwhile, upstairs, a lone candle lit up the kitchen nook. Chetan sat in its corner, keeping his eye on Nick, who had come out of his stupor and was now cognizant. Chetan had become increasingly afraid of him. The protégé's hunger was growing at an alarming rate, even for Catherine's taste.

Nick licked his lips and stared at Chetan like he was a steak. "I'm hungry."

"Why are you looking at me?" Chetan responded, shrinking in his chair like an ogled woman.

Nick wasn't his only concern. Catherine had been acting strangely as of late. It was noticeable that she was distancing herself from Chetan. He could tell she was scheming something when she looked at him.

Chetan picked up the candle and excused himself to get away from Nick. As he hurried out of the kitchen, he looked back to make sure Nick wasn't following him. All he saw was the protégé's black silhouette against the window, watching him back. Chetan jittered and scurried out. Crossing into the living room, he quickly shut the door and fell back on it, thrilled to be alone in relative safety.

"Whew! That crazy motherfucker." He lifted himself off the door and waved the candle around. That was when he saw Catherine standing right in front of him.

"Where did you come from?" he asked.

Catherine had no time for small talk. "It's time. I know where Grace is."

Chetan could tell Catherine was chillingly wound up. "Okay, let's go then," he replied, trying to sound ambivalent.

Catherine studied him for a bit. She then opened the door with wave of her hand. "Nick, could you come here, dear?" She addressed Chetan again, "You've done your job well, but it's time now for you to complete it."

Nick came in and stood next to her.

"How? Do you want me to kill Grace for you?" Chetan asked. A sense of dread cascaded upon him.

"Oh, you fool, you know *I* have to do that. No, no … Come here," Catherine said. With her bony finger, she beckoned to Chetan. Stroking his face, she sweetly smiled. Chetan knew he was in trouble then. "You have to die."

Suddenly, Nick grabbed Chetan and locked his arms behind him.

"Haven't you wondered why I kept a witless hack like you around? Do you think it's because you're so awesome?" Catherine asked.

"I thought it was because I was the only witch who'd go along with your plans," Chetan prattled.

"Partly. See, you served a purpose. I needed to have a readily available energy source—like a backup generator, so to speak. A witch's blood to consume. That blood would make me stronger when the time came for me to confront Grace. That time is now, and that witch is you."

Chetan tried to break free of Nick's grip. "Catherine? I can't believe you."

She mocked him with a fake pout. "Why so surprised? You know I'm bad. What did you expect?" She slashed his throat with her long nail.

Chetan was very much alive as Catherine sucked his blood. Nick, still propping him up, found it nearly impossible to fight off his desire to devour him.

Catherine raised her face, and through bloody teeth and fangs spoke to Nick. "Here … Your first taste."

Nick was like a wild animal as he chomped down on Chetan's shoulder, taking out a chunk. He let the body drop to the floor and pounced on it, biting out large portions.

"Ah, ah, ah … We must share," Catherine said, her body contorting as she transformed into her demonic appearance. She ripped out Chetan's chest muscle and held it in her hand. It looked like a tender roast, marbled with fat. "Take him to the children," she instructed.

Chetan's life was fading fast as Nick hauled him by his ankles to the bonus room. Catherine followed, eating the delicious piece of muscle, savoring it like petit filet. Chetan's head bounced up and down on the stairs as Nick dragged him.

On Catherine's way down, she noticed a discarded, rusty, cast iron skillet hanging on a wall. She used the hammer hanging next to it to make an impromptu dinner bell, banging on it loudly to rouse the sleeping protégés. "Wake up, children. It's dinnertime."

"No! No! Catherine … Nick …" Chetan pleaded.

Nick tossed his body into the swarming horde below. They converged on it and finished eating him alive. As they did, their physical strength grew into superhuman power.

Catherine was delighted. "They are fed. Tomorrow night, Grace and I finally meet."

James and I rode in the car alone on our way to the reservation. The others had decided it was best for them to ride separately in Aunt Evelyn's minivan; they were trying to avoid James's bad vibe.

Ever since he had found out Adrian had attacked me, James had been my shadow—to the kitchen, the yard, the bedroom, everywhere. I drew the line when he wanted to sit in the bathroom while I took a shit. Although James was with me physically, his mind was elsewhere. He barely spoke and took in no food or drink. I could see he was devising a plan to find and destroy Adrian.

I drank the sheep's blood he brought home, but it did me no good. I was weak, and my stomach was churning with nausea. Everyone was telling me I needed to feed; however, I still refused to eat another human being. I figured willpower would get me through it, but it wasn't working. I reasoned I had to give it more time.

Up ahead and above the forest, I could see smoke billowing from the bonfire. I'd never actually been on the reservation. The few times I had come into the area, it was only to go to Julie's house, which was down the street. It still surprised me that no one in town had any idea werewolves lived there.

Our caravan pulled up to the reservation's behemoth gate. An acne-faced young man acted as a guard of sorts—more of a welcoming committee. The gate was actually two large swinging doors made of white wooden panels. On them was painted the wolf insignia of Julie's tribe. This entrance was not built to keep the world out. It was constructed in honor of tribal heritage and nature.

The young man radioed to someone up ahead and waved us in with a friendly smile. The newly paved road was shaded by a canopy of aged oaks and elms. It led to the main area of the reservation, where there was a bustling general store, a small bank, and a gas station. We drove deeper into the residential area dotted with mobile, small ranch, and bungalow-style homes. I was able to catch the coded wolf sign that was strategically yet subtly placed on each building.

The residents were a joyful people, sitting on their front porches, enthusiastically engaging one another with lively chatter. They waved as the minivan carrying Julie and Hari drove past them. This was the first time I'd seen Julie put on a genuine smile since our fight.

As we drove by her old elementary school, I was reminded that I'd never really known her at all. She had a whole other life I was not privy to … and that life was good. These Native Americans were not the downtrodden victims I was so often told about. They were a proud, capable, and strong people. It was obvious where Julie had inherited her fortitude from.

We pulled up to a modest, two-story house. "Well, are you ready to meet the chief?" I asked James.

"Yeah, sure," he said. "As soon as we're done, I can take care of some other business."

I decided to give him his space—a little time to find his composure. I got out of the car.

Oops, forgot the knife. I went back to the car and got the blade Amari had given me. Sliding it into my boot, I made sure my jeans covered it. I almost hadn't brought it, believing I'd be amongst friends. However, Aunt Evelyn had told me to get used to carrying it because "you never know."

I joined the others, who were already out of the minivan. Aunt Evelyn looked at James, raising her brow. She was not happy that he was still in a funk, and went straight over to him. James huffed when he saw Aunt Evelyn coming his way. His mind was already preoccupied, and the last thing he wanted right then was a speech.

But, as usual, that didn't deter Aunt Evelyn. "Take the scowl off your face. I know you're upset over Adrian. However, you cannot let that impede our mission here. We need the chief's help and can't give him any inkling that there is discord among us. Let's not give him a reason to change his mind. Too much is depending on this."

James put on a front and pretended to relax. "See? I'm smiling. I'm okay. I'm not going to mess any of this up. I promise." Inside he was churning with too much animosity to simply wish it away, and he didn't fool Aunt Evelyn.

"There's nothing we can do about you now. Get the gifts," she said.

As we all gathered the peace offerings, James held my hand. "I love you. You can never know how much," he said.

"I do know. I love you, too."

We followed the others up the winding walk lined with solar garden lights. Little children watched us, looking fascinated. However, as soon as they sensed James's angst, they scurried away in fear.

A wolf symbol hung like mistletoe over the front door. "Here goes nothing," Hari said right before he banged on the door with the huge, wolf-faced knocker.

After some time, Chief Weylen opened the door. He was a large, jolly man with a full mane of grayish-white hair. With a wide smile and opened arms, he first welcomed Julie and Hari inside the house. "Oh, children, welcome home. We've missed you."

The three of them huddled in a three-way hug. Then, in line with protocol, Julie and Hari took their places behind the chief. He turned his suspicious attention toward James and me.

"Well, I guess it's safe for me to let you in," the chief said. I could hear the acrimony in his voice, and that he had second thoughts about us being there. As we witches walked past him, he peeked outside and looked at the sky. It was a sunny day, but a dark cloud seemed to be hanging over the reservation. He took note. "Hmph."

We only took a few steps into the house when the chief stopped us. "Wait," he said, then went over to a table and lit up a tight wad of dried sage. He came back to us and performed a smudging, swiping the sage's smoke all around our bodies.

Chief Weylen swiped over James more than anyone else. "You have many bad thoughts, young man," the chief said to him. Aunt Evelyn gave James a disappointed look.

"I guess you're all okay now," Chief Weylen said. "Except you, young buck. But I'll let you stay anyway," he said to James.

The chief started toward the back of the house. "Well, don't just stand there. Come on." I could feel he was still being very cautious with us as he led us to his kitchen. He made special efforts not to touch us. If one of the witches got too close, he skirted us like a running back going for a touchdown.

Hari saw my confusion. "He doesn't want to be contaminated by evil," he explained, half joking and half serious.

We all piled into the kitchen, which was the size of a sardine can. "We brought you some gifts," Aunt Evelyn said to Chief Weylen, still trying to sway his favor in our direction. I saw the chief's shoulders relax as his heart softened—not because of the gifts, but because Aunt Evelyn was trying so hard to impress him.

"It has been a long time since we've interacted with our long-lost brethren," he stated. "Too long."

Chief Weylen paid no mind to the gifts, but put a comforting arm around Aunt Evelyn's shoulders.

I noticed that there was a large, skinned hare splayed on the newspaper-strewn table. "That morsel is for the bonfire tonight," Chief Weylen explained, as if he could taste it already. We all took seats and watched him perform culinary alchemy. With the precision of Joël Robuchon, he chopped up the rabbit with a meat cleaver. He kind of reminded me of Leatherface the way he brought that big-ass knife down. He then threw the pieces into a stewpot of searing olive oil until they developed a golden-brown crust.

"Thank you for allowing us to come to your home. We appreciate your help," Aunt Evelyn said. She closed her eyes and enjoyed the aroma of the rabbit.

Chief Weylen julienned carrots, onions, and celery. "Apparently I had no choice." He started a roux. "It appears we are all in this together."

The smell of the vegetables as they hit the roux was heavenly, even to my sickly stomach. I thought this surely must have been the ideal way to hash out world differences: over a pot of homemade stew.

The chief wiped the juices from the rabbit onto his apron, and addressed me, "I didn't know what to think of you, but the spirits tell me you have a good heart ... A heavy heart, but a good one nonetheless."

A young girl, about six or seven, bounded in. "Julie!" she screamed. She leapt from clear across the kitchen, strong and high, into Julie's arms. Even at such a young age, she was mastering her wolf powers.

"This is Kaya, my granddaughter," Chief Weylen said, his eyes brimming with adoration.

Kaya was one of the most beautiful and happiest children I'd ever seen. Her eyes were oddly shaped—totally round, like black buttons. Her jet-black side ponytail skimmed her sun-drenched shoulders. She had dimples that ran a mile deep when she smiled.

"She was all I had after the death of my son and his wife. She's my life," the chief explained with a mixture of joy and pain.

Kaya hopped out of Julie's arms and took center stage in front of all of us. "Papa, I learned it."

"Okay, show us then." The chief plopped down on a chair with all of the usual parental expectation. As a result, we were squeezed in tighter than before.

"What's she talking about?' Hari asked.

The chief responded, "Kaya has learned words from our sacred text. She'll read them to the tribe at tonight's bonfire."

Kaya held up her hand, her fingers tipped with multicolored nail polish from a kiddie makeup kit. "Hail, hail, great Wolf Spirit, within this circle I have made. Great Spirit, beseech me when my night duty calls. For by day I walk as man. When I die I will serve thee evermore with haste."

Though the spell was to be powered by the participation of all the wolves during ritual, *something* was summoned. The trees outside rustled, and the wind moaned and kicked up in response.

"So you conjured wind," Hari joked, causing everyone to laugh. James even smiled sideways.

"Oh, you be quiet, Hari," Kaya said, punching him in the side.

The chief's laughter was interrupted when he happened to glance out the window. The ominous cloud had descended upon the reservation even more. Without a doubt, Chief Weylen knew something terrible was coming.

The picnic benches were lined up in rows; it reminded me of my old high school cafeteria. *Shudder.*

At every place setting, there was a mat made of oyster shells woven with tan muslin. They looked pretty, but I could tell they would be impossible to eat on. The elders sat at tables draped with deer skins. The coverings smelled like putrefied roadkill, and that did nothing to alleviate my sick feeling.

I noticed a group of deeply wrinkled women sitting in a circle. They had been diligently making pretty, beaded bracelets for this occasion for weeks. I looked around and saw that some of the adults already had enough bracelets to cover their arms from wrist to shoulders.

The most elder of the women hobbled over to me. She didn't speak; she just slid a bracelet on my arm.

"Grace, consider yourself fortunate. That is a badge of honor. I've never seen one offered to an outsider," Hari stated.

The elder woman hugged me, but quickly pulled back, disturbed. "Hari, she is so thin. Haven't you been feeding her?"

Hari and I looked at each other. "It's complicated," he said.

The elder woman could not tolerate my skeletal frame, and dragged me to the food. Amused, James followed. The large buffet table had traditional dried beef and pork. Smaller tables had grilled and smoked meats and fishes. And, of course, there was Chief Weylen's rabbit stew. There were definitely no vegetarians on this reservation.

The chief stood on a raised platform and called everyone over. He said a moving blessing over the food and then encouraged us all to dig in. The guests converged on the food with gusto. However, I was so tired, all I could do was sit on a bench.

James brought me a plate of food—the rarest meat of the carnivores' feast he managed to snatch up. "You look horrible," he said, holding a forkful of deer tenderloin in front of my mouth.

"You say the sweetest things." I managed to eat the deer, but I still wanted to throw up. It was so undercooked that its juices flowed down my chin.

"You've got blood all over you." He seductively ran his tongue across my chin, licking the blood off. He was coming out of his funk, and that made me start feeling a wee bit better.

I glanced over at the chief. His attention was diverted from the celebration. He was looking around as if he sensed something. He moved closer to the tree line and peered deeper into the woods. Staring back at him from the darkness were many glowing eyes.

The chief signaled to the others with a warrior yell. From then on everything seemed like it was moving in slow motion. Catherine's protégés stormed out of the woods in an immediate and fierce attack. The natives all instantly morphed into wolves and responded in kind.

And then there she was. Finally, after a twenty-one year wait, I saw her. With profound greatness and evil, Catherine emerged from the darkness.

It took only seconds for our eyes to meet. Each of us seemed paralyzed by the other's presence. Our fangs popped out with thick venom dripping—that had never happened to me before. Catherine twitched and squirmed until she broke free of her bewilderment. I was still fighting to break out of mine as she ran toward me with some kind of terminal velocity. However, James was moving just as fast, and tackled her. It sounded like he hit a brick wall.

Catherine was so frenzied by my presence, James was having a terrible time controlling her. She couldn't even speak; all she could do was screech.

Meanwhile, Addison, Hari, Aunt Evelyn, and Julie fought off protégés who were busy gorging on the weaker wolves. It became clear to them that these were not average protégés. They were staggeringly powerful, and more hungry than usual. Catherine must have imbued them with extraordinary strength.

"Hide, Grace! Hide!" James screamed as he held Catherine down by her neck. I could see he was having difficulty keeping her down, and I didn't have much time to get away. In my severely weakened state, I summoned any power I could. Seeing a boulder, I focused on it. It lifted and floated over to James and Catherine.

"James, move!" I yelled. He did so just in time for the boulder to fall on Catherine.

Surrounded by chaos, he stood there minding the boulder, waiting to see what would happen. There was no movement underneath. Then the rock wobbled some. He knew Catherine would emerge with a more pitiless attack.

"Grace, run," he said, readying himself for the fight.

I ran past the chief. He was trying to save Kaya from the jaws of a protégé. He made a spectacular wolf—tall, strong, and lean, unlike his human form. He grabbed the protégé and broke its neck. The protégé released Kaya's mangled body from its drooling mouth, and the chief's devastated emotions caused him to morph back to his fragile human form. He picked up Kaya and rocked her in his arms. She smiled at him, and then passed away.

The chief didn't even have a chance to grieve as another protégé came toward him. The chief grabbed a stick. Just as the protégé was about to pounce, he stood the stick straight up. The protégé landed on it, and it went straight through its heart.

Nick and Tamara stalked toward me, and Julie saw it. The enchantment that forced her to protect me kicked in. At the same time, she saw Hari running a protégé down in the sparse part of the woods, unaware that another protégé pursued him. Julie was conflicted. She wanted to rescue her brother, but was spellbound to help me instead.

"Hari, get out of there! Someone's on your tail," Julie screamed. He didn't hear her.

Nick and Tamara circled Julie and me. "All you have to do is go after your brother. Let me have Grace," Tamara said.

If Julie could have, she would've left me there to fend for myself and gone to save Hari. I couldn't blame her; I would've done the same thing.

"Okay, I'll go get him for you." Tamara snickered. She ran at top speed after Hari. Julie was left there to protect me from Nick.

Her eyes welled up. "Please, Hari … Please run faster."

The protégé Hari was chasing made a sudden turn into the woods and disappeared. Tamara and the protégé who were after Hari caught up with and surrounded him. Tamara took a close look at Hari. He resembled a younger version of her daddy. Therefore, in her mind, he *really* had to die.

"Let's get this son of a bitch," she told the other protégé. They ran Hari into a tree with a thundering crash, causing long splinters to stab into his arms.

"Pup, you're out of your league. And I have no problem with euthanasia," Tamara said to him.

Hari was limp and broken. He barely had breath in him, but he wasn't going down without a good fight. He lashed out blindly. Despite being able to hear his cracked bones scraping together under his skin, he made his fist connect with the protégé's concrete body. Hari heard deafening snaps as the bones in his hand crushed.

Not deterred, he garnered his energy, howling to summon and release his concentrated life force. Tamara was unimpressed, and overconfident in the protégés' positions, figuring Hari had only one shot at the two of them.

Hari also knew that if he didn't kill both of them, it would be over for him. He ran to the closest tree, jumped, and ricocheted off two others. He soared through the air with the protégés' faces inches away from his grasp.

Tamara slapped him mightily. He hit a tree with such force, its trunk splintered. Hari couldn't move. His breathing became shallow and erratic. He tried to get away with a slow crawl as the protégés stood over him, but Tamara held him down firmly into the dirt.

Meanwhile, Julie fought off Nick with skill while I tried to get the knife out of my boot. It was stuck. We both heard Tamara laughing from the woods.

"See? It's over, Julie," Tamara said. "You should've just given me Grace in the first place. You know we'll win in the end. Now you'll have the pleasure of listening to your brother's last breath."

Julie turned her head away. She refused to watch the protégés tear Hari apart. She took it out on Nick, and chopped him in the temple. Grabbing his head, he fell to the ground.

Back at the bonfire, Catherine tossed off the boulder and threw a magic circle around James. It acted as a bubble and trapped him. Catherine then threw black magic bolts at Julie, who was about to kill Nick, and knocked her unconscious. Just as Catherine was about to fly over to me, Addison and Aunt Evelyn combined their energies and put her in an invisible chain. With Catherine incapacitated, the magical bubble around James burst, lights falling out like firecrackers.

While Nick writhed on the ground, I took refuge behind the rock. I was still struggling to get the knife, and cursing myself for wearing such tight boots. Just as it was about to slide out, a phantasmal figure came out of the darkness. As it drew closer, it coalesced into a solid form.

"We meet again," Adrian said. I was very weak, and still didn't have the knife out to protect myself. My only option was to run. Unfortunately, Adrian had no trouble taking me down. I fought him off the best I could, but he controlled me with punches to the head.

With Aunt Evelyn and Addison managing Catherine, James flashed over to Adrian and me. They exchanged no words. Adrian let me go to engage in some mortal hand-to-hand combat with James. They did not use magic spells or tricks because this was personal. It required skin-to-skin, soul-to-soul contact.

The fight was barbarous. Both men, now in their monstrous forms, bit and chewed on each other. Ham-fisted blows skyrocketed them deeper into the woods, away from me, leaving me alone. They fought to exhaustion, and James emerged the victor. He had Adrian on the ground in a headlock.

"Why, Adrian? You were my brother. I loved you."

Adrian let go of his last smirk. "I always hated you."

The brothers had no more to say. James twisted Adrian's head off, and wept as it rolled into a creek bed.

Meanwhile, Tamara and her protégé partner helped Catherine get leverage over Addison and Evelyn. Catherine was free to get me—and she did. At the same time, I was able to yank the knife out of my boot.

"You have to know how to use that knife for it to work," she said to me.

I slashed the air wildly. "You didn't have to hurt all of those people. This has always been about you and me. So come on with it."

Catherine moved closer to me. "My, what a brave one you've grown into. I'm going to enjoy killing you."

"Not today, bitch. Not ever."

All of a sudden, I saw a blur, and Catherine was on me. I dropped the knife as I tried to fight her off. She accidently ripped a hole in my abdomen with her longest claw during the struggle.

"Oh, you idiot! See what you made me do?" she screamed.

I was bleeding out like a sprinkler, and my intestines were exposed. Catherine knew if she wanted my power, she couldn't let me die there. She had to eat me during a specific ritual.

"Hurry, children!" she said to her two remaining protégés, Nick and Tamara. Her minions came to her side.

"Why aren't you eating her?" Tamara asked.

"I have to heal her and then perform the ritual. Not before a lot of torture, though," Catherine explained, then dug her claw-like nails deep into my arm so she could handle me better. She created a crackly, five-dimensional portal for us to transport through. Spotting the knife, she picked it up.

The vortex whirled up, and I could feel my molecules compressing.

James made it back to me just in time to reach into the vortex. I could see the atoms of his hand dematerializing as he pulled me out right before I reached my event horizon.

"The knife!" I yelled.

Catherine and her protégés were already pixelated. She was holding the still-solid knife. James reached back in, but couldn't remove it from her puzzle-pieced hand. With a puff of smoke, Catherine and her protégés disappeared—along with the knife.

And I was dying.

"You're not leaving me now," James said as he picked me up. He ran me back to the bonfire area. It was filled with injured and dead wolves, and wailing survivors. Somehow the wolves had managed to kill almost all of the protégés.

James spotted a dying, young tribeswoman. He put me down next to her. "Eat," he stated. "It's the only way to keep you alive. She's going to die whether you do it or not. Feed. Right now, Grace."

I tried to stall. "You said feeding was only to be done in ritual."

"This is an emergency."

"No, James. I can't do that. It's wrong. It's murder," I whispered, feeling myself slipping away.

James tore some of the young woman's flesh and put it into my mouth. It tasted good, and I could feel my body healing itself. My hunger rose up and compelled me to take more. As I sank my fangs into her and ate, I changed into the same gargoyle-looking creature the other witches had when they'd eaten the little man. The young woman passed away, and I was satiated on her blood and flesh.

And I was totally healed.

Chief Weylen was horrified by what he saw. He still had the stick he'd used to kill the protégé, and beat me away from the young woman's body with it. He chased me, giving my body swats and lashes. "You all are nothing but devils. Pure devils!"

The rest of the wolves chased us off the property while performing some sort of exorcism. As we were running off the field, I could see the blood-stained sheet covering Kaya, and Julie exiting the woods carrying Hari's dead body.

She yelled at me, "All of this … for you! I hope you're happy."

The chief went to Julie and helped her carry Hari away.

"She needs me," I said to James, but he was pushing me toward the car.

"That's really not a good idea right now. Let her be with her people."

I broke free and ran toward Julie, but the other wolves stopped me.

"Devil! Leave," Julie demanded before disappearing into Chief Weylen's house.

"Come on. We've got to go," James said. "Don't look back again."

This was not part of the plan. I existed to save life, not take it away from those who were only trying to help me. Maybe the council, Amari, and Chief Weylen were right after all.

Maybe I really was the devil.

Chapter Twenty-Four

We're born alone, we live alone, we die
alone. Only through our love and
friendship can we create the illusion for
the moment that we're not alone.

—Orson Welles

If they had chased us with pitchforks … If they had swung ropes to
lynch us … If they had mobbed and beat us down mercilessly … I
would have understood.

After Catherine's gruesome attack on the tribe and my subsequent
feeding on the young woman, we had to make a mad scramble to our
vehicles. It wasn't so much that we were afraid of the shape-shifters.
The escape was necessary for us to avoid defending ourselves against
them. If that unfortunate situation arose, the catastrophic result would
have been more unnecessary loss of life—theirs, not ours.

I was running hard, trailing James. He gripped my hand so tightly I
thought it was breaking. As if he were Lot and I was his wife, he
ordered, "Don't look back." I did as I was told, but noticed that the
impenetrable, dark cloud that had settled over the reservation seemed
to be following us. Its movement was imperceptible to an undiscerning
eye, but I caught it. It scared me, so I ran ahead of James and started
dragging him instead.

The berserk chants of the tribe seemed to be right at our backs. The
faster we ran, the more incensed and agonized their conjurations
became. Our brothers and sisters in wolf's clothing had retained their
occult abilities, though they weren't as strong as ours. Their whammy
generated an unseen wall of hands that literally pushed us—the evil
spirits—off their property. The hands' slaps drove stinging, ghostly
bristles deep into our backs.

Without any of us dying or having to kill more of the shape-
shifters, we finally made it back to our vehicles. In somewhat of a
panic mode, Aunt Evelyn and Addison both struggled with their door
handles before jumping into the minivan. Directly behind them James
helped me into the car and buckled my seatbelt for me. He was

meticulous about it. He took the time to make sure I was strapped in tight, in total disregard of his own safety.

The wolves hung back. "You okay?" he asked while looking over his shoulder at the mob of shape-shifters practically foaming at their mouths.

"I'm good," I said quickly, so he'd hurry and get into the car.

I could see some of the shape-shifters still hadn't retracted their fangs, and I wondered if they were for us. The chanting had stopped, but some in the crowd still heckled. "Good riddance!" shouted an anonymous voice while someone else spit on our tracks. No matter how much they assailed, the shape-shifters never advanced. They just wanted us gone.

Shaking, Aunt Evelyn turned the ignition and put her hands on the steering wheel, but quickly removed them. She rubbed her fingertips against her palms. The sparkly yet gritty traces of killer-defensive magic were still on her hands. Disturbed, she reached into the backseat for her purse and searched through it.

From James's car I could see her muddling about. I was sure the shape-shifters saw her as well, and were wondering what the heck she was doing. What I didn't know was that Aunt Evelyn was thinking her magic didn't do much good, seeing that Hari was gone, and she just wanted the useless conjury off her hands.

Aunt Evelyn squirted a glop of Purell onto her grainy palms and furiously rubbed them together. The magic was thick and did not come off easily. She reached for one of the countless fast-food napkins she had stashed in the glove compartment. As she did this, she noticed one of Hari's hairs lying across the center console.

"He was shedding ... That little puppy," she said with bittersweet remembrance in her voice. She drew a deep breath through her nose as she thought of the beautiful boy they had lost. A visceral cry strived to explode out of her body, but she stifled it, thinking about the loss Addison had just endured as well.

Aunt Evelyn looked at her. She had settled down quite a bit. In fact, she was acting very strange. Instead of lamenting Adrian's death, she sat in the passenger seat just staring out the window. A faraway look shared space on her face with a scant smile.

"It's kind of strange, huh? That this van arrived this morning with four people, and now we're leaving with only two," Addison remarked. Her words were somber, and in no way matched her slightly up tone.

"Yes, very strange," Aunt Evelyn responded, realizing that Addison had disconnected from reality.

Meanwhile, I was fighting to keep my emotions from shutting down. In a psychosomatic response, my body was numbing, so much that I felt like I was floating over my seat.

"Why is Aunt Evelyn just sitting there? We gotta get out of here," I said to James. He was quiet. He was so overcome with sorrow, he couldn't even grieve; he was well past that point. It was like he had pulled the pin on a grenade of misery, but would not—could not—let it go. We were just waiting for the inevitable explosion.

Not only James, but Aunt Evelyn, Addison, and Julie were all now in the throes of hell. Like bicycle spokes, all of this staggering pain branched out from me. I'd had one job: to take Catherine down. And I had failed. Miserably so. Hell, I'd all but gift wrapped and handed the knife over to her.

Aunt Evelyn finally cranked up her minivan and pressed hard on the gas. The van lurched forward and immediately accelerated toward the exit. James took up the rear. Our vehicles sped to the open gate, which was now unmanned. One of the protégés had killed the young guard effortlessly. Aunt Evelyn and James swerved to avoid running over his partially eaten body in the middle of the road. The only untouched part of his carcass was his heavily pomaded hair, which was still very much in place. No doubt the gate that had welcomed all would now become a heavily armed portal to a hermetically sealed compound.

I held on tight as the car fishtailed out of the reservation, leaving tire tracks in its wake. Trees whizzed by in a collage of green and brown blurs as James raced down the narrow backwoods road. It was eerily quiet, except for the calling songs of crickets and the popping of rocks and gravel hitting the wheel wells. The steadily rising temperature inside the car, generated by James's despair, was no match for the air conditioner. He had to keep wiping steam off the windshield so he could see. Not wanting to sound like a nag, I refrained from telling him simply to put the windows down.

The road and trees quickly receded to a single point behind us. The swirling smoke of the extinguished bonfire was eerie against the pinkish-gray sky. Despite James's previous instructions, I looked back. No one was chasing us. For a moment, I allowed myself to believe everything was okay. Twisting back around, I relaxed my shoulders and eased up, sliding comfortably down into the seat.

James was absorbed in getting me home safely, all the while trying and failing to block Adrian out of his mind. I figured I had to do something for him. After all, it was my fault he was in that state in the first place. I pondered my tremendously limited options as I looked at the back of Aunt Evelyn's minivan. James was tailgating, and I had to close my eyes to shut out the blinding glare of the red rear lights.

After turning over solutions to my quandary, the most obvious were the only ones available: get the knife, and kill Catherine. Duh.

Unfortunately, she sure as hell wasn't just going to hand it over. She was stronger now, and we had lost some of our team. The only thing that was certain was that between Catherine and me, one of us would be dead at end of this. Which one? Well, she had the upper hand now.

Fucking A! I wished there was a way to fast-forward past all of this shit.

James and I did not find it necessary to talk during the long ride home. Stone-faced, he kept his eyes on the road. The only time his expression changed was when we crossed over from the blackness of the woods to the bright lights of Massapequa. And that was only to squint at the fluorescent glow.

I gazed out the splotchy window, dirtied by splatted bugs and my greasy face. In it I caught my reflection superimposed against the backdrop of shopping centers, grocery stores, and gas stations streaking by. I touched my cheek, hardly recognizing myself. I looked so sad … old … put-upon.

Oh, God. What's happening to me?

Before I had time to mull that over, we arrived at Aunt Evelyn's house. Over the course of my life, this home had taken on many personifications. It had been an abode that evoked wonderment and joy while I was growing up. It was a place of solace after discovering my magical path. Then it became a house of horrors when I'd witnessed my first ritualized killing. Tonight it took on what would be its last incarnation: the seat of wretchedness. This house was now a sarcophagus that would contain all of our pain and dread. Not even James's love could prevent that.

He parked next to Aunt Evelyn. His body was rigid, and he kept his hands on the steering wheel for a while as if he were contemplating an escape plan for him and me. I watched his eyes moving about the way they did when he was having an internal dialogue. I knew it was the end of his conversation when he let go of the wheel and smirked a little; he must have determined there was no place for us to run to. He coaxed himself out of the car, and I watched that terribly sad man cross over to my side. He looked like he like he had been hit by a truck and was wracked with pain, but holding it in. I knew it was not a physical pain he suppressed, but a heartfelt one.

Aunt Evelyn and Addison took their time getting out of their minivan, too. Aunt Evelyn was obviously distraught. However, Addison had an odd, calmly indifferent attitude. We all avoided eye contact, ashamed of destroying the trust of Chief Weylen and our inability to stop Catherine. We walked to the house with the speed of turtles and snails.

I watched the others as they plodded along. Tonight they had been thrown too much to deal with at one time and had reached their limits. It frightened me some to see how they, my protectors, had been humbled. I was realizing they were not gods or perfect beings. They were just plain witches coping the best way they could.

Once inside, I couldn't help but notice how hollow-sounding the house was. Somehow it had become empty and devoid of life. The house, so desperate for any sign of liveliness, started sucking up all of what we had remaining. We went into a freefall of depression.

Aunt Evelyn meant to drop her keys in the bowl on the desk, but she missed it all together. The keys fell to the floor with a loud, jingling clank. In the emptiness of the foyer, it sounded like cymbals crashing in my ears. Aunt Evelyn didn't give a care about the keys, and left them right where they landed.

"Well, I guess that's that," she said. She shrugged her shoulders and raised her open palms like she wanted to say more, but did not have any words to give us. She simply walked away. The rest of them followed suit. They were islands breaking off and floating away from each other. They separated into different parts of the house to escape the extra burden of absorbing one another's pain; they had too much of their own to deal with.

James squeezed my hand and went up to my room. I noticed that Addison did not go to her room upstairs, but down to the basement.

I was left alone in the foyer. Although I hadn't a clue what to do for the others, I thought I was handling myself just fine. Then my face flushed and my stomach tightened. My eyes darted about, making sure the foyer wasn't closing in on me. My throat was parched, and I had to take large, dry gulps. I felt like I was being buried in the sand, confined and suffocated. A brick of incapacitating gloom had been thrown at me, and I had to dodge it. I needed an immediate distraction.

"Addison," I yelled. I started down the basement stairs slowly, because I didn't want to catch her in a private moment.

"Come on in," she said, sounding almost normal. In no way had I expected that, and I knew I had to watch her closely. After all, who knew what reaction would come out of her next? However, my main concern was that gloom brick that was still hurtling toward me. I had to get out of the way. I hurried down the remainder of those basement stairs, trying my best not to trip. The basement was still in disarray from Hurricane James. Piles of debris from his rampage littered the floor. I used my foot to push some rubbish to the side, and made my way over to Addison.

"I'm just going to pack up some of Adrian's stuff," she said. She was so nonchalant, like she was talking about getting him ready for summer camp. "I have to get it out of sight so James won't see it. Wouldn't want him to be more upset than he already is."

The thing was … Addison wasn't moving. She was just standing there, kind of smiling.

"No, we wouldn't," I said.

Addison looked at me, and her eyes perked up as if she had just remembered to do something. "Oh, please … help, won't you?"

One of the last things in the world I wanted to do was touch Adrian's shit. I wanted to be as far away as possible from anything even remotely related to him. But what could I say? No? No to a woman whose baby brother had died because of me? I couldn't think of a humane way to refuse her request, especially since she was so vulnerable and trying to carry on, albeit in a strange way.

"Sure, no problem," I said.

Apparently that was what it took for Addison to move. She drifted over to a paint-chipped, wooden, sliding closet. It was hard to shift, and she had to continually yank at the bulky door until it flung open. The interior of the closet was larger and deeper than the exterior gave away. Addison walked into the mouth of darkness, and disappeared into the black abyss. I could hear her foraging. Then a light came on.

"Don't just stand there. Grab some boxes. There's plenty in here," she chimed.

I entered the closet, which was filled with discarded Christmas ornaments, old books, tools still in their plastic sheaths, and a bonanza of brown boxes that were squashed and torn. That didn't seem to matter to Addison. She passed them off to me in assembly line fashion, and I tossed them to the middle of the basement.

Some landed on Adrian's bed. Each time a one hit that velveteen cover and brushed loudly over the top, I cringed.

Addison airily headed over to his suitcase next. She started taking out items of clothing and folding them neatly. "You can pick up his things from the floor," she said.

Awesome! I had the dubious honor of picking up Adrian's dirty drawers. I flinched with each pair of silk boxers I touched. All of them reeked of sleaze and left a slimy film on my hands. My teeth clenched so hard, I swore they started to crack.

"You okay over there?" Addison asked, not even looking my way.

"Sure. Cool as ever." I wanted to say to hell with it, but I knew I wasn't there for myself. I was helping Addison.

Taking some of Adrian's possessions off a low-hanging shelf he'd installed as a shrine to his narcissism, she wistfully reflected on each piece, sighing lightly with fond memories. She skimmed through a large stack of self-adoring photos Adrian had taken of himself. In some he was onstage in front of packs of swooning girls. Other photos featured his topless torso, taken with his cell phone in random bathroom mirrors. However, a somewhat sweet photograph was tucked inside that ode to self-love. It featured a candid shot of the three siblings, smiling and happy together on some ordinary day. It surprised me that Adrian could be that sentimental.

Addison let go a barely audible chuckle and went back to a box she had already halfway packed. I thought she was adding more to it. Instead, she pulled out a gray polo coated with Adrian's scent. She put it to her face, nuzzling and sniffing it. Then she turned to me, her face now a bit sad and definitely accusatory.

"I know he hurt you, and I'm …" her next word came out with difficulty, "*sorry* for that. But he wasn't all bad. He was my brother."

I could see it coming. *Wait for it. Wait for it.*

"His only real crime was loving you," Addison finished.

Boom.

I couldn't get how she could even allude to Adrian's nonexistent goodness. And if her definition of love was rape, well damn love. I wanted to scream at Addison, tell her what a fucking prick he really was. He was nothing more than a betrayer. Not only did he betray the witches, but he betrayed those who tried to help us. Many people died because of him.

But I didn't feel like getting into it with her, and kept my mouth shut. I just kept shoving Adrian's shit into boxes, and snatched the packing tape. The sticky sound as I snappily unrolled it agitated Addison even further.

"I'm sorry I was not sensitive to your plight." I could tell she wasn't sincere. Hell, she was actually mocking me.

I looked at her sideways as I tried to rip the packing tape with my hands. She handed me a pair of scissors with the blades pointed in my direction. I tried to take them, but she didn't let them go. We both held the scissors, engaging in a tug-of-war for a few seconds. Addison released the scissors while cocking her eyebrow a fraction.

"Thanks," I said, peeping at her, too.

"No problem. Anything to help you." Addison strode to the other side of the room, to Adrian's CD player. She put on a recording of one of his songs. Surely an attempt to make me feel guilty.

The music started, and I must admit if things had been different, I would have fallen under the trance of the surreal, haunting melody. The orchestration consisted of a hypnotizing twelve-tone atonality that had the ability to bewitch most people. Adrian's angelic voice came in so innocently. I squirmed, becoming more uncomfortable with each note and chord. I tried to put a force field around me to prevent Adrian's voice from entering. It didn't work, and I was violated a second time.

"He was so great," Addison said as her smile grew inordinately wide. She was trying to stop the pain from coming, but she gasped as the grief clutched and stilled her. She stared at me with a maddening mix of resentment, compassion, and sadness.

"You know, Adrian and I only volunteered for this because of James. We didn't want him to go it alone. We went against our family for you, and we lost everything. Do you think it was worth it?"

Her sorrow visibly emanated out of her in whirling, yellow tendrils that reached around the room, trying to latch on to me. One found its target. It was sharp, and my flesh burned at its very touch. I could see more tendrils coming at me. I was not about to stick around, getting poked and burned by a multitude of etheric octopus arms. Without even giving Addison a good-bye, I got the fuck out of there.

The tendril arms followed me up the basement steps. As soon as I entered the hall, I slammed the door behind me. I could see a faint yellow glow peeking from under the door and then receding back down to Addison.

Relieved that I'd dodged that psychic onslaught, I went straight to the kitchen to get some comfort from Aunt Evelyn. However, that voice inside of me advised against it. Of course I did not listen, and went in anyway. It didn't take long for me to figure out that something was up with Aunt Evelyn, too.

She didn't even notice I was there. She was intently going through cabinets, searching for something. Not finding it, she slammed the doors, each slam louder than the one preceding it. Stepping back, she saw what she wanted not in the cabinet, but on top of it. She got on chair, but it was too short; her arms could not reach. As she got off the chair, the thong of her flip-flop slipped from between her toes, causing her to almost fall off the chair. And that pissed her off. She threw her hands up, and with a magical swoosh flung a hodgepodge of cereal boxes off the top of the fridge. Then Aunt Evelyn swiped again, this time over the kitchen table. A plate Adrian had eaten off of flung against a wall, along with a cup Hari had drank out of. All of the cabinets opened, and pieces of ceramic tableware flew about the kitchen. Aunt Evelyn stood amid the jagged pieces. She was spent. She put her face in her hands and broke down in tears.

I quietly removed myself and went up upstairs, quite horrified by the way everyone around me was falling apart. At the same time, however, something wonderful was happening to me. I was growing physically stronger due to the infusion of blood from the young woman I'd cannibalized. With each step my spine straightened, making me walk taller and more square-shouldered. I felt like I could run a marathon and climb Mount Everest all in one day. I was a dichotomy. Emotionally I was hobbled by grief and guilt, but my body was enjoying the power and prowess gained from the shape-shifter's blood.

"What the fuck?" I said to myself. I felt like such a hypocrite. I had to get to James. He would know how to handle my predicament. He would tell me what to do.

I entered my bedroom filled with the expectation that James would make it all right. I knew he'd tell me it would be okay and only good would come out of this. He would tell me to take it easy; he'd handle it. Like he always did.

"James, something weird is happening to me," I said as soon as I got into the room. He was standing at the window with his hands in his pockets.

"What's wrong?" He didn't turn around.

I went to him and presented myself, programmed to get a hug. He still just stared out the window.

"James?"

He turned to me. He looked so lost. "Something's wrong, you said?" he asked as if he'd just caught on to what I'd told him.

I knew then that I could ask him for comfort, and he would try his best to give it to me, but he would fail because he needed his strength to come to terms with killing his brother. This was an extremely disturbing revelation to me—that there would be times when I couldn't even rely on James.

"Oh, nothing. Can I get you anything?" I asked.

He turned back to window. "No."

I walked out and closed the bedroom door behind me. I didn't know what to do or where to go, so I just stood at the door and looked down the hallway. I hoped Aunt Evelyn or Addison would snap out of their funks and come to my rescue. I waited and waited. No one came up those stairs. For the first time since all of this got started, I had no one to lean on. And I had absolutely no clue what to do next.

The number was thirty-three. Catherine and her minions had devoured thirty-three innocent men, women, and children that day.

Chief Weylen stood amidst dried pools of blood and bits of graying flesh. Body parts were strewn about the reservation in arrangements that almost seemed purposeful. The few whole corpses were collected in a collage of sheets from survivors' houses.

The injured were gathered up on makeshift stretchers and carried to a provisional triage. This was necessary, as they could not be taken to any mainstream hospital or clinic. Not only would the shape-shifters have to explain how they were injured, but there were the exams and blood work to be reckoned with. Those clinical tools would show that the wolves were in no way normal physiologically.

Chief Weylen had foreseen the need for medical care a long time ago and financed two young shape-shifters' medical-school educations. These doctors lived double lives. In one they were both prominent New York City physicians. In the other they were holistic medicine men for the tribe. The two doctors, despite the catastrophic injuries, worked adeptly to service the wounded. With the rest of the tribe acting as impromptu physicians' assistants, everyone dealt the best they could with missing limbs, massive blood loss, contusions, bruises, and broken bones.

The hours of caring for the infirm went well into the night. After they were all attended to, Chief Weylen and the elders prepared the dead for the next life. The chief took out an eagle's quill that had been passed down for centuries, and used only during times of death. After dipping it in ink, he wrote names in the Book of the Dead. He had never had to write more than one name at a time ... until now. The bodies were cleaned, anointed in essential oils, and dressed in traditional regalia. As the elders adorned the bodies, the common thought was how only ten protégés could kill so many.

Though the shape-shifters were Native American in descent, the origins of their lineage could be traced back to the original coven. Many of their burial practices reflected this. Thirty-three funeral pyres were surrounded by dazed family members. The fetid smell of gasoline emanating from the kindling did not bother them at all. A few young wolves brought Kaya's body over to the chief. She was dressed in a simple pink dress with a garland of baby's breath around her head. To the chief she looked like a napping flower girl. He was thankful her face had not been disfigured in the attack, and her injuries had been concentrated from the chest down. Kaya's beautiful face, so peaceful, would be his last remembrance of her. The chief fixed her hair and kissed her forehead. Before he became overwhelmed, he signaled to the young wolves to place her atop the pyre.

Duty called, and Chief Weylen steadied himself. His presence loomed large as he adroitly addressed the grieving crowd. The spirits were with him as he found just the right words to guide and support his people. As the tribe followed him in fervent prayer, the elder woman who'd given Grace the bracelet looked on. Being wise, she saw how her people's anger and hate boiled within them so strong it poisoned the air. She knew she had to do something to repair the damage done to their once-tranquil souls.

Julie stayed inside the chief's house for the duration of the ceremony. In no way could she could bear seeing Hari laid out like a butchered piece of meat. She watched her parents gripping each other as if they were facing a ferocious storm. Her mother wore her open-sored grief like a shroud for everyone to see. Her father, however, closed his up, knowing if he let his agony go, he'd die right there himself.

Each family selected someone to take up a torch. The chief was the last one. They all held the flames to the incendiary kindling under the corpses. Thirty-three fires blazed up, hauntingly illuminating the bodies' white coverings. The wails of women and usually strong men echoed throughout the clearing.

As the fires consumed the pyres, the once-bright linens wrapping the bodies changed colors: from stark white to spotty beige, to dark brown, to black. The red glow of the fires reflected off Chief Weylen's eyes as he breathed in the smell of incinerating flesh.

"Good-bye, Kaya, my love," he said with dying embers falling around his face.

The next morning, the reservation was a virtual ghost town. There were no children playing. No joyful, chattering adults sitting on porches. The birds couldn't even bring themselves to sing.

The elder woman opened her cottage door and was immediately struck by the morose atmosphere. She turned right back around and emerged from the house a half hour later. She carried a water bottle, a hand towel, and a small bucket of water. Trudging past the smoldering remains of the pyres, she headed toward the sweat lodge.

Though the lodge was primarily a male domain, the old woman had a rebellious streak. She had been breaking the traditionalist rules about women communing with the spirits in the lodge since her teens. The spirits that came through to her during trances gave her not only spiritual knowledge but scientific information. Outsiders were always amazed by how she had no formal schooling but was able to tackle problems like engineering, chemistry, math, and such.

Before entering the hut, the old woman smudged with sweet grass and left her slippers outside. She entered, and once she closed the flap, the area was nearly pitch black. The interior was lined with a tarp, and there were many ancient buffalo hides on the floor. The elder woman ducked down as she made her way to the altar space in the middle of the hut. She was mindful as she lit the twigs in the pit and heated the carefully selected stones. When they were red hot, she ladled the purified water from her bucket onto them, creating a remarkable sauna. It took her old bones a while to sit down, but once she did, she began to pray her way into a contemplative state, and finally into a total trance. As more and more steam rose from the stones, the ancient spirits awakened.

"Great spirits, I come to thee in great peril and distress. Our people have been attacked by the vilest of evil. Many have been lost."

The foggy condensation was aglow with crimson from the rocks. The figures of spirits snaked through the vapor, appearing and disappearing intermittently.

"My family is trying to deal with the horrible occurrence, but the thought of hateful vengeance is overtaking their minds. It will consume them and snuff out their goodness. Tell me what to do."

A humanoid form smoked out from the rocks. It was small and did not speak, but the old woman understood it all the same.

Later on that night, Chief Weylen mindlessly rocked in his favorite chair with a stiff, blank expression. The television was tuned to a cartoon on some kids' channel. He couldn't think of the name, and had always thought it such a silly show. Regardless, he had watched it so many times with Kaya. He looked over at her empty beanbag chair and imagined she was there watching it with him.

There was a weak knock on the door. In his dissociated state, the chief thought it came from the TV. After a few seconds, there was another knock, harder this time. This finally roused him. He slowly stood, as if he carried a weight of sadness across his back. He walked past Julie, who was staying with him. She stared out the window to where Hari's body had been cremated. She wanted to remain close to his ashes until they were cool enough to collect.

The chief knew it was wrong, but he hoped it was not a tribal member seeking council or comfort about what had happened at the bonfire. He had nothing to give anyone else. Opening the door, he was surprised and relieved it was the old woman. She had no immediate family affected by the massacre, so she would not need much.

"Evening, Chief. I don't mean to bother, but may I come in?" the elder woman asked.

The chief looked with confusion at the still-beading sweat on her brow. "What is this about?"

"I was concerned about our tribe, and spoke to the spirits on what to do. They have a message for you." The elder peeked around the chief at Julie. "And for her, too. You both cannot let evil turn you into scornful people. You have to allow peace to reign, and help the young woman named Grace."

The chief gave an unconvinced laugh. "Help those monsters? Did you not see what they did? They infiltrated us."

"Aberrant creatures attacked us. The visitors did not."

"If you are referring to the one called Grace, I beg to differ. She ate one of us."

"True. I had to overcome much opposition within myself to get past that. However, the spirits have told me she is true, despite what she did." The old woman pointed at Julie. "She has to go back to the witches."

The chief stepped onto the porch with the old woman. "Are you crazy? I won't let Julie go back into hell."

"The spirits said she has to go back. That is what she's has been fated to do. She plays an important part in this."

"You want me to send her back to the evil ones."

"She has to go back."

The chief crossed his arms. "And what if I refuse?"

"There will be a great judgment upon you. For not doing what is right. Opting for what was easy. The lazy path has always been being hateful and vengeful. You must overcome your human instincts and go to your higher ones."

Chief Weylen knew the old woman had been endowed with special spiritual power, and if she said it, it was right. Nevertheless, he still did not want to accept it. "They don't deserve our help. They were the ones who let those Ancients—those evil beings—into their bodies, so consumed with revenge they were. And this is the result of it. We and all the earth have to suffer the consequences of it."

"That is why it is so important for Julie to go back to them."

The chief looked at the piles of ashes that were once bodies in the clearing. "Kaya was all I had."

The old woman put her thin-skinned hand on his shoulder. "Let Julie go back. She has to. There is no other way."

"Julie is suffering at the loss of her brother. And with her strong will, she will balk at your request."

The elder woman smiled. "The spirits anticipated that. That's Julie's nature. You must understand that her pain goes deeper than her brother. Her love for Grace was strong, and she feels her friend left her behind, and now sees her only as a servant. Despite that, with prodding, Julie will go back."

The chief looked at Kaya's pyre. "I guess that's all then."

Throughout the night, not one hour passed that James did not shout out. And he only screamed one word: "Adrian!"

His oceanic rocking back and forth made me seasick in my own bed. Gathering my pillow and the comforter, I left James with the thin sheet. I tried to escape the room quietly, but he sat straight up and looked at me.

"Adrian?" he asked.

"No, honey. It's only me. Go back to sleep."

He grinned at me with half-closed eyes and put his head down. Fuck, that really creeped me out. I got out of there as quickly as I could.

The hallway was faintly lit with tiny wall lamps. I started toward the stairs, the lamps acting as guideposts. As I drew closer to the ritual room, I noticed James's bloody handprint was still on the door. Why hadn't I paid attention to it before? My first thought was simply to hurtle myself over the banister to avoid passing it, but I wasn't too sure of my skills as a trapeze artist.

"Just don't look at it," I told myself as I got closer to the door. I passed it with a little hop, landing in front of the door leading to the attic. *Whew.* I walked down the hall a little farther, but stopped. The pendant around my neck started to glow. Mother was calling me. I turned and gazed at the attic door.

It suddenly dawned on me that through all of this bullshit, one person had never showed up to help. No words of encouragement or sage advice, let alone protective influence. That absentee person was my mother, Ilan. My lip quivered as anger rose up in me.

Who the hell did Mother think she was? She was the one who had started all of this long ago, and I was owed some answers as to why she was MIA. I marched up the attic steps, making sure not to wake the others. I didn't want them to try to stop me from cussing her out.

The mirror was still uncovered from when I'd spoken to her for the first—and, might I mention, the last—time. I closed my eyes and tried to summon her. "Come on, Mother. Show yourself." I was being as cordial as my anger would allow me. But nothing happened. I rubbed the pendant, thinking that would help. "Where are you?" Still nothing. Now I was really pissed.

"I don't even know you all that well, but this is probably so typical. You fuck people over, disappear, and expect them to do your dirty work for you. Fine! Whatever." I ripped the pendant off my neck and threw it at the glass. The only thing I wanted was to destroy that mirror so Mother would never have any more influence on me.

I put all of the force I could muster behind a kick aimed directly at the center of the mirror. However, instead of breaking, the glass warped and liquefied. It looked like an aqueous wall of silver. When I tried to touch it, I was sucked into the mirror. My body compacted into a long cylinder the diameter of a pencil lead. And then I turned into pure light.

Like popping out of a vacuum, I arrived at what appeared to be the Valois castle garden, but it wasn't. I was surrounded by a hyper-real world. The colors were exceedingly exaggerated, with an intensity almost too great to bear. The ground was soft and cushy like condensed foam, but covered in the most-lush grass imaginable.

I was drawn to a narrow path that led into the woods. Deep inside there was a gazebo where a figure sat serenely, her back to me. I recognized her immediately as Mother and realized I was not on the Valois estate, but her personal realm. It existed somewhere between heaven and earth, life and death.

Though the sun was shining, diamond-like snowflakes fell. As I tried to storm over to let Mother have it, I saw the snow miraculously dissipating right above my head. None ever hit the ground.

"I've always loved the snow," Mother said in the softest voice.

I stood in wonder for only a brief moment, as I had a more pressing issue to take care of: getting some answers from my mother. However, the closer I got to her, the harder it became to walk. I looked down, and the grass was like green molasses sticking to the bottoms of my feet.

"What in the heck are you doing to me?" I asked.

Mother did not turn around. "The grass is a safeguard. I will not permit anyone, including you, to approach me in anger. I am not only your mother, I am a high priestess in the Valois court, and I will be treated as such."

Really? Now's the time you pick to power trip?

"Yes, ma'am," I said sarcastically. The grass turned back to blades, and I was allowed to regain my footing. As I walked toward Mother, she stood and turned to me—smiling, of course.

"I see you are angry, my dear."

"Angry? Naw. Things are really swell right now."

I waited for her to come down and at least give me a hug. She stayed rooted. "How do you like this place?"

"What are you talking about?" I wondered why we were discussing nonsensical stuff.

"My heaven. You're in it."

"Okay, so?"

"I created it. Don't you think it's beautiful?"

"I don't care about your heaven. I'm here to tell you about yourself. You lied to me."

Mother went on with her own conversation. "I created it like I created you. And what I create is beautiful and has purpose. And I didn't lie."

"Everything has gone wrong. You said you'd be there. Instead, you sit here in your storybook paradise. It was selfish and stupid for you to create me. You should have dealt with Catherine on your own. Putting it off on me wasn't fair."

"You were not only made for a mission. You were made out of love. You were always more than a golem."

Oh, here we go again. Some other shit I don't want to know about myself. I took the bait and asked anyway. "What's a golem?"

"A golem is a being made to serve its creator. You're more like a half golem. I needed something that had the potential to be more powerful than any of us natural-born witches could ever be. That's why I created you. That's why you are unique. That's why other witches are terrified of you, yet hate you at the same time."

All I could do was laugh and cry at the ridiculousness of all this.

"I know your confidence is low, but you can do this. You're the only one who can achieve the task. "

"How could you do this to me?" I asked.

"You will come to understand that sometimes being there means *not* being there."

What the fuck with the damn riddles?

Mother finally stepped off her gazebo, but she didn't look like she was coming over to give me a hug.

"There's something else. You have done a grave wrong that has endangered the mission. You fed on an innocent."

"You mean the shape-shifter girl?"

"We only eat in ritual, and we only eat those who deserve punishment. You fed like Catherine feeds. Now there is an imbalance that has caused the future to favor Catherine. You've weakened not only your chances of success, but the energy of those sent to help you. The scales are heavy on the side of evil."

"I was dying," I stated, totally exasperated.

"I am telling you the consequences. Catherine now has the knife, and on top of that, you ate like an animal. There is only one way to combat this."

"What? Feed more?"

"You can't just go feeding on people. Feeding is only to be used on rare occasions and always during ritual. In fact, too much feeding will cause your demise. You will have to become ingenious enough to find other ways to solve your problems."

"Okay, is there some book with all this information?"

"What I've discovered since I've been in this place is that witches never learn it all. Everything is on a need-to-know basis."

I couldn't be a bitch anymore. I had to get over myself and get on with the task. "How do I fix it? I'll do anything."

"You have to go see the Three Sisters. They have something you need and I can't give you. That's the only thing left to help you defeat Catherine."

Shit ... More fucking riddles.

The Three Sisters? No one had mentioned them to me before. "Who are they? What do they need to give me?"

Mother didn't answer my questions, but said, "And you must go alone. No Evelyn. No Addison. And especially no James."

Before I could ask—or rather demand—any more information, I felt a pull from my navel to my spine and was yanked backward through the dimensional warp. I reached out toward Mother, but she just waved good-bye.

"Wait! I need you. I can't do this alone. Not now. Please!" I pleaded.

I was thrown through the mirror like I was surfacing in a silver pool, and landed hard on my belly. "Next time tell me to buckle up."

The pendant was right under my face. It was still glowing lightly, but then it extinguished. Once again Mother had flashed in and out of my life.

When I opened the attic door, I could see the faint glimmer of dawn. I must have been up there for a few hours. As I stepped out into the hall, I heard something bumping around. The sound came from a bedroom. I figured Addison must have decided to forego sleeping on Adrian's bed and get in her own. Opening the door, I was met by Julie's glowering eyes.

My body went forward and back as I tried to decide whether to enter or retreat. "Uh … I didn't know you were here."

Julie looked away and continued going through her dresser drawers. I noticed she was still wearing what she'd had on at the bonfire. I didn't wait for her to welcome me in. If I had, the invitation never would have come.

"I'm sorry about Hari," I said.

Julie huffed. "Are you also sorry about eating my tribe?"

Aw, shit. Julie just had to start something. "I was dying. The girl was going to die anyway. I took a life that was already in the process of expiring."

"Another excuse," she stated, holding up two shirts in comparison.

"Julie, why are you here? I mean, if you've only come to rag on me—"

She dropped her arms. "I'm forced to be here, not only because of Ilan's magic, but also by request of the chief. He made me come back to help save your ass."

I tried to move closer to her, but she gave me a back-it-up look. "I am trying to make it right, and I do understand what you're going through," I told her.

"Understand? Really? How?"

"I lost someone, too."

Julie sucked in her cheeks. "Who? Your mother? I already know that. Remember, I was there risking my life for you. Just like now. But see, that happened when you were a baby, so her death didn't exactly rock your world." Downy fur started to pop out all over her body. "You still have your dad and your aunt … and your stupid fuck buddy, too. You came out aces on this one. You get to eat my family, fuck around, and shit all over your friends. All in the name of a mission."

I didn't get mad. Julie had just lost her brother and was venting. I would be an asshole to try to argue her down.

"I have lost everything because of you. When this is over, however it ends, I'm through with you." Julie said something under her breath. I couldn't exactly hear it, but it sounded a lot like "better hope I don't try to kill you myself."

"What can I do to make it right with you?" I asked, and I meant it. I not only wanted to get rid of my guilt, which I admit was selfish, but I wanted us to be right again. I was craving her. Not in some lustful, sexual way. I just needed her so badly. James was wonderful, but I missed what Julie and I had shared.

She smirked. "What can you do to make it right? Well, to start you can get the hell out."

I held up my hands to let her know I had no fight left in me. I wasn't going to resist her resentment or try to change it. "Bye, Julie." I went back into the hall, and she slammed the door behind my back. As I walked away, a shift in my outlook occurred.

No that bitch didn't.

Fuck being nice. Fuck being sensitive to Julie's feelings. I already said I was sorry, and now I was mighty damn tired of her melodramatics. There was a mission to accomplish, and I needed all of the help I could get.

Yeah, I ate the shape-shifter girl. And yes, Hari was dead, but it was time to move forward.

I wondered for a moment if I was just throwing my own little temper tantrum. Maybe it was James's blood in me. Maybe it was my Ancient spirit growing stronger. Whatever it was, I felt my guilt fading fast. I was no longer going to tolerate Julie's pouty crap. Damn that.

That decision was alarming and freeing at the same time.

Later on that morning, I relayed what my mother had told me to the rest. Aunt Evelyn squeezed her fists like she was holding a stress ball. "The Three Sisters? Are you sure Ilan said the Three Sisters?"

Addison, James, and even Julie looked alarmed. With the exception of Julie, everyone seemed to be coming out of the doldrums.

"The sisters? There is no way Ilan would send you to them. You must have heard her wrong," Addison said.

"I heard her just fine. Wow, these chicks have got you guys in a tizzy. Who are they?" I asked.

Aunt Evelyn looked at me through eyes that were bloodshot and swollen from crying all night. "We're not really sure *who* or *what* they are. They always were and always will be."

"Well, that cleared it up," I said.

"They're a tricky sort. Definitely beings you have to handle with care. All of their assistance comes with a price or a trick attached to it," Addison stated, like she was describing a horrible accident.

"Well, if Ilan said we should contact them, we must do it, and do it now." Aunt Evelyn went to a closet and dug around. Pulling out an old, dusty phone book that came straight from the '70s, she dropped the tome on the table. It was a directory for the greater Los Angeles area.

"What? A phone book? No magic ceremony to summon the Three Sisters?" I joked, making spooky hands.

Aunt Evelyn flipped through the pages. "Their number never changes. So there's no need to expend the energy."

I waited a moment before I told them the rest. "Mother also told me I have to go alone."

James's reaction was swift. "There is no way! The sisters are much too dangerous. We all know Grace's powers aren't strong enough. They fade in and out—and more out than in. Besides, all witches are aware of her presence, and you know they pretty much all want to do harm to her, both the good ones and the bad ones. It's like we're sending her to slaughter."

"We are at our wits' end. We've run out of options. If Ilan says she goes alone, there is nothing else we can do about it," Aunt Evelyn explained.

"Fuck that. I'm going," James said, and was about to head to the basement to pack.

Aunt Evelyn took his arm. "No, you're not. You can't jeopardize this. We have to trust. Ilan must see some sort of trap waiting for us if we all go. Or something even worse."

"I think we should have faith in Ilan's judgment," Addison stated. She looked at James and could tell he wasn't having it. "Please follow directions on this. I've already lost one brother. I don't aim to lose another."

He deferred to Aunt Evelyn. "I can't let her go. Grace is too important to risk. Too important to the world. Too important to me."

I stepped in. "Let me go. I have to. There is no other way. If I need help, I can always telephone or summon you guys. Okay?"

James rested his chin on top of my head. I waited for some long speech or plea not to go. Reluctantly, he said, "Okay."

As much as it was mourning time over at Aunt Evelyn's house, it was a time of celebration at Catherine's hideout.

She sat on a castaway sectional left behind by the previous tenants, savoring a bit of Grace's blood acquired from when the girl's abdomen was sliced open. The tip of Catherine's mucky tongue probed the blood. With every taste she gained the tiniest bit of Grace's magic. She discovered that her own profound powers grew threefold from what may have added up to less than a drop of blood.

Meanwhile, Tamara and Nick reveled in their own increases in power due to the ingestion of the shape-shifter's blood.

"Mistress Catherine, watch," Tamara said. She swooped behind Nick and picked him up. She twirled him over her head like a ballerina, purposely trying to punk him out to impress Catherine. Nick jumped out of her hands and growled at her.

"Nick, behave," Catherine demanded. She so loved playing puppet master.

Nick wiped down the front of his clothes to regain his composure. Giving Tamara the side-eye as he rolled up his sleeves, he bent down and pressed his pinky finger into the concrete floor. The surface indented under the tremendous concentrated force, and cracks spread out a few feet. He then pounded his fist down and caused the house to shake. A deep hole was left, as if a small meteor had crashed into it.

Catherine clapped. "Oh, my little pets! You are stupendous. That dog blood has made you unstoppable. You are the best protégés by far." Catherine waved Tamara and Nick over. "Come, come closer now." Her hands lowered as if instructing an audience to quiet down.

Tamara and Nick honored the request by sitting obediently on the floor. Both looked at their maker with adoring reverence. Catherine took center court. "Children, we are now in the final stages of our endeavor. This is an extremely tenuous time. Though they are weakened, the witches are anticipating an attack and are preparing for it. They know they are at a disadvantage if they come after me now, but engage me they must. I, on the other hand, want a confrontation *now* because I will most assuredly win. So we will force their hand. Make them come to our turf."

"How?" Tamara asked.

Catherine rubbed Tamara's head. "Throw a twist at them. I will send my two remarkable babies out, but I will not go."

"You won't go? Don't you have to get Grace?" Nick asked, cocking his head to the side.

Excited, Catherine threw her hands in the air. "Oh, you are an inquisitive fellow. All right, here is the plan!"

Chapter Twenty-Five

It's always darkest before it turns
absolutely pitch black.

—Paul Newman

Typically, at any airport, Arrivals is a happy place. Having been freed from the stale confines of the airplane's cabin, flight-weary passengers have achieved the goal of reaching their final destinations. Most likely, loving friends or family members will be there to greet them with open arms and smiling faces.

However, I wasn't at Arrivals; I was at Departures.

Departures at JFK International Airport was where bustling hoards of maniacs swarmed in a competitive, agitated state of desperation. Being the end of the school year, harried parents were forced to spend quality time with their miserable children, ranging in ages from wailing infants to smart-assed teens. Haughty business travelers acted as though they owned the airport as they callously plowed through the crowds to bum-rush the airport lounge and guzzle down their frequent flyer miles. Tourists and foreigners were lost puppies with mouths agape, wondering which way was up. The rest were thousands and thousands of solipsists who bumped and pushed, apparently not having the ability to perceive anyone else.

And I thought Catherine was hard to deal with.

The line for the first TSA checkpoint was long. James and I stood on the outside of the stanchion, allowing others to skip ahead. I stroked the retractable belt of the post in a futile attempt to stall getting on the plane.

James was trying to get more time in too, but he played it off by giving me directions about the trip. "Remember, be careful with the Three Sisters. They will give you what you came looking for, but always at some dangerous price."

"James, I don't even know what the hell I'm supposed to be getting."

"Yes, I know. All the more reason to use extreme caution." He paused. "I can't understand why Ilan is sending you there, and without help. It doesn't make any sense. She knows your magic is not up to par."

I couldn't sleep the previous night thinking the exact same thing. Why was Mother sending me to three women who were supposedly as bad as Catherine? Especially with my spastic powers and no backup?

"Have you ever met anyone who had contact with the Three Sisters?" I asked James, all the while trying to ignore the airport clock.

He looked up as he went through his extensive memory bank. "Well, no, I reckon. But I've heard enough about them to know to watch out."

That made me wonder. Maybe the witches had the Three Sisters pegged wrong. I mean, that had to be why Mother was sending me. And James just said he'd never met anyone who had been hurt by them.

"You said there's always a trick with their gifts. What exactly did you *hear* happened to the others?" I asked.

"Well, I guess what I know is hearsay. Urban legends. Rumors. Those who went to the Sisters got what they came for, but they returned in a terrible state—like they had a pseudo-stroke with total amnesia. Others didn't come back at all."

"Then why the fuck go to these crazy bitches?" I wondered loudly. People looked at me, and I spoke more softly. "Why even risk it?"

"If you and yours are in trouble, the Three Sisters are the last resort. They always seem to have the very thing you need. And whatever you need is so valuable, it's worth the risk. Plus, everyone thinks they'll be the one that won't get got."

"So Mother decides to send me."

"Because you're not like the others. Maybe Ilan believes you can come back with the prize unscathed."

"Or maybe the Three Sisters are just an urban legend like you said."

"I don't know about all that. If enough witches say there's trouble, something's got to be wrong."

James and I had taken too much time, and a kindly security officer in a blue sweater and a badge came over. "Excuse me. Who is flying today?" she asked with a sunny grin.

The uniform looked so official, I raised my hand like I was swearing in at court. "I am."

"Miss, you need to move it along then," the officer stated. She directed me to get in line.

My stomach tightened into a knot as I held back tears. No way was I going to let a bunch of strangers see me bawl. "Guess it's time."

James looked at me, thinking of ways to prevent me from getting on that plane. None came to mind. "Be on the lookout for other witches who want to do you harm." He kissed my waiting lips, and kind of sucked them when he pulled away. "I love you, hero."

I gave him a wink. "Back at you."

Our fingers slid apart, and I walked away before the next wave of flyers converged on the line. I heard James say, "Make sure you come back to me." I didn't turn around for fear I'd say "to hell with it" and run straight back into his arms. I could feel him watching me until I was out of sight.

I was nervous as I moved through the line with multiple S-turns. Not only because of the gravity of meeting the Three Sisters, but because of flying. The last time I'd been on a plane was before 2001, and I didn't have time now to learn about the new restrictions and guidelines. On top of that, I was notoriously known for having motion sickness. In anticipation of that, I kept biting the dry skin off my lip.

Apparently that made me look suspicious enough to catch the attention of a tense TSA agent. He watched from afar as I mimicked what the other passengers were doing. They took out their licenses; so did I. They had their itineraries at the ready; so did I.

The airport must have hired psychics, because another worker—a perceptive attendant at a podium—knew something was off with me. She never looked away from my face as I handed her my license and other information. She glared at me some, and glanced down at my ID. Something made her hold my license up against the lights, as if that would help anything. And it was embarrassing.

"Is there a problem?" I asked.

The podium attendant said, "No." I could tell she wasn't convinced my license was legit, but she had no reason to hold me back. "Okay, go on."

As I cleared the podium, I looked at all of the other people in line and wondered if any of them were witches, and, if so, if they would try to kill me on the spot. I started to perspire with nervous energy as I made my way to the TSA scanner. Again I copied the others and took off my shoes. They were smart or well-traveled enough to wear footwear that easily slipped on and off. I had on high tops, double knotted because the laces were too long. I had to hop on one foot as I tried to unlace each one, and nearly fell on my face more than once.

I finally was down to my stretched-out socks and thought it would be smooth going from there. Wrong. I was faced with all these gray bins, and realized I had to dump all of my shit in there. However, there was a problem: I couldn't be separated from my wand, and it was in my bag. I didn't know if the screener would see it as a weapon or some other kind of threat. What if they decided to search the bag? No one was to touch my wand except for me. I stood totally still for a moment, internally freaking out over what to do.

That was when a loud bitch behind me said, "Fuck, I hate flying with retards." With that I snapped back into reality and put my bag and shoes in a bin. Off they went on the conveyor.

"You have to put them in separate bins," an authoritative voice snarled.

With no time to look for the voice's origin, I raced back to the beginning of the conveyor, bouncing into whiney-ass people along the way. I separated my items and proceeded to go through the body scanner. I could no longer see my bag, and those few seconds seemed to last forever.

Emerging from the scanner, I found that my stuff was still in the X-ray ... and the conveyor had stopped. The screener was keyed in on my bag. She leaned in to the monitor; her eyes narrowed, and the corner of her mouth suspiciously rose. She waved someone over—a little woman with a nametag reading "VALEZ". It was plain to me that Ms. Valez had much attitude, and I didn't want to deal with her.

The closer Valez got to that monitor, the more I chewed the inside of my mouth. My eyes got large, and I started blinking hard. I concentrated, trying to change the outline of the wand's image to something else. The screener pointed at the monitor. Before Valez could look at it, my magic concealed the shape of my wand.

"Look at this. Tell me what you think," the screener said. Then she and Valez looked at the monitor. Only small containers of shampoo and lotion appeared in the bag. A perplexed look fell over the screener's face, but she shook it off immediately and started the conveyor again. However, Valez stared straight at me.

After I grabbed my shoes and bag, I could see her looking past but pointing at me. I glanced back and saw the lurking TSA agent nodding. Valez motioned to me.

"Ma'am, could you come here please?"

"Yes," I said.

"I have to check your bun."

"My bun?"

"Your hair."

Oh, yeah. I had put my hair up in a tiny bun on top of my head. I hadn't felt like washing it that morning, and just piled it up. Valez put on gloves and poked and prodded my dirty mess. I didn't have Snookie-type hair, and my bun was the size of a golf ball, so this should've been quick. However, Valez's spidey senses were activated just like the podium agent who had checked my license. Her thin lips disappeared as she spent an inordinate amount of time searching my hair.

Witch? Terrorist? Drug mule? I wondered which one she thought I was. I could understand how a person could confuse the three. *Snark.*

"So, where are you traveling to?" Valez asked.

"Los Angeles."

"What's in Los Angeles?" she asked, still poking at my hair.

Shit. I was being interrogated. Valez just knew I was up to no good, and she was determined to find out what my plans were.

I held my bag close to me. "I'm sorry. Did I do something wrong?"

"I'm going to have to pat you down. Do you agree?"

Okay, I'd dated Rafe long enough to know when someone was trying to pull a mind fuck on me, and Valez's question was a trick. If I refused, she would try to humiliate me or claim I must have had *something* to hide. I decided to play along, only because I wanted to get out of security as fast as I could. "Sure, whatever."

Valez snapped the cuff of her glove as if she were about to perform a rectal exam. "I will be using the backs of my hands to touch your crotch and buttocks."

Sure ... That makes having you all up in my stuff that much better.

"Fine."

Valez molested me twenty different ways and still found nothing. I tried to use my magic to get her off, but it flaked out on me. "May I go now?"

"No," she snapped. She wasn't near done yet. "Follow me." She called over to another TSA agent—an older gentleman who looked like every day was just a hindrance to his retirement.

"Swab her," Valez instructed him. Now, I admit, with my fear of flying and going to meet the notorious Three Sisters, I might have looked a bit intense, but come on now. Swabbing me?

The old man was burned out. He couldn't even fake interest as he instructed, "Put your palms forward, please." Valez stood to the side, salivating. And by some miracle, no explosives were found. Go figure.

Frustrated, and with much reluctance, Valez told me I could go. I hurried up and got the hell out of there before she changed her mind and decided to do a cavity search. She watched me as I headed toward the gate. Even though I was trying to save the human race, I would let Catherine eat the shit out of her ass.

As it happened, I was the second to last passenger to board, thanks to buying a ticket at the very last possible moment. This airline had no assigned seating, so I knew I would be stuck with a crappy seat.

The walk down the vibrating, claustrophobic jet way was already making me queasy. I was so glad to see the lithe flight attendant with the syrupy voice. Like a nodding robot, he said to each passenger, "Welcome aboard."

With a right turn, I faced a cabin filled to capacity and stretched my neck out to see how far back the line went. It didn't look like it had an ending. Like the jet way, the plane was vibrating under my feet. I started having visions of barf bags.

The movement of the line was stop and go through the tight-fitted fuselage. Every time we abruptly stopped, the erect penis of the man behind me stabbed me in the back.

After waiting patiently for the other passengers to force their luggage into the overhead compartments, I was saved from Mr. Penis as he disappeared somewhere on the plane. Finally, I found a place to sit two rows up from the rear restroom. My seatmate, a businessman sitting on the aisle, had his tray down for some quick work.

"Excuse me," I said, pointing at the other seat. He sucked his teeth and put up his tray, but he didn't stand up to let me pass. I had to squeeze by him, and accidently stepped on his foot. And he grouchfaced me.

Motherfucker, why didn't you just move in the first place?

The turbulent flight was everything I'd expected it to be—absolutely atrocious. My Dramamine kicked in too late, and I ended up monopolizing the toilet, chucking up in-flight peanuts and ginger ale. The few times I was at my seat, the businessman and I jockeyed for position over the armrest. I nearly had a panic attack due to feeling so out of control.

Never mind Catherine's evil ways. Hell, I wanted to kill her just for making me go through all this bullshit.

Landing couldn't come soon enough. After disembarking, I went to baggage claims, where I was to meet a driver sent by the Three Sisters. I looked through a sea of cardboard signs and caught sight of one with the initials GV on it. A young male held it up—a model type. I thought the sisters must have been hideous if they couldn't even come out in the light of day to pick me up.

I ended up in the backseat of a stretch limo headed up the 405, to a few blocks off Sunset going toward Holmby Hills. We went up winding, narrow canyon roads, passing other mysterious limousines along the way. From what I could tell, the neighborhood was populated by only gardeners and nannies.

The limo arrived at a black-gated entrance at the bottom of a hill. The property was surrounded by a brick wall that, along with bushy trees, hid it from prying eyes. The driver pressed the gate opener, and we entered the grounds. A gargantuan building loomed in the distance.

"Why is there a hotel in the middle of a residential neighborhood?" I asked.

"This is the house, mademoiselle. Welcome to Eternity Hill."

"Well, Goddamn."

He drove the car halfway around a graveled, circular drive that enwrapped a marble fountain, then parked directly in front of the castle-like manse, a celebration of Baroque architecture. The house featured a domed tower, with its central entrance three floors below. Grayish columns accented the otherwise flat-faced front. The house had no sharp edges, only rounded corners. The expansive landscaping looked more like a gigantic botanical maze than a yard.

The driver helped me out of the limo like I was royalty, even with my ratty suitcase.

"Here you go," I said, offering him a five-dollar tip.

"That is not necessary, mademoiselle." Instead of taking the money, he went up the grand stairs, and I followed him. He did not knock, but the door opened anyway. No person was present, just a hyper, young voice. "Oh, you made it!"

Seemingly out of nowhere, a platinum blonde appeared, sucking vigorously on a Dum Dum lollipop. From the smell I figured it was cream-soda flavored.

"You can take Grace's things upstairs," she instructed the driver, who took my suitcase. I held on to the bag that contained my wand.

The young woman appeared to be about twenty, but acted twelve. She wasn't shy about her body either. Her outfit consisted of a tight tank top, a plaid miniskirt, and knee socks. She was short, but stood average height on high, cork-heeled platforms. She was a real-life anime character. However, she had two distinguishing characteristics. First she looked to be about five months pregnant. Second she had something wrong with her left eye. It jumped all over the place. She grabbed me as though I were her long-lost friend.

"Ooh …welcome! We are so excited to meet you, Grace."

"Likewise … uh …"

The young woman hit herself on the forehead. "Oh, yeah. I didn't tell you my name. It's Sarine." She rubbed her belly. "This here's Lily."

"Nice to meet you, Sarine." I looked down at her pregged-out pooch. "You too, Lily."

Sarine had that weird, flirty-girl sashay. She exaggerated the up and down movements of her gait to make her ponytail swing from side to side. I thought it was dumb when girls did that, but from what I'd heard, Sarine was no ordinary girl. She was one of the Three Sisters. I kept a close watch on her as her large hoop earrings swung off the side of her face.

"Did you eat? I know that airport food is very expensive," she said.

"Just some peanuts and ginger ale."

"Well, come on now. I'll get you fed."

Man that Sarine didn't waste any time. I followed her through the house, which on the inside looked more like a church. There was what appeared to be belladonna in every corner. The checkered floor was a nice contrast to the grand, arched doorways. Electric stars dotted the walls throughout, while a replica of Michelangelo's *The Creation of Adam* adorned the ceiling.

Sarine looked over her shoulder like she was so thrilled to see me. However, I could only focus on her crazy eye. That damn thing was dancing.

"You can imagine how surprised we were to hear you were coming. Evelyn was so secretive. She said she you need something from us? For the life of me, I don't know what she's talking about." Sarine paused. "Your mother told you to come, didn't she?"

I didn't want to give her too much information, and braced up. "So are you and the father excited about the baby?"

"Father? Oh, I never talk to him."

A multitude of servants dipped in and out of rooms, and none of them looked at us. They were dressed in old-timey maid's outfits, with long, white aprons covering their black dresses. Black stockings and Mary Janes completed the look.

To the right of yet another arched entranceway was a sunken kitchen. It was a gourmet's delight, jam-packed with the latest and greatest in large and small appliances. As I rubbed my hand across the Electrolux stove, I gazed out of one big window. And when I say one big window, I mean the entire wall was a window that opened up to a courtyard.

Sarine, so unaffected by all the opulence, indifferently opened the fridge. She presented me with three white, paper-wrapped options straight from a professional butcher—free-range turkey, Virginia ham, and prime rib.

My mouth watered, and my fangs tipped out a little bit at the glorious smell of that meat. "All of it sounds so good. I don't know what to pick."

"Why not pick it all? A super-sub!"

Sarine made my sandwich. She set out the mustard and homemade mayonnaise along with heirloom tomatoes and watercress. She even put some gherkins and dirty potato chips on the side. This was served to me on some bone china that had to have been handed down from Mount Olympus.

I didn't even bother sitting before sinking my teeth into that sandwich. Mayo and mustard dripped luxuriously down my chin, and Sarine wiped them off of me.

"I know. It's good, right?" She went right back to the fridge and took out the components for her own California-chic salad.

"Where are the others?" I asked. I barely finished the question before I heard someone coming in, shuffling their feet.

"Speak of the devil. Here's my sister," Sarine stated. A morose female came into the kitchen, dressed in some sort of black smock and barefoot.

"This is my older sister, Clea," Sarine said, beaming.

Clea glared at me. Her head was shaved, with a little peach fuzz on top, and she was slightly overweight. She had perpetual dark circles under her eyes and a just-sucked-a-lemon expression. I figured she must have been adopted, since she was Asian. She too had eye issues like Sarine, but more profound. She had no left eye at all. No socket or anything. There was just smooth skin where an eye should've been.

With a mouthful of salad, Sarine instructed, "Clea, don't be rude. Say hi. This is the one who's causing all the fuss with the witches."

"Why is she eating all our food?" Clea asked. She went straight to the fridge and started taking account on how much was left.

Sarine shoo-shooed the situation. "Never mind Clea," she whispered to me. "She's just a big, old grumpy pants."

Meanwhile, Clea took out a permanent marker and drew lines on the milk and juice containers to mark how much was left.

I tried to blow off this way-too-obvious diss. "This house is huge. How many bedrooms do you have?"

Sarine put her finger to her cheek. She was mouthing numbers and having a hard time remembering. "I don't know. Twenty-two, I guess. Who counts?"

A piece of tomato fell from my sandwich to the spotless floor. Clea's one eye twitched really hard about that.

Sarine caught on. "Grace, why don't you have a seat in the nook?" She led me around a separating wall to the supposed breakfast nook. This space was large enough to house a twelve-seat dining room set. The table was adorned with two gigantic, feet-high vases and a damask runner. The tapestried chairs looked like seating for heads of state.

"Dude, seriously, you really eat here?" I asked. I so tried not to goo goo too much.

Sarine gave Clea a mischievous look. "All the time."

I sat on the end chair and took to finishing my sandwich. Sarine and Clea stood rather close to me and watched with intense interest. With every bite they looked fascinated, like I was some beast at the zoo.

To make them back up off me, I decided to rely on a social blooper. "So, how much is your mortgage?" I asked. This rude question most definitely would insult them, and they would storm away, leaving me and the sandwich to have some alone time.

However, Sarine took it in stride. "There is no mortgage. Daddy got the house for us a long, long, *long* time ago."

"Your daddy must have some hellacious money."

Sarine replied, "We guess you could say that."

I looked out the window at the gardener who was maintaining the courtyard's koi pond. "What's it like to be one of you?" I asked rhetorically as I also admired the ivy growing tall along the courtyard walls.

"It's lovely. Unlike witches, we don't *have to* get involved in human affairs. Ultimately, whatever happens to them is no never mind to us," Sarine answered.

My mind was reeling. One thing was certain: the Three Sisters were not witches. However, Sarine spoke as though they weren't all human either.

"So what exactly are you?" I asked, trying to act as blasé as possible.

"Well ..." Sarine said, "we are—"

Right then one of the maids rushed in. "Madame Gem is home," she said with a curtsy.

Clea and Sarine straightened up like devilish students do when the principal is coming.

"Time to meet Gem," Sarine stated. She offered me a linen napkin and wiped the side of her own mouth, indicating I had mustard crusted up on mine.

I followed Sarine and Clea to the den. We passed many Gustave Dore-like paintings that seemed to be telling a story. Unfortunately, we were in too much of a hurry for me to figure it out.

Sarine and Clea entered the massive den first.

"Dear sister, we're so glad you're back home," Clea said with adoration. Was this their sister or their ruler?

"Grace Valois is present," Clea finished. She stepped off to the side, and, with a move resembling a bear clawing, ushered me in.

The two-storied room smelled of fading incense with a barely noticeable undertone of charcoal. Walls of humongous cherry wood panels enclosed an elegant French Renaissance décor. There was no overhead lighting, just floor and table lamps delicately illuminating the room. I was hesitant to even put my nasty high tops on the expensive, room-sized Oriental rug.

Sarine nudged me. "This is going to be so good."

I moved deeper into the room, looking for this awful creature to jump out at me. However, the door to a dressing room opened and a tall, twiggish figure glided into view. The figure was backlit, and presented itself by dramatically putting both hands on the sides of the door frame. The figure's Kimono-sleeved dress made it look like a gigantic butterfly.

The figure then spoke with a beautiful soprano voice. "Well, hello there, darling!"

Sarine was tickled, and clasped her hands in front of her chest. "This is our elder sister, Gem."

Gem sauntered into the den, looking more like RuPaul's long-lost sister than Sarine and Clea's. This chick was fa-bu-lous and she knew it. I was expecting Molly Shannon to follow behind her saying, "Superstar!" Gem came at me, batting her long, fake eyelash. Yes, eyelash—singular. She too had left eye issues. She wore a rhinestone patch over hers. On top of that, Gem had a curly afro that boldly reached for the sky. Her thick, Fashion Fair foundation and rouge must have been put on with a putty knife. If she had tried to kiss me, her overly glossed lips would have slid right off my face.

"Well, let me have a look at you." Gem put her hands on her perfectly hour-glassed hips. "You are something else, aren't you?" She then grabbed my face and gave me a hard, pressing kiss on my forehead. "Let's have a drink, shall we?"

I took a seat on a chaise lounge with Gem's lip print on my head, and watched her pour various liquors into a cocktail shaker.

"I was quite surprised to hear from Evelyn. She sounded so desperate. How could I refuse her request to let you come to my home?" Gem added some bitters to the mix and shook it some more. "So, young lady, we are supposed to be taking care of you. That's very curious, don't you agree?"

"Uh-huh," I replied.

Gem poured the drinks and topped them with fresh orange slices. Sarine and Clea took theirs while Gem handed me mine. I hesitated to drink it. I didn't want to find myself in some filthy motel tub with my kidneys cut out.

"Baby, it's okay. I can only imagine what horrible things you've heard about us, but I'm not going to poison you. We are very honest, and very upfront in everything we do. Whether or not you take what we offer … Well, freewill, right?" Gem said. She then gave me a broad smile.

I sipped the drink, and it was delicious.

"Sweetie, for the life of me, I have no idea what I'm supposed to be giving you. Until we all figure that mystery out, let's enjoy each other." Gem sat down next to me with her legs tucked under her. The slit of her dress opened, exposing her thighs. I couldn't help but notice how her flesh looked like chocolate pudding.

Gem circled the rim of her glass with her slender finger and spoke in an offhanded way. "I'm sure my sisters have informed you that we typically don't get involved in witch affairs. We are only concerned with our own agenda. Your plight doesn't serve us one way or another unless your agenda benefits ours. However, if we do become involved, this is a barter system, so to speak. We give to you—you give to us."

I put my glass down. "Aunt Evelyn didn't mention anything about a trade. What exactly do you want?"

Sarine stifled an alcohol-induced burp and rubbed her round belly. I was about to ask if she should be drinking in her condition, but saw Clea's sour face glaring at me and decided to mind my own business.

"Evelyn didn't mention it," Sarine said, "because she didn't know. And the price is different for everyone."

"I need to call my aunt. Excuse me." I went to the corner of the room and tried to make a call on my cell. I just got some loud static.

Gem said, "The reception in this house is terrible. You can try later. Come back and sit down," Gem instructed.

"Do you have a phone I can use?" I asked.

Gem patted the couch insistently. "Come on and sit down," she said with a sweet, melodious voice.

Clea was still looking at me like she wanted to rip my head off. I didn't want to spook her, and decided to cooperate—for now. I sat back down next to Gem, who put both her hands gently on my shoulders.

"Do we frighten you?" she asked.

I was quiet.

"Back-fence talk. That's the price we pay for keeping to ourselves so much. When others describe you, they fill in gaps with faulty information," Gem murmured sadly, shaking her head.

"What about those who have been hurt or never come back after seeing you?"

Gem sighed. "Grace, have you ever met anyone who has experienced us directly? Better yet, can anyone produce proof that dealing with us does harm?"

Then I remembered what James had said. He'd admitted he had never known or even seen anyone who had dealt with the Three Sisters.

Gem continued, "I never tell anyone what to think. But now that you've met us, I think you're smart enough to form your own opinion."

Yeah, Gem used a dangerous amount of foundation, and her perfume was air pollution. However, at that point, I could not see what the hoopla was all about. But there was one thing that was irking me. "Your father? He must have been a very loving man to have adopted three girls."

"Adopted?" Clea interjected. "What do you mean adopted?"

"Uh, you're all so ..." I had to find the right word. "Different."

Gem laughed. "Oh, you are so extraordinary, and yet so handicapped by your limited human understanding. We are full-blooded sisters. Through and through."

I had to slurp down the rest of my drink on that one. "Okay, then could you tell me about your father?"

Gem put her drink down on the coffee table. "Well, he's serving a ridiculously long prison sentence. He was framed by his boss. Daddy worked for a highly profitable company and thought he could run it better. He rallied a few other employees, and this caused a mutiny. About one third of the staff left with all of the company secrets. Daddy gave the information away to lower-level employees, and that created much competition for his old boss. Next thing you know, Daddy is in jail for insider trading."

"That sucks," I said.

"He may be in jail, but he still runs things the best he can," Sarine explained.

Clea spoke up with passion. "We're going to break him out."

Gem looked around the room. "Luckily, he set us up rather nicely, didn't he? One of his last endeavors before he went to jail was in the music industry. In fact, we received a demo from Adrian once upon a time."

Ugh ... that name. Adrian. Again I couldn't escape him.

"We were very, very interested in Adrian. Just the type Daddy scouted for. Too bad he died," Gem said.

I changed the subject. "Do you get to see your father often? What jail is he in?" I thought I had overstepped my boundaries, but Sarine didn't have any problem answering.

"We see Daddy all the time," she said. She looked at her sisters, and they returned her gaze. "And the prison? It's really close by."

I could see from the Three Sisters' faces that this was some sort of inside joke.

The sisters set me up in a bedroom that was more like a deluxe suite. A California king bed was its centerpiece, raised on a round platform with a drapey canopy and peachy, satin sheets.

On an exquisite dresser lay a pure gold comb and brush set that I just had to try out. I took the brush and let the natural bristles run through a portion of my greasy tresses. Somehow, it cleaned that section of my hair, leaving it shiny and bouncy. "I'll be damned."

I fell into the bed and rolled around like a kid. I happened to go over a remote control; however, I didn't see a television. I pressed "ALL ON" and heard a buzzing sound. At the foot of the bed, a large-screen TV came out of a lift cabinet with one of those Maury Povich "who is the daddy?" shows playing.

"A girl could get used to this," I said, looking over to the empty pillow next to me. "James!" I instantly remembered that I hadn't spoken to him all day. Pulling out my cell phone, I tried to call again. An automated message said, "All circuits are down. Please try again later." I searched the room and found two phone jacks, but no phones.

Later I went downstairs to join the Three Sisters for hors d'oeuvres. I was good for a few hours, actually managing small talk, but speaking to James was foremost in my mind. "I don't mean to be rude, but do you have a phone I could use? I'm trying to call home and can't seem to do it on my cell."

Clea and Sarine gave me "don't look at me" looks and turned their heads to nibble quietly on their brie and rye crackers.

Gem pleasantly answered for all of them, "The house phone is strictly for business use only. That's how Evelyn was able to get through … Your being here … well, that's business."

"I don't mind paying the long-distance fee."

"That's not it. Again, the house phone is for business only," Gem said with more light in her voice.

Frustrated, I reached for my wine and ended up knocking the glass over. The liquid flowed to the floor and seeped under a potted plant. "You guys must really have a thing for this. Belladonna isn't it?" I asked as a maid wiped up my mess.

"Look closely at the tips of its leaves. Notice the pricks? This is not quite belladonna, although it strongly resembles it," Gem said, stroking one of the plant's branches. "It happens to be one of the few plants Daddy managed to bring over from our old home. It is a deadly plant that can strip a witch of all of his powers, leaving him exposed to the possibility of death. We are the only ones on earth who have it."

At that moment, the pendant around my neck glowed a little and faded out. It dawned on me that the plant was what I'd come for. That was what the Three Sisters had to give me.

Gem noticed my pendant. "What is going on with your necklace?"

"Oh, my necklace?" I muttered, quickly changing my body position.

"Yes, it lit up."

"No, it was the light from the lamp glinting off of it." I moved to allow the lamp's light to reflect off my pendant in such a way it looked like it glowed.

"Hmmm." Instantly, Gem went right back to her vivacious self.

"May I have some of your plant?" I asked abruptly.

"Absolutely … *not*," said Clea. "It is for our use only."

Gem chimed in, "Besides, you don't want to deal with that. Witches have to handle it with extreme care. Just one prick of its thorns and your powers are zapped. Plus, enough of that venom and you're dead."

The next morning found me completely bleary-eyed. I did not sleep at all that night. Thoughts of James consumed me.

Gem and Sarine, meanwhile, breezed down the stairs with sullen Clea following close behind. Sarine ran up and gave me a tight hug. "We're going out today. To show you the town and go shopping!" she squealed.

"Yay! Can't hardly wait," I said with fake enthusiasm. The only things on my mind were getting to a phone and snatching up some of that mock belladonna.

Sarine looked at my attire and shook her head. "No, no. This will never do. Come with me." She took my hand, and the next thing I knew, I was sitting in a makeup chair in their in-house beauty salon. Sarine brought over what appeared to be an overnight bag. She opened it, and it was filled with eye shadows, blushes, and lipsticks of all kinds.

"You have a cool undertone," she said, holding a magnifying mirror up to my face. Immediately she dumped a shitload of makeup on me in an attempt to make a carbon copy of herself. As I looked in the mirror—thinking I looked like Bozo—Sarine was busy in the closet picking out clothes. She found some, and wound up dressing me like a sexy schoolgirl; I even had ribbons in my hair. Because I had a plan, I did not make a fuss, and gave superficial approval.

Later I stood outside with the Three Sisters, waiting for the driver to bring the car around. Gem, Sarine, and I looked like Pretty Women, while Clea was a total emo. The car arrived and the good-looking driver assisted all of us in. He avoided all the major traffic, and we ended up in an exclusive retail spot. The Three Sisters treated me to a lavish shopping spree at Maxfield and a hoity-toity lunch at Katsuya. I had to admit, I was having a pretty damn good time. However, I still wanted to make that call.

"I need to make a trip to the ladies' room. If you will excuse me?" I said, standing up from my plate of sashimi.

Sarine backed up her chair. "You want me to come with you?"

"No, no. A girl needs her privacy," I replied while trying to walk away.

Gem raised her glass of port. "I'll drink to that."

I pretended to go to the restroom, but made a detour to the hostess. "Do you have a phone I could use?"

Without looking up from her seating chart, she pointed me in the direction of a phone. I hurried to it and dialed James's number with lightning speed. However, I just got a dial tone. I tried again with the same result.

A fancy-pants woman was going into the restroom. I figured she was my last chance. I ducked behind plants and booths to prevent the Three Sisters from noticing I had not gone to the restroom in the first place.

I must have terrified the woman—as soon as I got into the bathroom, I was on her. "Please, I don't have much time, but may I use your phone?"

She handed it to me like I was about to jack her for it. I dialed not only James, but Addison, Aunt Evelyn, and Julie too. I couldn't get through to any of them. "Thanks," I said quickly, handing the phone back over. As soon as I left the bathroom, I could hear her say, "What the fuck was that all about?" I gathered myself and returned to the table as if nothing happened.

After we left the restaurant, the Three Sisters informed me they had some business to attend to, and allowed me to tag along. We ended up at Rumyel Records, the biggest label in the industry. The sisters had a meeting with a flamboyant music executive who did a lot of reality TV hosting on the side. I couldn't believe I was really meeting him. He was not impressed by me at all. Go figure.

The exec was asking Gem for more money to produce his new act, a sixteen-year-old girl who gyrated around like she was working a pole. I vaguely knew who they were talking about until Gem demanded the young act be trotted out. I recognized the singer instantly from her dollar-sign tramp stamp.

"Hey, y'all," the singer said.

Gem had one question: "Has she been schooled on the nuances of our business?"

The exec replied, "Yes. She will do anything to make it big."

"I guess you will have your money then. I'll have accounting set that up immediately." Gem put her face extremely close to the singer's. "I'll even throw in a nice advance for you. Do you realize what team you're playing for?"

The singer nodded.

Sarine, Clea, and I followed Gem into a small room that contained only a desk.

"Grace, would you be a dear and come here?" Gem asked me.

I went over, and she handed me what looked like a black Rubik's cube. "No one in the world has been able to open this. Can you try?"

I could never solve one of those things, but figured what the heck. "Sure, why not?" I said.

After a few twists and turns, one of the middle squares slid out. I put the cube down, thinking I'd broken it. "I'm so sorry. I can buy you another one."

The whole room was dead quiet. Inside the square was a key. Gem immediately took it. "You really are something special. No one has been able to open that. Not since Daddy went to jail."

James paced back and forth. He hadn't heard from Grace in days, and had been trying desperately to contact her. He looked in the phone book for the Three Sisters' number, but it had somehow disappeared.

Aunt Evelyn saw how antsy not only James was, but the others, too. "We're going out for dinner," she said. The others grumbled at that proposition. "I insist. No need to sit around here like old fuddy-duddies. Get your shoes on and let's go."

After much protesting, the witches and Julie were ready. James pulled Aunt Evelyn aside. "I've been trying to call Grace, but I can't reach her. What's going on?" he asked.

"Things must be rigged so we can't interfere. That's the only thing I can think of," Aunt Evelyn said. James blew out his breath hard. "We have to have faith that Grace will be fine."

James exited to the porch with Addison. Julie followed, but stopped in her tracks. She looked around the porch and fixed her gaze on one spot.

Addison, who was already at the minivan, glanced back at her. "James, notice how Julie is just staring out into space? What's wrong with her?"

James, who was more concerned about Grace, shrugged his shoulders. "How would I know?"

Julie stood a few feet away from the screen door, which was taking its sweet time closing. She reached out at the air as if she were grasping at something. When her hand came back empty, she thought her imagination had gotten the best of her, and she headed to the minivan.

Little did Julie know that as the screen door slowly closed, something invisible had made its way into the house.

Aunt Evelyn was on her way out and didn't notice anything. By that time the screen door had closed, and she flung it back open. Taking in a deep breath, she said, "Smell that fresh air." She then trotted over to the minivan and got in.

It was a pleasant day for the witches and Julie. After a few gleeful hours, they returned home with smiles, their spirits feeling much lighter. When everyone got out of the minivan, Aunt Evelyn put her arms around Julie to let her know all was forgiven between them. Julie reciprocated.

Addison was eating right out of her Styrofoam takeout container filled with leftover steak and potatoes. She handed a sporkful of meat over to James, but he refused. He was still thinking about Grace, and had hardly touched his own dinner.

"Today was a good day," Aunt Evelyn said. The others agreed and went off to their rooms for the night—clueless that death was waiting for them.

The stroke of midnight came fast. Addison was in a relatively deep sleep when she heard a thud in her room. She pulled up her eye mask and scanned the darkness. When she didn't see anything, she closed her eyes. Something in the room thudded again.

"Julie, is that you?"

However, Julie was asleep on the couch downstairs. Addison heard something shuffle from one side of the room to the other. She fumbled with the lamp, but just coming out of sleep made her clumsy, and the lamp fell to the rug. Addison immediately perked up. She swiped her hand, causing the room to haze over with light. Climbing out of bed, she held up her hand, ready to perform defensive magic.

Nick was behind her. Catherine's newly enhanced magic allowed her to cast a very powerful invisibility spell over him and Tamara. It was so powerful that not even Addison could detect him. As she walked through the darkness, his body materialized. With his powerful hand, he grabbed her from behind, and with a clean, swift swipe, slit her throat from ear to ear. He let her body slide down his as her blood squirted onto the wall. Not wanting to let fresh meat go to waste, Nick ate some of her.

Aunt Evelyn was awakened by Addison's body hitting the floor. "What in the world?" She put on her robe and slippers and went to investigate. In the hall, she listened hard for more noise. She noticed that with every step she took, there was another one that echoed it. And it didn't belong to her. Aunt Evelyn turned around with magic hands ready to go. However, there was only darkness behind her. She turned back around and ran right into Tamara and a baseball bat. The bat immediately struck Aunt Evelyn in the head, cracking her skull and knocking her out.

Julie startled out of sleep. Her internal alarm screamed that Grace's life was *about* to be in danger. She jumped up and transformed into the shape-shifter, but what could she do? Grace was so far away.

Then Nick jumped out of the darkness and pounced on Julie. Their bumping around woke up James. Without even thinking, he ran up the stairs as if he had never been asleep. He jumped into the fight, with Tamara joining in, too.

Meanwhile in Los Angeles, I was snooping around Eternity Hill. I was determined to find Gem's phone. I snuck into the den—with my wand, just in case something went down. It was so dark I had to wipe the walls looking for a light switch. Unfortunately, I could not find one. I felt my way to the middle of the room, bumping into all the furniture in my path.

I found a lamp and twisted on the switch. "Okay, if I were Gem, where would I keep my phone?"

Gem was such a strange character, though, it seemed that a logical line of thinking would not work. I walked along the walls and finally saw a white telephone cord. "Bingo!" I rushed over and followed the cord all the way to its plug. Of course there was no phone at the end of it ... just another dead end.

Exasperated, I leaned against a wall panel and accidently fell through. A gush of cold wind chilled my skin. I had stumbled into a hidden chamber.

I thought, *You know, you really shouldn't go in there.* But since when did I take anyone's advice, including my own? I stepped inside a black, candlelit corridor. The deeper I went, the more it smelled like the spray of a skunk. I covered my nose as I made my way to a door. "Go back! Go back now. Pretend you didn't see any of this," my intuition screamed.

"Shut up," I told my inner voice.

Opening the door, I went in a few steps. I didn't get too far before I saw the preserved bodies of those rumored missing witches who'd had dealings with the Three Sisters before. I ran backward out of the chamber in horror. Stunned and disoriented, I stumbled onto what appeared to be a burial chamber. In it stood a solitary coffin, and something was moving in it. I looked above the coffin and saw another painting—one of William Blake's *Paradise Lost* illustrations. And it hit me. Lucifer was in that coffin.

"Daddy posed for that personally," Gem explained as she came up behind me. The other two sisters followed her.

"Who are you?" I asked. My wand was ready to go.

"I told you she was slow on the uptake. Our father is Lucifer, and we are his fallen angels," Clea snapped.

"Daddy was sentenced to one thousand years in prison for asserting his individuality and giving humans choices. What's so bad about that?" Sarine said.

I realized that the entire house *was* the prison. Lucifer was trapped in that coffin, and that smell was not a skunk, but brimstone.

Gem approached me like a buddy. "Grace, we know a heavy burden has been put upon you. It need not be that way. You really don't want to fight Catherine. You want to be free—free of a destiny not of your choosing. You want a life with no pain. No suffering. No sorrow. Bliss … It can be yours right now. We can give it to you. Let us give it to you. All you have to do is make a choice."

I did want bliss. I did want to be free. And I found myself tempted.

Sarine came over and spoke, too. "Even though Daddy is in jail, this is still his world. The humans always choose him. We influence them through food, drugs, sex, war, politics, but mostly through music."

"Daddy is the Prince of the Air," Clea added. "The air*waves*, that is. You can embed the air with anything you want. The human mind is extremely malleable, but rarely in the direction that benefits all. Really, humans have never wanted to be good. They like being bad."

"When you opened that puzzle cube and rescued the key to get Daddy out, we knew you'd be an excellent addition to our team. Join us, and you can have everything. See, we can't use the key ourselves. It won't open the lock for us. We need you to do it," Gem stated.

"And if I don't?" I said, getting my right mind back.

"You did come for *something*. We ascertained that it must be the plant. Well, we just won't give it to you. Plus, we can't let you leave knowing our secret. Remember, there is a trade. Either join us, or lose your mind or your life."

"I won't be one of you, and I don't choose either of the other options," I said. Then, in a flash, I whipped out my wand and hit each sister with a blaze of fire. Grabbing the key, I ran out of that pit and straight into the hall. As I looked at the paintings, I understood the story they told was of Lucifer's fall in the Book of Revelation.

The Three Sisters put the fires out and transformed into human-like jackals with wings, and flew after me. I knew I had to get two things: the plant and the limo's keys. I booked it through that labyrinth of a house, taking my chances on getting pricked with the plant as I grabbed as much as I could. I must've done it right, because I didn't get as much as a scratch.

I finally made it to the garage, where three stretch limos were stored. I grabbed a set of keys and tried the first car. No go. I could hear the jackals tearing up the house and screaming like banshees as they looked for me. I tried to calm myself as I put the key in the lock of car number two. That didn't work either. And the shrieking of the Three Sisters was getting closer.

Car number three was my last hope. "Oh, God, please let it work," I begged. I put the key in the lock, and it turned. Quickly opening the door, I tossed in my wand and the plant. I put the key in the ignition and turned on the car. There was no time to let up the garage door, so I put the limo in reverse and floored it. The door shattered into a million pieces as the car screeched out of it. I put the gear in "D" and burned rubber down the driveway.

The jackals flew out of the obliterated garage door and caught up with me. With large talons, they ripped metal off the car's frame. One of the jackals flew right next to the driver's-side window. She kept ramming it with her massive body. The window cracked, and I nearly rolled over as the limo careened down the canyon hill.

I was now out of Holmby Hills and on a main road. Because it was the middle of the night on a weekday, there was—thankfully—no traffic. I glanced down at the speedometer—eighty-two on a city street. And I sure as hell didn't bother with red lights.

The jackals then started to tear at the tires. I made a sharp turn to shake them off, and only succeeded in tilting the limo on two wheels. After it fell back onto all fours, one tire blew out, and I briefly lost control, swerving onto the sidewalk. I took out a mailbox and a newspaper container.

After a considerable distance, one of the jackals finally pulled the rest of the roof off the car, which meant the limo had lost most of its body. She grabbed my shoulders with her claws and was about to pull me out of the speeding car like an eagle capturing its prey. That was until the car crossed out of the Los Angeles city limits. The jackals bounced backward like they had flown into an unseen wall. I braked hard and looked back.

The sister-jackals were squealing and trying to break some sort of force field they could not cross. I took the opportunity to escape, and drove away as quickly as I could in that wreck of a car.

After a few miles, the three-tired limo sputtered out on me. I pulled over, hoping the Three Sisters hadn't escaped their boundary. I tried to call home, and again I couldn't get through.

I got out of the car and looked for a safe place to spend the night. This was no easy task, because I had apparently ended up on Skid Row. I had no ID or even cash for an hourly rate motel, so I had to make due in an abandoned tunnel. Using my nose, I searched for a spot that wasn't saturated in piss or diarrhea. I found a discarded paper bag and wrapped the plant, making sure the pricks didn't stick me. I set it behind me, and after keeping watch for a couple of hours, I fell asleep.

The next morning I woke up with a homeless guy sleeping on my lap. I pushed the sewer-smelling man off me.

"Hey, what's the matter with you?" he said as if I had fucked up. I checked for my wand; it was still hidden in my waistband. *He had better be glad, too.*

I walked out of the tunnel, blocking my eyes from the intense morning light, and climbed up to the street. With the plant in one hand, I hitchhiked with the other. After a few motorists stopped to ask how much I was selling my flowers for, a semi stopped for me. The truck driver was a middle-aged woman with a Buddha belly.

"Hey, I'm Nellie. Where you headed?" she asked cheerfully.

"East … to New York."

"I'm not going to New York, but I am headed east. You can go as far as I can take you."

"Sounds good."

I hopped into the truck and felt oddly calm with Nellie. "Do I know you?" I asked.

"No, but I know you. I'm a witch."

I backed up. James had told me that all witches, good and bad, wanted to kill me.

Nellie laughed. "Don't worry. I'm not going to hurt you. I always thought Ilan was right with what she had done. I never thought I'd be picking up a legend like you. Not in my lifetime." She glanced at me. "You look like you've been in a fight."

"I have. Ever heard of the Three Sisters?"

Nellie shuddered. "Yup. No one ever gets away from them. You must be very lucky."

"Yeah, I guess. They were chasing me, but something stopped them, like they got stuck behind a wall."

"I drive this route all the time, and from what I can gather, they are confined to the limits of Los Angeles. I don't know why. Maybe another witch can answer that. I dropped out of the witch life a while back. Too much for my nerves. I live a low-profile, mortal life now. Start talking witch stuff and bad things start to happen."

I took that as my cue to stop talking about the Three Sisters. As I watched Nellie handle the big rig, it dawned on me why Mother had sent me to LA. I had to get the plant. But, more importantly, I had to learn independence. I would need to have confidence in my own skill if I were to defeat Catherine.

A car passed by, and a little boy in the backseat gave Nellie the "honk the horn" gesture. She gladly pulled the chain, and the horn blared. We were now far away from Los Angeles—the City of Angels.

However, no one ever specified what kind of angels they were.

Chapter Twenty-Six

God grant me the serenity to accept the things I cannot change, the courage to change the things I can, and the wisdom to know the difference.

—Reinhold Niebuhr

I was on the last leg of my hitchhiking trek across the country, and my current driver was Mandy. Though I deeply appreciated the ride, I was not enthused over the suffocating vapors emanating from her three-to-a-pack, strawberry-scented air freshener. I watched it dangle off the rearview mirror and wondered why a strawberry air freshener was shaped like a leaf.

"I hate to be nosy, but you never said why you're hitchhiking," Mandy said, bobbing her head to some Maroon 5. She had been asking me in roundabout ways about how I'd ended up on Interstate 80, in the middle of nowhere, with my thumb in the air.

"It's a long story. You wouldn't be interested," I answered, trying to tune her out.

"We've got at least two more hours to go. Plenty of time for you to spill your secrets." She followed that up with an involuntary, bizarre laugh that sounded like a giant tortoise having sex.

Suddenly, I totally got why Mandy was trying so hard to engage me. She was an extremely lonely girl who'd do anything for any sort of human contact. I figured she must have had a mild form of Tourette's syndrome, judging from the way her mouth twitched. She also had to keep an industrial-sized jar of cream in the car for her psoriasis, which left her with large, silvery-white patches all over her body—particularly on her hands. Ever since she'd picked me up on the outskirts of Chicago, I'd been forced to slather the gloppy cream on her exposed areas. That way we wouldn't have to waste time pulling over so she could do it herself. Gross.

I sat there, still trying to wipe that greasy shit on to my dirty pants. Out of the corner of my eye, I could see Mandy looking back and forth between the road and me.

"Well?" she asked.

Once again, I answered obliquely about my life situation.

And once again Mandy wasn't satisfied, and wanted to probe even deeper. "Maybe you'll feel more open if I tell you about me?"

Aw, Goddamn. Mandy had already told me about herself ... the same story four dozen times. Here was the abbreviated rundown: She was an only child, an accidental conception for parents who had never wanted kids in the first place. And they let her know it. She'd never had a boyfriend, and channeled all of her energy into her schoolwork, which had allowed her to graduate high school and college early. She'd driven to Chicago for an internship, but they'd thought she was not enough of a people person and sent her back home. And she'd even had the nerve to throw in a few catty comments about my needing a shower. Mind you, I had been hitchhiking for the past three days. Now, was there any more to Mandy? I don't think so. However, if she unzipped her pants and pulled out a surprise dick ... Now that would have been something to talk about.

Under different circumstances I would have felt guilty about my malicious thoughts, but I knew Mandy's picking me up was not an entirely charitable gesture. She believed her supposed act of generosity toward me would pay off in a reciprocal relationship. She was so desperate for companionship she'd go oven shopping with Gil Valle as long as he promised to call later.

So, after fifty years—I mean two hours—Mandy and I finally arrived in Massapequa. I gave her directions to the main road adjacent to Aunt Evelyn's driveway. No way was I letting Mandy come near the actual house.

"You know, I don't live too far away from here. I can come by anytime and hang out," she said.

I looked at the nonexistent watch on my wrist. "Ooh, it's getting late. You'd better hurry and drop me off so you can get to *your* house ... like *really* fast. You don't even have to stop the car. I'll jump out."

Mandy let out that atrocious laugh again. "Grace, you're so funny."

"Yeah, heh heh."

Mandy did deliver me to my destination—the entrance of Aunt Evelyn's driveway. To my chagrin she stopped the car to let me out instead of keeping it moving as I'd suggested. This led to an uncomfortable good-bye.

"You actually live here? I heard about this place. Supposed to be real witchy," Mandy said, scoping out the property.

At first I thought Mandy had outed me, but I looked at her clueless face and realized she was still none the wiser. However, she reached into her console and pulled out an anti-Halloween booklet from her church. It was titled *Exodus 22:18*. She handed it to me.

"We just had them printed up and will be distributing them in October," Mandy explained.

I skimmed through the booklet. The narrative and scary pictures featured a defiant little girl who decided to go trick-or-treating and ended up in hell instead.

"Gee, thanks for the gift. You shouldn't have. Really," I said.

"I've got an idea. You can tag along with me as I hand them out. It's easy. Just put them under windshield wipers."

I hopped out of that car in one seamless sweep. "Gotta go."

"Hey, give me your phone number."

"I don't mean to be cold, but no," I said while blocking out her clinging-crab energy.

"But I gave you a ride," Mandy protested.

The last thing I needed was a zealous stalker with a girl crush. Plus her associating with me would put her life in peril, and I did not want to be held accountable for that. My response had to be swift, leaving nothing to misconstrue. I had to be cruel to be kind.

"Mandy, let me make myself perfectly clear. I'm sure you'll make a wonderful pal for someone else. But you and me? It ain't gonna happen. We don't have anything in common, and quite frankly, I can't even stand to hear you breathe. You have as much chance of being my buddy as an apple has of turning into an orange. Therefore, disappear."

Mandy didn't get it. Filled with delusional, codependent hope, she stated, "But with grafting and gene splicing, an apple *can* become an orange."

A slow, inarticulate groan slipped out of me, and I turned my back on her. However, she didn't drive off, and was still making plans for our future together. "I'll see you later," she said cheerily.

Mandy was becoming a ridiculous memory as I scampered toward my reunion with James. Abstinence was not my friend, and my body had been craving his touch ever since I'd left.

Aside from hearing Mandy's car creep away, I was glad to be back in the stillness and solitude of the country. And I was amazed that the plant was still as fresh and vibrant as it had been when I'd stole it from the Three Sisters.

I traipsed down the driveway, relishing the utter peace and quiet, but as I got closer to Aunt Evelyn's house, I was struck by how *something* was off—way off. Everything was too quiet. No squawking birds. No chirping insects. Not even the rustling of the wind. I walked faster and arrived at the mailbox. Its lid was wide open from the eruption of envelopes stuffed inside.

All I could think was, *James*. Without any hesitation I ran toward the house. The first thing I saw was the screen door lying busted up on the porch. The main door was off its hinges, too.

Shit ... This is bad.

I dropped my bag and pulled out my wand, but I never let that plant go. I cautiously peeked inside both the minivan and James's car, hoping like hell no one was dead inside. Although nothing was amiss with the vehicles, the house was a very different story. I slowly climbed the steps and got a closer look at the screen door. It was punched up with holes, and the mesh was torn away at the corners. As I made my way to the front door, large chunks of broken glass crunched under my feet. It had been busted out from *inside* the house. Because the front door was diagonally leaning across where it should have been standing, I had to crawl into the house through a gap at the bottom.

All I could hear was the unnerving drone of the refrigerator. I didn't have to go too far before I saw a blood-scrawled taunt on the wall: "COME AND GET HIM." The letters were tall and uneven, as if written by a madman in an insane asylum. Holding the plant and the wand was a hindrance to me, so I had to make a choice between the two. I chose my wand. I secured the plant in a desk drawer—knowing that if I became endangered, I could make my way back to it—and went deeper into the house.

There was blood, so much blood, as if the house itself were bleeding out. No piece of furniture was left unturned, and body-sized holes peppered every wall. Bookshelves were broken like they'd been karate chopped in half. Fluff billowed out of scored slices in the sofas and couches. I skimmed the wall like an undercover cop going into a raid. At every door I made a sudden roll into its framework, with my wand ready to go. I went through every room on the first level and found no one. I swung open the door leading to the basement; a slight yellow undertone from Addison's grief tendrils still inhabited it. I went down anyway, braving the possibility of being stung again, but there was no one down there either. It looked exactly the same as the last time I'd seen it.

I started toward the upper level of the house. I had to be extra careful because the posts and banister had had been ripped off the staircase. The creaking steps under my feet prevented me from launching a sneak attack, so I had to be ready for anything. Making it to the top floor, I headed down the hall.

I peeked into Aunt Evelyn's room. Her bed, covered in a flowery duvet, was neatly made, with an open book pyramiding on the pillow. I stepped out and closed the door behind me, figuring I wasn't going to let something run out of there at full speed.

Julie's bedroom was next. I pushed the door open with my wand, and saw her sitting on the side of the bed, keeping watch over Aunt Evelyn. Julie was all messed up. Deep cuts and contusions were spread all over her exhausted body. Her dislocated shoulder was set in a homemade sling, and her face looked like it had been gnawed on.

However, Aunt Evelyn's condition was worse. She was in a semi-coma, and almost unrecognizable from a blow to the head. Her entire face was swollen like a balloon, and her eyes were totally blacked out. She probably needed a ventilator for the staggered breaths that clicked out of her mouth. Someone else's blood and flesh were still wedged under her nails, and her wrist bore multiple abrasions from defending herself.

I rushed over and dropped to my knees, holding Aunt Evelyn's ice-cold hand. "What happened?"

Julie was in so much pain, it hurt to even speak. "Catherine's protégés ambushed us. They had some mighty powerful magic on them that made them invisible. Grace, those protégés are wicked strong. I don't know what kind of magic Catherine is using, but they're almost unbeatable."

I knew what kind magic Catherine was using. She was using my magical power that she'd hijacked from my blood, which she'd obtained during our last confrontation.

Julie's eyes were fighting sleep. She hadn't had a decent night's rest since she'd started keeping vigil over Aunt Evelyn. I could see that one of her cuts was bleeding. It was obvious she needed stitches. I didn't care if she still resented me; I was going to care for her.

"Julie, let me fix that for you."

I found a tiny, plastic sewing kit in a dresser drawer and picked out some beige thread and a needle. I then searched the room for alcohol. Instead I came across some antiseptic Aunt Evelyn had been given when she'd had her ears pierced at Claire's Boutique. I held the needle over a tissue and poured the antiseptic right on it.

"This might hurt a bit," I said. I expected Julie to knock my hand away from her face in anger, but she calmly sat there and let me close her wound. She stared at me as if she was thinking about everything that had gone down between us.

"Thank you," she said humbly.

"For what?" I asked.

"For putting up with my bullshit. I know I've been tough."

Was this an actually apology? With Julie it was hard to tell. My stitching started to zigzag as I tried to figure it out, but that didn't stop me from agreeing with her. "Yeah, you have."

We both chuckled, and then Julie put her hand on my lap.

"Grace, I'm sorry for all I put you through. I was jealous of your relationship with James. I thought he was taking my best friend away from me, and I was fucking pissed about that. And then when I lost Hari, I took it out on you. Can you forgive me?"

"I already did." I didn't want to disrupt this profoundly sentimental moment, but I did need to know something.

"Where's James? I haven't seen him yet."

Julie gazed at me sincerely, preparing me for bad news. "They took him. Catherine has been waiting for more than twenty years for a showdown with you. She's taking every opportunity to savor it. She wants you to suffer as much as possible."

"So that's what that scribble-scrabble message was about. All right, if that's the way she wants it, that's the way she'll have it. I'm going to go get James and bring him home safe. That's not a problem for me, but a humongous one for her."

I finished the stitches with a crude knot on Julie's face. I got up, ready for battle, as if I already knew where Catherine was.

"What do you think you're doing? You don't even know where to go," Julie said.

"Logically James has to be in the vicinity if Catherine is goading me to come and get him," I replied with my muscles flexing.

"Despite what you might think, Grace Valois, you are not invincible. You need help. I'm not going to let you deal with that old hag by yourself. Give me a chance to rest up and get stronger, and we can roll out together."

"Plus, we'll have Addison for backup."

Julie's head dropped. "Addison is dead."

"What?"

"They killed her."

I lost my balance and plopped down on the bed, not wanting to believe we had lost another member of our team. "Where is she?"

"Do you really want to do this right now?"

"Why not? It's going to hurt no matter if it's now or later."

Julie wobbled to her feet and I followed her to the back porch. Addison's body was wrapped in a blue bed sheet that had turned purple from all of the blood. I put my hand over my mouth as the awful smell of decay triggered my gag reflex.

"I was going to bury her, but I was too tired and sad to do it," Julie whispered brokenly.

"We'll do it together."

We went back inside and found handkerchiefs to tie around our faces in an attempt to block out the putrefaction. Then we both grabbed an end and took Addison to the clearing where James and I had almost made love for the first time. I dug while Julie took a much-needed break.

It took me an hour to dig that six-foot hole. I jumped into it, and Julie gently and respectfully lowered Addison into the ground. Doing a quick squat, I used my new strength to jump out of the hole. We held hands, said a prayer, and covered the body with dirt. It seemed like such a mundane, anticlimactic ending for such a dramatic life.

"Good-bye, Addison," I said to the mound of dirt. Julie and I turned back toward the house. As soon as we got there, I ran her a steamy bath and took the liberty of washing her hair and back for her. As I took the washcloth and squeezed water onto her skin, I was appalled to see that her back looked like she had been whipped. After I cleaned her up, I helped her into her favorite shorts and T-shirt, and got her into bed.

"I missed you," Julie said through a yawn. We kissed, and I pulled the covers over her. Before her head hit the pillow, she was sound asleep.

To alleviate my anxiety, I decided to clean. I swept up the broken glass, ripped-up sheetrock, and tiny bits of tchotchkes. I mopped the floor with pine-scented cleaner to take the edge off the funk of rotten blood and soured sweat. I wiped the walls down to remove the massive amount of blood smear, but ended up just making them turn a repulsive pinkish brown. What furniture I could salvage, I put right-side up and back in place.

I dragged a full trash bag to the kitchen. Of course there was cleaning to be done in there too, but I was thankful for it. I went right to washing the dishes in the sink, scrubbing hard to remove dried-up, soft-boiled yolk from breakfast some days ago. Wiping my dishpan hands on my shirt, I went to the refrigerator and started throwing away food that had gone bad. I came across a Styrofoam container with "Addison" written daintily across the top. I couldn't even cry; I had no more tears left in me. I tossed her leftovers into the trash without a second thought. All I knew was that I was going to get my man and kill Catherine once and for all.

But how was I going to locate her? It wasn't like I could ask random people, "Hey, do you know this witch bitch named Catherine?" I thought about just driving around Massapequa, but seriously, it wasn't not like Catherine was hanging out at Duane Reade. Maybe I could simply lie low and wait for another attack.

As I weighed my options, I tossed the trash bag into the refuse container behind the house. I went back inside and saw I had not dumped the contents of the dustpan into trash. After putting another bag into the can, I started to dump the dustpan's contents into it. However, I noticed some yellowish, Chiclet-looking thing falling in and dug it out. It was a tooth, and I sensed it belonged to Tamara. I figured Julie must have knocked it out in the scuffle.

This was the boon I needed to help me locate Catherine's lair. I took the tooth to the parlor, sat on the couch, and closed my fist around it, concentrating. Cloudy visions of a cul-de-sac drifted through my mind. The images became more detailed. I saw a house with a realtor lockbox on the door. There was a murky basement that felt like much death had occurred there. And then I saw James, tortured and near death. My psychic tour ended with a glimpse of a street sign: Tunglemans Court.

I finally knew where James was.

Julie and I were in the living room going through Hari's clothes. We pushed aside all of the shorts, Hawaiian shirts, and flip-flops to get to the BDUs.

"Grace, do you think it's necessary for us to dress up in soldier clothes?" Julie asked.

"What would combat specialist Hari do? We would honor him by wearing these," I said.

Julie nodded in agreement. "Hari wouldn't allow us to wear anything else. BDUs it is then."

We both grabbed some camouflage pants and T-shirts. Julie found some grease paint—green and brown—and smeared it on her cheek with a determined stroke.

"Really?" I shook my head, smiling.

"Hey, if we're going to soldier up, we might as well go all the way."

I followed suit. When Julie and I looked in the mirror, we saw a couple of tough chicks. We fist bumped, slapped hands, and snapped our fingers.

"Let's do this," I said.

We jumped into the minivan, remarking how hilarious it must have looked for two supernatural fighters to hop out of a Dodge Caravan. Unfortunately, the superficial lightheartedness didn't last long. Following the minivan's navigation system, we found Tunglemans Court. We did a drive-by creep and opted to park one street over. Covertly, Julie and I made our way on foot back over to Tunglemans. We stayed at the entrance of the cul-de-sac, doing surveillance with the newly fallen night acting as our cover. We were on our bellies, lying low under a bloom of tree limbs that were writhing in the wind.

There were only two houses on the street, and a woman dressed in scrubs came out of one. She looked frazzled and was in a hurry. Some older, power-walking woman was trying to talk to the younger one as she got into the car. The scrub-bedecked woman furiously backed out and took off, getting as far away from the old woman as fast as she could. Meanwhile, Julie and I hid our eyes so the driver couldn't see the whites as she passed. The older woman was oblivious to the fact that she had just gotten checked, and left the cul-de-sac with a speed-walking stride.

"Unless Catherine has aged forty years and taken an interest in aerobics, she must be in the other house," I whispered.

Julie and I skulked over to the foreclosed home. I cringed with every cracked twig I accidently stepped on.

We crouched outside the house, near a hibiscus bush. "Okay, we need to find weak spots and points of easy entry. You go that way. I'll go this way," I said. We briefly clutched hands in a sign of solidarity.

I walked around the house, waving my hand to softly light up weak spots on the house. I could tell Catherine had covered it with a protection spell at some point, but she must have lifted the veil in anticipation of my arrival. I continued to survey the front, and bent down to look into a dirty basement window. As I tried to look into the dark room, I could see the specter reflection of someone coming up behind me. In a nanosecond, Nick swept me up from behind.

"What are you doing, little girl?" Nick said. As he turned me around, I quickly used charisma. When he saw my face, I looked like the subject of his favorite wet dream. He put my feet back on the ground while keeping his arms firmly wrapped around me. I could sense his predatory sexuality rising up. The more aroused he became, the tighter he held me. I noticed he had actually gotten stronger since the attack at the reservation.

I could see Nick was thoroughly entranced. This gave me the chance to dig into my pocket and grab a handful of pixie dust. I flung my hand out, though my arms were still pinned down at my sides.

Slowly the dust rose from the grass and started taking shape. Nick's attention was divided between the pixie dust and me. Growing, growing, the dust manifested as a hyper-demonic version of Catherine. Nick let go of me and fell to his knees.

"I'm sorry. It's not what it looks like. I didn't want the girl. I was only keeping her for you. I love only you," Nick said. He glanced back at me. The charisma had worn off, and my true identity was revealed. He turned back to "Catherine" as she disintegrated. Nick yelled, and swiftly came after me with a profound vengeance.

Oh, shit.

I held up my hand and screamed the first thing that came to my mind, "Freeze!" Nick abruptly stopped, and all of his movements ceased. He then turned into an ice statue of himself. I looked at my hand in amazement.

"Not what I intended, but it'll do," I said. Finding a tree branch, I picked it up and positioned myself behind Nick like a player going up to bat. "Here goes nothing."

I swung back wide, and struck him as hard as I could. Nick broke up into thousands of ice cubes. I had a sense of relief, a feeling that maybe it would not be so hard killing Catherine after all.

Now, unbeknownst to me, Julie—being brave and hardheaded as usual—had somehow made her way inside the house. She knew we were not to go in separately, but she felt confident that she'd be okay. And her guilty conscience compelled her to clear the path for me as penance for how she had treated me.

The house was filled with a strange hum, like the resonating frequency right after a gong has been hit. Catherine's maniacal energy was thick in there. Moreover, the house's musty odor was accented by something that smelled like an overcharged battery.

Julie edged forward on noisy floorboards; the fur started growing on her skin as she sensed someone was there with her. Covering herself, she turned in a circle as she walked. What she didn't know was that Tamara was watching her from the infinite blackness. Julie stopped turning and walked forward into the unknown.

Tamara, however, scaled the wall and crawled stealthily behind her. Tamara smiled; she enjoyed stalking Julie as a hunter does its prey. She wanted to take her time and play. Tamara blew lightly in Julie's direction. Julie felt it and jumped into a defensive posture, and then decided to move on to a side room.

The streetlight streaming into the tiny window illuminated the room with a grayish light. Julie stepped in with Tamara following. Julie looked around, but she failed to look up at the ceiling. Not seeing anything of interest, she started out of the room, but Tamara jumped down on her. Julie reeled around and transformed into the shape-shifter.

Tamara piggybacked Julie, choking her. Whirling around, Julie futilely grabbed at Tamara. Julie's ever-increasing momentum sent both of them crashing into a hallway wall. As Julie continued to try to get Tamara's strong arms from around her, they crashed into the walls and floor. They moved erratically down the hall and dove into the dining room. They fell to the floor, with Tamara rolling off Julie. They both turned their heads and looked at each other. Julie now recognized her assailant as the woman who had killed Hari. She sprung to her feet, as did Tamara.

"What a treat. I get to kill you like I killed your brother," Tamara gloated.

Julie didn't take the bait, and kept a cool head. They both sized each other up as they circled.

"Oh, you look like you want to cry," said Tamara. She lunged at Julie in a game of chicken, but Julie was focused, strategizing.

"Even though I prefer lobster, your brother was delicious. Mighty fine dining," Tamara went on.

That was it; Julie lost it. She charged with brutal animal instinct, and delivered a high kick to Tamara's head. Julie didn't give her anytime to recover, and jerked her up by the neck. She raised Tamara up overhead and slammed her back to the floor. Then Julie crouched down and delivered blows to her kidneys. Every punch broke one of Tamara's ribs. One went straight though her body. Julie flipped her over.

Tamara was beginning to succumb to her injuries. She laughed with an open mouth, showing the empty space where the tooth Grace had found had come from. "Fuck you."

"How about I fist fuck you instead?" Julie said. She pulled her fist back and drove it into Tamara's mouth, going all the way back to her spinal column and severing it. As Julie tried to remove her fist, it got caught behind Tamara's teeth. She had to yank her hand out, and took more of Tamara's teeth with it. Julie stood up and gave the corpse a kick for good measure.

Then she stepped into the hall. She looked back at Tamara and smiled with satisfaction. Unfortunately, she turned right back around into Catherine, who punched her on the side of the head, and Julie dropped.

"You killed my baby. That will never do," Catherine said.

Julie was disoriented by the abnormally powerful blow. Catherine pushed up her sleeves and took Julie's knee.

"It's time to fix the dog." Catherine twisted. Julie screamed bloody murder as her knee popped out of the joint. Catherine started whistling as Julie's lower leg twisted backward.

Meanwhile, I entered the house and whispered, "Julie." Catherine's supersonic hearing caught this, and she instantly became more interested in me.

I carefully made my way through the house. "Julie, where are you?"

Up ahead, I could see one of her legs sticking straight out. I tiptoed over to her as quickly as I could. "Julie, you weren't supposed to go in without me," I said. However, I stopped my chastisement when I saw her other leg bent backward at a most atrocious angle. "Dear God, what happened?"

"Catherine," Julie muttered, trying to not wail.

"Where is she?"

Julie pointed at a door leading to the basement. "Down there."

I was about to storm down when Julie grabbed my pants leg. "Don't go. It's a trap."

"It's not a trap if you know it's there."

Julie reached up and gave my hand a squeeze for encouragement. I made my way to the door and flung it open. I held out my wand, pointing into the darkness. Moving into the basement, I made sure to stay low and slow.

I made it to the floor and found myself stepping over what felt like piles of fat sticks. I conjured the tip of my wand to light, and pointed it down. I was stepping on bones; the basement was filled with them.

Suddenly I heard James's distant screams. He sounded like he was in horrific pain. I listened closely, and followed the sound. It took me to a door. At first I thought it was a closet, but when I opened it I saw that it led down into an empty stairwell. I walked down and entered a subbasement. I had read about these in history class. The original owner of this house must have gotten caught up in the pandemonium of the Red Scare and built this as some sort of fallout shelter. Instead of focusing on life in a newly developing suburb with dreams of backyard barbeques, this guy was waiting for an atomic bomb to drop. Funny how *now* a war was taking place within the confines of the house instead. Got to love the irony.

There was a narrow door directly at the bottom of the stairwell. I didn't know what waited on other side, and took a deep breath to prepare myself.

"Oh, fuck it."

I went for broke and rushed the door. I burst through, and had to make an abrupt stop before I hit a concrete wall directly in front of me. I looked around and discovered I was in a tight tunnel. I could only go right or left. On a hunch, I went right.

The subbasement was more like a cinderblock catacomb. Following naked, lit lightbulbs, I walked through what seemed like endless tunnels with small recesses dotted throughout. There was very almost no ventilation, and the smell of battery acid filled what little air there was.

I finally entered some sort of enchanted chamber. In its center a gigantic, blue pentagram blazed on the floor with an unearthly glow. On the other side of it, I could see James. I ran as fast as I could to him. He was bound with an etheric cord. He had been charred by battery acid and had third-degree burns all over his body. He had lost so much blood, he was nearly drained.

"James," I exclaimed, squatting down. I kissed him. His mouth was full of blood, but I didn't care.

"Hey, stranger," he said; he used the last energy to say those words. I tried to remove the cord, but it was as hot as boiling water.

"I can't get it off." While I still tried, James slowly pointed, indicating that something was behind me. I whipped around and heard something move away from me; I could see it standing in a dark corner. I moved toward it, and with no hesitation, shot my wand. It emitted crackly light and lit up the corner. The thing was revealed: it was a coat tree covered in plastic. Alas, I didn't notice the outline of something *else* coming at me from the darkness.

It was Catherine.

I backed away from the coat tree, right into Catherine's frigid body. I flailed around, and she disappeared. I remembered a trick Aunt Evelyn and James had done many times. I waved my hand and hazed the room like they had done. Against the darkness, the outline of Catherine's shrouded body glinted in response. I immediately threw magic at her. She jumped up like a cat, and with extremely fast speed, blurred past me. She was laughing ... more like cackling. She *really* cackled. I tried to use telekinesis to throw her off her feet, but the power sputtered out on me.

"Why don't you face me instead of running like a wuss?" I taunted. This burned Catherine the fuck up. She was no longer merry. It was on.

Out of nowhere, she plunged down at me. Picking me up, she threw me to the corner of the ceiling. As I came back down, the back of my head barely missed a hook hanging on the wall. Though dazed, I picked myself up immediately. I flicked my wand and sent a wave of liquid crystal toward Catherine. It landed on her like glue, dripped to the floor, and stuck her in place.

I pitched toward her. However, she broke free and threw magic at me. An orb resembling a smoke ring hit my stomach and went in me like a shotgun shell. I doubled over as her hocus pocus bounced off my insides, doing major damage to my organs.

"You! You are what has stood between me and greatness," Catherine bellowed, sending another smoke ring of devilry into me. I could feel myself withering from the inside out. She grabbed me by the hair, taking me down, and hauled me across the floor.

"Don't worry about what's inside of you. It's just going to rip you up. However, it won't kill you before I get a chance to. When I get you in that pentagram, I'm going to take your blood and eat you. And I swear there will be nothing left to say you even existed—except your soul and powers inside of me."

She continued to drag me to the pentagram. My liver was severed and leaking bile. My blood was now poisoned, and my internal bleeding was catastrophic. I looked at James, who was also dying.

"I love you," he whispered. And he closed his eyes.

There was no way was I going to let James die. With a newfound strength, I managed to grab Catherine's wrist, breaking it. My hand cut through the air, and wavy energy shot out, grabbing hold of her. With my telekinetic powers magnified, I was able to toss her around the room with mighty force.

I summoned all of my fortitude and courage, and used telekinesis to pin her up against the wall, leaving her feet to dangle. As I stumbled to stand, I wrapped my hand in my shirt's cuff to protect me from the mock belladonna. Taking the plant out of my pocket, I headed straight for Catherine.

Catherine bucked against the wall as I sliced her across the face and chest with the mock belladonna. She screamed as her power drained out like it was her life's blood. I let her fall to the floor and watched for any sign of life, but she appeared to be dead.

I rushed over to James, who barely had a pulse.

"Come on, baby. Come on," I said. I tried old-fashioned CPR on him like he'd done on me so many months earlier. He was still slipping away. I cut my wrist and fed him my blood, which was still coursing with his. James sucked weakly at first, and then harder. He looked at me, and his eyes were no longer the eyes of a dying man. They were coming back alive.

Our blood tie had saved him.

However, behind me, Catherine defied gravity and raised straight up—stiff like a plank rising from the floor. She was so powerful and psychotic, not even the plant could kill her. Luckily, what the plant *had* done was buy me some time, and that was exactly what I needed at that moment.

"Is that all you've got?" Catherine said in a guttural, evil voice.

For the first time, I transformed into one of those gargoyle-like creatures like the other witches had done at the ritual. However, my form was more hideous, more beastly. I grew extremely tall and lost all of my recognizable facial characteristics. All that pent-up fear I had for Catherine changed my body. However, the fear was gone now, and I was the embodiment of abject rage.

I jumped on her like a starving animal and held her down with my saber-length fangs. Her foul-tasting blood seeped into my mouth, and I swallowed it as a show of dominance. Removing the knife Amari had given me from my waistband, plunged it into Catherine. There was no pattern to my stabs; I was just jabbing. Through each one of her cuts, some weird, nefarious light shined out. The knife had a strange effect, like it was radioactive to her. Her flesh boiled as if she were in a nuclear reactor. We both concentrated on each other's eyes. Catherine saw her executioner; I saw fear incarnate.

"It's over," I said. I picked her up with telekinesis and floated her body over the pentagram, which seemed like it was starving for her. I dropped Catherine into its center and watched her take one final breath, her eyes wide open.

Then her body exploded. The bits of annihilated flesh were sucked into a dimensional field in the pentagram. In a weak puff, Catherine's Ancient spirit rose in a last attempt to escape and kill me, but was hindered by the pentagram's gravitational force. I never saw Catherine's soul. She had lost it a long time ago.

There was a tectonic shift under the pentagram, and it imploded, disappearing into another dimension. The floor closed back up, and all that was left was a faint trace of the pentagram's outline.

I morphed back into my normal self. The etheric cord holding James disappeared, too. I ran over and helped him up. I put his arm across my shoulder. His hand draped down and accidently brushed my breast.

"Really? You had to go through all of this just to cop a feel?" I joked.

It took us a long time to make it back up to the main floor. Julie had somehow managed to put her broken leg straight in front of her. I sat James down next to her.

"I'm going to go get the car," I stated. As I hurried out, I couldn't help but be proud of myself. I'd walked into that house with an uncertainty about the outcome, but I was leaving a success. Yeah, I kind of did the hero walk all the way out the door.

Julie looked over at James and said, "That's a bad bitch."

And I just had to agree.

A few days passed, and the house was slowly coming back together. James placed a large sheet of wood across the front door until a contractor could come out and fix it. Julie had moved back into the room she and Addison had shared. Remarkably, it didn't bother her that Addison had died in there, and she always had a restful night's sleep. She said she could feel Addison's spirit and it was comforting to her.

Sometimes it felt like it had all been a dream—like it had never happened—but there were those heavy moments when memories came crashing back with excruciating pain. I often wondered what would have happened to me if none of this had occurred. I would have been sitting behind a desk, my accounting diploma looming behind me in some cheap frame. And I probably would have still been messed up in the head, pining over Rafe. Instead, I ended up freer than I'd ever been, and with a love that went beyond the scope and breadth of the universe itself. That was more than an acceptable trade-off.

I was upstairs with Aunt Evelyn, feeding her soup for breakfast, and later would do the same for lunch and dinner, too. She was propped up on one of those TV pillows. Her swelling had gone down, but she still suffered incredible headaches. Regardless, Aunt Evelyn was more concerned with everyone else's welfare, as usual. James was in the room, too. He kept looking out the window as if he were expecting something.

The smell of Aunt Evelyn's soup was making me starved. Julie had gone out for some burgers and fries, but that was hours ago.

"James, have you heard from Julie yet? She said she was just going to Micky D's. She should've been back by now." However, James was watching something from the window, and it brought a wide smile to his face. I was too hungry to get up and go see what he was grinning about.

Suddenly, there was a ruckus at the door. "We're home!" Julie shouted from downstairs.

"It's about time," I said somewhat brusquely.

Aunt Evelyn passed a sneaky smile to James, and flashed me a regular one. "I've had enough. You go on downstairs and eat your food."

I didn't hesitate. With my stomach growling like a big bear, I trotted toward the stairs. Then I stopped to think. *We're?* Julie had said. *Who is 'we're'?*

I walked down the stairs and saw her standing there with *him*. My dad! I was stunned, shocked that he was there.

"Come here, baby girl!" he said with open arms. Running to him, I tripped over my feet. Dad swung me around like he had when I was five years old.

"Where have you been?" I asked, still in awe.

"At an Extended Stay America in Pittsburgh."

He was still twirling me around, and I was getting dizzy. "You look so different. So grown," he said as he put me down.

I patted his belly, which had grown, too.

"Too much delivery. You know I can't cook," he said. However, his extra weight didn't bother me one iota. My dad was back, and I was thrilled.

Fall came to Massapequa in bursts of orange, brown, yellow, and red. James and I celebrated the change of seasons with a romantic walk in town. Even with construction going on, it was wonderful.

We passed the Buttered Bagel. "Want one?" James asked.

"Sure, with a schmear," I replied.

"Will do."

As James went in, I noticed Rafe across the street, leaning against a wall. James was barely in the store before Rafe ran over to me.

"Hey, Grace. Long time, no see," he said.

"That's a good thing, don't you think?"

Seeing me with another man made him jealous. This ass was convinced I would never get over him. "So is that you new boyfriend?"

"Mm-hm."

"He's all right," Rafe leaned in, "but I bet he can't do you like I did."

Just then Tiffany showed up like a ghost popping out of thin air.

"Really, Grace. Are you so desperate that you have to flirt with my man? It's not going to work. What would he want with some hoggy trash like you?" Tiffany asked with a flip of her hair.

Rafe, knowing he'd been busted, acted like a jerk to me—as if that were something new. "Like I would lower myself to be seen with you again. Come on, Tiff."

I let it go, taking the high road. I could now see how silly Rafe was, and how insecure Tiffany had been the whole time. All I did was stand there and watch them walk away. As I observed the exaggerated switch of Tiffany's nonexistent ass, I suddenly started thinking:

Oh no. Wait a minute. Fuck the damn high road. After what these assholes did to me? I am not that big of a person yet. And it's time for some payback.

Rafe and Tiffany were approaching the construction site's Port-O-Potty just as the truck had arrived to empty it. When those two creeps were close enough, I waved my hand, causing the hose to dislodge. Piss and shit spewed all over my nemeses.

I so wanted to run over there and scream, "In your face, motherfuckers! In your face—literally!" But witch decorum, which included anonymity, frowned upon such a display. So I just reveled in the spectacle from afar. Satisfied, I laughed it up. *Now* I could be the better person, and meander down the high road.

James came out with a bag of bagels and saw me chucking it up.

"What's going on?" he asked. He looked down the street at the two piles of shit, Tiffany and Rafe. "Wow! What happened to them?"

"Who knows?" I said, shrugging. I gave James a light peck on his cheek.

"What was that for?" he asked.

"Just because I love you."

"I love you, too. Forever and with everything."

James and I went on, only looking back occasionally at Tiffany and Rafe. During the rest of our walk, I thought about how wonderful it was to be there with him. However, there were still ominous things to deal with. I did have to become the leader of the council. I had acquired a taste for human flesh and blood. Mandy was still driving past my house. And I now had Catherine's blood in me, and there was no telling what effect that would have.

James and I came upon a cement bench. He pulled out some bagels, very fresh and chewy. He had already smeared on his cream cheese. As he was about to put the bagel in his mouth, I pulled it toward me and seductively licked off some of the white stuff.

"I hope that's a prelude of things to come," he said.

"You'd better believe it," I responded.

As I took a bite of my own bagel, I decided to worry about all that other stuff later and, for once, let everything be all good.

The End